D0996880

This book is due for return by the last date shown above.
To avoid paying fines please renew or return promptly.

Portsmouth
CITY COUNCIL
LEISURE SERVICE   CL-1

NAVIGATOR

TIME'S TAPESTRY: 3

NAVIGATOR

TIME'S TAPESTRY: 3

Stephen Baxter

GOLLANCZ
LONDON

Navigator © Stephen Baxter 2007

The right of Stephen Baxter to be identified as the
author of this work has been asserted by him in accordance
with the Copyright, Designs and Patents Act 1988.

First published in Great Britain in 2007 by Gollancz
An imprint of the Orion Publishing Group
Orion House, 5 Upper St Martin's Lane, London WC2H 9EA
An Hachette Livre UK company

A CIP catalogue record for this book is available
from the British Library.

ISBN 978 0 57507 6 754 (Cased)
ISBN 978 0 57507 9 915 (Trade Paperback)

1 3 5 7 9 10 8 6 4 2

Typeset by Input Data Services Ltd, Frome

Printed in Great Britain by Mackays of Chatham plc, Chatham, Kent

www.orionbooks.co.uk

The Orion Publishing Group's policy is to use papers that
are natural, renewable and recyclable products and made from
wood grown in sustainable forests. The logging and manufacturing
processes are expected to conform to the environmental
regulations of the country of origin.

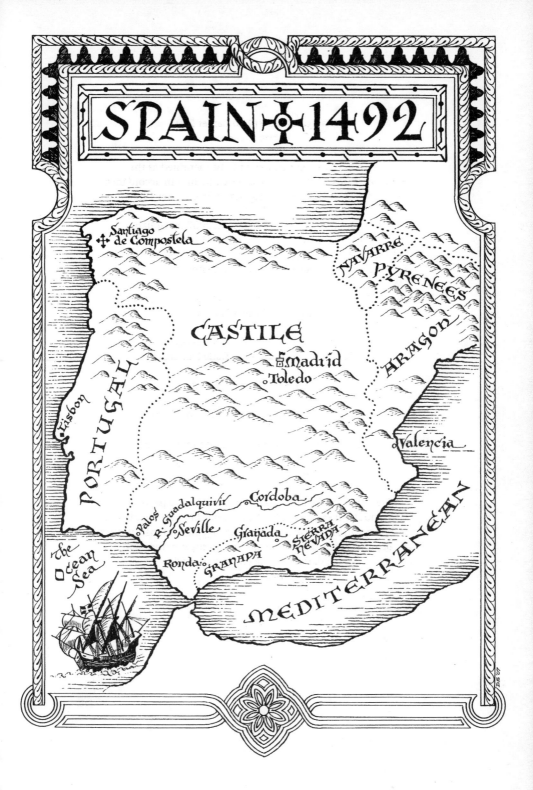

SPAIN ✠ 1492

Santiago de Compostela

NAVARRE
PYRENEES
ARAGON

CASTILE
Madrid
Toledo

PORTUGAL
Lisbon

Valencia

Cordoba
Palos
R. Guadalquivir
Seville
Granada
SIERRA NEVADA
Ronda
GRANADA

The Ocean Sea

MEDITERRANEAN

Timeline

AD 622	Beginning of Islamic era
AD 711	First Muslim armies land in Spain
AD 732	Battle of Poitiers; furthest extension of Muslim advance
AD 756	Politically independent realm of al-Andalus established
AD 929	Cordoba caliphate declared
AD 1031	Collapse of Cordoba caliphate; emergence of *taifas*
AD 1066	Danish and Norman invasions of England
AD 1085	Alfonso of Castile conquers Toledo
AD 1096–99	The First Crusade
AD 1187	Saladin reconquers Jerusalem
AD 1212	Las Navas de Tolosa: key Christian victory in al-Andalus
AD 1236	Christian conquest of Cordoba
AD 1242	Death of Ogodai; Mongols turn back from Vienna
AD 1248	Christian conquest of Seville
AD 1260	In Holy Land, Mamluks inflict Mongols' first defeat
AD 1291	Crusader states eliminated
AD 1347–52	The 'Great Mortality' – the Black Death
AD 1453	Ottoman Turks conquer Constantinople
AD 1479	Union of Castile and Aragon
AD 1492	Christians conquer Granada. Columbus's journey begins

The Testament of Eadgyth of York:

(Lines revealed in AD 1070)

In the last days
To the tail of the peacock
He will come:
The spider's spawn, the Christ-bearer
The Dove.
And the Dove will fly east,
Wings strong, heart stout, mind clear.
God's Engines will burn our ocean
And flame across the lands of spices.
All this I have witnessed
I and my mothers.
Send the Dove west! O, send him west!

(Lines revealed in AD 1481)

The Dragon stirs from his eastern throne,
Walks west.
The Feathered Serpent, plague-hardened,
Flies over ocean sea,
Flies east.
Serpent and Dragon, the mortal duel
And Serpent feasts on holy flesh.
All this I have witnessed
I and my mothers.
Send the Dove west! O, send him west!

The 'Indendium Dei' cryptogram:

(Source: the 'Engines of God' Codex of Aethelmaer of Malmesbury,
c. AD 1000)

BMQVK XESEF EBZKM BMHSM BGNSD DYEED OSMEM HPTVZ HESZS
ZHVH

PROLOGUE
AD 1070

Orm Egilsson was among the last to reach the village this bright February morning, and the place was already a ruin. The wooden houses had been set alight, the stone barns cracked open like eggs, the winter food robbed, the seed corn torched and the animals slaughtered or driven off, even the pregnant ewes and cattle.

And the bodies were everywhere. Men and boys had been cut down like blades of grass. Some of them had makeshift weapons in their hands, scythes and rakes, even pikes and rusty swords. They had been useless against Norman warriors. But these farmers had to fight, for there was no English army to fight for them, no English king since Harold had been destroyed at Hastings more than three years ago. And once the men had fallen the women and girls were kept for the Normans' usual sport. Orm looked away from the twisted bodies in their bloodied rags, the mud scuffed around them by the knees and feet of the soldiers.

It was like this all across the land. Whichever way Orm looked he saw smoke rising, plumes of it dominated by the tremendous column that rose up from York itself, a few miles away. It was the Normans' intention to ensure that this country could not support any more rebellion, not even the furtive pinpricks of the wildmen, not for a generation or more. And the Normans pursued such goals with relentless efficiency.

At a command from his officer Orm dismounted and tied his horse's rein to a burned stump. The job of the mop-up party was to ensure the work was finished thoroughly. The heat from the smouldering fires made Orm sweat inside his heavy chain-mail coat, and the sooty air was gritty under his conical helmet. But he prodded at charred ruins with a stabbing-sword and kicked over bodies with the rest of them. It wasn't as bad as taking part in the slaughter itself.

3

He came to one ruined hovel, actually a little Christian chapel, devoted, he saw from the remnant of a dedication stone, to Saint Agnes, a Roman martyr. Orm kicked away the debris of the fallen walls, exposing an earth floor covered with a layer of straw. Here was a hearth, the stones still warm from the night's fire, a couple of wooden chests already broken open. Nothing left of value.

But something moved under the straw, a rustle in the dirt. Perhaps it was a rat. He stepped that way.

And he heard a voice, a woman, softly, rapidly chanting English words:

> In the last days
> To the tail of the peacock
> He will come:
> The spider's spawn, the Christ-bearer
> The Dove.
> And the Dove will fly east . . .

A prayer? Not one he knew – but as a pagan, he wouldn't expect to.

He stamped hard. His boot clattered, a hollow sound. The voice fell silent.

He kicked aside the straw and exposed planks, roughly cut. In the gaps between the planks he saw a flicker of movement, a flash of a blue eye.

Orm braced himself, his sword raised in the air, ready to stab down. But he hesitated, sick of blood. He leaned down, slipped his gloved fingers between the planks and pulled them up.

A woman huddled in the hole, dressed in a grimy black habit. She flinched from the light, her hands over her face. In the hole with her was a half-chewed loaf of hard winter bread, a wooden pitcher of water, and a discoloured patch of ground that, from its stink, told him she had been in here some hours.

He ought to finish her off. It would be kinder than to let the Normans have her. He hardened his grasp on the hilt of his sword.

She lowered her hands and looked at him. She had bright blue eyes, a round, sturdy face, short-cropped hair.

He gasped. 'Godgifu,' he said. And he lowered his sword.

The woman in the hole watched him, her gaze fixed on his face.

'But you are not Godgifu,' he said in English.

She thought that over. 'Are you sure?'

'You can't be. I saw her die.' No, his pitiless memory informed him. More than that. Orm had killed her, or his murderous machine of a body had, in the blood-lust on Senlac Ridge, during the slaughter men had come to refer to as the Battle of Hastings. Killed the woman he loved, without thinking. He had never forgiven himself, even though he had obtained absolution of a sort from Sihtric, Godgifu's priest-brother.

'Well, you're right. My name is Eadgyth. I wish I were your Godgifu, though.' Her voice was scratchy from disuse. She wasn't much older than twenty.

'Why do you wish that?'

'Because you would spare Godgifu. You will soon kill me.'

'Why are you here, Eadgyth?'

'I'm hiding.'

'From the Normans?'

'From the Normans, and my parents.'

'Why your parents?'

She shivered in her hole. 'I want to give my life to God. They want to give it to the Conqueror.'

He glanced around. The other troopers were busy with something they had found on the far side of the village, a cache of money, or a woman still alive. There was nobody near Orm, nobody watching. Orm squatted down, stiff in his grimy mail coat. 'Tell me.'

It was a familiar story. Under Harold and his predecessors Eadgyth's family had been land-owners, well-to-do. But more than three years after the Conquest, any vague intentions King William might have had for rapprochement with the old English aristocracy had been burned away by rebellion. All over the country there were wildmen operating from the woods and hills and marshland, places the heavily armoured Normans could not follow. The sons of dead King Harold had been raiding from Ireland. The Scottish King Malcolm had married his sister to Edgar the Atheling, the relative of Edward the Confessor who some argued had a better claim to the throne than even Harold had. And so on. As one rebellion after another was put down, very few of the native English nobility retained their positions.

Eadgyth's parents' intention was to survive under the new regime. And their main asset, as they saw it, was their only daughter.

'They brought me back from my convent. I was told I must marry the son of the Norman lord who now owns us. I met the boy. No more than seventeen. He tried to rape me before I told him my name. He's a bishop now.' She laughed, not bitter.

'So you ran away.'

'I've travelled from safe-house to safe-house, sheltered by the clergy and by the people of places like this.'

Orm had heard of this. For peasants stripped of custom and English law, hermits like Eadgyth were a reminder of the old days, the old English ways.

She said to him, 'And you—?'

'Orm. My name is Orm Egilsson.'

'Why are *you* here? You are not Norman, or English. This is not your home.'

'I am a mercenary. I fight for pay.'

She shifted in her cramped hole. 'You were at Hastings?'

'I was.'

'On such a day it was better to fight for the winner. Why have the Normans brought you here?'

'To put a stop to the rebellions.'

Eadgyth said, 'My own uncle is a wildman, in the fen country of the east.'

'Yes. The Normans call them *silvatici*. People of the woods.' All over England the wildmen had taught the Normans another new word: *murdrum*, furtive slaughter. 'The north has been worst, though. This country. And so it will suffer most grievously. Everywhere it is like this, from Durham to York – burned – uninhabited.' There would be no harvest this year, no lambs or calves; famine would follow the steel.

'So at last the Conqueror has come here,' Eadgyth whispered. 'From Hastings all the way to this remote place of farmers and sheep and cattle.'

Orm heard voices calling. 'We have no more time,' he said.

'Then you must earn your pay.'

He looked into her calm eyes, so like Godgifu's.

'What's this?' The voice was heavy, the accent crude French.

Orm was dismayed to see Roger fitz Gommery standing over him. Roger was a common soldier, a slab of hardened muscle from toe to brain, and an ardent rapist. The crotch of his leather trousers was already smeared with blood and ordure from his day's sport. 'Have I broken into your party, Orm Egilsson? Let's see what we've got.'

He closed his leather glove over Eadgyth's short hair, and dragged her to her feet. She screamed, and her legs flapped, too weak to support her weight.

'Roger—'

'You'll get your share, Orm.'

With his gloved hand Roger ripped at the neck of Eadgyth's habit. Old, much patched, the material gave easily. She was left naked save for pants of stained wool, which Roger pulled away. Her body was skeletal, her skin pocked by lesions, her breasts shrunken mounds behind hard nipples. She whimpered, her eyes closed, and she seemed to be praying:

> And the Dove will fly east,
> Wings strong, heart stout, mind clear.
> God's Engines will burn our ocean
> And flame across the lands of spices.
> All this I have witnessed
> I and my mothers . . .

As she gabbled these words, Roger looked her up and down, contemptuous. 'Skin and bone. Chicken legs. You know what, Dane? I can't be bothered; I've had my fill today. But we can still have a little sport. Have you ever carved a chicken?' He took a knife from his belt and, almost thoughtfully, drew it across Eadgyth's back. She jerked rigid at the pain, and warm blood poured.

And her eyes snapped open.

She stared directly at Orm. 'Egilsson,' she said. 'Orm Egilsson. Can you hear me? Are you there?' All the weakness had gone from her voice, despite the way Roger held her up by her hair, despite the wound that crossed her back. It didn't even sound like her voice any more, but deeper, heavier, the accent distorted. *'Are you there,* Orm Egilsson?'

Roger gaped. 'Is she possessed?'

'Orm Egilsson. Listen to what I have to tell you. Listen, and remember, and let your sons and their sons remember too.' And again she began to intone her eerie, unfamiliar prayer.

> In the last days
> To the tail of the peacock
> He will come:
> The spider's spawn, the Christ-bearer
> The Dove.
> And the Dove will fly east . . .

Roger crossed himself. 'By God's wounds, she's a prophet.'

She spoke on in that clear alien voice, of fires consuming an ocean, of war.

> All this I have witnessed
> I and my mothers.
> Send the Dove west! O, send him west!

Orm was unaccountably afraid of this naked, helpless woman. 'What peacock, what dove? I don't know what you mean.'

'Find him,' Eadgyth said, and her voice was a hiss now.

'Who?'

'Sihtric.'

It was the name of Godgifu's brother, the priest. He had not told Eadgyth of him. The name shocked Orm to his core. 'But Sihtric is in Spain,' he said weakly.

'Find him. And stop him.'

Roger lost his nerve. He let go of the woman's hair and she crumpled into a heap. 'Screw her, kill her, or marry her, she's all yours, Dane. I'm having no more of this.' He turned and stomped off, massive in his armour, obsessively crossing himself.

The woman was huddled over on herself, her back bright with blood. Orm lifted her face with a gloved hand. Spittle flecked her lips, and he saw blood on her tongue. She had bitten it while speaking. He said, 'Who are you? By whose authority shall I command Sihtric?'

She looked at him. 'Orm?'

'Who are you?'

'I am Eadgyth. Only Eadgyth.' She frowned. 'I – have I fallen?'

'Do you remember what you said to me?'

'What I said ... What's happened to me, Orm Egilsson?'

He stood up. The bright February day became insubstantial around him, and a harsher light shone through its sparse threads. He remembered all Sihtric's talk in the days before Hastings, the mystical babbling of a possibly heretical priest – talk about the tapestry of time, and how its weave might be picked undone and remade by a god, or a man with sufficient power. The Weaver, Sihtric had called him. And now Sihtric and his mysteries had returned to Orm's life.

But on the ground before him was a woman, helpless, naked, shivering, bleeding. That was the reality. He reached up to his horse, pulled a blanket from the saddle, and draped it over her shoulders. The Norman soldiers, drunk on blood and rape, drawn by Roger's gabbled account, gathered around curiously.

I

MUSTA'RIB

AD 1085

I

The north Spanish country did not interest Robert, son of Orm.

Why should it? Green, damp, mild even in July, it was too like England. And besides, Robert, fourteen years old, believed that his soul yearned for spiritual nourishment, not for spectacle. So he was glad when he and his father reached Santiago de Compostela, the city of Saint James of the Field of Stars, where he would be able to prostrate himself among the flocking pilgrims before the tomb of the Apostle, Santiago Matamoros, James the Moorslayer.

As it turned out, it was not his soul he would give up in this city, but his heart, and not to the dusty bones of a saint, but to the sweet face of a half-Moorish girl.

The three of them, Robert, Orm and Ali Ibn Hafsun, their guide, sat on little stone benches in the shade of an apple tree, resting bodies weary from the day's ride from the coast, and sipping a vendor's sharp-flavoured tea. Saint James's city was small, shabby, somewhat decayed, as if nobody had repaired a wall or fixed a broken roof tile since the departure of the Romans. But this little square bustled, as pilgrims in travel-stained dress queued to pay homage, children chased chickens, women shopped for food, and men in loose white clothes conducted business in various tongues.

And in the shadow of the squat church, camels groaned and jostled. The camels were extraordinary. Robert thought they looked *wrong*, somehow, as if put together from bits of other creatures.

Orm laughed at the camels. 'I always heard that Africa starts on the other side of the Pyrenees. Now I know.'

Ibn Hafsun was studying Robert. About Orm's age, somewhere in his forties, Ibn Hafsun dressed like a Moor, and yet he had greying blond hair and blue eyes. He seemed to sense Robert's restlessness. 'You are distracted, boy. I can see it in the way you gulp down that hot tea, the way your gaze roams over every surface, looking at all and seeing nothing.'

Orm had always said Robert had the spiritual soul of his long-dead mother, Eadgyth, who had once been a hermit. But Robert had the build and temper of his father, who was a soldier. 'What's it to you?' he snapped back, fourteen years old, bristling.

Ibn Hafsun raised his hands. 'I mean no offence. I am your guide in this strange country. That's what I'm paid to do. And though I have delivered your body to this place, I'm doing a poor job if I allow your spirit to wander around like a chick that has lost its nest.' He spoke an accented Latin dialect. Robert had expected everybody to speak Arabic, but there were two tongues in Spain, Arabic and this diverged version of Latin, which the people called *aljami* or *latinia*.

'I'm not a lost chick.'

Ibn Hafsun smiled. 'Then how do you think of yourself?'

'I am a pilgrim. And I'm here in this city of Saint James to visit the tomb of the brother of Christ, who came here to die.'

Orm murmured, 'You must forgive him, Ibn Hafsun. It's the fashion these days to be pious. A generation after the Conquest, the English kings are forgotten and every boy in England wants to be a warrior of God like King William.'

'But this is only a way station,' Ibn Hafsun said innocently to Robert. 'Your first stop in Spain. Your destination is Cordoba. And as I understand it you are here in Santiago to meet not a long-dead apostle, but a living priest.'

Robert snorted. 'If it isn't all some elaborate hoax, devised by some trickster to empty my father's purse.' They had quarrelled over the purpose of the journey many times in England.

Orm shifted on the bench. He was still a big man, but his body, battered and scarred from too many campaigns, was stiff, sore, uncomfortable even in rest. He said firmly, 'I wrote to Sihtric, and he wrote back, and I recognised his writing. Oh, Sihtric lives. I'm sure of that.'

And he shared a look with Robert, for the central truth went unsaid: what had drawn them here was Orm's story of the 'Testament' spoken by Eadgyth, Robert's mother, when Orm had first found her hiding from Normans in a hole in the ground. Now, after years of saving and preparation, Orm was ready to fulfil her command to seek out Sihtric.

Robert only half believed all this. But when he had been very young his mother had drifted away to the old church of Saint Agnes near York, now rebuilt by the Normans, and had crawled back into that hole in the ground, ignoring her distracted husband and distressed young son. And Robert had been only six years old when she died, her lungs ruined by her years of flight from the Normans.

Ibn Hafsun watched the silent exchange between them, and Robert saw a calculating curiosity in those pale eyes. 'Well, you're here, Robert, whatever the motivation. So what do you think of the country?'

'Not much. It's like England.'

Ibn Hafsun laughed. 'I won't deny that. Yes, this corner is like England or Ireland. Wet, windy, dominated by ocean weather from the west. But very little of the peninsula is like this. You'll see.'

'I think he's not quite sure what a "peninsula" is, Ibn Hafsun,' Orm said.

'At least tell me this: what do you call the land to which you have come?'

'Spain,' Robert snapped back.

'Ah. Well, it's had many names. The Romans called it Iberia, named for a river, the Ebro, which drains into the Mediterranean. Later they called it Betica, after another river that drains to the west into the Ocean Sea – the river that runs through Cordoba, in fact. Later still it became known as Hispania, or Spain, after a man called Hispan who once ruled here – or perhaps it was named for Hesperus, the evening star. Many of these names were invented by even older people, of course, the folk who lived here before the Caesars came. And the Moors call it al-Andalus.'

'The Moors are in the south,' Robert said. 'They never came here.'

'Didn't they?' Ibn Hafsun grinned. 'Once there was but a tiny salt crystal of Christianity in a cupful of Islam, here in the north, after the Moors overran the peninsula in just a few years. And once, oh, this is only a century ago, a great Moorish vizier called Al-Mansur sacked this very city and carried off the bells of Saint James's church to Cordoba where they rest to this day.'

'I don't believe you,' Robert said.

'About what?'

'That the Moors took only a few years to overrun the whole of Spain. The Romans would have pushed them back.'

'I'm afraid it's true,' Ibn Hafsun said. 'It was only a hundred years after the death of the Prophet. The kings then were not Roman, for the empire had lost the west, but Gothic. We ruled as the Romans did, or better, for centuries. But we could not stand before the Moors.'

Orm asked, 'Why do you say "we"?'

Ibn Hafsun said proudly, 'My family were Gothic counts. Our family name was Alfonso.'

'Like the King,' Robert said.

'In my great-grandfather's time we converted to Islam, and took an Arabic name. The Moors call the likes of us *muwallad*, which means "adopted children". And now I find myself a left-behind Muslim in what is once again a Christian kingdom. You see, history is complicated.' He smiled, a Muslim with blue eyes and blond hair.

Robert said rudely, 'If your family were once counts, why are you reduced to escorting travellers for pennies?'

Behind him a new voice said, 'Because in al-Andalus, it's hard for anyone but a Moor to get rich.'

Robert turned. A man approached them, short, not strong-looking, with a pinched face worn with age. He wore a modest priest's black habit, and his tonsure was cut raggedly into a scalp that was losing its hair. A girl followed him, in a simple flowing gown. She had her face downcast modestly.

Ibn Hafsun stood, and the others followed his lead. 'Sihtric. The peace of Allah be on you. And your daughter.'

'And God go with you too.' The priest was a skinny man, Robert saw, but with a pot-belly that spoke of indulgence. He studied Orm, who towered over him. 'Well, Viking. When did we last meet?'

'William's coronation. Nineteen years gone, or the best part of it.'

'I wish I could say I was glad to see you. But life is more complicated than that, isn't it? And this is your son.' He turned to Robert, grinning. 'The ardent pagan spawned a devout Christian. How amusing.' He laughed out loud.

Robert was irritated to be spoken of in this dismissive way.

But then Sihtric's daughter lifted her head and looked directly at Robert, and he forgot his irritation. Surely she was only a little older than he was. Her face was a perfect oval, the colour of honey, her lips full and red, her nose fine, and her eyes bright blue.

'Her name,' Sihtric said drily, 'is Moraima.'

Robert barely heard him. He was already lost.

II

They stayed a single night in Santiago de Compostela, and then formed up into a party to ride south. They planned to travel all the way to Cordoba, no longer the capital of a western caliphate, but still the beating heart of Muslim civilisation in Spain.

And, Robert learned, 'ride' was the correct word.

They would all be on horseback, their goods carried on the backs of two imperious-looking camels. When they set off, Ibn Hafsun led the way. Robert was expected to bring up the rear, with his eye on these camels. He quickly found it was no joy to plod along immersed in camel farts and hot dust, with nobody to speak to.

What was worse was that the girl, Moraima, rode at the front alongside Ibn Hafsun, never closer than two or three horse-lengths from Robert.

'For such an advanced civilisation,' Sihtric observed, 'the Moors are oddly reluctant to employ the wheel.'

Ibn Hafsun just grinned. 'Who needs wheels when Allah gave us camels?'

'So, a daughter,' Orm said to Sihtric. 'I wasn't expecting that. She's a beauty, priest.'

'Ah, yes. There is beauty in my family, of a sturdy sort – as you know all too well, Viking, God rest my sister's soul.'

'And the mother is a Moor?'

'Was. Moraima has grown up a Muslim.'

'I thought the bishops discourage you priests from ploughing your parishioners.'

'Well, she wasn't my parishioner. And a man gets lonely, so far from home. You have to live with the people around you; you have to live *like* them. The Moors call me a Mozarab – *Musta'rib*, a nearly-Arab ...

The bishops are a rather long way from Cordoba, Orm.'

As the day wore away and the sun sailed over the dome of sky, the country changed gradually. They passed through the foothills of a sharp mountain range and crossed into drier land, dustier, where the grass was sparse or non-existent, and the hills were like lumps of rock sticking out of the dirt. The towns were tight little clusters of blocky houses the colour of the dust. In the land between the towns olive trees grew in swathes that washed to the horizon, and herds of bony sheep fled as they passed. The people here were different too, their skin darker, their teeth and eyes bright white. On the road they occasionally passed muleteers, hardy, wizened men driving little caravans of laden animals; the bells around the mules' necks rang mournfully. *This* was not like England, Robert thought.

As the afternoon darkened towards evening, they stopped at an inn. Ibn Hafsun handed over some coins, and they sat on upturned barrels in the shade of olive trees while a woman cooked for them over an open fire. She threw garlic, aubergines, peppers and flour-dipped anchovies into olive oil that spat in a hot pan. As the anchovies fried, a smell of the sea spread through the air.

Ibn Hafsun came to squat on a blanket beside Robert. He dipped bread into a bowl of something foul-smelling; it turned out to be sheep's-milk cheese laced with crushed fruit. He offered some to Robert, but Robert refused.

Even here, Robert couldn't get close to Moraima, who sat modestly with her father.

Not far from the road a party of boys worked through a grove of olive trees. They collected the fruit by throwing sticks up into the branches. They were skilful, each throw dislodging many fruit. It looked a good game, and Robert wished he were a couple of years younger so he could join in without embarrassment.

Sihtric and Orm began at last to speak of the business that had brought Orm here.

'I told you of the Testimony,' Orm said.

'Your wife's prophecy, before she was your wife. Who spoke my name to you, long before she could have known of my existence.' Sihtric shivered. 'It feels uncomfortable to be under such supernatural scrutiny. But why did it take you fifteen years to get around to doing something about it?'

Orm shrugged. 'I had a living to make. Funds to raise. A family.' He glanced at Robert. 'I considered forgetting about it, giving it up without ever coming here.'

'So what changed?'

'I met a traveller – a mercenary who had fought with King Alfonso in al-Andalus. And he told me a fragment of a Moorish legend. There was a line of Eadgyth's prophecy I had never understood, amid much talk of doves and oceans.'

'What line?'

'"The tail of the peacock." That was what she said. And that was what my traveller finally explained to me.'

Moraima smiled. 'I understand. I have heard the story . . .'

According to an old Arab myth, she said, after the Flood the habitable lands of the world were shaped like a bird, with its head in the east and its arse in the west.

'So much for what the Arabs think of western Europe,' Orm remarked.

But as al-Andalus became magnificent under the Moors, the land was reimagined as a peacock's tail.

Robert listened to Moraima's voice, entranced. She'd hardly spoken since joining the party with her father – and hadn't said a single word to *him*.

Orm said to Sihtric, 'You see? *I* knew you were in Spain, but Eadgyth didn't. She said your name without ever meeting you. And when I came across the business of the peacock's tail – it all seemed to fit together and I felt I had to follow it up.'

Sihtric smiled. 'Typical of the Weaver to be cryptic – if it is the Weaver. Let's refer to the agent who put these words into your wife's head as, let me see, a *Witness*. He may be the same as the Weaver, or he may not.'

'She.'

'What?'

'When I showed Eadgyth my transcript of the words she spoke – she had no memory of it – she always called, um, her *visitor* "she".'

'She it is,' Sihtric said. 'And what do you believe the Witness has mandated you to do?'

Orm looked at him. 'Stop you.'

Sihtric gazed back. 'Well, you'll have to find out what I'm doing here first, won't you?'

If Ibn Hafsun was curious about their talk, he didn't show it. He worked his way through his sheep's-milk cheese silently.

Somewhere a wailing voice cried. It was a muezzin, Ibn Hafsun told Robert, calling from his tower in the nearby town, summoning the faithful to prayer. Ibn Hafsun fetched his own blanket from his horse, and knelt and faced east.

In the dusty heat, with the alien song in his ears and the exotic scent of the Arab food in his nostrils, Robert had never felt so far from home. And when Moraima glanced at him, her pale blue eyes were the strangest thing of all in this strange new world, and the most enticing.

III

The next day Robert ignored his duty with the camels. He pushed his way up the column so he rode closer to Ibn Hafsun, and spoke to him.

The Spanish peninsula, he learned, was like a vast square, all but cut off from France by a chain of mountains, the Pyrenees. More chains of mountains crossed the interior, running roughly east to west, and in the lowlands between the mountains rivers snaked over the land. Four of the five greatest rivers drained west into the Ocean Sea.

The north-west corner, around Santiago de Compostela, was green and temperate, and many people made a living from the sea. In the south-east was more greenery, and there the Moors ran market gardens, rich with fruit trees. But here they were passing through the heart of the country, a vast extent of arid lowlands cut through by the mountains and rivers. The Christians in their degenerate descendant-tongue of Latin called it *meseta*. The winters were long and bitterly cold, the summers dry and intense. There were no woods here, and little in the way of grass, only patchy scrub. No small birds sang, Robert noticed, for there was nowhere for them to nest; only buzzards wheeled, and eagles scouted the hills.

'And the Christians and the Moors?'

Ibn Hafsun said, 'You must think of Spain as sliced into three: the Moors in the south, Christian kingdoms in the north, and a kind of frontier land between. As the Christians have gradually grown stronger, the frontier has, with the centuries, been pushed southwards. Now that the Castilians have captured Toledo the frontier roughly cuts the peninsula in two, east to west: the north Christian, the south Moorish.'

Robert nodded, picturing it. 'And one day that frontier will be pushed all the way south, and Spain will be free of Moors once more.'

'Are you sure? Look around you. Look what the Moors made of this country.'

They happened to be following a river bank. Robert saw that irrigation systems striped the countryside, and along the river itself huge water-wheels turned patiently.

'All this is Moorish,' Ibn Hafsun said. 'There was a high civilisation here, Robert son of Orm. The highest since the Romans. Higher than Christendom.'

'Not so high,' Robert said fiercely, 'that Alfonso's Christian armies could not drive the Moors out.'

Ibn Hafsun shrugged. 'Well, that's inarguable.'

'Must it be so?'

The soft voice startled Robert. It was Moraima, who had come to ride alongside the two of them. She spoke English, her father's language, but heavily accented.

Robert said to her, 'Those are the first words you have spoken to me. And must they be about war?'

'But it's all you talk about. You and our fathers.' Her voice, like her face, was delicate, and yet Robert thought he saw a strength beneath the fragile surface. It only made her more desirable.

'We weren't talking about war. Ibn Hafsun was telling me about the country.'

'Ah,' said Ibn Hafsun, 'but you are a warrior of God – a warrior cub at any rate. Tell me that you aren't dreaming of riding across this land in your mail coat, your sword in your hand, at the side of Rodrigo, El Cid, "The Boss", the greatest Castilian warrior of all!'

Moraima laughed, a sound like bubbling water. 'I ask you again, Robert: must it be so?'

Robert said reluctantly, 'The Pope himself says that if you fight to reclaim Christian lands from infidels, you are fighting for Christ.'

'Well, the Pope would say that,' Sihtric called back from his own mount. 'But the Pope has wider ambitions.'

Across Europe the conflict between Christianity and Islam was already four centuries old. Now the Seljuk Turks, ferociously warlike, had taken the Holy Land itself, all but extinguishing Christianity in the country that had given it birth. And they pressed on the East Roman Empire, long the bulwark between west and east, taking the rich province of Asia Minor. Alexius, emperor in Constantinople, had appealed to the west for help. But after centuries of invasions and war, the post-Roman states of west Europe were like armed camps, fractious and suspicious, bristling with petty armies any of which would have been dwarfed by the legionary forces of old. The Pope, spiritual leader of all these domains, longed to unify them in a great cause.

'And what better ambition for a pope than a war against Islam?' Ibn Hafsun murmured.

Moraima eyed Robert again. 'I ask you once more: Must it be so?'

Robert said, 'I hope not.'

'You do?'

'I would rather you and I were friends, than enemies.'

'Then we will have to see how this little adventure of ours unfolds, won't we?' And she trotted back to her father's side.

The older men exchanged bawdy glances, but Robert ignored them.

IV

In the days that followed, as they pushed steadily south, the country became rougher. The olive groves and vineyards grew wild, the scrub encroached on the roads, and many of the towns looked abandoned. There were some inhabited communities, but all were heavily defended: fortified hilltops, towns with complicated systems of walls and towers. Ibn Hafsun and Orm kept their swords exposed.

Ibn Hafsun said, 'This is the boundary, Robert. This is what you get when great civilisations rub against each other. The Arabs have a word. They call this the *tugur*. The front teeth.'

At last they party approached Toledo. The party drew to a halt, all of them subdued.

It was mid-afternoon, and the sun was in the south, so that, approaching from the north, Robert saw the city in silhouette. The heart of Toledo was a fortress that sat on a promontory, with a river glistening at its feet. And on the plain outside the town, across a stout stone bridge, an army had gathered, pennants glittering in a cloud of dust, tents fluttering in the soft breeze. It was a Christian army, gathered under the cross of Jesus.

Ibn Hafsun came to Robert. 'What do you make of it, soldier?'

Robert glanced around. 'A naturally defensible site, on that rock. The river guards it on three sides. The walls are Moorish?'

'Roman, then Gothic, then Moorish.'

'And yet the town fell to Alfonso.'

'Only months ago. The wounds are raw. You have come to the very edge of Christendom, young soldier. We will stay here only one night. The city is a place of narrow streets, winding, many shadows. Watch your back, and your father's. And tomorrow – al-Andalus! Or what is left of it. Now, come. Have you any coin? I have a feeling those soldiers of the King will extract a toll from us for crossing their bridge ...'

The next day, beyond Toledo, they pressed on, further south again. With every plodding step of the camels the heat gathered, and Robert Egilsson felt as if he was being walked steadily into some great hearth.

They were deep in the territory of the Moors now. That became apparent the first time they stopped at a small town to replace a lame camel. Marwam, a dark, skinny, rodent-faced man, insisted on replacing both their camels with fresh beasts, and for the price he threw in his own services as an escort.

'It might be wise,' said Ibn Hafsun. 'We're a long way past the border with the Christians, but relations are tense among the *taifas* – I mean, the Moorish kingdoms. You never know when you might cross the wrong border, or fail to pay the correct toll.'

But Sihtric snorted his contempt. 'Waste your money on this weasel-eyed camel-driver if you like. I'll have nothing to do with it.'

So Marwam joined the party. As they left, a gaggle of little children ran out onto the road to wave them off, shrieking and jumping, all of them as rodent-faced as Marwam.

Marwam was the first authentic Moor Robert had met – not a mixed-blood like Moraima, or a descendant of a Gothic Christian like Ibn Hafsun – and Robert watched him curiously. Dressed in swathes of grubby white cloth, Marwam was a wiry man who looked as at home on a camel as on foot. As they rode along he sang wailing, nasal songs, the songs of a desert people sung in a country that had once been Roman. But Robert thought that sometimes he was singing to Moraima, for he would gaze at her with deep brown eyes, his words sung in an unfamiliar tongue making Moraima blush.

Robert muttered to his father, 'If I knew the Moorish for "remember your wife and kids" I'd sing that back to him.'

Orm grinned, tolerant. 'I wouldn't worry. She's a city girl. I don't think she has any interest in camel-drivers. He's just flirting, and so is she. Besides, shouldn't you put such things out of your head? Jealousy is a Christian sin, I imagine. As is lust.'

'Most things are,' Robert conceded gloomily.

In all this business of borders and tolls and *taifas*, Robert was learning, to his surprise, that there was more than one Moorish country here in Spain. He had imagined that all of Islam would be united like one vast army, without individual faces or minds, under the orders of the caliph in Baghdad.

In fact the Muslims were diverse peoples. Even the armies who had originally invaded Gothic Spain three hundred years ago – whom the

Christians called Moors, imagining they came from the old Roman province of Mauretania – had not all been Arabic. The leaders had been Arab, yes, but they had been outnumbered by their Berber warriors, who came from the harsh lands of the Maghrib just to the south across the Pillars of Hercules. Many of the Berbers' descendants were prone to complain, even fifteen or twenty generations later, how they had been tricked by the Arabs when it came to parcelling up the old Gothic kingdom.

And, Robert learned, Muslims went to war with each other, as well as with Christians.

It had been fifty years since a single ruler, in Cordoba, had controlled all the Muslim lands in Spain. That ruler, remarkably, had been a second caliph, independent of the one in faraway Baghdad. 'It is as if,' Sihtric said, 'a city like Paris or York hosted a second pope of its own.'

When the caliphate fell, al-Andalus splintered into *taifas* – so many of these little statelets that nobody had been able to count them; there may have been three dozen. But as is the way of politics and war the *taifas* had squabbled among themselves like fish in a pond, eating each other up until there were only half a dozen left.

As they drove steadily south the land became ever starker, drier, dustier, baked in the heat. And yet the irrigation channels brought green life to the land in great broad strips. Sihtric said that 'water courts' sitting in the towns supervised the upkeep of the irrigation systems, which were a communal treasure. The land actually seemed richer than England, where the peasants toiled with heavy ploughs. But then this land was not as God had designed it but as people had made it, people who had walked out of deserts, who knew how to extract life from the slightest drop of moisture.

In one place where they stopped for the night, Marwam paid a farmer a few coins for them to pitch their blankets under the shade of fruit trees. Robert had never seen such fruit, heavy and bright. They were *oranges*, Moraima told him, an Arabic name for a fruit brought here by the Moors. She clambered up a trunk and picked a couple of samples, and showed him how to remove the thick peel. When he dug in his thumbs he squirted her with zest, and when he bit into the fat segments, juice gushed out and rolled down his chin. The orange was bitter, making his tongue curl, but the flavour was like light in his mouth.

So they ate their oranges, their faces plastered with sticky juice and zest, laughing at each other. It was a simple, wordless moment between the two of them which even the faithless camel driver couldn't spoil.

V

At last the party came to Cordoba.

Approaching the walled kernel of the city, they passed through a hinterland of cultivated country. Farthest out estates sprawled, astonishingly green, with hanging gardens and citrus groves crowding the river banks, and with buildings like blocky jewels shining in the sun. These estates were like the villas of the long-gone Romans, Sihtric said. He called them *munyas*, country houses.

Then the old roads brought them through suburbs of the city itself, communities of mud-brick houses that jostled by the road. Sihtric said that the city had long outgrown its Roman walls, and many of its necessary functions had been transplanted out here: residential areas, markets, bathhouses, industry, gardens. Most of the buildings inside the city walls were official, such as palaces, a chancery, the mints, prisons.

But the place had seen better days. The travellers passed burned-out buildings, and even some grand estates looked abandoned. These wrecks were nothing to do with the Christian armies but were scars of the wars between Muslims. Cordoba was no longer a capital of anything, not even of its own destiny, for it had been absorbed into the rule of a *taifa* run out of another Moorish city called Seville.

As they neared the city, vendors of water sacks, meat on sticks, and even bits of sparkling jewellery crowded around the travellers. Beggars too pushed forward, holding up the stumps of severed arms, or stretching open hideous wounds on their faces. Old soldiers, perhaps, or refugees from the cities the Christians had occupied to the north.

At last Cordoba itself loomed before them, a walled forest of minarets and domes and cupolas. They approached a gate in the walls, one of seven. Traffic streamed through it, pedestrians, horses, mules, the camels towering over the rest.

Soldiers stood by the gate, languid. Robert studied them. They wore quilted jackets over long mail coats, and round helmets, and they had mail masks they could pull up over their faces. They carried shields of wood, long spears, stabbing swords and complicated-looking bows. Some of them carried crossbows, which Ibn Hafsun said were of a design that dated back to the Romans. It seemed odd to Robert to see a soldier without Christ's cross emblazoned anywhere on his costume.

They lodged their animals at a stable, and left instructions for their goods to be brought after them. Robert was surprised to find slaves working here; there weren't many slaves in England.

Then they walked into the crowded city itself, Sihtric leading the way. The streets were so narrow that in places two people couldn't pass without brushing, and woven into a network of dead ends and double-backs so dense that Robert was soon lost. His nose was filled with the spicy scents of unfamiliar cooking, and his ears rang with the muezzin cries that billowed out from the towers of the city mosques. Marwam had already turned back, to Robert's relief, but the faces crowding around him were like a hundred Marwams, dark, sharp, their alien language studded with bits of Latin.

They passed an arched gateway in a wall, lobed, delicately shaped of soft stone and covered with intricate carvings. Robert's gaze was led through the arch from the shadow of the street into a sunlit courtyard, where a fountain bubbled in a square garden of tiles and green plants. There was nothing like this in Robert's England, a place of gloomy fortified towns and brooding Norman keeps, nothing like this garden full of water and sunlight. It was like looking through a hole in the wall of the world, a glimpse of paradise.

'This is how we do things here,' Moraima said, watching him. 'Our gardens are the hearts of our homes. Our wealth, poured into beauty for those whom we love to enjoy. Is it different where you live?'

He saw the light of the secret garden reflected in her deep eyes, as if they too were doorways he might enter.

Ibn Hafsun nudged Orm and sniggered, and the girl laughed, and the moment was lost.

VI

They spent a day resting.

Robert, unable to sleep late for the heat, was up at dawn. He went walking at random.

The city was awake before he was, the streets bustling, the markets and mosques busy in the blue-grey light, the muleteers driving their beasts out of the city gates. As he walked he gradually got used to the layout of streets. Moorish houses were knots of buildings gathered around a court-yard, to be reached by narrowing paths that budded off wider highways. There was a logic to it, but it wasn't the straight-line logic of a Roman city like London; here the streets branched like the limbs of a tree, leading to endless dead-ends. The people weren't like English people either. They were a mixed-up sort, the result of generations of intermarriage between the invaders and the old Gothic peoples. Not everybody was Muslim either; there were Christians here, and many Jews.

The city nestled within the circling safety of its old Roman walls, which ran down to a river where waterwheels turned languidly, and which was still spanned by a stout Roman bridge. The city's heart was full of grand buildings, finely tiled, intricately adorned with carved stone and moulded plaster. The greatest building of all was a vast mosque that sprawled in its own compound close to the river: a temple to a god who was not God, a firm Islamic statement planted proudly in a Roman city. There was a sense of wealth here, Robert thought, of care, of intensive labour over every detail. And yet it was an architecture born of war. The buildings had stout fortress-like walls and towers and gate-ways, but these warlike structures were made elegant by their pro-portions, and the fine embellishment of fretwork and stucco and inscription.

As the day wore on he learned the cycle of the city. Because of the heat and the light the very rhythm of life here was quite different from any English city. As noon approached the people retreated to the shade of their homes, windows closed and shutters drawn. Even the animals grew quiet, as if the whole city slept beneath a shroud of dense, dusty orange air. But as evening approached and the first whispers of coolness arrived, the city began to stir once more. The street lights were lit, and the city came alive as a firmament of light and movement, of music and laughter.

Robert was entranced.

On the second morning they made their way to Sihtric's small town house. Robert's heart quickened when Moraima joined them.

Sihtric served them watered wine, and announced that later in the day he would introduce Orm to his sponsor, one Ahmed Ibn Tufayl, a vizier of the emir of the *taifa* which now owned Cordoba. 'When he heard you were coming, Orm, the vizier demanded I bring you to him. The caliphs always saw off the Vikings; this wasn't Alfred's England, weak, backward and divided, and there are few Vikings here. So you're an object of curiosity!'

'I hope I don't disappoint,' Orm growled ungraciously. In the bright Spanish sunlight he was massive, heavy, somehow dark, Robert thought. He wasn't comfortable here. And his head probably hurt from the monkish wine he and Sihtric had consumed the night before. Orm said to Robert, 'Don't you notice anything different about me today?'

'By God's eyes. You cut your hair.'

He stroked his chin. 'Look, a good shave too. And I had a bath.'

Robert was genuinely shocked. 'You didn't.'

'I went to one of those bathhouses the Moors have. Quite pleasant it was, if you can put up with smelling like an East Roman whore.'

Ibn Hafsun smiled. 'You have to make yourself presentable to meet a Muslim ruler. Clean clothes, a wash. The envoys of the Christian kings, even of the Pope, have always known this. Of course Christians aren't quite as in awe of the Moors as they were in my father's day.'

Moraima, serving more wine, passed Robert. 'I'm glad *you* haven't bathed. I quite like the way Christians smell.' And with a fleeting, luring smile, she turned away.

Sihtric lectured them about Cordoba's magnificence. 'At its peak, only a generation ago, it was the greatest city in the west. Why, its population even matched Constantinople. Five hundred mosques. Three hundred bathhouses. Fifty hospitals. Do you even know what a "hospital" is, young Robert?

'And the greatest library in all the world, it is said, flourished here in

28

Cordoba, under the caliphs. It all started when the East Roman emperor sent the caliph a copy of a pharmacology text by Dioscorides – have you heard of him? It was like dropping a bit of hot iron into a pan of water. Scholarship *boiled* in al-Andalus ...'

The caliphs, rich and at peace, embraced learning as an emblem of power and sophistication. And they were much better placed to do so than western Christendom, for they had access to the surviving works of antiquity. Employing legions of copyists and translators, the Moorish scholars merged Greek and Roman learning with what their cousins in Damascus and Baghdad had acquired from the Persians, and they built on what they learned. The result was a flowering in astronomy and physics, medicine and philosophy.

Sihtric said, 'The library itself grew to *four hundred thousand* books. The catalogue alone ran to forty-four volumes! This was at a time when the kings of England were entirely illiterate. But when the caliphate fell the library was broken up. How I wish I had been born a generation earlier. But there are still books milling around the city, as if released into the wild. It is my skill at tracking the books down as much as my learning that makes me so useful to Ibn Tufayl, I think ...'

Sihtric was a man of contradictions. For all his admiration of Cordoba's Moorish achievements, he was keen to play up its deeper Roman origins.

'All of western Europe is the same. All of us dwelling in the vast ruins of the empire, four centuries after some German brute pushed aside the last boy-emperor from his throne. Did you know that the philosopher Seneca came from this very town? And the Emperor Hadrian himself, who made his mark on Britain as you know very well, Orm, came from the Spanish city the Roman called Italica, which is now the capital of our local *taifa*, *Ishbiliya*, or Seville ...'

As he droned on, Moraima, without warning, grabbed Robert's hand, held her finger to her lips and hauled him out of the room. 'Come on. By the time they notice we've gone we'll be far away.'

Robert was thrilled to be off on an illicit adventure with Moraima – to be alone with her at last, with no fathers or lusty camel-drivers in the way. But a lingering sense of duty prompted him to say, 'We have to see this vizier—'

'I'll get you to the palace in time. I thought you were a warrior – you're very timid. Come *on*.'

So they set off, holding hands, giggling and half-running like children.

She led him to a market, crowded and noisy, where stalls were piled high with tiles and bowls, with fine velvets and felts and silks. Moraima said that Cordoban shoes and carpets and paper were famous throughout the Muslim world. There were exotic imports to be found too: the fur of walrus and polar bears from Scandinavia, carved ivory and gold trinkets from Africa, silk, spices and jewellery from the east, even fine wool from England. One stall had a pile of fruit that Moraima had to name for him, save for the oranges: lemons, limes, bananas, pomegranates, watermelons, artichokes. Not even the Norman kings, Robert imagined, ate such exotic stuff as this.

Moraima said, 'They say Cordoba is more like Africa than Europe. That Paris is not like this, or London.'

'Africa starts at the Pyrenees,' Robert said, echoing his father.

'I've never travelled beyond the Pyrenees. I'd love to see London. Or York.'

'I've seen those places, and more.'

'You're lucky.'

He shrugged. 'My mother died when I was small. I go where my father goes. He's a soldier. Somebody's always rebelling, and he goes to sort it out.'

'And London—'

'Big. Dirty. Crowded. A cathedral like a big black pile. The Normans are building an immense fort in the corner of the old Roman walls. And York is a midden. It never recovered from the Normans' harrying twenty years ago.'

'"Harrying"? What does that mean?'

'Ask my father. He was there.'

But that wounded country seemed far from this light-filled city, very far and somehow unreal. 'You know, you aren't much like your father,' he said.

'How so?'

'You seem full of ...' He sought the right word. 'Joy. Your father doesn't seem joyful at all.'

Moraima shrugged. 'He admires the city, the Moors' accomplishments. He relishes the learning. But he despises it at the same time. I think he *has* to despise it, for it is not Christian.'

'And yet he stays here,' said Robert. 'Why? For you?'

'Yes, for me.' But she said this without emotion. 'And he has his projects. Something to do with the library, the books. History.'

'All for the vizier?'

'Paid for by the vizier, yes, but not all *for* him.'

'What projects, then?'

'He doesn't tell *me*.' That seemed to embarrass her, and she said, 'What about your father? Why is he here?'

Robert sighed. 'Something to do with your father, and what he's up to. Though how a bit of book-reading in faraway Spain can affect him I don't know.' He looked at her. 'Moraima – we keep talking about *them*.'

She said coyly, 'So what do you want to talk about?'

He dared to say, 'We could start with the way your eyes match the blue of the sky.'

She gasped, and he saw he'd pleased her. 'You'd like our poetry,' she said, recovering quickly. 'It's full of lines like that. Eyes like stars and breasts like billowing clouds—'

'Maybe I should read you some,' he said.

But she wasn't to be snared so easily. 'Well, how about the colour of the vizier's eyes when we turn up at his palace late? Come on!' And she turned and ran through the market crowds.

Utterly lost in the heart of the city, he had no choice but to follow.

VII

Robert and Moraima found their fathers at the gate in the city walls. Ibn Hafsun the *muwallad* stood by with horses.

Sihtric was impatient, fretting. 'Where have you been? You do not keep the vizier of an emir waiting.'

'Ibn Tufayl will understand,' Moraima said, unconcerned.

Sihtric fumed, but his anxiety to be away got the better of him. They mounted their horses and rode out into the dust of the country.

They headed west, following a road that climbed away from the city by its river. Buildings trailed along this road, some grand residences; evidently it was a road often travelled by the wealthy. But many of the houses looked abandoned, their pretty patios overgrown.

They came to what Robert thought was another town, smaller than Cordoba but still extensive. They paused on a ridge, looking out over this place. Surrounded by a complicated double-wall system, it was largely ruined, buildings burned out, ponds and canals choked with weeds, the wild greenery taking back the gardens.

'This was no town,' Sihtric said. 'It was a palace. Its name is Madinat az-Zahra. Built a hundred and fifty years ago by the caliph, so that he could rule the most prosperous and best-governed land in the west in a manner befitting its grandeur. The whole civil service was moved out here. There were mosques, baths, workshops, stables, gardens, houses.'

'And,' Ibn Hafsun said, faintly mocking as always, 'there was a menagerie stocked with exotic animals from Africa and Asia, and an aviary, and fishponds like lakes.'

Orm said, 'So if it was all so magnificent, what happened?'

Ibn Hafsun said, 'The Berbers smashed the palace up. Those black-eyed savages of the desert.'

'I blame al-Mansur, who brought the Berbers here from Africa in the first place,' said Sihtric.

'He who stole the bell of Saint James,' Robert said.

'Yes. A vizier who, under a negligent caliph, built a private army, gorged on wealth, and attacked the Christians. And in doing so he fatally undermined the caliphate itself. Al-Mansur! What greed! What arrogance! What folly! What suffering he caused!'

'The people loved him, of course,' Ibn Hafsun said drily.

Moraima said to Robert, 'It is said that the fish in the ponds needed twelve thousand loaves of bread every day to feed them. Maybe they should have employed your Jesus as a baker, just as when He fed the five thousand!' She laughed gaily.

Robert grew hot. 'That's blasphemy.'

Sihtric said, 'Yes, well, the Pope's a long way away. Come now, we're keeping the vizier waiting.'

They rode on.

One part of the ruined palace compound had been roughly walled off. They left their horses here and were met by a servant, a shaven-headed man of perhaps forty, who led them further on foot. The servant said nothing, but treated the Christians to withering looks of contempt. Robert grew angry, but Orm whispered, 'Smooth as snot, isn't he?' That made Robert laugh.

Some effort had been made to restore the buildings in this part of the compound. The paths and patios had been cleared, and the ponds scraped clean of rubble. But there was no water, save that brought in pots by servants from the river. The Berbers, in their gleeful orgy of destruction, had wrecked the aqueducts that had once fed the clogged fountains.

They were brought through a series of rooms which were more or less intact. They were box-shaped, almost cubes, with open archways connecting one to the other, so that for Robert it was like wandering through a puzzle. The walls were covered with fine tiles up to about shoulder height, and above that the surface was rich with filigree and intricate plaster mouldings. The arches especially, some of them double or triple, were very finely made. All the rooms gave onto a patio or a garden, and the bright light reflected through the arches, filling the rooms with a golden glow. It struck Robert that there was not one human image to be seen in the decoration, not one face or figure. But the Prophet's words were etched in long stripes around the walls and over the curves of the arches, so each room was like a page from a vast book. It was a written building.

These rooms weren't perfect. In all of them there was scarring, the

33

scorch of fires, damage to the tiling, holes in the ceilings. But still the maze of beautiful rooms somehow drew out Robert's spirit.

And the soft, indirect light washed over the smooth perfection of Moraima's skin. He smiled, and she smiled back.

VIII

So they were brought into the presence of the vizier Ahmed Ibn Tufayl. This was the best room of all, Robert thought. Hangings of Damascus silk covered the upper walls, lamps of silver and crystal gave out a pure light, and an ornate ceiling sparkled with what looked like stars, studs of coloured glass embedded in polished wood.

The vizier himself lay on a couch. 'Sihtric, my friend and colleague. Welcome.' He was a thin, elegant man of perhaps fifty, with a pale colouring, though his nose and cheeks were blotched red. Servants, or guards, stood to either side, scimitars showing at their waists.

Led by Sihtric, the party approached the vizier one by one. Sihtric bowed before him and kissed his hand. Ibn Hafsun followed suit, and then Orm. Robert saw, though, that his father treated the two guards to a challenging stare. Orm was here as an equal, not a supplicant.

The vizier greeted Moraima more tenderly, patting her hair and cupping her cheek. Moraima submitted passively. Robert felt a stab of jealousy, but the vizier's attention was more affectionate than lustful – like a relative, not a lover.

At last it was Robert's turn. Ibn Tufayl's eyes were watchful but blood-shot. When Robert bowed to kiss his hand, on the vizier's fingers he smelled spices and perfumes, but an underlying stink of piss. And Robert was faintly shocked to smell wine on the vizier's breath.

Ibn Tufayl waved a hand. 'Sit, please.'

There were no seats, only couches, and a scattering of cushions on the floor. Sihtric and Moraima and Ibn Hafsun sat cross-legged with the ease of long practice. Orm and Robert followed their example, Orm stiffly. Servants circulated with drinks and sweetmeats, the juices of crushed fruit, and dried figs and grapes.

When Ibn Tufayl spoke, in clear Latin, Robert was surprised it was to him. 'So you're the Christian soldier I've heard so much of from Sihtric. Mother a mystic, father a Viking warrior – yes? A potent mix in young blood.'

'Now, you mustn't tease him, Ibn Tufayl,' Sihtric said. 'His faith is strong. He's probably the purest Christian here – purer even than me.'

Ibn Tufayl arched an eyebrow. 'Well, that isn't hard, Sihtric old friend, as you and I both know. But you don't know much about us infidels, do you, boy? I can tell from your round eyes.'

'I've never seen a place like this before,' Robert blurted.

'Of course you haven't. Beautiful, isn't it? And of course it was far more so before the *fitnah*. By which I mean the turbulence, the fall of the caliphate. I am determined to restore what I can, before the memory of it is lost.

'This is not like your architecture, boy, that you inherited from the Romans, or that your ancestors brought with them from the German bogs. My ancestors were people of the east, of the sun, of the desert. They came to Spain only a century after the death of the Prophet. They had been nomads; they lived in tents! And their architecture reflects that. Think of this room as a fine tent of stone. To do business we sit on the floor, or lean on the walls – which is why they are tiled to your shoulders. The arches let the light and warmth of the world seep in. And in the patios water played, cherished, for in the desert water is the most precious substance of all.' He sighed. 'Some day it will be restored as it was, but perhaps not in my lifetime.'

Orm said mildly, 'But the Christians are strong now.'

Ibn Tufayl was dismissive. 'Let me tell you the truth about Christians in al-Andalus. Have you heard of the Martyrs of Cordoba? Christians have always been tolerated here, as you are *dhimmis*, People of the Book, like the Jews. But these "martyrs", fifty or so, began to challenge the authorities, and to insult Islam. In the end they got what they wanted: a glorious public death. Such self-sacrificing idealists are trained in the Christian monasteries, which we continue to tolerate in our territory. Hotbeds of violence and rogue clerics and the extreme preaching of hate. Thus it goes when an inferior civilisation, yours, meets a higher one, ours. Your only weapon is your own petty lives. But these attacks are pinpricks. Nothing.'

Orm said, 'I don't think I would call the loss of Toledo a pinprick.'

Ibn Tufayl smiled. 'It is a setback. Nothing more. There is talk of summoning help from across the strait. In the Maghrib there is a new movement called the Almoravids. Fierce, strong Muslim warriors. It won't be long before the old city is in the hands of an emir, and the muezzin rings out across the rooftops once more.'

'We'll see,' Robert said, and he glared at the vizier, who laughed at him.

After more talk of this sort, with Ibn Tufayl pressing Orm over details of what he called Viking ways of life and of making war, the little meeting broke up. They were all dismissed, save for Sihtric, who said he had business to discuss with the vizier.

'I'd like to know what kind of "business",' Orm muttered to Robert.

'I don't think I'd trust that vizier,' Robert said. 'He had wine on his breath. Muslims don't drink.'

'No, they don't. Or aren't supposed to. There's more to the vizier than meets the eye. And I'd like to know more about the relationship he has with Sihtric. What hold does Sihtric have over him?' Orm sighed. 'I suppose it was foolish to think there would be anything simple about all this. Sihtric is a complicated man, and this is a complicated place.'

'But you're going to try to resolve your business with Sihtric even so?'

'I think I have to. I'm going to wait here for Sihtric. What will you do?'

Robert grinned. 'Go back to the city with Moraima.'

Orm nodded. 'I thought so. Just be careful.'

'My arm is strong.'

'But your heart isn't, no stronger than mine ever was. Be wary, son.'

IX

'Take your boots off,' Moraima whispered.

They stood in the walled courtyard of Cordoba's great mosque – the Court of the Orange Trees, Moraima called it. It was crowded with the faithful, who washed in the fountains before entering the mosque.

Robert peered nervously through a narrow door into an interior of shadows and columns. 'Are you sure about this? This is a mosque – I'm a Christian—'

'But Jesus is revered in our theology. He was a great prophet. Of course a Christian may enter a mosque.'

'Besides, the mosque is the greatest religious glory of all al-Andalus,' said a boy, approaching them. 'You must see it before you come to conquer us, Christian.'

And a second boy said, 'Just don't go shouting out "Jesus Christ the King" in the Mihrab and you'll be fine.'

These two were about Moraima's age, perhaps a year or two older than Robert. They were slim, dark, dressed in brightly coloured clothes. Healthy, loose-limbed, they were not especially handsome, but they seemed intelligent, good-humoured, confident. Even their Latin was fluent. And they had the air of wealth, of easy riches. Before them Robert felt dull, cloddish, like a lump of earth.

'These are my friends,' Moraima said. 'Ghalib. Hisham.' Robert wouldn't have remembered which was which, save that Ghalib wore a bright red turban. They were sons of courtiers who served Ibn Tufayl, she said.

'I didn't know we'd have company,' Robert said, and he struggled to keep the disappointment out of his voice.

The boys noticed, and they grinned. But what had he expected? Of course Moraima had friends here; of course she had a life of her own, that had nothing to do with him.

Moraima said, 'Oh, come on, Robert. I thought you'd like to meet new people. And they've been eager to meet you. Hisham is studying philosophy, and Ghalib's training to be an astronomer, like his father.'

Ghalib said the word slowly and heavily. '*Astronomer*. I don't suppose you have many of those in England, do you?'

'You'd better write it down for him,' said Hisham. 'Oh, I forgot. You don't read in England either, do you? So what do you do, English Robert?'

Ghalib said, 'There are only two jobs in England. Farmers and whores.'

Robert said tightly, 'Watch your mouth, pretty boy. My mother was English.'

'So what kind of plough did she drive?'

Moraima stood between them hastily. 'That's enough. You're like children – like all men! Come on. Let's go into the mosque, and be respectful with it.'

So Robert entered the great mosque, with Moraima at his side, the stone floor cold under his bare feet, and the two boys sniggering at his back.

But in the mosque's calm spaces, he soon forgot all about the boys.

It was like walking into a forest of slim pillars, linked by arches as delicate as the fronds of palm trees. Moraima said there were more than a thousand pillars in this one building. There were people walking everywhere, respectful, barefoot. Not a priest, or rather an imam, to be seen. The building was full of light, coming from windows and arched doorways, a light turned golden by reflection from the stone. Every way he looked the lines of pillars led his gaze away, deeper and deeper, until he saw walls adorned with inscriptions in beautiful Kufic script, words he could not read but which exhorted the faithful to raise their hearts to Allah.

He was grateful when Moraima's hand slipped into his, for he felt he would soon be lost.

'What are you thinking?' Moraima asked softly.

'That it's beautiful,' he said. 'And that I don't understand it. Of course I could say the same about you.'

She ignored the clumsy compliment. 'It isn't so hard. There is a central axis leading to the Mihrab. That points the way to Mecca; there the imam calls the faithful to Friday prayer. But you may pray wherever you like. The priests don't get in the way here. My father says it's a "different geometry of worship" from the Christian.'

'This is nothing like a Christian church.'

'Well, no. Christians build their churches as Romans once built their basilicas. That's what my father says. The first emirs of al-Andalus started with nothing. They borrowed ideas – the round arches of the Romans, for instance. They even reused what the Romans and the Goths had left behind.' And she showed him how many of the columns, of jasper and marble, were subtly different, in their proportions, their capitals; they were Roman and Gothic relics.

'The arches are meant to look like the branches of palms,' Moraima said. 'It is an oasis in stone.'

'Yet it's centuries since your people came from the desert.'

'Yes. We were thrown down here and *changed*. Isn't it funny? Now we are not African any more, but not European – just us, something different in the world ...'

They walked further, and Robert learned to read the history of al-Andalus in the slim columns of stone.

At first the Muslim conquerors had been in a minority, a few hundred thousand in a Christian population of millions. But that proportion grew quickly, thanks to massive immigration across the straits from Africa. And though tolerance of religion was practised, Islam was the religion of the state, and conversion was a useful step on the road to power. Ibn Hafsun's family had been one Gothic dynasty who had abandoned the cross for the crescent. And as the numbers of Muslim worshippers in Cordoba grew, so the great mosque was extended several times to accommodate them – most recently by al-Mansur, the over-reaching vizier who had brought the calamity of the *fitnah* upon al-Andalus.

They walked still deeper into the mosque. In places there were multiple arches, arches built on top of others like children standing on each others' shoulders, all exquisitely carved. And the Mihrab, another arch adorned with gold leaf, was like a gateway to paradise. Its materials were a gift to al-Andalus from Constantinople, said Moraima.

Lost in the mosque's cool spaces, Robert realised he hadn't been aware of the two boys, Ghalib and Hisham, for some time.

'Oh, they got bored long ago,' said Moraima when he mentioned them. 'Come. Let's get some air.'

X

When Sihtric was done with the vizier, he had suggested to Orm that the two of them should take a ride, further out into the country.

Orm mounted his horse suspiciously. 'Where are we going?'

'You'll see. Go ahead, boy . . . So, what of Robert? He seems drawn by the Moorish world.'

'He's his mother's son, may God help him. He's a confused young man – more confused than he knows. But it's the fact that he's drawn to your daughter that concerns me more. No good will come of it,' muttered Orm.

'He's his father's son too. You were just as young and foolish once, Orm.'

'Yes,' Orm snapped. 'And it led to tragedy.'

Sihtric said testily, 'But if we ban them from seeing each other they will just ignore us. We'll have to find a way of coping with things as they unfold.'

'So what do we do in the meantime?'

'I suggest we pursue the business for which you came all this way.' He grinned. 'I think you are going to enjoy this.'

They topped a small rise, and Sihtric reined in his horse. He pointed. 'There. What do you see, among those olive trees?'

Orm stared. There was much activity going on in the olive grove. The centre of it seemed to be a kind of machine that nestled among the trees, a long cart that rested on three sets of widely spaced wheels. A large wooden crescent-shape dominated one end, and its upper surface was meshed by ropes and gleaming metal. The whole was obscured by a kind of scaffolding, through which a boy clambered, fixing ropes.

The machine was the product of a kind of open-air workshop, Orm saw now. Men and boys moved between furnaces, lathes, piles of timber, and tables heaped with gleaming metal components, and scholars came and went between rows of tents among the olive trees.

'Quite a sight,' he said, non-committal.

'It is, isn't it? What are we building, do you think?'

Orm shrugged. 'Some kind of wagon?'

'Come, Orm, stretch your limited imagination. Just look at it. Never mind the scale: tell me what you see.'

The shaft, the bow, the ropes. 'It looks like an arbalest,' Orm said. 'Which the English call a crossbow ...' But an arbalest was a gadget small enough for a man to hold in his arms. This machine sprawled across a field, and had a boy actually walking along its back. Orm muttered prayers to the pagan gods of his childhood. 'By all that's holy—'

'Oh, there's nothing holy about it.'

'Aethelmaer?'

'Aethelmaer. Come, let's ride down.'

Orm remembered Aethelmaer.

In the last days of the reign of King Edward the Confessor, Sihtric had attached himself to the court of Harold, Earl of Wessex, as a priest-confessor – and as a prophet of sorts. He believed he was in the possession of a prophecy already four centuries old, a calendar-like vision called the Menologium of Isolde, whose sole purpose was to ensure an English victory over the Normans in the year of the great comet – the year of Our Lord 1066. Not that it had done much good. Harold, who had refused to take all the prophecy's advice, had fallen to defeat by the Normans.

But during his career as a court Sibyl, Sihtric had learned of the existence of a rival.

'Aethelmaer! A fat, crippled monk from Wiltshire,' he said with some bitterness. 'Who had also been uttering prophecies about the comet. I've since found his very words, among his papers.' He quoted from memory: '"You've come, have you, o comet? You've come, you source of tears to many mothers. It is long since I saw you; but as I see you now you are much more terrible, for I see you brandishing the downfall of my country ..."'

'And you summoned him to Westminster.'

'Yes. You were there, Orm, you remember.'

His useless legs stinking of rot and unguent, the monk had wheezed his way through an account of his prophecy – which turned out not to have been his at all, but gabbled out by a young man called Aethelred, who had been abandoned as a child, taken in by the monastery at

Malmesbury, and then had his short, unhappy life curtailed by debauched brothers.

'But not before he had left behind a remarkable body of work, studied and preserved by Aethelmaer and others.'

'I saw them. Sketches of machines. Siege engines, catapults ...'

'I call the designs the Codex of Aethelmaer.' Sihtric smiled. 'The Engines of God.'

Orm struggled to remember the fantastic designs he had glimpsed just once, decades ago, and had never understood even then. 'But they were just scribbles on parchment. In a lifetime of study, Aethelmaer could build none of them.'

'Not quite,' Sihtric said. 'He did try to build one, remember? That was how he became crippled.'

Orm shook his head. 'I never understood that. Why would you *want* to fly like a bird? Of course none of this means a thing unless you can actually build these mechanical marvels of yours.'

'True enough,' Sihtric said. 'And I think you would be pleased to learn that I too have failed like Aethelmaer, wouldn't you, Orm the Viking? Well, you're about to be disappointed.'

Orm stared at him. 'You mean the arbalest? Sihtric, can you really be developing gadgets, weapons, from the plans you stole from that mad monk?'

'Interesting choice of words,' Sihtric said. 'Stole? I hardly think so. You met Aethelmaer. Old, crippled, he could do no more than have his arse wiped by some young novice, and probably enjoyed it too.'

'Your talk is sometimes filthy for a priest,' Orm said.

'Well, I'm a filthy sort of priest. Anyhow Aethelmaer's laborious mechanical sketching would have gone no further when he died, if not for my "stealing". Am I not honouring his legacy, by trying to pursue the designs he left?

'And, "gadgets"? You make them sound like toys. These are engines, Orm. Engines of war – and, perhaps, of peace. Come now. Let me show you.' Sihtric spurred his horse forward.

Orm, overwhelmed, followed.

XI

Robert and Moraima walked out of the mosque into dazzling daylight.

They headed down to the river, where waterwheels turned with a creak of wooden gears – Moraima said the wheels were called *norias* – and boats with colourful sails steered through the arches of the Roman bridge. On the bank, amid a clinking of coins, vendors sold food and water and parasols.

Moraima said, 'You were affected by the mosque, weren't you? Not everybody is. I think you're deep, Robert son of Orm.'

'Am I?' He laughed. 'Well, maybe compared to Ghalib and Hisham.'

'Now you're being jealous, and that's *not* deep. I can't always tell what you're thinking, though. What you're feeling.'

He thought it over. 'My time in Spain – I didn't know what to expect. That journey down through the country, the emptiness, the heat ...' He was shy about this, but he tried to express himself. 'And when I walk into these marvellous places, the mosque, the palace – something inside me – it's like a bird fluttering in my chest.'

She astonished him by placing her hand over his. 'My father said you would be like this. You have your father's muscles, but the soul of your mother.'

'Whose soul does he say you have?'

'His sister's. My aunt, Godgifu, who died before either of us was born. And who loved your father, Orm.'

That was a shock. 'I knew nothing of that.'

She looked at him directly. 'Do you think love can cross generations?'

Confused, he turned away. 'I didn't come here for love. I came here because of my father's business with yours.'

'Yes. Our fathers are both veterans of Hastings, and I suppose something like that shapes you for ever. But the past is dead, gone, and they are old men. Who cares about our fathers' business? We are young. We are the future.'

He looked at her. 'You're talking about us.'

'What about us?'

He sighed, faintly irritated. 'There you go again. You drop hints, and when I respond you turn away and go all coy.'

She smiled. 'Don't tell me you don't like it. Would you like there to be an *us*?'

He gazed at her, hot in his tunic of English wool. 'You know I would, or you wouldn't talk like this.'

She said, '*But* . . .'

'But we're so different. Muslim and Christian!'

'There are ways around that. The People of the Book are tolerated here.'

He grunted. 'Not in England, they're not. And you're becoming a scholar, as far as I can see. While I will never be anything but a soldier.'

'There's plenty of work for soldiers in Spain,' she said.

He smiled. 'Let's keep it simple. Do you think it would be a sin before God or Allah if I kissed you?'

'We could always find out.' She stepped towards him. Her skin was the smoothest surface he had ever seen, utterly flawless, and as her full lips parted he could smell the subtlest spice, a pepper perhaps.

But there was a rude cry. 'Hey, Christian! Take a look!' It was Ghalib.

XII

Orm paced out the mighty weapon.

The body of the shaft was forty paces long, perhaps two wide, and mounted on three axles. The bow itself, twenty paces from tip to tip, was made of wood layers, finely cut and polished, that ran in smooth, pleasing curves, gleaming in the intense sunlight. It was like a section of a boat, perhaps, or a monstrous piece of furniture.

'You've used arbalests,' Sihtric called. 'Tell me about them.'

'The bow is usually made of metal.'

'Not here. We couldn't cast such an immense bow, and nor could it be bent back if we did. Look here, we use laminated wood, layers pasted and nailed together. We hired boat-builders from your Viking homelands.'

'The vizier's pockets must be deep.'

'And how do you load a crossbow?'

Orm grunted. 'Depends. The old-fashioned sort, you bend over, put your foot on a stirrup, catch the bowstring in a hook on your belt, and straighten up until you've got the string in the lock. The newer sort you have a little hand-crank to draw back the string. You put your bolt in the groove, and press a lever to release it.'

'The principles are just the same here. Look at this.' Long metal screws had been built into the body of the stock. 'These are used to draw back the string. It isn't hard; a single man can turn that wheel, down there. Or you can use a mule. And look, see how the carriage wheels tip outward? That's to give the base more stability. Here's a tilting platform so you can raise the bow, and aim the flight of the bolt. And here, you see, anchors lock the crossbow to the ground and reduce recoil.'

'And have you fired such a thing?'

46

'Only in tests. We're still refining the design. How well do your hand bows perform?'

Orm shrugged. 'A range of two or three hundred paces. You can pierce chain mail.'

Sihtric grinned. 'This beauty should have a range of *miles*. And it will pierce masonry. Thus, one of Aethelmaer's designs, all but realised – all but ready to be deployed in war. Tell me you're not impressed.'

Orm pursed his lips, and walked around the machine once more. 'Yes. I'm impressed by what you've built. But imagine this in war. It would take a long time to load, longer to haul it around the countryside to aim it – and it could be destroyed by a single burning arrow.'

Sihtric sighed. 'All right. But what if I told you that instead of just knocking down a bit of wall, my arbalest could deliver a bolt capable of laying waste an entire fort, even a city? *A single bolt*! What then?'

Orm grimaced. 'That sounds a fever dream, and an ugly one.'

'But Aethelmaer had such dreams, or Aethelred did. I can show them to you, sketched in the notes. Dreams of a super-weapon – Aethelmaer called it *Incendium Dei*, the Conflagration of God. Perhaps it is something like Greek fire – I don't know. But the only clues he left for it are encrypted, and it remains beyond the capabilities even of the scholars of al-Andalus to decipher. Later I'll show you the Codex itself – much study remains to be done on it. But first, come. I'll show you how we work here.'

Leading their horses, they walked away from the mighty arbalest and through the open-air workshop. Orm glanced with interest at the tools of the carpenters and metal-workers. He had ordered several swords in the course of a long fighting life, and had come to appreciate the metal-workers' art; casting the immense screws of the arbalest must have set them significant challenges.

On some of the tables models were set out, intricate wooden toys that looked like birds or beetles or fish. They were models made from designs even more astonishing than the great arbalest, Orm saw, engines that flew and swam and crawled. Some of them were sliced open so you could see the wooden skeleton within, and the bodies of tiny men working oars or hauling on wheels. The boy trapped in Orm's battered warrior's body longed to hold these gadgets, to play with them.

In one of the tents a wooden floor had been set down, a few paces across. Its surface was incised into rows, along which stones the size of fists painted black or white were lined up. Two scholars argued in rapid Arabic over a parchment. In response to their commands a boy jumped about over the board, moving stones from one row to the next.

Occasionally he apparently made a mistake, and his reward was a volley of abuse, but when he got it right the scholars forgot the boy and argued over the patterns he conjured.

'So,' Sihtric said. 'Any idea what this is, Orm?'

Orm shrugged. 'Some kind of game?'

Sihtric snorted. 'This is deadly serious. The scholars are working out the trajectories of an arbalest bolt. We are developing an aiming system, you see. And the boy with his counters on the board is figuring the numbers for the scholars as they call out the sums.'

Orm frowned. 'I don't see any numbers.'

'But they are here nonetheless, represented by the beads in their columns. This is called an abacus, Orm. It's a counting system. You can add, subtract. You can even multiply numbers together with ease.'

Orm scoffed. 'Everybody knows you can't figure numbers beyond nine hundred.'

'Using this, you can go as high as you like. With such gadgets a ten-year-old Moorish child can count better than the King of England. I'm not surprised *you* haven't heard of this, or of Arabic mathematics in general. Mark my words, one day everybody in Europe will be counting this way.'

'Turning prophet again, Sihtric? Well, we won't be around to see it, one way or another.'

'True. But it's this sort of learning I came here to discover, and to exploit. Ah, here we are. My copy of Aethelred's original sketches.' It was a well-thumbed compendium of parchments – a document Orm hadn't seen for twenty years, since the day he had met Aethelmaer in Westminster. 'The Engines of God . . .'

XIII

At Ghalib's mocking call Robert turned away from Moraima and looked towards the river. Hisham was standing on a wall along the bank.

And Ghalib had somehow climbed up onto a waterwheel. As it turned, he was climbing up from one spoke to the next, as if clambering over a treadmill. He was soaked to the skin, his red turban bright, and he was laughing. 'Hey, Moraima – hey, God's warrior! Look at me, look at me!'

Moraima laughed, but she clamped her hand over her mouth. 'Allah preserve him. He'll get himself killed.'

Robert strode towards the waterwheel, pushing through a gathering crowd of laughing onlookers. 'Get down off there, you idiot!'

Hisham threw a mock punch at Robert. 'You're just jealous because Moraima's looking at him, not you.'

Robert glared. 'Unless you shut up she will be looking at *you* when I push your teeth down your throat.'

Hisham returned the challenge for one heartbeat, then backed off.

'Hey, Christian.' Ghalib was calling again. 'Watch this.' Now he was heading for the wheel's mighty axle. He was spun around the hub, turning head-over-heels with each revolution. The wood was soaked by spray and was slippery.

Moraima ran forward. 'Get down! Oh, get down, you fool!'

Ghalib grabbed a strut with one hand, then threw himself backwards, flinging out the other hand, so he was splayed out over the hub, turning over and over on the wheel. 'Hey, look at me! I'm crucified! I'm Jesus on the cross!'

He actually got a laugh from the onlookers, and a smattering of applause. Hisham played up. He pulled his shirt over his head, and wailed in a loud, high voice. 'And I'm His mother the Virgin! Oh, my son, my only son, what have those awful Romans done to you?'

On the wheel, Ghalib kept grinning, but his expression was forced, and Robert saw he was tiring.

Then his right hand slipped from the wood. He dangled from his left arm, and flailed, trying to get a fresh hold with his right hand. But the wheel turned remorselessly, and he flipped over, and his left hand started to slip too. He tried desperately to grab onto something, anything.

And he pushed his right arm inside the wheel, into the machinery. Robert heard a distant crunch, like an owl chewing a mouse's bone. Ghalib didn't even scream. He fell down the face of the wheel, his right arm dangling like a blood-soaked rag, and splashed into the water.

The watching people just stared. The wheel turned as if Ghalib had never existed.

Robert ran over the cobbles and climbed onto the bank wall beside Hisham. There was barely any room between the wall and the turning wheel. But there was Ghalib, floating in the water, apparently unconscious. The water all around him was stained red. And soon he would be drawn into the wheel's machinery again.

Moraima grabbed Robert's arm. 'You must help him.'

Cursing, he kicked off his boots for the second time that day. Then he jumped, feet first, his arms tucked in at his sides, and plummeted down into the water.

XIV

Weary from the heat and light, Orm and Sihtric sat in the shade of an awning and sipped water laced with lemon juice. They looked out over the scaffolding that encased the arbalest.

Sihtric said, 'The principles are simple, but the devil is in the detail, Orm. Our ambition constantly outruns our capabilities. On the arbalest, for instance, I've lost count of the number of spring shafts we've stripped, the bow arms we've fractured. We learn, step by step.' He riffled through the much-thumbed sketches of Aethelmaer's designs, with elaborations and annotations added by Moorish scholars. 'It is as if the wretched Aethelred was given a glimpse of the future. And we poor fools labour to build the machines of another century with the tools and materials of this.

'But there remains the central mystery of the *Incendium Dei*, which will give the punch to these weapons. Look, here is the scrap of cipher Aethelmaer left.' He pointed to a line of spidery lettering, headed simply *Incendium Dei*:

BMQVK XESEF EBZKM BMHSM BGNSD DYEED OSMEM HPTVZ
HESZS ZHVH

'I saw this before, at Westminster,' Orm said. 'It meant nothing to me then, nor does it now.'

'Nor me, and that's the problem. Well, nobody said it would be easy.'

'And you've devoted your life to this stuff ever since Hastings?'

Sihtric shrugged. 'After Harold fell, after my Menologium lost its value, I had no purpose. I needed a new goal.'

'You could,' Orm pointed out, 'have found some parish to serve. There has been plenty of suffering among the English these last twenty years.'

Sihtric smiled, almost sadly. 'Me, a humble parish priest? After I was nearly a king-maker? I don't think so. I wanted power – that's the truth and I don't deny it. I had no other purpose in mind. And I saw Aethelmaer's designs as a way to achieving that power.'

'So you found a way to live here.'

'It took time. You may remember I had a contact in Ibn Sharaf of Toledo, the noted astronomer, who corresponded with me in London. He gave me a start. After that I found a place in a monastery. I quickly learned Arabic, which is the language of government here. I made some money translating the Bible into Arabic, for other Mozarabs. There are Christians here who have grown up reading only Arabic. Imagine that!'

'And you too are a Mozarab,' Orm said. 'A "nearly Arab". You are defined by what you are not. Tolerated or not, I don't think I would like to live with such a label.'

'Few do,' conceded Sihtric. 'And there are boundaries to that tolerance. The Moors are clannish, Orm. You can't just find the local lord and offer him your services, as in England. With the Moors it's all family and patronage and who you know – devilish hard to break into. And under Islamic law there are limits to the tax you can impose on a Muslim, but you can tax Christians as much as you like. And then, Mozarabs are excluded from the higher levels of government, from power. It's actually a good career move to do as Ibn Hafsun's family once did, and convert. But then I am a priest; that course is excluded to me.' The bitterness in his voice was obvious. 'We survive, we Mozarabs. But we are a cowed people.'

'And yet you prospered.'

'Well, I formed a relationship with the vizier, Ibn Tufayl. I told him my goals; I showed him Aethelmaer's designs. He sponsored my work. This is an age of war. I think he regards my work as a worthwhile investment: a relatively small outlay for a possibly handsome return.'

Orm frowned. 'What sort of relationship?' This seemed to him the central mystery of Sihtric's life here.

But Sihtric would only say, 'There are some things it's better an innocent like you never learns, Orm.'

Orm, irritated and patronised, tried another approach. 'Ibn Tufayl works for the emir in Seville. If he turns your arbalest on other Moors, that's one thing. But what if he turns it on the armies of the Christian kings? Have you thought about that? You're building these machines with Moorish money. But *who are they for?*'

Sihtric glanced around, as if they might be overheard. 'That particular truth is murky. I came here seeking power and influence for myself, that's all, ignoble as it is. But while here I have discovered a higher purpose.'

Orm laughed. 'You always did have ideas above your station, priest.'

'Yes, well, I'll have to show you, in good time, and then we'll see what you have to say about it. And in the meantime, we have another murky truth to explore. Don't we, Orm?'

'You mean Eadgyth's Testament.' He felt uncomfortable, even though he had come all this way to discuss this.

Sihtric scoffed. 'What do you think about that, Orm? That you, a Viking whose father worshipped trees, married a woman who was given a vision of God?'

Orm's discomfort deepened. 'Isn't that possible?'

'*You know the truth already*, Orm. You have seen it. You know all about the Menologium, and indeed the Codex of Aethelmaer. You know they were authored by an agent, or agents, intent on deflecting destiny. And now you have felt the cold hands of another history-meddler on your shoulder. Yes, *another*, Orm, I'm convinced of that. For your Witness seems opposed to the intervention made by the author of my Codex, doesn't she? We're caught in a war of meddlers, it seems.'

Orm stared at him. '"Meddlers"? That's a very human word.'

'I use it intentionally. There's nothing divine about the Weaver, Orm. He fiddles with history as a poor painter adds one brushstroke after another, never satisfied, for he has no true vision. And not only that, the Weaver fails to achieve his goals. William won at Hastings despite the Weaver's tinkering. No, Orm. The Weaver may not be human; he may be more – or less – than that. But I am convinced he is not God – and nor is your Witness.'

Orm's shock deepened. 'But how can he send words through time, into the head of another, save through a miracle? I have seen it myself, in Eadgyth. When she spoke her prophecy, *they were not her words*.'

'Trickery!' Sihtric said. 'Machinery! Working on my machines with the Moors has shaped my thinking, Orm. Think of it. You can build a machine that can throw a bolt miles. Waterwheels and canals that can turn a desert green! If you can do all that—'

'It's one thing to throw a bolt,' Orm protested. 'Another to throw words across centuries.'

'I can't imagine how it's done. But I also can't imagine what our machines will be capable of in five hundred years, or a thousand. I can put no limits on them, any more than I put limits on God.' His tone was edgy, uneasy.

'Is that heresy, priest?'

'Ah, that's a good question, and I'm a long way from any bishop who might be able to answer it for me.'

Orm stared at him, trying to pick his way through this morass of theology and speculation. 'You know, I used to talk about you with your sister, before Hastings. Even then we thought your ambition, that whole business of the Menologium, was destroying you. Turning you away from God. That was twenty years ago.'

'Well, perhaps you were right.' Sihtric laughed darkly. 'Nothing changes, does it?'

They were disturbed by a horseman, who came galloping in a cloud of dust. He was hot, bedraggled. 'Father! They said I would find you here.'

'Robert? What's wrong?'

'There has been an accident. A boy, Ghalib—'

Sihtric frowned. 'I know him – the son of a court favourite. Is he dead?'

'Not yet. But he is so badly injured he soon will be, that's for sure.' Robert told them what had happened. 'I got him out of the water – I tied off the damaged arm. I tried to save him, Father.'

Orm stood. 'We must sort this out,' he said to Sihtric.

'Of course,' Sihtric said. 'But, Robert, nobody will blame you if you tried to save this boy. And besides, the doctors here are better than you can imagine. Don't despair – leave that to me.' He winked at Orm. 'Let's go!'

They ran to their horses, and the three of them galloped away, leaving the scholars to clear away the drinks, to wipe the horse-raised dust from their plans and models and tables, and to return to their patient work on the tremendous arbalest.

XV

Ibn Tufayl had ordered a hospital to be set up for his court in the ruined palace at Madinat az-Zahra. It was just a collection of tents, erected in the shelter of the walls of roofless rooms. Here Robert had to wait with Orm while Sihtric made inquiries about Ghalib.

After the hasty ride back from the arbalest, Robert was hot, dirty, his clothes still stinking of river-bottom mire and soaked through by Ghalib's blood. He tried to think.

How would it be if Ghalib died? Of course it wasn't his fault that Ghalib had fallen – it wasn't his fault that Ghalib had been mucking about on the waterwheel in the first place, and he had risked his own neck by dragging Ghalib out of the water. But the fact was he had been flirting with Moraima, a Muslim girl, and the two boys wouldn't have trailed around after them if not for that. Robert didn't want the death of Ghalib on his conscience. And he didn't want his burgeoning relationship with Moraima, such as it was, to be hauled into the light.

This was going to take some sorting out the next time he was in a confessional box.

Sihtric beckoned, and led them into one of the tents.

Robert was hugely relieved, if astonished, to find Ghalib sitting up in a chair. But his right arm terminated just below the elbow, a stump wrapped in clean white bandages. The boy looked pale, his gaze wandering; perhaps he was drugged. But he was alive, indeed he was conscious, and he didn't seem to be in any pain. And when he saw Robert, Ghalib's eyes filled with shame and anger.

Hisham stood beside Ghalib. Attendants fussed around, orchestrated by a portly man in pristine white robes. When he saw the visitors this man approached them. His face, round and sleek, looked as if it had been dipped in oil. He held his hands before him; small like a child's, they were scrubbed pink-clean, and showed no signs of calluses or scars. He said to Sihtric, 'Father. We have met before.' His accent was strange. 'My name is Abu Yusuf Yunus.'

'Ah, yes. The Egyptian.'

'My grandfather was Egyptian,' Abu Yusuf Yunus said stiffly. 'I am related by marriage to the Banu Zuhr family. I am a close friend of Abd al-Malik, while my father studied general medicine with his father, Muhammad Ibn Marwan Ibn Zuhr. Furthermore my grandfather studied with al-Zahrawi. We followed the prescripts of the *al-Tasrif* in treating this poor child . . .'

Orm grunted, impatient, and he pulled Sihtric aside. 'What's he babbling about?'

'Just establishing his credentials. Making sure I know who he is and where he stands. I told you, Orm, it's all family with the Moors. They're all Ibn this or Abu that, the son of him or the father of the other, their lineage carried like a flag. And these scholars are the same, all boasting about their academic lineage, who taught who what.'

Abu Yusuf Yunus, unable to make out their English words, walked towards the injured boy. In stilted Latin he said, 'The arm was almost severed below the elbow by the waterwheel's machinery – muscles, arteries and blood vessels all lacerated, the bone, too, all but cut through. To that extent the injury was like the result of a blow with a sword. But the lower arm was crushed, the flesh pulped and the bone ground up, as if the boy had been trampled, say.' Ghalib looked up at him dimly, and submitted passively as the surgeon began briskly to unravel the bandages on his arm. 'Your young Christian—'

'Robert,' Orm growled. 'My son.'

'Robert didn't save the boy's life merely by dragging him from the water, but by stemming the blood loss from the damaged arm. He tied it off with a bit of rope below the shoulder.'

'I did that,' Hisham said promptly. And he stared at Robert, as if daring him to contradict this naked lie.

'Then you are a hero, as much as Robert – more so, perhaps, for you used your brain rather than your muscles. Well done. Well done indeed.'

Robert looked away. Orm put his hand on his shoulder.

The bandages removed, Abu Yusuf Yunus exposed the wounded arm. Flaps of crudely cut skin were folded over the stump and stitched with gut. The seams leaked blood and a yellowish pus. Abu Yusuf Yunus clapped his hands. Attendants came bustling up with bowls of water and oils, and began to mop the wound. Ghalib twisted, but the attendants held him down.

Abu Yusuf Yunus said, 'I had to amputate the crushed lower arm, of course. Such was the damage, the main challenge was to leave flaps of skin intact enough for the later closure. It took some work, then, to find the severed blood vessels and arteries and stitch them closed. Those arteries have a way of drawing back from a cut, and you have to rummage around in there.' Gruesomely, he wiggled his pink fingers. 'With that done, it was a case of clean out, cauterise and stitch closed. The danger now is infection – that immersion in river water won't have helped – but we do have treatments for gangrene, should it develop.'

'You've done a remarkable job,' Sihtric said effusively.

The surgeon nodded, his eyes half-closed, accepting his due.

Orm growled to Robert, 'Doctors, they're all the same. Never trusted them. Look at this oaf. Cares more about preening and posturing and taking the credit than about his patient.'

'Is that what you think?' The voice was low, silky, but faintly slurred. 'Perhaps you really are a barbarian, Orm the Viking.'

They turned, and Robert found himself facing the vizier.

Ibn Tufayl's eyes were bloodshot and staring. His face was deep red, his hair mussed, his black robe subtly disarrayed. He looked as if he had been woken in a hurry and dressed too quickly. And once again his breath stank of stale wine.

The surgeon and his attendants shrank away, bowing.

'I have just heard of the accident to the eldest son of my friend Ibn Bajjah. How did this happen?' He turned on the surgeon. 'Whose fault was this?'

Abu Yusuf Yunus showed the vizier the repaired wound. 'The boy is in no danger. I, Abu Yusuf Yunus, have saved him.'

The vizier grabbed the surgeon's jaw with his cupped hand, gripping so hard that his fingers made white indentations in the surgeon's flabby cheeks. 'Of course you saved him, doctor,' Ibn Tufayl said harshly. 'That's your job. If you had let him die, you would soon have followed him to paradise, believe me. I didn't ask you how you did your job, Abu Yusuf Yunus. I asked you whose fault it was.'

The surgeon's hands flapped like a bird's wings. 'Lord – I can't say – I wasn't there.'

'It was him.' Ghalib had spoken. In his chair, his face pale, his eyes glazed, he pointed straight at Robert. 'He caused this. He is to blame.'

The vizier pushed the surgeon away, and Abu Yusuf Yunus stumbled back, shaking.

Robert, unable to imagine the consequences of this moment, prepared to defend himself.

Orm stepped between the vizier and his son, with his cloak thrown back so that the hilt of his sword was revealed. 'This is a false accusation. My son saved this foolish boy. He did not harm him. Quite the opposite. Perhaps Ghalib is addled by the pain and the drugs.'

Ibn Tufayl said to Ghalib, 'Tell me what happened. What are you accusing this boy of? Did he push you into the water – hurl you at the waterwheel – what?'

'None of those things,' Ghalib said, his own speech slurred. 'But we would not have been at the river at all if not for him.' Ghalib glared at Robert, and Robert recognised real hatred shining through the fug of the morphia. If he had despised Robert as a Christian and a foreigner before, now he was humiliated that he owed his life to him. Ghalib said, 'We were trying to protect her, from this English animal. That's why we were following him. For *her*.'

'It's true,' Hisham gabbled now. 'I was there. He was trying to seduce her. Robert the Christian.'

The vizier was having trouble following this. 'Who? *Who* was he trying to seduce?'

'Moraima,' Ghalib said bluntly.

The vizier howled, and lunged at Robert. Orm blocked his way. The vizier's own attendants ran up, and tried to separate the men.

Amid this shouting and chaos, Ghalib cried out, and slumped forward in a faint.

XVI

'I was lonely,' Sihtric whispered. 'In the end, it comes down to that, and my own weakness. And the result was a new life.'

'Moraima,' Robert said.

'Yes.' Sihtric smiled wistfully. 'And now I will never be lonely again.'

'I think,' Orm said sternly, 'that you had better tell us the whole truth, Sihtric. About you, Moraima, and the vizier.'

Robert, Sihtric and Orm had been escorted to a battered, fire-damaged room. Here the three of them sat, on worn floor coverings and baggy cushions. Bright daylight filtered through more of the charming archways that had so entranced Robert. But now massive soldiers stood in those arches, silhouetted.

Orm had growled at being put under armed guard. The nervous attendant who had brought them here assured them it wasn't like that, they had been brought here for their own safety at a time of disturbance.

Sihtric had advised them just to put up with it. 'They've done this before. I've seen it. Just freeze the situation for a few hours, while they get him sobered up. And I've seen some of the potions they use. Even tried some myself. Sometimes they will bleed you, or rub ground-up elephant tusk onto your teeth. So decadent were some of the caliphs that the task of making them sober enough to be seen in public inspired a whole library full of medicinal wisdom.'

Now Orm said, 'Just tell us the truth, Sihtric.'

Sihtric eyed him. 'What do you imagine that truth is?'

Robert blurted, 'That they are lovers. Ibn Tufayl and Moraima. Or perhaps it's worse than that. Perhaps that old goat of a vizier took her by force.'

Orm eyed the guards. 'I assume our guardians do not speak any English. But I wouldn't be prepared to bet my life on it. Think about your words, Robert.'

'Lovers?' Sihtric sighed. 'If only it were that simple . . .'

He said it all began with his own loneliness.

'You must remember I came here as a scholar. My sketches of war machines intrigued the vizier, as I had hoped, and he gave me a small stipend. As I told you I had ways to make more bits of money independently, from selling Arabic translations of the Bible to Mozarabs, and from administering to their spiritual needs. And as I began to gain access to the libraries of the emir I developed my own interests, outside the narrow scope of Aethelmaer's designs. Interests in the career of the Moors in Spain, for instance. And the secret history I discovered – well. That's for another day, Orm, but we must speak of it, for it forms my whole purpose.

'What I did not anticipate was that these small signs of independence on my part were troubling to a man like the vizier. These are fractured times in al-Andalus, a time of turmoil and threat. With enemies both within the *taifa* court and outside, the vizier needs to know whom he can trust. No, more than that: he can trust only those whose souls he owns entirely.'

'And so,' Orm said, 'he set out to own you.'

'Yes.' Sihtric sighed again. 'For he sees my weaknesses more clearly than I see them myself – you can ask my confessor, it's true. I was alone, Orm. Nobody even *cares* about England here. To the Moors the civilised world stretches from Damascus to Cordoba, and Europe is a cold, dark place full of squabbling little statelets, far away and of no importance save as a source of slaves. And I am a man,' he whispered, as if this were the worst confession of all. 'A man alone, in an atmosphere of remarkable sensuality . . .'

The rulers of Seville, like some of the caliphs that went before them, were extravagant, indulgent, given to gesture and spectacle and pleasure. Their hedonism was spoken of throughout al-Andalus – indeed throughout the Muslim world. 'Let me give you one example. There was a prince whose wife, a Christian from the north, wept because she missed the snows of winter, which she would never see again. So he ordered a legion of gardeners to transplant a whole forest of almond trees, *in blossom*, and move them to the square beneath her bedroom window. They did this at night, and in silence. And when she woke up, her husband was able to say, "There, my beloved, I have brought you your snow!" I can't imagine William the Bastard making such a gesture, can you?'

Orm didn't smile. 'And so, in this atmosphere of indulgence, your soul softened.'

'I was seduced,' Sihtric said. 'The first to come to me was a boy, slim, dark, with eyes like a deer's. He was a student. As we worked he sat close to me, he brought me presents – flowers in glass bowls, that sort of thing. I didn't really notice, to tell the truth; the work was everything. Then one night he slid into my bed. I was half asleep – I thought it was a woman, or a succubus perhaps, sent by the devil to tempt me. Well, I had a devil of a shock when I slid my hand down that oil-smooth belly and found six inches of stiff cock. I nearly yelled the place down.'

Robert laughed.

But Orm said grimly, 'So the vizier, having determined that your inclination was not towards boys, sent you a woman.'

'She was a copyist at the library. She was called Muzna. But she said that was a corruption of Maria. Once her family had been Christians, become *muwallad* long ago. The combination of that dark beauty, and the chink of Christian light that might still lodge in her soul, compelled me. When she stayed when the others had gone, when she laughed at my foolish jokes and brought me gifts—'

'When she came to your bed,' Orm said. 'You never could get to the point, could you, priest?'

'She was an addiction, a drug. The smoothness of her skin, the scent of her hair – I had known nothing like it. I would have given my immortal soul for her; indeed, perhaps I have done just that. I was *happy*, Orm. I was as happy as I have ever been – happy with her, happy to be alive and breathing, and my head not addled as usual with dreams of power and gain. You of all people know me well enough to understand that. But then three calamities happened, in quick succession.'

'Go on.'

'First I was called into the vizier's presence. He had Muzna at his side. She was crying. She stood with him.'

Robert saw it. '*She was his daughter* – the vizier's.'

'Yes. He had manipulated her; he had had her seduce me; he used his own daughter to unlock my weakness. I protested that love between a Christian and a Muslim was not unknown. Indeed there was some such love in Muzna's mother's ancestry. But times are changing. As the Christian armies roll down the peninsula like a great smothering carpet, in some *taifas* the seduction of a Muslim woman by a Christian can be punishable by death – an execution by stoning.' He shuddered. 'And besides, as the vizier pointed out, I am a priest. He could ruin my ecclesiastical career with a word. I could even be excommunicated.'

'But this was all kept just between the three of you,' Orm said.

'Yes. For, of course, the vizier's purpose was not to destroy me but to *own* me. That was why he used his own daughter. And it worked.

'After that he insisted I showed him all my work. He even asked for a tithe, a share of the income I made from my Arabic Bibles!' He grinned. 'I survived. It just made it harder to conceal my other projects from him. But of course I was never allowed to be alone with Muzna again. Our love had served its purpose, for him.'

'So,' Orm said, 'the first of your three calamities was to learn that Muzna was the vizier's daughter. And the second?'

'To learn she was pregnant.'

It was an accident. The Moorish doctors were as expert in contraception as in so many other fields of medicine, but no method was foolproof.

Sihtric's eyes were bright now. 'Of course she could have got rid of it. Her father's doctors could have helped her with that too. But she wouldn't allow it. She hid away, until the baby was born.'

Robert said, 'Why would she do that?'

'I can only guess. We were never allowed to talk. I believe she wanted the baby as something of her own. She was a good woman, and intelligent. She was sickened at being used by her father. It wasn't much of a plan, but at the very least the baby would make her less useful as a pawn in a marital alliance of lineages – or, worse, a whore.'

Robert said, 'She may have loved you. She may have wanted to keep the baby because it was yours.'

Sihtric bowed his head. 'I can never allow myself to believe that.'

Orm said grimly, 'And your third calamity?'

'She died in childbirth. The baby survived. Not my Muzna.' He said bitterly, 'Again we were let down by the glories of Moorish medicine. The doctors can save a fool of a boy who throws himself at a waterwheel, but not my Muzna!'

Robert said, 'And the child?'

'Was Moraima. My daughter. And the granddaughter of the vizier.'

Robert sat back, shocked.

'So that's why the vizier cares so much about her,' said Orm. 'And why he reacted so strongly when a young Christian buck like Robert came sniffing around.'

Sihtric said, 'And I, I who had found love and comfort, had it snatched away from me. Oh, God is cruel if He is defied!'

Robert, on impulse, touched his shoulder. 'To despair of God is a sin.'

Sihtric looked up, his face full of anguish. 'Yes. But the trouble is, I think He has despaired of *me*. Well. Now you know it all.'

'Not quite all.' The vizier walked into the room, making the guard step aside.

Robert saw that Moraima waited outside, a flower in the sunlight. Her face was blotchy, as if she had been crying. But she saw him, and smiled weakly.

The vizier walked steadily, apparently sober, but he was pale, drained. 'You haven't told the whole truth, Sihtric,' he said in Latin. 'I know enough English by now to understand that. Isn't a lie by omission still a lie?'

Orm said, 'What whole truth?'

The vizier faced Sihtric. 'The truth of how he took his revenge.'

XVII

They were brought out of their battered cell, and returned to an audience room with the vizier. Ibn Tufayl sat on a couch, and sipped a steaming potion. Orm and his party were offered no refreshment.

Moraima stood beside her father, her slim beauty somehow high-lighted by the cool abstraction of the patterns on the tiled wall behind her. Robert couldn't take his eyes off her.

'So,' Orm said. 'Let us speak of revenge.'

The vizier glanced around the room, at attendants and soldiers, a doctor who fussed at his elbow. He dismissed them all with a gesture. The soldiers left reluctantly, and Robert saw they took station just outside the room. Ibn Tufayl said, 'Tell them, Sihtric. It's the story of your cunning, after all. And it worked so well!'

So Sihtric, reluctantly, began. He said that after Muzna's death, the two men were locked together in grief and in blood, through Moraima, daughter of one, granddaughter of the other.

'He sent Moraima off to an aunt in Seville,' Sihtric said. 'He promised me he intended nothing but the best for her, but that wasn't good enough for me. I wanted Moraima in my life – *she was my daughter*, a child for a man who had never expected such a blessing. She was all I had left of Muzna. And besides I didn't trust him. Moraima inherited her mother's beauty – you can testify to that, Robert! I didn't like the idea that in twelve or fifteen or twenty years Ibn Tufayl might use her as he once used her mother.'

The vizier said languidly, 'Don't pretend it was for Moraima or Muzna. It was all for you. Is revenge-taking a sin in your church? It should be.'

'Tell us what you did,' said Orm.

With Muzna dead and Moraima gone, the two men continued to work on their shared project, Aethelmaer's designs.

'I used the opportunity of my time alone with the vizier,' Sihtric said. 'I interested him in the work. I tried to become his friend. And I began to bring him gifts.'

'What gifts?'

'Wine,' said the vizier bluntly.

Wine, forbidden under Muslim custom and law but manufactured in the Christian monasteries still permitted within al-Andalus, and smuggled into Madinat az-Zahra by Sihtric.

'I was a Muslim savouring communion wine – the blood of your Christ! Ironic, isn't it? But it was more than a taste that Sihtric cultivated in me. You are a good judge of men, priest. If I saw a weakness in you, you saw one in me, one I didn't know I possessed.'

'You became a drunk,' Orm said.

'The priest was the only route through which I could obtain the wine I needed. Thus I gave him power over me.'

'But,' Robert said, 'what did *you* want, Sihtric?'

'Moraima,' Sihtric said.

The two men struck a deal. Moraima would be brought back to Cordoba and raised as Sihtric's daughter. She would be a good Muslim, though: the vizier would not tolerate his granddaughter being raised a Christian.

'The girl would be known as my daughter,' Sihtric said. 'But her descent from the vizier was to be kept a secret. Ibn Tufayl let my reputation suffer rather than his. The Christian community was scandalised.'

'So,' Orm said. 'You, Sihtric, armed with your control of the vizier through his drunkenness. And the vizier knowing that you fathered a child by a Muslim girl. The two of you locked together in your weakness, mutually dependent, mutually loathing. I should have known I would find you in a situation like this, priest. It's just the sort of mess which always gathers around you.'

'It's almost a work of art, isn't it?' Sihtric said bitterly.

'I don't want to hear any more of this.' Moraima stepped forward, anger bringing colour to her cheeks. 'I don't want to be discussed as if I were just another barrel of wine, a business deal between two weak old men.'

The vizier said, 'Now, Moraima—'

'Oh, let her go,' Sihtric said. 'Why should she hear this painful old rubbish hashed over once again? Go, child; find yourself something more pleasant to do.'

'And me,' Robert said impulsively. 'Let me walk with her.'

Ibn Tufayl studied him. 'You must be even more stupid than you look.'

Robert blurted, thinking as he spoke, 'I can never have Moraima, and she can't have me. How we feel doesn't matter. It's over – indeed, it never was. Just let us walk together for an hour. Let us say goodbye.'

Orm said, 'Vizier, I take it you've no plans to punish the boy over Ghalib.'

'For what? He behaved nobly enough.' Ibn Tufayl's raging temper had vanished with his intoxication. 'Besides, the fault is ours, mine and Sihtric's, for allowing such situations to develop. That is what we must discuss. For as Moraima grows older—'

'Yes,' Sihtric said. 'We need to work out a way to manage her heart.'

'But for now,' Orm said, 'let them go.'

Ibn Tufayl clapped his hands to summon in his guards. 'Very well. Go, you two. Be aware you will be watched, every step of the way.'

Robert, hugely relieved to be getting away from Sihtric and the vizier and all their murky compromises, followed Moraima to the door.

But as he passed his father, Orm whispered, 'Just be careful.'

XVIII

Outside the light of the low afternoon sun seemed dazzling bright. The guard stood just a pace away, his arms folded, glaring.

Robert faced the girl. 'Moraima, I—'

'Hush. Don't talk. Not here.'

They walked across the palace compound. They soon reached ruins, for only a fraction of Madinat az-Zahra had been restored to habitability by the vizier's workmen. But Moraima knew the way, and led Robert further. Following rubble-strewn paths they came to a complex of high walls and fallen roofs, where tiles and broken stucco littered a weed-cracked floor. 'Once a harem,' Moraima whispered. 'Complicated place. Easy to get lost. Come on.' She took his hand, and they ran, turning left then right and doubled back, hurrying between high walls and across empty, broken floors. Robert soon became lost himself, even though the afternoon sun hung as a constant beacon in the sky.

And before long the vizier's guard had been completely left behind.

She brought him to a ruined patio. Weeds clogged ponds long since stagnant, wiry little bushes pushed through cracks in the paving stones, and palms had outgrown the gardeners' neat configurations and gone wild. The walls of the rooms here were burned out and open to the sky. But some of the arches still stood, still serving as doorways to this secret garden.

For Robert, walking into this place with Moraima at his side was a fulfilment of the overheated, fragmentary fantasies he had had since he first arrived in Cordoba.

They found a stone bench and sat. A small bird fluttered away, disturbed. Somewhere a guitar played, and a thin voice sang a plaintive song.

'I like it here,' Moraima said. 'Even though nobody has touched it for fifty years. I like the idea that a place can be beautiful even when the people have vanished, that things will go on when all our fussing and fighting is over. If this is all we leave behind when we've gone, a pretty place where the birds can nest, perhaps that's enough.'

He took her hand. In fact it felt like a bird in his palm, the bones thin, fragile, the flesh warm. 'That's a melancholy thought.'

She smiled, enigmatic. 'But you've seen how I live. They say they love me, the two of them.'

'Sihtric and Ibn Tufayl.'

'Father and grandfather. I sometimes think that all they do is use me to hurt each other. And sometimes, it's awful, sometimes I think they don't love me at all. That they blame me for killing my mother, who they both loved more than they love me.'

He wanted to comfort her, to reassure her that couldn't be true. But the priest and the vizier were complicated, ugly creatures, locked together, feeding off each other's weakness and pain. How could he say if they loved her well or not? No wonder she dreamed of a world without humans.

'Moraima, I've heard what they want. But what do *you* want? What kind of life?'

'I don't know,' she said honestly. 'I can't imagine it. Things are too complicated. *But . . .*'

'Yes?'

'It doesn't feel complicated when I'm with you.'

His heart hammered. 'If it wasn't for the others – my father, yours, the vizier – if things were different—'

'If Jesus and Muhammad had never existed? What's the good of talking like that? Things are as they are; you can't change the past.'

But her father, he thought, seemed to believe that the past *could* be changed. 'But even so. If it was only a question of the two of us, could we make a life together?'

She said firmly, 'We can never know. Because it isn't going to happen, is it? All we have is this moment.' Her face was before his, softened by nearness, her eyes huge, the colours of the wild garden reflected in her smooth skin. 'That's all anybody has.'

'Then we should grasp it.'

Their lips closed together. Her breath was like the breeze off the desert. 'I don't even mind,' she whispered into his mouth, 'that you smell so bad.'

They kissed again, and he felt as if he was passing through another arched gateway into a still more wonderful place yet.

XIX

Orm and Sihtric sat on floor cushions inside the priest's study, as he called it, in a corner of the palace complex. It was a nest of shelves heaped with books and parchments, and there was a lingering smell of lamp oil and candle soot. The room was in poor condition, the ceiling blackened by some ancient fire, the wall hangings musty and frayed; this part of the ruined palace was only poorly restored. But the room was far from the bustle of the vizier's court, and Sihtric said he liked it this way.

'For I have secrets in this room,' said Sihtric. 'Secrets I've shared with no one – certainly not the vizier. You want to know *why* I stay here, why I live among Moors who speak of Allah, and Christians who speak no Latin? Why I have let myself become locked into a damaging relationship with a snake like the vizier . . .' He glanced upwards to the darkened ceiling, as if challenging God. 'You see, Orm, I've found a rent in the tapestry of time. *Another* one, a third or a fourth, to add to the ripping-open of the Menologium of Isolde, and the Codex, and your poor wife's Testament. And through that rent I have glimpsed horror. But from that horror I have conceived an ambition as big as the world, Orm. It is nothing less than the final defeat of Islam, and the preservation of Christendom into the far future. What higher goal can there be than that? Is a man justified in giving up his very soul to achieve such an aim?'

A month had passed since the incident of Ghalib and the waterwheel. A month in which Orm had continued to learn uncomfortable details of Sihtric's murky career in Cordoba. And now, he said, Sihtric was going to tell him the whole truth. Orm wasn't sure he wanted to hear it. He shivered, obscurely frightened. 'You always did talk in riddles, priest.'

'Well, the whole business is a riddle, isn't it? But then it always was.'

Sihtric got to his feet and crossed to the wall. He pulled away a crate stacked with books, then hauled aside a shabby hanging to expose tiles with geometric patterns, a kind of trefoil in black and white that, repeated, covered the wall area. Sihtric dug his fingers into the edge of a tile and with some effort picked it away from the wall. 'I have a habit of biting my nails,' he said. 'Makes this tricky.' A hatch, concealed by tiles, now hinged down to reveal an iron door. Sihtric extracted a key from his robe, unlocked the door, and it swung back to reveal a compartment inside the wall. Sihtric began to rummage in the dark space, which Orm saw was full of books, scrolls, heaps of parchment and vellum. There was a musty smell, of rot and age.

Sihtric drew a flat wooden box from the wall compartment. He placed this on a table, unpicked ties of copper wire, and opened up the box like the covers of a book. Leather hinges creaked slightly, and a smell like stale meat flooded the room.

Inside the box was a wooden frame over which was stretched a sheet of what looked like vellum. Orm peered closely. Words had been marked onto the vellum, pricked in some black ink. The small, closely spaced letters were lined up in neat rows, but had been distorted by the stretching of the vellum, and in places the skin was pocked and broken, crudely stitched. There was nothing else in the box.

With faint dread Orm reached out and touched the vellum. It was dry, rough. 'What is this, calfskin?'

Sihtric would not say. 'When I found this object it was rolled up inside a wooden cylinder, for it had been preserved as a holy relic. It is old, three centuries or more.'

'So you stretched it on this frame.'

'With infinite care, yes. But I couldn't help a little distortion of the letters.'

Orm looked closely at the first few lines. 'Is this Latin? "My name is al-Hafredi, as the scribes tell it, and Alfred, as my family knew me. That liveth, was dead, evermore . . ." I don't understand. A riddle? The name, though. Al-Hafredi is a Moorish name. But Alfred—'

'English, of course. The name of our greatest king.'

'Here is a man who lived under the Moors, then,' Orm said. 'His name, Alfred, was rendered in a Moorish way. Just as our guide Ibn Hafsun's name was a corruption of the old family name of Alfonso.'

'You should have been a scholar.'

'Don't mock me,' Orm said mildly. 'However my scholarship doesn't extend to puzzling out the rest. "That liveth, was dead, evermore." It's not even a sentence. What does it mean?'

'There lies the cunning. The manuscript isn't in any kind of code. But it does contain fragments like this. They puzzled me too, until I saw that the intention of this man, a Christian living under the Moors, was to speak clearly to other Christians, in a way that his Moorish masters would not understand. So, pagan, what piece of literature do all Christians share?'

'The Bible.'

'Correct. And I realised that what we have in this line is a fragment of the Bible, a quotation, compressed and embedded.'

'What quotation?'

'From the Book of the Revelation of Saint John.' He closed his eyes. '"I am he that liveth, and was dead; and behold, I am alive for evermore." Liveth, dead, evermore. You see?'

'If you say so.'

'The quotations come from both the Old and New Testaments. With patience I riddled them all out. It would take a Christian to do so. The Muslims do study the Bible, you know; they call it the "Holy Book". However no Muslim scholar will know the Bible as intimately as a Christian. Of course the quotations are allusive rather than literal. Puzzling out the story al-Hafredi wished to tell; that was the real challenge.'

'But you did it.'

'Oh, yes. Given time.'

'Then tell me what you learned.'

'Ironically it was an assignment by the vizier himself that set me on this course ...'

After the *fitnah* the *taifas*, coalescing and competing, had struggled to develop scholarship as a way of achieving dominance over each other; there had even been something of a renaissance as the monopolistic power of a corrupt caliphate collapsed. Seville was not to fall behind. Ibn Tufayl had the backing of his emir, and the funds to progress scholarly projects.

'Among other things, Ibn Tufayl decided he wanted a new history of al-Andalus to be written, from the day three centuries past when Tariq led his armies of Arabs and Berbers across the strait, up to the present. It would be the first significant survey for more than a century, since the time of one Ahmad ar-Razi.'

'And he commissioned you to do that.'

'It was part of the condition of his funding my work on the Engines of God. I think it amused Ibn Tufayl to have a Christian working on a history of the greatest enemy of Christendom itself. But I was happy enough to take the job, as it was an excuse for me to burrow into the mountain of scholarship the Muslims accumulated over the centuries of the caliphate. Knowledge, Orm, knowledge, the greatest power of all. You never know where it might lead! And so the vizier and I came to a mutually satisfactory arrangement.

'The work went smoothly enough. But I soon became aware of a great mystery.'

'What mystery?'

'Why it is that I was born a Christian and not a Muslim,' Sihtric said. 'Why I grew up, in England, speaking English. *Why Christianity survives at all.*'

XX

The great expansion of Islam had begun within a generation of the death of Muhammad. It became necessary, for the first caliphs, like Roman generals, quickly came to depend on plunder to survive. 'It was conquer or perish,' Sihtric said. So the armies of Damascus exploded out of Arabia, swept west across North Africa, and stormed across the Pillars of Hercules and through the Gothic kingdom of Spain.

And, with al-Andalus under the control of governors appointed by the Damascus caliphate, the raiding armies went further north still. The Muslim armies crossed the Pyrenees to attack Septimania, a Gothic domain within Gaul. They were Arabs and Berbers, men of the east and of Africa, now pouring into the green belly of Gaul.

Soon, under an able general called Abd al-Rahman, all the cities of the Mediterranean coast of Gaul were in Muslim hands. It was the eighth century. Less than a decade since the first crossing of the strait.

'There were fault lines, on both the Moorish and Christian sides,' Sihtric said. 'Abd al-Rahman always had trouble with the Berbers. One Berber general called Munuza managed to carve out an independent kingdom for himself in northern Spain, bordering Gaul. And his neighbour in Gaul was the Duke Odo of Aquitaine, who had nominally pledged allegiance to the French kings, but like Munuza craved his own independence. Both pebbles in the shoes of their respective rulers, you see.

'Well, Abd al-Rahman had a tidy mind. He shook out both these pebbles. He killed Munuza, and then crossed the mountains into Aquitaine. Odo's forces were defeated, and Abd al-Rahman, leading his army in person, drove forward, thrusting deep into Gaul. Fifteen thousand men he had, to carry out the usual burning, looting, massacring, enslavement and so forth. And he advanced to within two hundred miles of Paris, to a place called Poitiers.'

'I know it. Not far from the sanctuary of Saint Martin of Tours.'

'And there, history turned,' Sihtric said. 'The Muslims were at the door to the "Great Land", as they called it, of western Europe. Perhaps they could go further – perhaps they could advance all the way to Constantinople.

'But there, on the Roman road north of Poitiers, al-Rahman faced the army of the Frankish king, the last significant obstacle between the Muslims and all Europe.'

Orm knew the story. 'Charles Martel. The Hammer.'

'Well, Charles became known as "the Hammer" only *after* his great victory, after he saved Europe for Christendom. A story told to every young Christian warrior since! *But it need not have been so*. This is where we come to the rent in time's tapestry, Orm. This is what happened . . .'

Odo of Aquitaine, his army defeated by the Moors, his cities stormed, his people slaughtered or enslaved, was in despair. His only possible ally was Charles of the Franks, on whom Odo had previously made war himself. Odo considered surrendering to the Muslims, who might prove more merciful to him and his family than the Christians.

Sihtric said, 'He seems to have been a poor sort of a man, and a worse ruler. But then he got help. A monk turned up at Odo's camp. He rode only a humble ass, like Christ entering Jerusalem, and carried nothing, no food, not even a bottle of water. He relied for his life on the Christian charity of the folk whose lands he crossed. He was a peculiar type, too well-fed to be a monk – and well-spoken, with a peculiarly accented Latin on his lips. He impressed with minor miracles – fortune-telling, an ability to predict bad storms and harsh winters, that sort of thing. He said his name was Alfred, he was from the famous monastery of Lindisfarne in England, and he had a message from Christ for Odo.'

'He was al-Hafredi.'

'Well yes, but don't run ahead of the story, Viking. He might have been killed, for Odo's troops were by this time cowering from shadows. He did have his wretched ass stolen, slaughtered and eaten by the starving warriors. But he was let live, and was admitted to Odo's presence. And there he changed Odo's mind.'

'How?' Orm asked.

Sihtric shrugged. 'I don't know what he said to Odo. I don't know what he promised him, what he showed him. But, Viking, if I knew your future, all of it, it would not be hard to manipulate *you*. Perhaps you can see that.

'In any event al-Hafredi persuaded Odo that he should not submit to the Moors, and despite his hostility to Charles he should throw himself on the Frank's mercy and face the Moors with him. And he whispered to Odo how the Moors might be beaten.'

'And Odo was convinced by this?'

'He must have been. For that's precisely what he did.'

So the Moors faced the Franks, that October three centuries past, the future of all Europe at stake. The two forces had been well matched. Charles was a proven war leader, as was Abd al-Rahman. There followed seven days of inconclusive skirmishes and scouting.

At last the combat came. Odo's weary forces made little difference to Charles's military strength – but the advice Odo was able to give on how the Moors fought, and how Abd al-Rahman thought, was much more valuable.

'The Moorish cavalry charged. But Charles's infantry held their ground. The Muslims were taken aback. They had been used to Christians breaking and running from their advances. In that one moment the battle turned, just as al-Hafredi said it would. And then Charles shocked the Moors by attacking them aggressively.

'In the combat that followed, Abd al-Rahman was killed. I have always wondered if al-Hafredi had something to do with it – perhaps that drab monkish habit concealed a knife. The Moors were not broken. They could have fought on, but without their leader, they chose to turn away.

'The battle itself was inconclusive. But it was a crucial day, in all our histories – Bede of Jarrow knew this, in faraway England. The Moors had come a thousand miles north from the strait to Africa. Now at last they had been turned back. And though they continued to raid southern Gaul, they were never to progress so far north again. Why, less than a century later Charles's grandson Charlemagne was mounting expeditions the other way across the Pyrenees.'

'Christendom was saved, then. And what became of al-Hafredi? How did his story come down to you?'

'He was wounded in the battle, it's said, an arrow in the back, but it did not penetrate deep enough to kill him. He survived, and, thanks to a grateful Odo, he was feted as something of a hero. He ended his life in Spain, in the city of Santiago de Compostela. He was never beatified, but when he died his relics were preserved, and stored in the cathedral of Saint James the Moorslayer.'

'I have always been faintly revolted,' Orm said, 'by the Christian obsession with bits of their holy dead.'

'Well, you should be glad of it. For, much later, when al-Mansur raided Santiago—'

'He who stole the cathedral bells.'

'Precisely. During that same raid he made off with the relics of al-Hafredi of Poitiers and brought them to Cordoba. So I came across the relics, as I followed hints of the story of al-Hafredi in other accounts – and so I eventually found the testament he left behind.' Sihtric stroked his bit of old skin.

'His testament. His story of how he came to Odo.'

'Yes. But there is more, Orm. In his testament Al-Hafredi goes on, beyond the events of the battle itself. He tells of *another* history. A history that would have come about if he had *not* come to comfort the defeated, suicidal Odo that dark October night. A history in which the Moors did *not* lose at Poitiers.'

This was the true history of the world, attested al-Hafredi of Poitiers, as it had been taught to him. It was a history in which no monkish wanderer had come to turn Odo's head.

Without the encouragement of the mysterious Alfred, Odo of Aquitaine surrendered to Abd al-Rahman, who used him as a hostage before casting him aside. When Charles of France faced the Moors without Odo, his numbers were not significantly weakened – but without Odo's whisperings about Moorish tactics he had a much poorer idea of the nature of the force he was facing. That inadequate knowledge led to crucial indecision. The Frankish force, rather than holding against the onslaught of the Moorish cavalry, broke and fled, as had all the Christian armies Abd al-Rahman had faced before.

'And it was not Abd al-Rahman who was killed that day,' Sihtric said grimly, 'but Charles.' The Franks, demoralised by defeat and convulsed by a succession dispute, could offer the Moors little further resistance.

And the gate to the Great Land was open.

The subsequent Moorish expansion across Gaul and then Germany was like the story of their conquest of Spain – if anything more dramatic. Then there was England. The Umayyad caliphate had long been a great naval power in the Mediterranean; the ocean between England and Gaul offered them no resistance, and nor did the squabbling Saxon kings when Moorish ships sailed up the estuaries of the Thames and the Severn and the Tyne.

'By the year of Our Lord 793,' Sihtric said, 'in which your Viking ancestors first raided England, Orm, there were Moors in Paris and in Rome. Even Constantinople had fallen, after a decade-long siege from both east and west. After that the political history of Moorish Europe was no simpler or less fractious than that of al-Andalus, but overall the Moorish grip on the Great Land never loosened.

'There was to be no Jorvik, no Danelaw, and no Normandy. There was no battle at Hastings, no Norman invasion of England – for there were no Normans! The emirs never allowed Vikings to settle on their territory as the Frankish kings did.'

Armed with the legacy of antiquity, the Moors were able to make the northern lands flourish as they had al-Andalus. Populations rose steadily, and gained in wealth and health – and, just as steadily, converted to Islam. There was an intellectual revolution, and marvellous medicines and machines transformed the lives of the people.

'The greatest mosque in Europe was built in Seville, but the second grandest was in Paris,' Sihtric said. 'The greatest library in the world was in London. Think of that!

'And it was in a Moorish London that a young man called al-Hafredi was to be born. In a few words he sketches his London for us, a London where minarets and marble-columned palaces rise within the old Roman walls, and the cries of the imams drift across the Thames.

'Al-Hafredi claimed he had come from a far future, a thousand years *beyond* the Muslim conquest. And he sketches that millennium – a future that was already history to him. There will be invaders,' Sihtric said. 'From the east. A wave of savage horsemen, bursting out of Asia. The Muslim rulers, fractious as ever, will be unable to stand before them. Al-Hafredi details their progress. But the nomads' world empire will be brief, gone in a few generations, leaving only memories of distant lands.

'In the next age, plague. Many will fall. It would have been far worse, says al-Hafredi, if not for Muslim medicine.

'And in the age after *that* there will be a terrible war, a war of the Silk Road, as empires of east and west fall on each other. The war will engulf the whole world, and will last another century. And it will be won by machines. I imagine engines like mine, like Aethelmaer's, or even more destructive, born in the fecund minds of warriors and those who serve them.

'The war, long and bloody, will be won by the Muslims. In the end Islam will hold sway across all the world as it is known, from Scandinavia to Africa, from Ireland to India and the lands beyond. And ships bearing the crescent banner will sail far beyond the horizon in search of new lands to conquer, new peoples to convert.'

'And somewhere in this future Islamic world,' Orm said, 'your friend al-Hafredi broods, unforgiving.'

'Yes. And here is the strangest part of the story. Just as in al-Andalus, Christianity will be tolerated – even a thousand years after Abd al-Rahman. But the bitter monks of Lindisfarne and elsewhere will be pinpricks of Christianity in a Muslim map. Christ will live on through them, for al-Hafredi quotes Matthew, chapter eighteen: "For where two or three are gathered together in my name, there I am in the midst of them." But Islam will be everywhere else. The situation will be intolerable, the whole world lost – and in the end, al-Hafredi feared, Christianity would be extinguished altogether. Something must be done.

'So the devious monks will steal one of the Moors' own marvellous engines, and hatch a plot to use against its inventors. Don't ask me how it is done – I barely understand the what, let alone the how. But they will find a way to hurl one man across history, just as my crossbow will hurl a bolt across the sky, just as your Witness sent her words across the firmament to Eadgyth – they will hurl him, naked and alone, into another time and place.'

Orm saw it. 'They sent al-Hafredi from Lindisfarne, in this future century, to Poitiers, in the deep past.'

'That is what al-Hafredi tells us happened to him,' Sihtric said firmly. 'And, following the mission that had been devised for him, he made his way to Odo, and turned that weak man's mind around.'

Orm tried to take all this in. 'If that was his mission, he succeeded. This other Europe is now extinguished altogether. The mosque of Paris, the great library in London—'

'They never existed – and never will.'

Orm thought of the beauties he had seen here in al-Andalus, and he remembered the Normans' harrying of the English north. 'Do you think this world, our world, is a better one, Sihtric?'

Sihtric sniffed. 'That other wasn't a Christian world; it deserved to vanish.'

Orm studied the vellum again, and stroked it gingerly with a fingertip. 'What is this stuff – goat, lamb? Why didn't your long-dead scribe use a better quality bit of leather? These wounds are odd. This one looks like an arrow puncture. Was this animal hunted down?'

Sihtric eyed him. 'Can't you guess what this is, Viking? A pity; I thought you were showing imagination for once. Think about it. Al-Hafredi brought back an account of his own lost future in written form; perhaps he feared that his crossbow-shot across time would leave him dead, but that his message might do some good even so ... And yet he travelled naked.'

Orm saw it. He drew his hand back. 'He bore his message on his body.'

Sihtric traced the letters on the bit of vellum with his finger. 'Tattooed across his back, compressed Bible quotations and all. This evidence of a stitched-up arrow wound is a detail that adds veracity to the whole saga, doesn't it? And when he died, stranded centuries out of his own time, the monks who tended him cut the skin off his back, and treated it as they would any bit of calfskin to be used for scribing.'

Orm stared at the bit of human skin, flayed off the body of a man from a vanished future. He felt obscurely angry. What strange world was he living in that such things could be possible? 'Tell me what you intend to do about all this.'

'I intend,' Sihtric said coldly, 'to follow al-Hafredi's example.'

'What do you mean?'

'I have seen an Islamic future, through al-Hafredi's words. The Moors may have been turned back at Poitiers, but Islam is still strong – rampant. I will not allow such a victory to come about.' He smiled coldly. 'Like al-Hafredi, I will use the Moors' own wealth and learning against them.'

Orm said slowly, 'So you intend to develop your engines with Moorish money. Then you will hand over the weapons to the Christian kings. And with those engines, all of Islam will be destroyed.'

'That's the plan. Simple, isn't it? It may be that I won't live to see the project completed, of course. But that's of no relevance. The march of Christendom transcends a mere human life.'

'But to betray your sponsor—'

'It won't be hard. You've met him. The vizier's no fool, but he is a drunk. He's not hard to manipulate.'

Orm wasn't so sure about that. 'And what of your conscience, Sihtric? What of the helpless millions whose destinies you plan to deflect? What of *their* souls? Does that not trouble you?'

'No, Orm, I am not troubled. There is another line from Revelation here. Chapter three: "I will not blot out his name out of the book of life." But al-Hafredi did, and I will. You came here with your head full of vague plans to oppose me, didn't you? Your wife's nonsense about the Dove. But you're full of doubt. Lesser men always are. But *I*, I am doing God's work – I am sure of that – that is all that matters.'

A shadow crossed the room; a candle flickered. The vizier stood in the doorway, an armed guard at his side. 'And all that matters to me, priest, is that at last I have proof of your treachery.'

XXI

Alone in the dark, Robert measured space and time.

The floor was square, thirty by thirty of his foot-lengths paced out toe against heel. He could not see the ceiling, but he knew that many of the palace's rooms were rough cubes, so he imagined the room was as tall as it was wide. He explored the walls with his fingers. The room had arched doorways, but they were bricked up, save one closed by the heavy wooden door that had slammed shut after he had been thrown in here by the vizier's guards.

And he measured time. There was no passage of day or night; the bright Spanish sunlight was banished from his life. But he counted the meals that were shoved through a hatch in the door – bread, rice, a bit of water, delivered with a precious splinter of light. He counted his own pissing, his stools. He counted the times he slept, but his sleeping was poor.

In the dark he became confused in his counting, which distressed him.

It took him some of that passing time to work out that he was, in fact, imprisoned. There were few gaols in England, no cells save for a few dismal dungeons beneath the Normans' keeps, where athelings or other valuable captives might be held. If you committed a crime you might be executed, or mutilated, or fined; if you lived you went back to work. There wasn't the spare food to feed a population of prisoners. In al-Andalus, it seemed, things were different.

And as the days wore away and it dawned on Robert that he could see no end to this captivity, a deep horror settled on him.

He prayed every day, of course. Prayed every hour. Prayed constantly. He tried to mark Sunday, when he thought that day came. He recited the words of the holy Mass, as best he remembered them. Praying was better than thinking. Better than wondering what had become of his father, or Moraima, better than endlessly speculating why he had been thrown into this hole. Better than wondering what might become of him when he was finally released. Or, worse, how it would be if he were never released at all.

After the first few days he decided that he should treat his captivity as a trial. He thought of heroic monks like Saint Cuthbert, who deliberately sought out purposeful solitude in order better to understand their own souls, and God. If he were to become a soldier of God, fighting in the Pope's armies, he would face far worse torments than this.

He longed to be with Moraima. And he longed for his father to come and save *him*. But these were the weak thoughts of a child and he put them aside. He would use these hours in the hot, foetid, alien dark to cleanse his soul of weakness.

By the time his captors came for him, he thought only of God.

The door opened, flooding the cell with light. Two burly guards dragged him out of the dark. He was dazzled by the brilliance of a low sun. But he thought the guards flinched from the new holy light that burned from his own eyes.

XXII

Robert was shoved inside a reception room. Released, he staggered, and stood upright.

He glanced around. Books, bound volumes and scrolls, were piled roughly in one corner. Four arched doorways were all blocked by the burly bodies of guards – dark, stocky, powerful men, Berbers perhaps. The room was beautiful. But he had no time for beauty now; this was just as much a prison as his own shit-filled cell.

But Moraima, sweet Moraima was here too.

Moraima came to him, her hands folded into an anxious knot. A delicate scent of jasmine hung around her. He longed to take her in his arms, to let out the warmth that surged inside him. But he knew he must not.

She stood before him, uncertain how to read him. 'Robert. It has been so long. I thought they might have killed you. The vizier is like the weather; he comes and goes in his moods. He got angry with Sihtric, and he just locked everybody away.' She said hastily, 'I don't know what's happening here, Robert. But we must talk.' And she placed a hand on her belly.

Now Orm and Sihtric were brought in. Robert saw that they, too, had been imprisoned. Orm's beard was ragged, his hair untrimmed, the dirt ground deep into his pores, and there was a sewer stink of the cell about him. The priest, too, was shabby, and he scratched himself under a grimy habit.

Orm ran to his son and took his shoulders. 'Robert. What did they do?'

'I was stuck in a hole. They kept me in the dark.'

'In the dark, and alone? And we thought we had it bad, priest.'

'I am not harmed.'

Orm looked deep into his eyes, troubled. 'Are you sure? You look different.'

'Harder, I'd say,' said Sihtric. 'Not necessarily a bad thing, a bit of toughening up.'

'Shut up,' Orm said. 'Come sit over here.' They settled on floor cushions. 'Robert, I'm sorry.'

'Why?'

'Because it's my fault.'

Robert felt impatient that his father and this flawed priest were drawing the crisis about themselves like a cloak. 'How is it your fault? You were imprisoned too.'

Orm scratched his stubble. 'But I fear all this came about because of my foolishness – ours.'

He told Robert about the conversation he had had with Sihtric in another corner of the palace, about the Engines of God, and the Testament of al-Hafredi, and Sihtric's real intentions.

'Evidently we were overheard,' Orm said.

Sihtric said glumly, 'I've used that room for years.'

'But that part of the palace,' Orm told Robert, 'was an ambassador's court. It is a warren of tunnels and spy-holes. Moraima knew all about it. And this priest never thought to inquire.'

Sihtric snapped, 'But the vizier learned nothing damaging before you showed up in al-Andalus, Orm, with your addled prophecy, your doves and serpents, your doubts. Nobody before you ever encouraged me to express dreams I had kept safely lodged in the silence of my soul all these decades. You upset everything, Orm, all my delicate arrangements. Now he knows it all . . .'

Robert looked at the two squabbling old men. They didn't matter to him now. Their babbling of history and prophecy was irrelevant – and so, he thought for the first time in his life, was his father. All that mattered to Robert was the cold steel of the piety he had discovered in himself during his solitude.

'What a touching scene.' The vizier walked into the room.

They all got to their feet.

Ibn Tufayl looked magnificent in his djellaba of the finest silk and spun wool and with his skin shining with oils, yet he swayed, subtly. 'Three shabby Christians. How low you are. How animal-like. And the *stink* of you.'

'If you're going to kill us,' grated Orm, 'get it over with.'

'Oh, I fully intend to do that. But there's no rush, Viking. After all this time we still have much to say to each other. Sit down, all of you.'

He crossed the chamber, alone save for a single servant who bore a tray of sweetmeats and drinks. He walked stiffly, his posture erect. But Robert saw the cautious pacing of a man concentrating on control.

'The man is as drunk as a Breton,' Orm murmured.

'Then God help us all,' whispered Sihtric.

XXIII

The vizier sat on a heap of cushions. The servant next to him knelt with head bowed, holding up her silver tray. Robert thought absently that she would tire very quickly in a posture like that; she must be hardened by a lifetime of servitude. Ibn Tufayl was of course aware of their hunger, and he ate his titbits slowly, with evident relish, chewing openly. But his face was flushed.

He indicated the arched doorways, where the guards waited, eyes white in desert-dark faces. 'We are effectively alone here. The guards are all Berbers. Almoravids, a fanatical bunch, but fierce warriors. And not a one of them understands a word of Arabic, let alone Latin. Not even this little one.' He stroked the head of the girl kneeling at his side. 'So you see, what we say in here will stay with us alone – or rather, with me.'

Sihtric waved an uncertain hand at the heaps of books in the corner. 'You have taken my books.'

The vizier nodded. 'Your Codex is here, the sketches you stole from Aethelmaer.' He held up a scroll. 'So are all your notes and commentaries, and the designs you have developed. All your work is here.' Ibn Tufayl smiled, malicious. 'And if I ordered it destroyed, perhaps on a mere whim, it would be gone for ever. The meaning of your life, priest, gone in a heartbeat.'

'You would not,' shouted Sihtric, his face reddening.

Orm said, 'Oh, calm down, priest. He's only goading you. It's obvious he won't destroy your work. It's far too precious to him for that.'

The vizier nodded. 'I'm glad one of you shows some wisdom.'

'But you have your own purpose for them, no doubt,' Robert said.

Ibn Tufayl half rose. 'Do not speak to me, you wolfling, or I will have you eviscerated before your father's eyes.'

Robert was shocked by the anger in his face, the crimson glower, the twisted lip, the bulging eyes. He flinched, unable to understand why he should be the focus of such rage.

Orm's grip tightened on his arm, hard enough to hurt. 'Stay calm.'

Sihtric said, 'He's right, though, isn't he, vizier? You have concocted your own scheme for the weapons.'

The vizier settled back. 'Oh, yes. Far beyond your petty notions. It takes a man of vision to see the true path. But oddly, it was you who put the vision into my head, priest. You and your muscled friend here. All your talk of al-Hafredi of Poitiers, this bizarre fantasy of men flung across time, a history averted. Nonsense! Irrelevant! No wonder you Christians fail if your heads are addled with such maundering. And yet the scheme you unfold, Sihtric, of a Muslim expansion across Gaul and Germany – now that is magnificent! The bones of a strategy – a grand one – and in your engines there is the means to carry it out.'

The vizier stood and paced around the room, energetic, vigorous, red-faced. The servant cowered every time he came close.

'I will continue the development of your engines, the crossbows, the armoured carts, the flying machines. And I will give them to the armies of Seville. Then, reinforced by our brothers the Almoravids from Africa, we will storm across the marches and scatter the barbarian hordes of the Christian kings. Perhaps our new conquest will be as rapid as that of Musa and Tariq – why not? And in five years, or ten, Seville will be established as the capital of a reclaimed al-Andalus, and the bells of the Christian churches will fall silent again.' He continued to pace, pace.

'And then?' whispered Sihtric. 'And then?'

'And then we will cross the Pyrenees. We will reverse the disaster of Poitiers, three hundred years ago. This time there will be no stopping our advance.'

'I wouldn't be so sure,' Orm said. 'I've fought with the Normans, remember. Why, they conquered England, the best-organised state in Europe. They'll put up a tough fight.'

'But they won't have Sihtric's engines,' the vizier said.

'And if you prevail,' Sihtric said. His voice was hoarse, his face drained of blood. 'On you will go, I suppose. Slaughtering, burning.'

Ibn Tufayl's voice rose, shrill. 'At last the solemn calm of a single caliphate will settle across the whole of the world, from east to west, from pole to pole. If it can be done once, as your madman wanderer seems to have believed, Sihtric, it can be done again.' He smiled. 'I would like to take Rome myself, I think. I will have to decide what to do with the Pope ... You see how you have inspired me? And it will be my honour to achieve it – my honour – I, a new al-Mansur.' He staggered, almost falling against a wall. He picked up a cup, drained it, found another empty, and cuffed his servant's head. 'More. Go, go!'

She scuttled out, head bowed.

Orm growled, 'Get to the point, vizier. What do you intend to do with us?'

'I need what you know. I don't need *you*. You will be – drained. And then discarded. But at least you know the great cause your deaths will serve.' The servant girl returned with a tray of fresh drinks; the vizier grabbed a cup and downed it in one gulp.

Moraima stared at him. 'Grandfather – I barely recognise you when you speak like this.'

He looked at her blearily. 'When you are old enough to understand, you'll thank me. And you'll tell your grandchildren of what you have heard today. But for now, this strange knowledge must be mine alone.'

Sihtric snapped, 'What does that mean? You say you have my plans. What of the prototypes I have built? What of the arbalest?'

'Destroyed.'

'And my scholars, my clerks, my engineers?'

'They will not speak of it,' the vizier said. 'My Berbers made sure of that.'

Sihtric's mouth dropped open, and he slumped, as if fainting. Orm supported him, but Sihtric pushed him away. 'There were fine minds among them, very fine young minds – the best in Cordoba. All sacrificed to your petty ambition. Murderer. Murderer!'

'Don't preach at me, you hypocritical fraud. You have ambition enough of your own. You were planning to arm Christians with your magic weapons.'

'I planned to serve Christ's holy purposes. I am no murderer of scholars and clerks and scribes, of carpenters and wheelwrights and metal-workers. You infidel monster, I will oppose you with every bone in my body.'

'And I,' the vizier roared, 'will extract every one of those bones if you stand in my way.'

The two of them faced each other, the tottering drunk, the portly, filthy priest, screaming at each other. They were so alike, Robert saw, two foolish middle-aged men who dreamed of reshaping the world. But he knew it was a world which no longer belonged to them.

Moraima stepped between them. 'Stop this, father, grandfather. I can't stand to see you fight.'

Robert stepped up and took Moraima's arm. 'Come away, Moraima. Leave them to it. You'll only get hurt.'

The vizier turned on him again, his flushed face a mask of ferocity.

'Get your filthy paws off her, you Christian animal. I know what you did. I know about the tainted spawn you have planted in her belly!'

That shocked even Sihtric to silence. Everybody stood still. Moraima covered her face.

Orm said darkly, 'Is this true, Robert?'

Robert looked at the girl. 'We've had no time to talk, no time alone – but, yes, father. I think it's true.' And now he understood why the vizier hated him.

Moraima said to the vizier, 'How did you know, grandfather? I've been to no doctor.'

'But you told one of your friends, who told *her* friend, who told the boy Ghalib, who, hating Robert, told me.'

Robert grunted. 'Ghalib will never forgive me for saving his life.'

The vizier shrieked, 'And I will not forgive you, or spare you, for you have defiled her, as this fat priest defiled her mother, my daughter.'

Robert boldly took Moraima's hand and drew her behind his back.

Orm said, 'Is that what this is all about? Are you really hungry to conquer the world for Islam, vizier? Or are you simply enraged that your granddaughter, like your daughter, loves a Christian? Is that what is driving you insane?'

The vizier stood tall, his mouth drawn wide, the muscles in his neck spasming. So deep was his rage, so toxic the drink swilling in his body, that for a heartbeat he seemed unable to act, even to speak. The guards fingered their scimitars uneasily.

But Sihtric was not frozen. He turned to Moraima. 'Goodbye, my lovely girl, my darling. All my life I have chased such grand ambitions. And yet in the end, if all I leave behind is you, perhaps it's enough.'

Moraima asked, bewildered, 'Father? What do you mean?'

'I will not see Christendom threatened – not through my own foolishness and arrogance. You say that everything I've achieved is gathered in this room, vizier. Then it must end, here in this room.'

And Sihtric jumped up at the wall, grabbed an oil lamp, and hurled himself on the heap of manuscripts in the corner of the room. The lamp broke under him, and fire blossomed around him, licking eagerly over the stacked scrolls and books, and Sihtric's robe. Ibn Tufayl let out a bellow of drunken despair, and threw himself at the fire. Orm grabbed him, whether to hold him back or to wrestle him Robert couldn't tell. But in a moment the two of them had toppled into the blaze on top of the squirming priest.

It had only taken a heartbeat. The room filled with smoke. The screams of the three men were high and terrible. Moraima lunged forward, but Robert held her.

The guards ran into the room. Some of them tried to drag the bodies from the pyre, only to be burned themselves and driven back, and others, with more presence of mind, ripped hangings off the walls and hurled them on the fire. The smoke was dense now, and, his lungs seared, Robert began to cough.

'Robert. Hsst. Robert!' The voice carried to Robert through the roaring of the blaze, the panicky shouts of the Berber guards. Ibn Hafsun the *muwallad* stood in an archway, only dimly visible through the billowing smoke. 'Let's get out of here. Bring the girl. Move, while you have a chance. Come on!'

Dragging an inert Moraima, Robert hurried that way. The guards were too occupied with the blaze, and the smoke too thick, for them to be seen and stopped.

But as he reached the arch the little serving girl stopped him. 'Please,' she said in heavily accented Latin. 'Please!'

Robert, anxious, tried to get past. But, her face soot-streaked, a burn livid on her right arm, she held up a scorched scroll, wrapped in an animal skin. She pointed at the blaze. 'Priest, priest!'

Robert grabbed the scroll and ran out, dragging Moraima, following Ibn Hafsun.

XXIV

Ibn Hafsun, Robert and Moraima slipped out of Cordoba. They rode down the Guadalquivir towards Seville, a bigger city where, Ibn Hafsun said, it would be easier for them to lose themselves, while the fuss died down.

Ibn Hafsun was vague about why he had saved them. 'I brought you across Spain, Robert, for a fee. I suppose I've always felt responsible for you. I didn't mean to lead you into such peril – and nor did I mean to play a part in the deaths of Sihtric and Orm.'

'It wasn't your fault,' Robert said.

'Perhaps not. But I'm a *muwallad*, Robert. A Muslim, but with a healthy dose of ancestral Christian guilt left in my bloodstream.'

As they journeyed along the course of the great river, Robert was distracted by the changing landscape. Al-Andalus might have declined since the end of the great days of the caliphate and the *fitnah*, but there was prosperity here. Huge ships sailed the length of the river, laden with goods. Near Seville the land was heavily farmed. Plantations of sugar cane sprawled amid ranches and stud farms where tremendous herds of horses flowed.

As they travelled, each morning Moraima was ill.

The two of them spoke little. Moraima was immersed in her loss and the churning of the new life inside her body. And Robert, brooding on Orm's death, his head full of the stern strength of his new faith, found he had nothing to say to her. In the evenings, in taverns or camped out in the open, Ibn Hafsun watched them sitting apart in silence, and sighed, and rolled over in his blanket to sleep.

Seville itself was bustling, prosperous under the Abbadids, the ruling family. Ibn Hafsun said that the river was navigable from the sea to this point, making Seville a natural port. There was a fortress here, built centuries ago by Cordoban governors. Now it was being extended by the Abbadids into a palace to be called al-Murawak – 'the Blessed'. If Cordoba's great days were over, it appeared that Seville's still lay ahead.

They came to a place a little way to the north and west of the fortress walls, where a small mosque stood. Ibn Hafsun said, 'You say Sihtric spoke of a great mosque to be built in Seville. If it is to be built anywhere, I judge it will be just here, for the position, close to the palace, is ideal.' He glanced around at the somewhat shabby mosque, the tangled streets. 'It's unprepossessing now. But it would be fascinating to come back in a century or two, and see what time has made of this place.'

Robert glanced at Moraima. 'We should make plans,' he said. 'Ibn Hafsun has brought us this far. Now it's up to us.'

'I have family in the city, on my mother's side,' Moraima said. 'The aunt who would have raised me. We could stay with her. She wouldn't betray us. She never liked grandfather much.'

'Or—'

'Yes?'

'Or we could take a ship for England.'

They eyed each other. Moraima's face was full of her loss, of her father and grandfather. A loss that, perhaps, she blamed him for, in some indirect way.

And Robert saw her from a distance, as if through a window of stained glass.

He was fourteen years old, and was battered by contradictory experiences. In a few days he had lost his father, but he had found a core of true Christian faith. When he had first travelled across al-Andalus his soul had opened up to its light and its beauty. But now he imagined a day when this country would be studded with solid churches and cathedrals, and the folk working these rich fields would all be good Christians. He imagined that future, and dreamed inchoately of playing a part in bringing it about.

And in the world as he saw it now, with a new clear vision and orderly head, he found little room for a Muslim girl and her half-Muslim baby.

She saw this in his face. She turned away.

He dug the scroll out of his pack. Badly scorched, it was crumbling. 'We must decide what to do with this.'

Ibn Hafsun glanced at it, interested. 'What is it?'

'It was saved from the fire. I think Sihtric thrust it out to a serving girl, who passed it to me ... I have told you of his visions, the engines. These are the original sketches, I think, taken from the English monk.'

Ibn Hafsun touched the battered scroll. 'The Codex! And nearly complete. Marvellous, marvellous. And it is wrapped in this bit of skin – is it tattooed somehow?'

Robert took the bit of skin, fingering it curiously. It was damaged by an arrow wound.

'But they are useless,' Moraima said. 'These designs. My father always said they needed the *Incendium Dei*, which his alchemists could never puzzle out.'

'Useless?' Ibn Hafsun laughed coldly. 'I wouldn't have said so. How many have already died as a result of this Codex?'

'It is useless,' Robert said. 'And my mother's vision even more so.' In the end, as far as he knew, Sihtric and Orm had never even discussed properly the 'Testament' that had brought Orm all this way in the first place. It had all been folly – a dreadful waste of life.

'Well,' Ibn Hafsun said, 'if you two aren't to stay together, what will you do with the Codex?'

'It's a Christian relic,' Robert said. 'I won't see it in Muslim hands. Perhaps we should destroy it.'

'It belonged to my father,' Moraima snapped. 'I won't see it destroyed.'

'That *would* seem a crime,' Ibn Hafsun said. 'It is a unique artefact ... Can I suggest a compromise? Let me take it. I will put it in safekeeping for you – or for your children, perhaps.'

'Safekeeping?' Moraima asked. 'Where?'

Ibn Hafsun thought it over, and had an inspiration. 'Right here. I'll put it in a box, and have it interred, under our feet. One day a great mosque will rise up here on this very spot. Surely it will be undisturbed there. And if you or your descendants ever want to retrieve it – well, you know where to look.'

'Are you an honest man, Ibn Hafsun?' Robert asked. 'You won't take it and exploit it for yourself?'

'Not I,' said Ibn Hafsun. 'I don't have the imagination for such things – or the stomach. After all I am caught between two worlds; who would I attack, my Muslim brothers or my Christian cousins? You can trust me, Robert Egilsson. I hope you know that of me by now.'

Robert and Moraima eyed each other. 'Agreed,' said Robert.

She nodded.

'And for you two,' Ibn Hafsun said sadly. 'Is there no hope?'

'No hope,' Robert said.

Moraima asked coldly, 'What of the baby?'

Robert shrugged. 'Have it born. Have it scooped out of you by your clever Islamic doctors. I don't care. It is your responsibility, only my shame.' And he turned to walk away.

'A shame that will haunt you, Robert,' she called after him. 'Haunt you!'

He kept walking, faster through the narrow streets, until he could no longer hear her voice.

As he approached the river he dug into his pack, checking his money.

And he found al-Hafredi's bit of tattooed wrapping skin, and scraps of the fire-damaged Codex, torn off. These fragments had been left behind when he had pulled out the scroll. He picked out the largest bit of the Codex, held it up in the bright Spanish sun, and studied it curiously. The words *Incendium Dei* had been ripped through, leaving incomplete letters, D, I, V, M. And there was a string of garbled lettering:

BMQVK XESEF EBZKM BMHSM ...

Perhaps he should discard these bits of grisly, enigmatic rubbish. But that felt wrong. After all men had died for this – his own father had.

He thrust the scrap back into his pack, with the bit of human skin. He could decide later. Then he walked along the river front, looking for a ship to England.

II

CRUCESIGNATI

AD 1242–1248

I

AD 1242

'On the day he left Seville Robert was only fourteen years old,' Joan said. 'A year younger than you are now, Saladin. He grew to become strong and pious – but a savage warrior, a driven man, it was always said. He took the Cross, and won Jerusalem. And he died on Temple Mount, far from home. This Christian country was his enduring achievement. Since then six generations of his children, six generations of *us*, have lived and died here. But Robert, that confused boy, has vanished into time, his life transient as a breath . . .'

Saladin sat with his mother on a blanket spread over the dusty ground of the Mount of Joy. On the hill a goat bleated, and their tethered horses grazed peacefully. The sun was high, the last of the morning's cloud was shredded, and a *sharav*, a desert wind, hot and dry and scented like spice, stretched the skin of Saladin's face tight as a drum.

All of Jerusalem was spread out before him, the domes of its mosques and churches and the swarming of its many bazaars and suqs all crowded within the wreckage of the old walls. Faint voices called the Muslim faithful to prayer, and somewhere the bell of a Christian church tolled. To the east he could see the Dead Sea and the Jordan. To the west the Mediterranean gleamed. It was hard to believe that any of this would ever change, that he himself would ever grow old. And he felt uncomfortable with his mother's talk of a long-dead boy.

'I don't like it when you say things like that,' he said.

'Like what?'

'Like a poet. "Transient as a breath." What does that *mean*?'

Joan sat wrapped in a loose white robe, with a scarf over her head to deflect the sunlight. While Saladin was dusky she was pale, her eyes blue, and the sun burned her easily. Saladin had heard it said that *he* looked as if he belonged here, but she did not, though the line of her ancestors since Robert the Wolf spanned a century and a half.

She was only thirty, he reminded himself. Her husband, his father, had died young, and she had worn herself out raising Saladin, and defending the family's wealth and position in Jerusalem. He knew all that. But her earnestness made him impatient. He felt like a slab of muscle, restless and confined.

She sighed. 'I'm trying to waken your soul, Saladin. Trying to give you a sense of the history in which we're all embedded.'

'Who cares about history? You can't change history, you're stuck with it. The future is all that matters.'

'Dear Saladin. You're just like your father, you know. His brain-pan was as hard as iron too. And he cared nothing for history either. But history shapes all our lives. The great currents of time have brought us here, you and I, to this hill over Jerusalem, far from the birthplaces of our ancestors – of Robert.

'And what's more it wasn't until your father died, and I had to take responsibility for his business affairs, that I learned that *all our family's fortune is based on history* – or rather our family's strange knowledge of it, and of the future. Your father kept that from me. Soon you will need to learn the truth. Saladin understood history, and his place in it, you know,' she said. 'I mean the first Saladin the Saracen, your namesake. That was why he spared the Christian population when he took Jeru-salem. It was a gesture which will cast a shadow across centuries.'

Saladin didn't always appreciate bearing the name of a Saracen, even the greatest and most honourable. 'Can we go back to the city now? You know how hot you get.'

'Not just yet. There's something I need to tell you. We are to receive a visitor. From England.'

Saladin was thrilled. To him, England, birthplace of Robert, and of Richard the Lionheart, the greatest Christian warrior of all, was as remote and exotic as the moon. 'Who? A knight, a prince?'

She laughed softly. 'Somebody much more useful. He is a man called Thomas Busshe. He is a monk, a friar in a Franciscan monastery near Colchester. But he also lectures on theology and philosophy in Oxford.'

Saladin's disappointment was crushing. 'A monk,' he said with disgust. 'A *scholar*. I don't even know where Colchester is.'

'It's an old city, north of London.'

But Saladin had no clear idea where London was either. 'So why is this fat old scholar hauling his backside from one end of the world to the other?'

She laughed again. 'Actually he has two purposes. He wants to speak of the Mongols, and our family's business. And he means to deliver me a letter. It was sent to his monastery, but it is intended for us. It comes from Cordoba.'

He frowned, thinking through his mish-mash geography. 'Cordoba? The city of the Moors in Spain?'

'Who would write to us from Cordoba, do you imagine?'

'Family? A Christian warrior?'

'No,' she said carefully. 'Quite the opposite. Our correspondents are Moors, Saladin. Muslims. And yet they are cousins. And yet they are descended from Robert the Wolf, just as we are ...'

II

The letter had come about because of a visit by an English scholar called Peter to his sponsor, Subh, a lady of Cordoba – and Joan's distant cousin.

It wasn't difficult for Peter to find his way through the dense heart of Cordoba. Though born in England, he had spent years in Toledo, and was used to tangled Moorish streets. But Cordoba had its own intricate beauty. As he walked, he came across little squares where the prospect would unexpectedly open up, and he found himself looking down sloping cobbled streets and under arches to silent crowds of rooftops beyond. It was May, and baskets of flowers added splashes of colour everywhere.

But the city seemed half empty. There were fewer people than flower baskets, it seemed, ragged children throwing stones into dry fountains, a firewood seller leading his donkey through deserted streets. Some of the grandest houses were abandoned, the gardens weed-strewn, the vines out of control, the ponds clogged.

He found his way to the River Guadalquivir, in whose embrace Cordoba nestled. The old bridge still stood proud, the labour of the Romans enduring centuries. From here he took his bearings. To the north-west was the Jewish quarter, to the east the Christian, and between them the Moorish quarter.

And there was the great mosque, with the cross of Christ fluttering on banners above its gates. There could not have been a clearer symbol of the Reconquest. Just six years earlier Cordoba itself had at last submitted to the armies of the Castilian king Fernando III, and the most beautiful mosque in al-Andalus had been reconsecrated as a Christian church.

Peter walked out of the centre of the city, looking for the home of Subh, the sponsor of his scholarship.

The house was well appointed in the old style, a remnant of the Moorish past. The gate was open, and he walked through an elaborate archway into a small but neat patio, where vines clung to slim pillars, and pot plants stood like soldiers around a pond where fish swam and a small fountain bubbled. Peter, in his woollen tunic and with his pack on his back, dusty from the road, felt shabby.

A woman came striding out of a doorway. A small crowd of men followed her, perhaps a dozen, mostly younger than her. They were nervous, agitated, and they chattered in dense Arabic. With his bright blond hair and blue eyes, Peter felt even more out of place.

When the woman saw Peter she stopped dead. 'Who are you?'

She was taller than Peter, and aged perhaps forty, judging from the lines that gathered around her full mouth. But her hair was as dark as her eyes, her cheeks were high and her nose strong, and there was a sway to her ample hips that was almost animal. Peter was twenty-two years old and a virgin. He was overwhelmed by her primitive force.

He bowed hastily, but in the process his pack tumbled over his shoulder and clouted him on the head. Some of the younger men sniggered. 'I am Peter,' he said nervously. 'A scholar from Toledo. We have been corresponding.'

'We've been more than just corresponding, Peter of Toledo,' she said. 'I've been paying your wages for the last year, and I've kept you alive from the look of your scrawny frame. Well, you evidently know who I am.'

'You are the lady Subh, who—'

'Oh, straighten up, man, I can't abide bowing and scraping.'

There was an amused glint in her eye that told him she knew exactly the effect she was having on him. He said, even more confused, 'I have brought the fruits of my studies into the history of your family—'

'I should hope you have or there'd be little point you coming all this way, would there? Look, young man, I'm afraid I don't have time for you just now. We have something of a family crisis going on.' She waved a hand at the men behind her. 'Look at this lot. All my relatives, nephews, cousins, even a few uncles. All flocking around me, the way they came huddling around my husband when he was alive, may he rest in the peace of Allah. I won't bother introducing you because they're not worth a clipped crown, the lot of them. All save this one, perhaps. Peter of Toledo, meet my son, Ibrahim.'

Ibrahim was about Peter's age, perhaps a bit younger. He wore a tunic and leggings of a severe black cloth. He bowed to Peter. He was

101

handsome, but his eyes, startling blue, were cold. 'What are you, Peter of Toledo? French?'

'English.'

Ibrahim grunted, uninterested. 'All Christians are the same.' He turned away.

'Ibrahim is as strong as his father,' Subh said, 'but ten times as difficult. Follows the teaching of the Almohads. Allah be thanked for sending me such a devout son.'

'Your mockery is inappropriate,' Ibrahim said sternly.

'Yes, yes. Well, we don't have time for this. Come.' And without another word she swept out of the courtyard and into the street beyond. The relatives followed her like baby geese.

Peter stood for a heartbeat. Then he dropped his pack in a shady corner and ran after the little mob, for he had no idea what else to do.

He found himself striding alongside Ibrahim. 'Where are we going?'

'To the mosque. Zawi is in trouble with the Christians.'

'Who is Zawi?'

'A cousin. Another one of the hapless flock who huddle under my mother's wing, and look for her protection when their foolishness and impiety leads them into trouble.'

He sounded stern and contemptuous, as only a very young man can be, Peter thought, aware of his own youth. 'You don't sound as if you have much respect for your family.'

'When the Christian armies came, my cousins did not fight for Cordoba as men. Now they cluster around a woman for protection. They are less than men.'

'And,' Peter asked carefully, 'did you fight?'

'I was too young,' Ibrahim said quickly.

Which Peter, versed in interpretation, understood to mean that his formidable mother had not let him fight. 'I would be interested to learn of your culture,' he said now. 'The principles of the Almohads, who see the whole world as a unity "plunged in God". A fascinating concept.'

Ibrahim glared at him with stony contempt. 'You know nothing of our culture. No Christian does.'

'That remark only shows that you know little of Christians yourself. I am a student, and a translator. I speak and write Arabic, pure Latin, and the dialects of the Castilians and the Aragonese, as well as Greek, French, English and other tongues. In Toledo I have translated works of Arab scholars into Latin, and Latin into Arabic, and—'

'You plunder the intellectual wealth of a higher culture as you plunder our African gold.'

Peter didn't rise to that. 'You can't translate philosophy without knowing something of its context.'

'Perhaps you think we all wandered in from the desert. Moors have been in this country for five hundred years.'

'I know that,' Peter said. 'But the Almohads *did* come from the desert, only a few decades ago – didn't they?'

Ibrahim was predictably offended, and stalked away after his mother. Peter was forced to hurry after them, his feet already aching from his journey.

III

A group of people, men, women and children, had gathered in a rough semicircle before the mosque's northern wall. Perhaps a hundred strong, they all seemed to be Christian. Many wore grubby crosses stitched to their shoulders, the papal symbol of the Reconquest. And they all seemed to be wielding stones, cobbles and lumps of concrete. Even the smallest children clutched pebbles in their tiny hands. It was a stoning, then. The Christians looked hungry for it to begin. There was no sign of any forces of order, of the Christian king's soldiers.

But Subh, without hesitation, marched straight into the middle of this mob. Subh's relatives hung back, but Ibrahim stayed with her, and Peter hurried after them.

At the centre of the crowd was a boy, dark-skinned, cowering against the wall. He stood awkwardly, dragging one wounded leg. His clothing was filthy and stiff with dark blood, and the left side of his face was swollen and battered. Two men stood near him, both stout and sleek, one expensively dressed, the other a Christian priest in his finery.

Subh stood proud before the cowering boy. 'You won't be harmed, Zawi. Stand straight, and stop that sniffling.' She glared around at the muttering crowd. The skin of her face shone with fine oils, and the slight breeze wrapped her loose white clothing around her so that her hips and breasts were prominent. In that moment of peril she looked magnificent to Peter, powerful, authoritative. Once again he felt a pang of helpless lust.

She called out clearly, '"He that is without sin among you, let him first cast a stone." Aren't those the words of Christ, recorded in the gospel of John? What, are you surprised that a Muslim knows the words of your holy books? I dare say I know your own creed better than most of you, and those tatty crosses sewn to your shoulders make no difference to that. Which of you fine Christians has condemned this snivelling boy?'

'I did, Subh.' It was the fat, finely dressed man who stood with the priest. His purple-dyed silk cloak must have been extraordinarily expensive.

'Alfonso,' Subh said with disgust. 'I might have known it was you. What do you accuse him of, *muhtasib* – mocking the size of your fat arse? If so you'll have to have half of Cordoba stoned.'

That actually won her a laugh.

Alfonso preened, plump fingers plucking at his leather belt. 'The crime is rather more serious than that, lady. This sand rat of a nephew of yours has fornicated with my granddaughter. *My* granddaughter, my Beatrice. Come here, child.' A girl, mousy, plain, stumbled forward from the crowd. 'Fornicated!' Alfonso thundered. 'What do you have to say to that?'

There was an angry murmur from the crowd.

Peter murmured to Ibrahim, 'In Toledo it's no stoning offence for a Muslim to sleep with a Christian.'

'In this town it is. And Alfonso is the *muhtasib*, who supervises the market. He is a man of influence in Cordoba.'

Subh was undaunted. 'And you have proof of this, do you, Alfonso the Fat? Oh, I'm prepared to believe that this wretched whelp of yours is no longer a virgin. But what else, beyond her word against his?'

'It was him,' Beatrice said, and she raised an unsteady finger to point at Zawi. 'He forced me!'

The crowd murmured again. But the priest looked down at his shoes, uncomfortable.

Subh, sharp, in control, noticed this. '*Forced you*? Ah, but that isn't the story you told earlier, I would wager. Is it, child?'

'Yes – no – but it was Zawi, it was!'

Subh snorted, but Peter noticed she did not call on the boy to deny it for himself. She stalked about, regal, sneering at the stone-wielding crowd. 'And if so, what did you think of his scars?' Beatrice said nothing, and Subh went on, 'Come, child. If you lay together you must have noticed *those*.'

Beatrice glanced at her grandfather, uncertain.

Subh turned to the boy. 'Show them what I mean.'

Zawi's embarrassment apparently overcame his fear. 'But, aunt—'

'Show them. Drop your trousers.'

The boy complied, to reveal bare legs and a grimy sash around his waist. The crowd hooted, mocking his skinny legs and his shrivelled cock, and the boy was mortified. But Subh plucked aside the sash, and the crowd gasped at a mesh of scars on his belly.

'The result of a pious mule-whipping,' Subh said. 'A childhood gift from one of your sons, I'm told, Alfonso. Child, how could you not notice *that*?'

The girl, confused, stammered out, 'But I did sleep with him. All right, he didn't force me. But I *did*. It was in the orange grove behind the—'

Subh drowned her out. 'Your word against his! That's all we have. Who are you protecting, Beatrice? Who? Somebody known to your father – one of his business associates?' She spat that out with utter contempt. 'And for that will you take the blood of a boy on your hands? Will you go to meet your Maker with that unforgiven sin on your conscience?' She turned on the crowd. 'Will you? And you?'

As Zawi pulled up his trousers, Alfonso made one last try. He cried, 'You will not contradict me, woman! The facts of the case are clear! This girl has been violated. *This girl*, of a line tainted by no Moorish blood or Jewish, a Christian line that has survived since the days of the Gothic kings . . .'

But nobody was listening. One cobble was actually hurled, bouncing off the mosque wall harmlessly. But the mood for blood was gone, washed away by the sheer power of Subh's personality. Even the priest walked away.

Subh approached Alfonso. 'Gothic kings, eh? Well, I,' she said, 'am descended from Ahmed Ibn Tufayl, vizier to the emir of Seville, and *that* is no lie. I know the truth about you and your family, *muhtasib*. For centuries you called yourself al-Hafsun. My family worked with yours, in those days. You were *muwallad*. But when the Christian kings returned, you conveniently called yourselves Christian once more. Your blood is no more pure than your slut of a granddaughter.'

And she turned her back on a fuming Alfonso. 'One of you,' she called to her hapless relatives, 'take Zawi home and clean him up. And tell him that if he gets up to this kind of mischief again, especially with a Christian, and *especially* with a granddaughter of that slug Alfonso, I'll cut off his cock myself.' She rubbed her hands as if to clean them of dust. 'Well, that's that sorted out. Now, what's next?' She smiled brightly at Peter. 'What are you waiting for? Come with me.'

He dared do nothing else but follow.

IV

In the patio of her home, Subh served Peter tea flavoured with the zest of an orange, and dried olives and apricots in thick cream.

It was May, and the garden was fresh, the leaves on the trees brilliant green, the roses flowering, the blossom on the pomegranates bright red. Somewhere a nightingale sang. This was a typically Moorish setting, Peter thought, an oasis-garden made by folk who cherished life where they found it.

But Ibrahim stalked about, restless. He seemed very angry that his mother had saved the life of his distant cousin. 'You lied shamelessly,' Ibrahim accused her. 'You knew very well that Zawi slept with that wretched girl. It was written all over him.'

Peter said, 'But the scars – the girl didn't recognise them.'

'He keeps the scars covered up with his sash,' Ibrahim snapped. 'Even while making love. Wouldn't you?'

'Oh, of course I knew he slept with the whelp,' Subh said. 'Why do you think I didn't question him? For fear he would blurt out the truth, or still worse profess some undying passion for the spread-legged little she-goat, and get himself put down.'

'And you made an unnecessary enemy of Alfonso in the process.'

'But he is already my enemy. You see, my son, I believe that to lie is wrong, but to allow a foolish boy to be stoned for a bit of careless lust is more wrong still.'

Ibrahim snapped, 'Our family has lived in this den of decadence for too long. It has poisoned our blood, which must be cleansed!' And he stalked off, unsatisfied.

So Peter was left alone with this woman, her languid form draped on a divan. Impossible fantasies ran through his head.

Subh sighed. 'It is a trial to have a son whose soul is so much purer than mine. A reminder of the time when the holy Almohads ran all our lives, and the Almoravids before them.'

After the fall of Toledo a century and a half earlier, a bruised al-Andalus had fallen under the sway of cultists from across the strait, Almoravids and later Almohads, men of the desert with veiled faces who dressed in skins and stank of their camels, devout, disciplined and cruel. Attitudes hardened on both sides. The popes granted crusading indulgences to knights who fought in Spain, challenging the fundamentalism of the desert warriors.

'The boy means well, of course. But he simply isn't *pragmatic*. Are you pragmatic, scholar? Or are you religious?'

'Not especially, though I do plenty of work for the religious houses, mostly the Franciscans. My ambition is to be a philosopher, for which I need to find patrons – like yourself, to whom I am eternally grateful.' Peter's career was a new sort, unimagined not so long before. Thanks to the injection of scholarship from the conquered regions of al-Andalus there had been an explosion of learning across Christendom, and all over Europe itinerant scholars like Peter were trying to make a living. 'Of course,' he went on, 'the task of the scholar is to reconcile all our philosophy with the revealed truth of God.' That was the official truth, but actually, it seemed to Peter, thanks to the Aristotelian studies of the Moorish scholars, across Christendom the close ties of devotion and scholarship were loosening.

Subh was still thinking about her son. 'Ibrahim can't see that the subtext of the little encounter today is my rivalry with Alfonso the Fat, and the long war he is waging to destroy me. That's why he was trying to have poor Zawi put down – it's nothing to do with the law, or what Zawi may or may not have actually done. It's all to get at me.'

'Why would he wish to do that?'

'Because I work against him. He offends me, in his hypocrisy, his exploitation of the mudejars, *and* the size of his arse.'

The term 'mudejar', *al-mudajjar*, meaning literally 'the tamed', referred to Muslims still living in Cordoba, Toledo and other territories reconquered by the Christians. There was work for them to do, as clerks, accountants, lawyers. The more enlightened Christian rulers and wealthy folk even employed mudejar artisans to restore or rebuild their houses and palaces in a Moorish style.

'And in Cordoba,' Subh said, 'Alfonso has spent the six years since the city's conquest establishing himself as a middle man. Wealthy Christians find it easier to deal with a man who presents himself as a Christian, you see, than with the children of the desert – even though ten years ago "Alfonso" was as Moorish as an Almohad. So Alfonso sells Moorish work at the highest prices, while paying the Moors a pittance, and growing rich himself in the process. Why, he even exploits some of my own family. Can you believe that? He despises me, you see, because I stand up to him.'

'You were very brave to face down the crowd.'

'Brave for a woman, you mean?' She snorted. 'Well, I have to be strong, for all the men have fled. It was a bad time when Cordoba fell. My husband was already dead, killed fighting the Christians. Then King Fernando laid siege to the city. We capitulated; after six months we had no choice.' She paused, and her eyes were distant. 'Best not to speak of those times. That first evening a bishop entered the mosque to "cleanse" it, as they put it, and rededicate it to Christ. And they took away the bells of the church of Saint James, and returned them to Santiago de Compostela from where they had been stolen by al-Mansur, more than two centuries ago. Christians don't forget, or forgive! – but then,' she said fiercely, 'neither do Muslims. When the city gates were opened to the Christians, those who could afford to do so fled south, to Seville or Granada, even across the strait to the Maghrib.'

'Why did you not flee?'

'Because,' she said grandly, 'those left behind, the marginal and the poor, the toy-makers and the saddlers, the farmers and the potters, good Muslims stranded in a Christian city, have nobody left to stand up for them. And besides I am the descendant of a vizier. As you, in your rummaging in the libraries of Toledo, have proven for me, I hope.'

Her warm look stirred his blood again. But he paused, for he knew that what he had found in Toledo was more complicated than that.

She recognised his hesitation. 'Don't tease me, Peter of Toledo. Did you find what I wanted?'

'Yes. And no.'

She made a gesture like swatting a fly. 'A typical scholar's response – infuriating! Is that all I get for my money?'

'In the archives I explored in Toledo,' he said carefully, 'I found answers to your questions – and more. Some of this will please you. Some of it will not.'

'Tell me, then. Did you find my ancestor?'

'Yes.' In fact that part hadn't been hard. Even in the fractured age of the *taifas*, the Moors had always been fine record-keepers. 'Yes, there was a vizier; his existence isn't just a family tradition. And his name, as you know, was Ahmed Ibn Tufayl. I can prove a direct line of descent, in places through the female line, to you.'

'Hah! I knew it! Oh, every Muslim in Cordoba claims descent from one royal lineage or another. But I knew we were different – I knew it.'

'I have some details of his career' – and Peter patted his bag – 'but what may interest you more is not how Ibn Tufayl lived, but how he died.'

V

'Much of this was written down after his death by his granddaughter, Moraima, who survived him.'

'My distant grandmother,' Subh breathed, eyes heartbreakingly wide.

'Over a hundred years dead.'

Peter summarised for her the story of Sihtric, the priest from England. 'Who as you know,' he said cautiously, 'fathered Moraima by Ibn Tufayl's daughter.'

She sighed. 'We've learned to live with that, I think.'

'The question is *why* Sihtric came to Spain. He approached Ibn Tufayl for sponsorship for a project: the development of designs for marvellous weapons called the Engines of God.'

Subh's eyes widened at that. 'Weapons?'

'These designs had a mysterious origin,' Peter said. 'Or murky, you might say. They were supposed to be the result of visions, divine or satanic, implanted in the mind of an English monk, now two centuries dead, who—'

Subh waved her hand impatiently. 'I've no time for visions and miracles. *Tell me about these weapons.* Did Sihtric build them? What became of them?'

He told her how Sihtric, with great difficulty, had got as far as a few prototypes. 'But there was something missing, so Sihtric came to believe. An agent he called *Incendium Dei* – the Fire of God. It was something like Greek Fire, perhaps – though there I'm guessing. It was mentioned in the designs, but nothing the alchemists could crack.'

'And then what? Get on with it, man!'

'And then,' Peter said, 'a man called Orm Egilsson, English or possibly a Dane, came to Cordoba in search of Sihtric. He brought with him his son, called Robert. Orm had a head full of a prophecy of his own, a "Testament of Eadgyth", or Edith, something to do with a mysterious figure called the Dove. And he seems to have been determined to put a stop to Sihtric's work.'

'Why? No, don't answer that. Prophecies and visions! Sometimes I think the whole world is gripped by pious madness. Did he stop Sihtric?'

'In a way. Orm's arrival upset everything – in particular the relationship between Sihtric and Ibn Tufayl.'

'So it all went wrong. Then what?'

'Ibn Tufayl tried to destroy the machines Sihtric had made, and to eliminate the scholars who had worked with him. He wanted it all for himself. He dreamed of being more than a vizier, lady.'

Subh nodded, matter-of-fact. 'He wouldn't have been the first. I take it he didn't achieve his ambition?'

'No. As they fought he burned himself to death, along with Sihtric and Orm, and the plans for the machines. All this took place in the palace of Madinat az-Zahra.'

Subh looked at him shrewdly. 'Not all the plans were lost. Or you would not be telling me about this now.'

'You're perceptive,' he said. 'No, not all of them. Ibn Tufayl doesn't seem to have been very competent. There are hints of personal weaknesses in the records – I suppose that doesn't matter. He was certainly not efficient in his elimination of Sihtric's work. I was able to find traces in the archives. For instance, one young clerk survived the vizier's cull, and, in bitterness, wrote down all he remembered to thwart the vizier's purpose. There are similar relics. It's all very fragmentary – most of it is just the point of view of one junior clerk – but—'

'You have these fragments?'

'Some of them. And, more than this – the blaze did not destroy everything. Moraima and Robert escaped. Between them they took away the Codex of the Engines of God – the original designs brought by Sihtric to Spain.'

'And what did they do with them?'

'The two of them fell out. They could not agree. The plans were buried – but what was buried was fire-damaged and not complete. One corner had been torn away by Robert, perhaps intentionally, perhaps not. This fragment contained the secret of God's Fire. Possibly – it is said. And it may be that Robert took away another treasure, another prophecy entirely, called the "Testament of al-Hafredi". I know little about that. But as for the rest of the engine designs, a man called Ibn Hafsun buried them for Moraima.' He thought it over. 'I suppose he may have been an ancestor of your Alonso the Fat.'

'How ironic that would be,' Subh said drily. 'And where did he bury the plans?'

Peter hesitated. 'Under the floor of the great mosque in Seville. In fact I have seen a fragment of memoir by Ibn Hafsun, in which he specifies exactly where the Codex can be found.'

Subh laughed. 'Now you're being absurd. Peter of Toledo, you must know that in a country where war has washed back and forth ever since Tariq crossed the strait, there are legends of buried treasure under every rock.'

'But it may be worth looking,' Peter said softly.

'You have an adventurous soul, for a scholar. And these sketches, the fragmentary plans you say you already have—'

'I'm no engineer. But I believe they could be developed into workable designs.' He said this with pride, and a certain longing, for it was a project he would find fascinating to pursue if he got the chance.

She clapped her hands, almost girlish. 'Oh, how marvellous. But you're telling me that even if I could get to Seville, even if we manage to dig up the mosque and find these plans – even if! – they will remain incomplete.'

'Because of the fragment taken by Robert, yes. But I have some news about that too. I was able to trace this Robert, son of Orm, and the family who followed him.'

She studied him. 'You are resourceful, aren't you? How?'

'It wasn't hard. He became known as Robert the Wolf.'

She sat back. 'Ah. One of the most notorious of the crusaders.'

'He settled in the Kingdom of Jerusalem, which he helped to found. His family live there still. Perhaps they know something of this Fire of God.'

'What do you suggest, Peter of Toledo?'

He shrugged. 'Write to the head of the family in the Outremer. She is called Joan. Tell how you may be able to help each other. I have a contact in a monastery in Colchester who could put us in touch.'

She scoffed. 'A mudejar of Cordoba writing to a Christian family in the Outremer? You really are a dreamer, aren't you, Peter?'

'Why not? You have two pieces of a puzzle, it seems to me, you and this Joan of the Outremer. And if you put them together it might be mutually beneficial.'

'And you, Christian Peter, would put these marvellous weapons in the hands of a Muslim? Would you have us make these weapons and slaughter each other?'

'The weapons may make war too dangerous to wage. Or the engines could be turned on the common enemy.'

'The Mongols,' Subh said. 'Now there's a thought. Well, don't worry, little Archimedes. I do sense an opportunity in these engines. But I'm no al-Mansur; business is what I know. All I want is to protect my family and my own. But if I can make a little money out of this I'll do it.' She smiled at him. 'You've done far more than I asked of you, Peter of Toledo. You've earned your fee.' But he kept his face serious, and, watching him, she grew grave. 'Ah. But you said you had something I would not wish to hear.'

'I do.' And, having witnessed a near-stoning that day, Peter knew how painful it was for her to learn that her ancestress Moraima was not just the daughter of a Christian, Sihtric, but the consort of another, Robert.

Subh was devastated. 'By Allah. But that means that Moraima's child, my distant grandfather, was *three-quarters Christian*. And by a brute of a crusader like Robert! No, no, it couldn't be worse. And to think I mocked that fool Alonso for the impurity of his blood!'

Peter said, 'All this was generations ago.'

She got up and paced, her movements hard, full of anger. 'You don't understand what it's like here, where Christianity rubs up against Islam. We are polarised. I have pinned my entire identity on my descent from the vizier. Nobody has heard of Sihtric, nobody cared about him. But if the vizier's granddaughter bore the bastard child of a notorious crusader, I am ruined in this city.'

'No one need know,' Peter said helplessly.

She laughed at him. 'Alonso will learn. He can afford better scholars than you, Peter. So that's that. I must flee Cordoba after all – and we may get a chance to explore Seville sooner than you expected.' She glanced at the angle of the sun. 'I have much to do. Scholar, find yourself a servant. Any of them will do. Have a room made up. We should still write to this Joan of the Outremer. Draft something for me, will you? Now you must excuse me. Ashmet? *Ashmet!*'

She stalked indoors, leaving Peter on the patio with the orange drink, and the dried fruit, and his pack with his notes.

VI

It was a deep shock to Saladin of Jerusalem to learn, from what Brother Thomas related of Peter's letter to Colchester, that Robert the Wolf, hero of the First Crusade, his family's saintly forebear, should be tainted by a liaison with Moraima, a Moorish girl.

'Now maybe you see what he had to run away from,' Joan said. 'All the way to the Holy Land—'

'Don't talk like that. Robert took the Cross. He didn't run anywhere.' Saladin got up, dusted off his leggings, and walked down the hill to the horses.

'I knew you'd react like this. You really are such a pious prig! But you don't need to worry,' his mother said, as she got up more stiffly. 'He tupped this girl, then left her in al-Andalus. He married your distant ancestress later, and she was a respectable Christian; there can be no blood of Muslim ancestry in you.' And she added, so softly he wasn't sure if she had spoken at all, 'Not from Moraima, anyway . . . Come. We must prepare for the arrival of Brother Thomas.'

VII

So Subh, descendant of a vizier, abandoned Cordoba, once the capital of a caliphate.

When Peter crossed the city on the day of her departure, the air was already hot, the sun intense, even so early in the morning. It had been late spring when Peter had arrived in Cordoba, with his mixture of hope and devastating bad news for Subh. Now it was midsummer and the fresh greenness had burned away, leaving the city parched and dusty, the blossom fallen, the patio gardens weary.

At the house Subh had already flung open the gates. Goods were heaped up in the narrow road: bags and packs and rolled-up carpets and wall hangings, even pot plants from the patio. Subh's household, with the usual gaggle of relatives, milled around. It was a day of defeat for Subh, of course. But she seemed as serene as always as she glided through the crowd, resolving disputes, solving problems, managing this last project in Cordoba as efficiently as she had handled all the other details of her life.

And as Subh supervised the abandonment of her home, Alfonso 'the Fat' and his ratty little granddaughter stood and watched. Alfonso didn't try to hide the look of triumph on his face.

The fleecing of departing Moorish refugees had become something of an industry in the conquered city. There seemed to be endless tithes to pay before you could get one mule-load of goods outside the walls. And Christians, never Muslims, were encouraged to buy up abandoned businesses and properties, usually at prices ruinous to the Muslim owners.

Even so Peter had been surprised when Subh sold her property to Alfonso, her rival.

But she had told Peter she was glad to do it. 'Alfonso was so determined to push my face into the dirt that he outbid everybody else and paid too much. Not as much as I'd have made if I'd sold up ten or fifteen years ago, before the siege, but far more than I expected. So let him have his victory; let him watch me walk away, no doubt fiddling with himself under that ugly cloak in his excitement. I'll take the fat fool's money.'

Muleteers drove their animals into the street to join the chaos, and gradually the backs of the patient beasts were loaded up. Peter, in his travelling clothes and carrying his pack, tried to master the mule he had to ride. It was a surly, truculent slab of muscle with sharp bristly fur and a stink of dried dung, and it was resolutely uninterested in Peter's plans for it.

Subh said to him, 'You don't have to come, you know. After all we are travelling out of the Christian territories. You could return to Toledo, and burrow back into your libraries like a worm into a book. If you decide to come with us you will leave behind everything you know, everything that is familiar.'

'I don't really make decisions,' he confessed. 'Not in that way. I do things step by step, depending on what seems right at the time. I left my birthplace near Bath to go to Oxford to study, and then on to London. And then I travelled to Toledo, where every scholar in Christendom wants to be for its translation schools. Then, when under your sponsorship I unearthed the story of your family's past, I felt I had to travel to Cordoba to meet you in person. And so on.'

She waved a hand. 'This is how the young plot their lives. You think you will live for ever; you think the future is full of endless possibility. So you follow impulses. You aren't old enough yet to understand that each choice you make in life in fact shuts as many doors for you as it opens.'

He felt put down by that; he had expected more gratitude, perhaps, for his loyalty. 'Well, lady, I have come across a trail of unanswered questions that I feel it's my duty to follow, regardless of where it may lead. That is not impulse, it's scholarship. And it is my instinct too,' he said boldly, 'to be at your side in the coming adventure.'

She looked him over. 'So sweet,' she murmured. And she cupped his cheek.

His flesh burned where she had touched it. But she had patted him like a child, not a lover. He turned to his mule, which seemed to look at him with sympathy, though it still resisted Peter's every attempt to climb on its back.

The caravan set off. There wasn't a single wheeled vehicle; everything and everybody was loaded on the back of a mule or a horse or a camel – even the magnificent Subh, who rode a delicate palfrey as if she had been born in the saddle.

They bumped their way out of Cordoba, met up with more mules and their drivers, and the caravan formed up for its passage along the banks of the Guadalquivir south-west to Seville – *Ishbiliya* – for the great river passed through both cities. The muleteers took over now, weather-beaten men with ragged clothes and faces like leather. They walked beside their lead mules, and the chiming of the bells around the animals' necks rose up into the dense, still air.

Peter looked back at the city as it receded, wondering if he would come this way again. Its walls were battered after the long months of siege, and the flags of Christ fluttered over its gates. But still the Roman bridge arched handsomely over the glimmering river, and when the muezzin calls sounded all the party paused to turn to the east and pray, all save Peter himself, who contented himself with the devotions of his childhood.

VIII

The maps which Thomas Busshe had studied in the monastery all showed the Holy Land as the centre of the world. But he felt as if his extraordinary journey took him, not to the centre, but to the very edge of reality.

Even to cross the water to France was gruelling for a man who had sailed nothing more ambitious than a leather-stitched rowboat across the Thames. Then came the slog through the splintered kingdoms of France to embark again at Marseilles, and a sea journey ever further eastward across a hot, flat Mediterranean which he knew to be largely a Muslim lake. He followed his maps as he passed along the coastline owned by the East Romans, Christians who did not bow to the Pope, and whose ancient city of Constantinople was now, shamefully, in the hands of the crusaders who had sacked it. But as he ploughed ever further east there was only the huge mass of the Sultanate of Rum to the north, under the Turks who had taken Asia Minor from the East Romans, and the Fatimid Caliphate to the south, where the crescent of Muhammad fluttered over the cities of the Nile. Great sprawls on the map these were, like enormous Muslim hands ready to crush his frail ship like a fly.

In Palestine, true, there was the Outremer, his destination, the remnants of the Christian kingdoms planted bravely by the soldiers of the First Crusade. But these domains were shrunken now, split up and reduced to fragments by the dramatic conquests of Saladin half a century before. Even Jerusalem itself was only nominally in the hands of Christians. Seeing these little islands of the faithful on his maps served only to convince Thomas Busshe that despite the Pope's ardent preaching, echoed in every pulpit in western Christendom, two centuries of

119

crusading had resulted in little solid achievement, indeed perhaps the very opposite.

But that could all change.

Thomas, over fifty years old, was no warrior himself. But he had formulated for himself a mission that he believed might yet reverse the fortunes of Christendom, a mission inspired by a relic of the past that had come swimming fortuitously to him out of the dark, like the finger-bone of a saint emerging from the muck of a drained pond. A gift that, if he used his intellect well, might yet win the epochal war of civilisations for Christ.

And so he drove on, determined, clinging to the ship's rail and trying not to vomit.

The climax of his extraordinary journey was at its very end. He landed at Jaffa, once more a Muslim city, and submitted himself to the ordeal of a trek across the dusty land to Jerusalem. And he met Joan and her son Saladin before the walls of the city itself.

The light was extraordinary in this holy country, thick and dense, crushing. It seemed to oppress the old city with its broken walls and shining domes, rather than illuminate it. Thomas, utterly exhausted, felt close to collapse. But here he was before Jerusalem itself, standing in the footprints of Christ. Overwhelmed, he brushed the dirt from his robes and scraped the sweat from his brow, and dropped to his knees to pray.

He was aware of Joan and Saladin, swathed in their white Saracen-like robes, watching him with some bemusement.

Joan led him into the heart of the city, with a serving boy who spoke not a word of English or Latin following behind with Thomas's pack. Thomas was soon lost in the maze of jumbled streets. There was a feeling of crush, of shabbiness, and Thomas saw that some of the buildings had been assembled from broken and ancient stones. Age lay heavy here.

To get to Joan's home he was led through a narrow alley to an inner court around which tall houses clustered. Joan entertained him in a large open room, with a thick carpet and heavy hangings on the wall. The windows, just slits, were so small that oil lamps burned despite the intensity of the light outside. It was a room that might have graced an English manor, he thought. But this was not England, where you strove to keep in the warm; the room was hot and stuffy, thick with smoke, and sweat started from his brow. It was an inappropriate, stubborn architecture.

Joan served him watered wine. 'You are an unaccustomed traveller, brother,' she said.

'I'm afraid so. I prefer to journey in the imagination, in the pages of my books, rather than to haul this weary carcass across land and sea.'

'And yet you have come as far as Baldwin, and those who first took the Cross.'

'The crusaders arrived fit to fight. They came to build kingdoms! I scarcely have the energy to make up a bed.'

'Oh, that is done for you,' Joan said. 'And while we don't expect you to conquer the city for us, you must see it. I want Saladin to show you around. No, I insist.'

Saladin nodded, looking surly, reluctant.

Joan's English was stilted, her accent a kind he had never heard the like of before. She was a slim woman, with a pretty, oval face and a pale, very English complexion – unlike her son, who was so dark he was all but invisible in the gloom of this absurd hall. The mother looked out of place here, a northern flower that ought to wilt in the sultry fire of the sun. Yet she was prospering, even though she had lost her husband and father before she was twenty.

This was a complicated place, he reminded himself, the Christian culture of the Outremer an exotic transplantation that had survived in this alien soil for nearly a century and a half. He must keep his wits about him.

'It is good to meet you, at last,' he said. 'I corresponded with your husband, and indeed your father before he passed your affairs on to your husband.'

Joan smiled at her son. 'Thus Brother Thomas has served our family's interests for generations.'

'You make me feel old,' Thomas said. 'But conversely your family's generous bequests have sustained the good work of my house for just as long.'

'Then we both benefit.'

The boy did not seem very interested. 'My mother said you have come to deliver a letter.'

'Among other things.' Thomas reached into his robe, and extracted a wallet of pigskin. He handed this wallet to Joan. 'It is from your cousin in Cordoba, as I indicated. Subh, a matron of that city.'

She drew out a bit of parchment, neatly folded but with a broken seal. She read a single underlined phrase. '*Incendium Dei*. I wonder what she means by that.' She held the letter before her small nose. 'I would like to imagine I can smell the oranges of Spain in the ink. Robert the Wolf would say little of his time in Spain, but he spoke of the orange trees. It's the sort of detail that survives in the telling.'

Thomas smiled. 'It probably smells more of the sea by now, madam. I have one other piece of news for you. The Mongols.'

'Their advance into Europe continues, does it?' Joan asked.

Thomas shook his head. 'They turned back at the gates of Vienna.'

'No!'

'It happened just this summer. It was on the death of the great Khan Ogodai. The Mongol generals immediately returned to their capital, for it is their custom to gather there to debate the succession.'

'Well, that's not in old al-Hafredi's foretelling.'

'Truthfully the document is unclear, madam. I may know more later in the year; I intend to meet with the Pope's legate, who was at the Mongol court when the reverse came. We must discuss the implications of this.'

'Of course.'

Saladin looked from one to the other. 'You realise I have no idea what you're talking about. Moorish cousins in Cordoba? The Mongols at Vienna? What does any of this have to do with us, here in Jerusalem?'

'It's a tangled story,' Joan said. 'It all stems from Robert and his strange adventures. You'll learn it all, Saladin.'

'I'd rather not,' the boy said briskly.

Thomas had come across warrior cubs like this before, who put sword-swinging ahead of scholarship. He saw it as part of God's purpose for him to correct such attitudes; he did not believe God wanted ignorant soldiers. And in this case it was essential that Saladin understood. 'It is your duty to hear.'

'Really.' Saladin got up abruptly. 'I've got things to do. Find me when you'd like your tour of the walls, Brother Thomas. Mother.' He nodded to Joan, and walked out.

'I would apologise,' Joan sighed. 'But he's always like this.'

'I sense he has a good heart.'

'And a strong soul,' she said. 'He'll do what's right.' She glanced again at her letter from Cordoba. 'Although I pray we will all find the way to do that.'

IX

Heading south-west along the bank of the Guadalquivir, Subh's caravan slowly moved out of the hinterland of Cordoba, with its sprawling farms and market gardens and groves of orange trees. The country broadened to an immense plain, the horizon obscured by a ghostly heat shimmer. It was an arid, open, severe land, littered with ruined forts like the hulks of wrecked ships.

Peter imagined it must be easy enough to get lost out here, on a land as vast and flat and featureless as an ocean. But not long after leaving the city they passed another mule train going the other way. The muleteers greeted each other noisily. In this sea of sand the muleteers were the navigators and the captains, stitching together the country with their endless journeying. And the muleteers sang, wailing muezzin-like melodies with earthy words in a rough Arabic. The songs were not so much long as open-ended, as one driver after another added a verse to an already complicated saga. So compelling were the choruses, so simple the melodies, that it was impossible not to join in, and the steady rhythm of the songs chimed with the pounding of the mules' hooves.

Peter, fanciful, found himself admiring the stoical simplicity of such a life. He envied the muleteers their sinewy strength, their obvious comfort on the rolling backs of their mules. To be bound into such a monkish routine, to learn to be able to do at least one thing exceptionally well, would itself be a kind of devotion. But he knew he could not bear such an elemental existence, not when there were cities full of books waiting to be read, a universe of philosophies to be contemplated.

And he was not so naïve as to idealise the muleteers' life. They were all heavily armed, with knives, swords and cudgels, and none of the caravans was small enough to be vulnerable to attack by the pirates of this desert sea. The shifting frontier line between Christendom and Islam made this a dangerous country to travel, and it was well known that refugees from the lost Moorish cities, always streaming south, were easy targets for killers, rapists and thieves. Subh had taken care to plan against such a calamity for her party.

On the second day Subh's son Ibrahim rode alongside Peter for a while. On his handsome charger he looked down on Peter, who thudded along on the back of his reluctant old mule. Ibrahim was provocative from the off. 'You are the only Christian in this caravan of Muslims. Even the muleteers are Muslim. Only you, out of place, and far from home. It is a certain kind of weakness, I believe, that drives a man to seek out the company of strangers. Why are you here, Christian Peter?'

'For the scholarship.'

Ibrahim hawked and spat. 'You could have enjoyed your scholarship without leaving London. Do you have a wife in London? A woman you love?'

'No wife or lover.'

'A boy—'

'I have no interest in boys, Ibrahim.'

'Then what are you fleeing from?'

'I'm fleeing nothing. I'm travelling in hope. I am following a loose thread in a tapestry, letting it lead me where it may. Your mother understands, I think.' Peter grew impatient with his pressing. 'Why should Christian and Muslim not share the adventure of life together? In Toledo, Christian and Muslim scholars meet and work together every day.'

'Under the banners of a Christian king.'

'Perhaps. But in the days of the caliphate Christian scholars similarly flocked to Muslim Cordoba.'

Ibrahim said, 'But there was no assimilation. Five centuries ago the Moorish armies marched north. The whole of Spain became a Muslim country, and Christians lived in a Moorish land. Now the Christians are scouring their way back down from the north, and Muslims will have to survive in a Christian country, as my family survived in Cordoba. No matter how long they cohabit, Muslim and Christian will not mix, any more than water and oil, whether there is more of the oil or more of the water.'

Peter considered arguing against this. But the evidence for it stood all around him, the bristling relics of warfare sticking out of the ground like broken teeth. 'All right. But here we are, Ibrahim, riding side by side. We don't have to fight, do we?'

124

Ibrahim eyed him, his eyes as bright as the sky. 'Perhaps not. But keep your gaze fixed to the backside of that mule in front of you, and off my mother's.' And he galloped away to rejoin his friends.

X

In the morning Thomas woke early, barely able to believe that he was really here. But even before he left his bed the wail of the muezzin calls told him that this holiest of cities was not Christian, not entirely.

Saladin came to find him. 'We should take that walk while the day is young. I don't imagine you will enjoy the noon heat.'

So Thomas ate his breakfast and hurried through his prayers, and followed Saladin out into the city.

Jerusalem was extraordinary, overwhelming, baffling, a warren of streets, a stew of history. On the Temple Mount, the gold cap of the Dome of the Rock gleamed like the sun brought down to earth, and beside it the silvery al-Aqsa mosque was light, airy, a dream in stone. The Muslims called the Mount *al-Haram ash-Sharif:* the Noble Holy Place. The Muslims were relative newcomers to Jerusalem, compared to the Jews and the Christians, but even they had already been here centuries.

The city was full of churches, of course. Some of them, built by the crusader kings of Jerusalem, were quite modern, with ribbed vaults and pointed arches, and would have graced any city of western Christendom. Others were older, more squat and monumental. These were Roman, many of them built during the long centuries *after* the legions had left Britain. Thomas poked around these buildings, fascinated.

But as he talked and analysed and speculated, Saladin hardly spoke. To him, Thomas thought, history meant little. Jerusalem was nothing but an arena for the warfare he expected to dominate his life, as it had the lives of his ancestors since Robert, who had come here with the First Crusade that had swept through the Holy Land like a fiery wind.

The Christian states the crusaders planted here had survived three

126

generations, until fortune threw up a great Muslim commander: a former vizier from Egypt, al-Malik al-Nasir Salah ed-Din Yusuf, known to the Christians as Saladin, who marched on Jerusalem. Even Richard the Lionheart was not strong enough to take back the holy city. Today Jerusalem was ruled under an agreement negotiated by the German emperor Frederick II, the nominal king of Jerusalem. The city had been left unfortified, and Muslims were allowed to remain; it was a shabby deal. Still, some of the old Christian families, like Joan's, had crept back into the city which they had regarded as their home for generations.

So much for warfare. But, Thomas asked himself, what kind of people were these folk of the Outremer?

The boy Saladin was an ardent Christian, that was certain; here on the front line of Christendom you would expect a sharpening of the faith. But he *looked* more Saracen than English, with his flowing robes, his dark skin, and Thomas had heard him jabber Arabic phrases as easily as he spoke his stilted English. Thomas guessed that there had been a few infusions of Saracen blood into his line over the generations. Saladin's deepest ancestry was English, but transplanted to the soil of Palestine for generations his kind had become something different, neither English nor Palestinian, something new in the world since the time of Robert.

And these new people of the Outremer were isolated, in a way that the Norman invaders of England, say, were not. King William's sons had taken English wives; after nearly two centuries their assimilation was complete. But Normans and English were both Christians. In the Outremer the remnants of the crusader kingdoms were islands of Christianity in a sea of Islam. This was Saladin's home, but his family would always be out of place here. And Thomas sensed that Saladin knew it in some deep part of his soul.

The day grew warmer, and the old city became a stone bowl full of hot, dry air. Thomas was grateful when Saladin took pity on him and led him back to the relative shade of Joan's house.

XI

As they rode steadily south-west and closed on Seville, the caravan entered Muslim lands.

Before the city they came upon an extensive Moorish army camp. It was a town of tents, men, horses, mules and camels, planted near the river bank; flags bearing the crescent hung limply in the heavy air. Weapons were piled up in huge mounds, shields and crossbows and spears supplied by the factories of Seville. Peter could hear the pounding of war drums, not coordinated but still a chilling sound, like distant thunder.

A party of troops rode out to meet the caravan, an officer and a small escort of hard-eyed desert horsemen. The officer wore a coat of quilted felt over mail armour, while the horsemen wore white robes and turbans; they carried spears and shields shaped like hearts. Subh had a letter, a conduct of safe-keeping from the emir in Seville. After an exchange of gifts – a bag of gold from Subh, some water carriers from the soldiers – the troops rode off back to their camp.

The muleteers made a wide detour away from the river to avoid the soldiers, and Peter was relieved, for everybody knew that the best-controlled soldiers were always liable to a little plunder, robbery and rapine. But he studied the camp, fascinated at the sight of a genuine Moorish army. It was odd that there were no wheeled vehicles to be seen, but along with mules the horses were gathered in great herds – imported from the Balearic islands, said Ibrahim, only the best for the army. And out of the ranks of the horses and mules rose the necks of haughty camels, brought over from Africa.

The core of the army was made up of levies raised on the provinces of al-Andalus, or what was left of it – cavalry from Granada, for instance.

Ibrahim pointed to groups of soldiers with dark faces, 'the silent soldiers' he called them dismissively, many of them Berbers who spoke no Arabic. But the most ardent fighters of all, said Ibrahim, were the volunteers who came here from across the Islamic world to 'the land of the jihad', as many Muslims called Spain. It was just as the crusading armies were made up of volunteers from across Christendom. Peter was awed to imagine the energies of two continent-spanning civilisations focused here on this place, this point in space and time.

The caravan was allowed to enter Seville without incident.

The city was more of a sprawl than Cordoba, and had long eclipsed its illustrious rival, becoming the capital of the Almohad rulers of al-Andalus. And, though Cordoba had fallen, this remained a Muslim city, not a Christian one; the crescent flew high over the domes and minarets, not the cross, and there was nothing plaintive about the muezzins' calls to prayer.

But there was evidence of the Christian Reconquest even here. Where Cordoba had seemed depopulated Seville struck Peter as very crowded. The towns and cities of the south had had to absorb the floods of refugees from the grinding advance of the Christian armies, and Subh said that she believed the population of the city might have doubled since the fall of Cordoba.

And it was a city under threat. Seville had the natural advantage that the Guadalquivir was navigable from the sea as far as this point, but that brought a certain vulnerability. So, near the heart of the city, two squat towers faced each other across the river. A massive chain stretched between them, that could be winched up to span the river to block the passage of threatening ships. Peter was taken by the brutal simplicity of the device.

As they threaded through the city Peter glimpsed the courtyard of the great mosque, crowded with fakirs and imams, and with the faithful who performed their ritual ablutions in the many fountains. It scarcely seemed conceivable that beneath the feet of those swarming faithful could be ancient plans for deadly weapons, plans lost and buried for more than a century, while this shining mosque had mushroomed over them.

Despite the overcrowding Subh had been able to secure a house, smaller than the one she had had to abandon in Cordoba but with a decent patio and fair-sized rooms, and not far from the great mosque. Here, once she had paid off her muleteers, she lodged herself, with Ibrahim and a few of her many family members.

And she gave a room to Peter. He peeled off his travel clothes with relief. He imagined he had sweated away half his body's weight into the fur of his wretched, patient mule. That night, in an airy room and on a soft pallet, out of the iron stink of the desert, he slept more deeply than he had since he was a child.

XII

Joan's smoky English hall was scarcely less tolerable in the evening's cool than in the heat of the day.

And here Saladin was told the strange truth about his family.

'It's a tangled story,' Thomas said, studying Saladin, trying to gauge what he understood. 'A story of prophecies – not one, but *three* of them, a whole sheaf.'

Joan told Saladin, sketching in brisk, efficient strokes, the story of how over a hundred and fifty years ago Robert the Wolf had travelled to Moorish Spain with his father, Orm the Viking, in search of a rogue priest.

Thomas said, 'Sihtric had come into the possession of plans for marvellous weapons. These plans were called the Codex of Aethelmaer, the weapons the Engines of God. But the Codex was compressed and enigmatic, and contained words nobody could read. So Sihtric went to Moorish Spain—'

'What? Why?' Saladin sounded outraged. 'To hand these weapons over to the caliphs?'

'The caliphs had gone by then,' Thomas said patiently. 'But, no, it was not Sihtric's intention to give his weapons to the Moors. He hoped to use the Moors' greater scholarship to help him understand the Codex and develop the weapons. And then, so his scheme seems to have gone, he would turn the weapons on his Moorish hosts.

'While he worked on these plans, as he researched the past, he came upon the *second* of the three prophecies – a sort of sketch of the future left by a wizard called al-Hafredi. More of that later.

'And then Robert and his father, Orm, turned up. Now Orm had a vision of his own – the *third* prophecy. He called it the Testament of

Eadgyth.' And he repeated Eadgyth's legend of the Dove, who must be turned to the west.

'Lots of prophecies, then,' Saladin said, confused.

'Orm believed his Testament of Eadgyth warned *against* the use of the Engines of God. That is why, armed with the Testament, a troubled Orm travelled with his son to the distant land where Sihtric was developing his weapons.'

'And in the middle of all this,' Joan said drily, 'our ancestor Robert found time to fall in love, and implant his seed in the loins of a Moorish girl, Moraima.'

Saladin was intrigued despite himself. 'So what happened to them all?'

'It all went predictably wrong,' Thomas said, and he sighed over the foolishness of the long dead. 'There was a fire. The result of some struggle, probably. Orm and Sihtric were both killed. The prophecies and plans were lost, or so it was believed ...'

Robert came home, seemingly full of disgust at what he had experienced of Moorish Spain. He became a warrior of God, eagerly taking the Cross when the Pope called the First Crusade.

Thomas said, 'But he never forgot his strange experiences, the tale of the magical engines, his father's prophecy, the future visions of al-Hafredi. In the end, driven by some sense of guilt perhaps – he may have felt it a betrayal of his father to just abandon it all – he told his own eldest son the whole story. And that son, mercifully for history and your family's fortune, was more bookish than his father, and wrote it all down for us.

'Now, by chance, not all of the Codex itself was lost. In the final struggle a scrap of it was torn away and ended up in Robert's possession. It bore strange words ...' Thomas rummaged through scrolls on a low table before him for his copy of the fragment. 'Ah, here we are.' He ran his finger along a line of text.

BMQVK XESEF EBZKM BMHSM BGNSD DYEED OSMEM HPTVZ
HESZS ZHVH

'There were letters nearby too, preserved on the fragment, but ripped through. AD, perhaps, a V and an M – nothing else could be made out.'

Saladin read this over. 'It's in no language I ever saw.'

'Reading isn't your strong suit anyhow, son,' Joan said, mocking him.

'This is no known language,' Thomas confirmed. 'I believe this is a cipher – a code, perhaps of the type Caesar once used. There may be some key, which is lost. At any rate it was preserved, thanks to the transcription of the bookish son.'

'Now,' said Joan. 'Here's the most important thing for us, Saladin. Another of the three prophecies, the Testament of al-Hafredi, also fell by chance into Robert's hands.'

'Written on a bit of human skin,' Thomas said with a certain morbid relish.

'And this al-Hafredi has become our family's own oracle.'

'An oracle?'

'I mean that literally, Saladin. One of Robert's grandsons gave the material to Brother Thomas's house to study and interpret it for us, and so they have, in the centuries since.'

Thomas said, 'Al-Hafredi told of events to come – very broad-brush, but reliable none the less. And in particular he spoke of the advance of the Mongols. This followed the Islamic conquest of Europe, and he described it step by step.'

Saladin was trying to work this out, his face twisting. 'The Muslims have never conquered Europe.'

'True, but we can believe that the Mongols' advance would have occurred as al-Hafredi described it, whether Islam conquered or not.'

Now Saladin seemed utterly baffled. 'And Robert lived and died long before anybody had heard of the Mongols!'

'He did indeed,' Joan said. 'It wouldn't be much of a prophecy if it was the other way around, would it?'

'But how can this be? Who but God can know the future?'

'Ah,' said Thomas. 'An interesting question.'

'Which,' Joan said hastily, 'we can explore at our leisure another time. For now, Saladin, the important point is that this information has proved useful.'

Saladin nodded. 'If you know the Mongols are coming you can arm against them.'

'We tried that,' Joan said. 'But nobody wants to believe in the coming of the Mongols until they are on the doorstep.

'What we could anticipate was the plight of the refugees – those poor folks driven ahead of the Mongols' advance, in Asia, Persia, Europe. So we set up caravan stops. We supplied food and water, blankets. We even hired Saracen doctors. And we bought up the land to which they had to flee.'

'We made money out of the terrified,' Saladin said. He seemed faintly disgusted.

'We saved lives,' Joan said sternly. 'There are far more ignoble ways of making a living, Saladin. And if we had not, our family could not have survived here.'

'Think of it as a miracle,' Thomas said to Saladin. 'Everyone knows that the First Crusade's dazzling successes all depended on miracles. Perhaps God has miraculously assisted your family, for purposes yet to be revealed. Think of it that way.'

'But now,' Joan said, 'things have changed.'

'How so?'

'For one thing,' Thomas said, 'the Mongols have turned back. We must discuss the meaning of this in due course.'

Joan said, 'And then there is this letter from Subh the Moor, our distant cousin. She drops a hint that the Codex, Sihtric's engine designs, may not be lost after all ...' Subh had said that a copy of the lost plans might have been buried under the floor of the mosque in Seville. 'If Robert ever knew this,' Joan said, 'he did not tell his son, or at any rate it was not written down.'

Now Saladin's face was full of a boyish wonder, pleasing to Thomas's dry heart. 'Buried under a mosque! What a story!'

'It may be just that,' Thomas warned. 'A story. But Subh has taken it seriously enough to write to you.'

Joan said, 'Subh believes that all these fragments of prophecy, in her possession and ours, may be put back together into a whole, the prophetic lore reassembled for the first time since the age of Sihtric himself.'

'And so that's why she wrote to you?' Saladin asked. 'But what does she want? We are Christian, she is Muslim. The Christians are destroying her country. Perhaps she intends to trick us, as that old priest Sihtric intended to trick the Moors.'

Thomas said, 'Even if that is her intention it need not be fulfilled. If we could get hold of these designs, if we could build the Engines of God, we could strike a devastating blow against Islam.'

Saladin studied him, curious. 'That sounds a very military ambition for a monk.'

'Not military. Evangelical.' He told them of Saint Francis of Assisi, founder of his order, whom Thomas himself had, thrillingly, met as a novice. 'The first rule Francis wrote for our order was a command for a global mission to "all peoples, races, tribes, and tongues, all nations and all men of all countries, who are and who shall be". Perhaps these Engines will enable my brothers to advance their most holy mission – even if not a life is taken with them.'

Joan said, 'So we share common goals, my family and your order.'

'Oh, yes.'

'So what do you think we should do about this, Thomas?'

'You could write to this cousin in Cordoba, or travel there. Or you could come to England – perhaps we could bring her there.'

Joan frowned. 'The Muslims would have us out of Jerusalem for good. It's not the best time to leave, chasing a dream. And I'm not sure if writing back to my Moorish cousin about this matter is advisable. For now, let us study the matter further. Subh can wait.' But she frowned again at her letter. 'You know, there are so many puzzles here. Thomas, what of this phrase, *Incendium Dei?*'

Thomas said, 'Something Subh's own ancestress, Moraima, evidently remembers of the lost Codex.'

'"The Fire of God."'

'More than "fire",' Thomas said. 'It is a word with passion. It means conflagration. Ruin. Perhaps it is a phrase associated with the bit of the manuscript from which Robert tore his corner ...'

A thought occurred to him. He pawed through his notes once more, looking for the transcription of the ripped-through phrase with the coded words. All those incomplete letters, I, V, M – was it possible that Subh's Latin phrase would complete that puzzle?

But he was exhausted by the heat. With apologies to Joan, promising to discuss all this further, he gathered up his documents and made his way to bed, his head buzzing with the enigma of the *Incendium Dei*, the Fire of God.

XIII

Among Subh's many admirable qualities was an antipathy to wasting time. And so, on only his second day in Seville, Peter was to meet Moorish scholars who would inspect the fragmentary weapons plans he had retrieved from the wreckage of the schemes of long-dead Sihtric.

He was in no state for this, with his hair and skin caked with dust and his clothes stiff with stale sweat. At Subh's suggestion, or perhaps it was an order, he took a bath, Moorish style. For the price of an English penny he had the dirt scraped and sweated out of his skin, he was shaved and his hair chopped back, and he had the ache of the mule ride kneaded out of his back by a masseur, a huge Moor with biceps like a bull's thighs.

When he got back to Subh's house he found his own clothes had been taken away for mending and cleaning, to be replaced by a set of clean, crisp white robes that would have suited any Moor. There was even a turban.

'My,' Subh said, when she met him at the gate. 'Has your skin been oiled? You even *smell* civilised.'

His head full of her perfume, he could only reply, 'Lady, I'll take that as a compliment.' He offered her his arm.

They walked the short distance to Seville's royal palace, which the Moors called the *al-qasr al-Mubarak*, the Blessed Palace. Somehow it didn't surprise Peter at all that Subh was held in high enough esteem by the emir to have been granted the use of rooms in his palace to meet her scholars.

They were met by one of the emir's staff, a sleek chamberlain with a scalp shaved smooth and polished oak-brown. He led them on a gentle walk through the rooms of the palace, which led from one to the other in the indirect Moorish style, filled with water-reflected light from patios and gardens. In some of the rooms they glimpsed people at leisure, wives and princes perhaps, and palace staff who worked on the business of running the emirate.

'I'm impressed you organised this so quickly,' he said.

'We may need to be hasty, if the rumours I've been hearing about the Christians' plans are true. We have a few years at best before Seville is besieged the way Cordoba was. So we must get on with it. But tell me – do you despair of the quality of our scholars in these latter days? After all the great age of the caliphate is long gone.'

'Not at all. I have studied Ibn Rushd, for instance, whom we know as Averroes. An astronomer, physician, philosopher, who is generally believed to have produced the best commentary on Aristotle since antiquity, and stirred up some trouble with it. Ibn Bajjah, a teacher of medicine, and tutor of Ibn Rushd. Al-Jayyani, who wrote commentaries on Euclid. Al-Maghribi, famous for trigonometry. Al-Zarqali, the fore-most astronomer—'

'Enough. You have convinced me. You know,' she mused, 'these scholars are heroes to you. But my son's heroes are men like Tariq and Saladin. Warriors. Makes you think.'

'I'll tell you something else about Muslim learning. Many Arabic words have no Latin equivalents, because the scholarship is so much more advanced. So when the work of Ibn Rushd, for instance, is trans-lated into Latin, the Arabic words are copied over as they are. Alkali. Camphor. Borax. Elixir. Algebra. Azure. Zenith. Nadir. Zero. Cipher—'

'Enough of your lists, boy!'

'Do you think that people in England and Germany will end up speaking Arabic without even knowing it?'

'Now that,' she said, 'is a delicious thought.'

They arrived at last at a patio with an elaborate sunken garden sur-rounded by graceful arches. Peter heard laughter, and in the shadowed spaces beyond he saw lithe running figures. At the western side of the patio they were brought through an elaborate horseshoe-arched doorway into a hall called the *turayya*. This grand hall was the emir's throne room; beneath a domed roof pillars of fine marble supported complex arcades. The chamberlain said it was named for the star system called in the west the Pleiades. It was so called because the rooms around this central hall were set out like those stars in the sky.

Peter's eye was drawn to the tile work which adorned the lower walls. A pattern of black stars, rich blue rectangles and white strips, repeating endlessly, somehow covered every scrap of the surface. 'I think I could spend my whole life,' Peter said, 'just looking at the tiles on that wall.'

'I'm afraid I have other plans for you,' Subh said. 'Enough gawping. Come now and sit with me.'

He joined her on floor cushions, and allowed a servant to pour him a glass of the juice of crushed oranges, as they waited for the first of their scholarly guests to come and talk of engines of war.

XIV

AD 1244

It was two years before Joan and Saladin saw Thomas again. They were years in which troubles more urgent than the vague promises of prophecies rose up and overwhelmed them – and, at last, after generations, the family of Robert the Wolf was forced to flee from Jerusalem.

Saladin thought of England as home, for this was the birthplace of his ancestor Robert; this was where his family had its deepest roots. But to a boy from the Outremer it was a strange, dark place. The sun never seemed to climb high in the sky, and was somehow dim even at noon. And Saladin felt *cold*, cold to his bones.

But as their ship sailed cautiously up a great estuary and into London he clung to the rail, staring out curiously at a city that sprawled across the horizon. Even the river was crowded, busy with trade, and upstream of a grim fortress called the Tower wooden cranes like long-necked birds pecked at ships laden with English wool, or with silk and wine coming into the country from the continent.

Thomas Busshe met them off the ship. Saladin was glad to see a familiar face in this strange country. Thomas had arranged lodgings for them for the night at a Franciscan priory. He had aged in the two years since their last meeting, and walked with a limp. But he seemed excited and pleased to see them – indeed, bursting with news, as he led them into the city.

As they walked, it was the filth that struck Saladin. All the narrow streets just ran with human sewage. And butchers worked out in the street, making the cobbles a mess of offal and bone fought over by rats and crows and bloody-handed urchins. Though squads of beadles, under-beadles and rakers swept gutters and drains clear of dung and hauled animal remains to the rivers for dumping, the stench of ordure and blood was overwhelming.

But, noisy, crowded, jostling, swaggering, stinking London bustled with commerce. In Jerusalem, tension simmered and arms and armour were everywhere. This sprawling city seemed to be run by merchants and shopkeepers, not by soldiers.

And there were no Saracens here, so Saladin's dark colouring stood out. A gang of well-dressed young men spotted Saladin and thought him a Saracen himself. 'Do you eat babies? Do you screw your mother? Get back where you came from, carpet-biter!' Thomas Busshe restrained him before he could draw his sword, but Saladin seethed.

That night he tried to sleep in air so dense and smoky he could barely breathe. He longed for the hot light of the Outremer, the iron scent of the desert.

In the morning, in Thomas's priory, they spoke of the fall of Jerusalem.

Joan bit into the tough bread softened by a bit of broth that passed for food here. 'Well, in the end we had to flee. We all did. Emperor Frederick's truce expired even before your visit two years ago, Thomas. But the Muslims were squabbling among themselves: brothers, rival princes in Damascus and Egypt, waging war on each other. That saved us for a bit. But at last, this year, one victorious princeling allied himself with the Khorezmians of Syria and took back Syria and Palestine, and – well. Reunited, the Muslims regained the Holy City too.

'We had warning. We fled with what we could carry, which was little enough. In Acre we bought our way onto one of the last ships – hideously overcrowded, you can imagine. The cost was obscene.'

Saladin was impatient. 'You talk of money, mother. What does money matter? This was not Saladin, not honourable. These Saracens burned the Church of the Holy Sepulchre. They massacred our people!'

Joan nodded, weary, grim, looking older than her thirty-two years. Saladin thought her experiences had hardened her, that she had come to hate the Saracens as perhaps she had not before. 'My son would have stayed to fight. I forced him to flee with me, for I needed his protection. Any shame in our flight is mine, not his.'

'Yes.' Thomas looked at Saladin. 'And this is what you must tell your confessor.'

Joan said, 'So Robert's blood descendants return to England half destitute. I may yet need the charity of your house, good brother.'

Thomas touched her hand. 'It won't come to that. Put away your despair; cling to hope. Your fortunes will rise again ... I have news for you.'

Joan studied him. 'You're being enigmatic, brother. Spit it out, man.'

140

'Not here.' He glanced around the empty room. 'London is a nest of spies.'

'Even here, in this priory?'

'Monks must make a living, lady. We must operate in the world of money and power. It's a corrupting environment. I will bring you to my own house, which is far from London. There we can talk with confidence.'

Saladin groaned. 'More travelling?'

'No more ships,' Thomas said. 'I promise you that.'

'But what is it you want to tell us?' Joan demanded. 'Give us a hint at least.'

Thomas smiled. 'Very well. I have come to believe more firmly than ever that your family legend of war engines and prophecies may have some truth in it. For I have stumbled upon evidence that *such things have happened more than once*. Warnings from the future, leaked into the past. No, not just evidence – I believe, proof. Eyewitness proof.'

Joan and Saladin stared at him. But he would say no more.

The next day they journeyed north out of London, jolting over an old Roman road, not repaired for centuries. Saladin longed for a camel's smooth gait, but there were no camels in England.

The country was green, and even away from the city the land was crowded, Saladin thought, full of people, carpeted with farms and studded with little towns and dung-coloured villages. Waterwheels creaked by the rivers, and windmills whispered as they turned in the breeze.

They stopped for a night at a city called Colchester. Set above a river, it was surrounded by bristling walls laid out in a vast rectangle, walls founded by the Romans but built up massively by the generations since.

Thomas said the history of England was written in those battered walls. William the Conqueror's descendants had been a sorry lot, and fifty years after William's death the country was racked by a long civil war between Stephen and Matilda, two of William's grandchildren. Thus, said Thomas, the ultimate legacy of William the Bastard: a once-prosperous country ruined by fratricidal warfare, famine, extortion, carnage and chaos. Saladin had heard of Matilda's grandson Richard the Lionheart. But King Richard died not long after his final crusade. His brother John was a weak, distrustful, treacherous, deeply unpopular king who was forced to cede power to his barons in a Great Charter, and under John's son, the third King Henry, a council of nobles, called a 'parliament', began to meet in Westminster. In England, then, power was shifting. But the latest King Henry favoured the church; great cathedrals sprouted like mushrooms ...

Saladin was disturbed by this bloody narrative. He had thought of England as a place of Christian peace and security – like a vast church, perhaps. But England was nothing like that. Wars had been fought out here and invasions mounted, and people were forced to huddle behind the walls of towns like fortresses. And it was all so insular. Did the posturing princes of this little country have no idea of the threat posed by the Muslims, who had taken three-quarters of Christendom – and, worse, the Mongols, who by all accounts had conquered three-quarters of the whole world?

At the very heart of Colchester was a Norman castle, a little like the brooding pile in London but even more imposing. 'The most massive keep in the whole country,' Thomas said. The castle's thick walls were heaped over a tremendous slab of concrete sunk into the sandy ground. Local legends had it that the slab had been the foundation of a great Roman temple. 'Think of the size it must have been! Who would build such a monument in this dismal place? But some of the locals claim that before the Romans came this town was already the capital of the whole of Britain.' Thomas shook his head. 'I suppose we would all like to believe we are descended from kings.'

Yet, Saladin thought, that mighty concrete slab had been poured into the ground by *somebody*, for some purpose. But his brief flicker of historical curiosity quickly died.

Thomas led them to his priory, a few miles outside the walls of the city. It was a modest house of a few dozen monks, supported by the sale of wool and tithes paid by the inhabitants of a small village, through which they had to walk. The houses were long, leading back from a central trampled track. It seemed that a family lived in each house along with their animals: there were no barns or sheep-pens or pig-sties, only the houses, for people and animals to share. The smoky air stank of the dung used to fuel the fires. A litter of grimy children followed the travellers, wide-eyed.

Compared to the aridity of the Outremer, the land here in the heart of England was green, and so wet that wherever you saw a ditch you had to assume it was for drainage, not irrigation. But the villagers scraping away at their long, skinny fields looked half-starved and exhausted. And there seemed to be an awful lot of children here, a lot of mouths to feed; no wonder the villagers had to work so hard.

The next morning was a Sunday, and Saladin and his mother worshipped in the village's small parish church. The church was dark and cramped, but its walls were brightly painted, covered with pictures based on Bible stories and the lives of the saints. Most striking was a very severe Christ, whose image stood above the chancel arch. The righteous climbed a ladder towards Him on one side of the arch, and the damned fell screaming into perdition on the other. The villagers, listening to their priest's mysterious Latin words, smelled of their fields, of grass and earth and dung.

After the service, Thomas said he would speak to them at last of his discoveries.

XV

In a cramped, smoky visitors' room in the priory, Thomas served them mead. Saladin sipped from his cup. The flavour was disgusting, the drink a kind of fermented honey, but it delivered a strong kick.

'Listen to the story I have to tell you,' Thomas said. 'Listen, believe, try to understand.'

He had come upon this truth by accident, when Thomas, in the service of Joan, was studying the progress of the Mongols.

Armed with al-Hafredi's glimpse of the future, Joan and her ancestors had been able to profit from a foreknowledge of the Mongols' advance. But in the year 1242 the Mongols had suddenly withdrawn from Europe. Thomas, digging into the reasons for this reversal, eventually found a man who had actually been at the court of the Mongols in that crucial season, two years ago. He was a knight called Philip of Marseilles. Devout, strong, fearless, Philip had taken the Cross more than once.

And he had agreed to serve as a legate for the Pope, in the pontiff's hopeful negotiations with the Mongol Great Khan.

The Mongols had been a nomadic people, one of many who hunted and warred across the vast grassy ocean of the Asian steppes. The Mongols' expansion across the world was the dream of Temujin, who called himself Genghis Khan, which meant 'the emperor of mankind', and he taught the Mongols to believe that they and only they were born to rule the whole world.

Genghis first unleashed his war dogs against China to the east. With one ancient civilisation reduced, the Mongols next assaulted the prosperous Islamic states to their west and south, especially Khwarazm, where they shattered an irrigation system that had endured since antiquity. Then Genghis's son Ogodai assaulted the Viking-founded cities of Russia to the north. Mongols cared nothing for cities or civil-isation; resolute nomads, they wanted only plunder, and space to graze their horses.

Then the Mongols turned west, to Europe, and Christendom.

The great general Sabotai led the attack. He split his forces into three, making diversionary thrusts to north and south while Sabotai himself led the main body of his forces across the Hungarian plain. Thus Sabotai controlled forces separated by hundreds of miles and by mountain ranges; there had been nothing like this coordination and control since the legions. And the forces of the Hungarian King Bela broke before these savage horsemen, their leathery dress strange, their horses small, fast and muscular.

Sabotai set up his yurts on the plain of northern Europe, and, in the autumn of 1241, prepared to overwinter before his next push west.

He was only a few days' ride from Vienna, along the Danube. No Christian army had even slowed the Mongol advance, let alone halted it. Now it was a dagger held over the heart of Europe, a world empire preparing to overwhelm the petty, squabbling states of Christendom.

And yet Pope Innocent IV tried to deal with the Mongols. Even as the horses of Sabotai grazed east of Vienna, Philip of Marseilles was attached to a party of clerics and knights despatched to the court of Ogodai, son of Genghis Khan.

Many Christians had applauded as the Mongol attacks thrust into the soft belly of Islam. There were even hopeful rumours that some of the Mongols were Christians, adherents of a heretical sect called Nestorians who clung to an obscure argument about the separation of the divine and human nature of Christ. And there was a popular legend of a figure called Prester John, said to be descended from one of the magi who attended the birth of Christ, a Christian ruler of a vast kingdom in the east. So in the Pope's counsels there was hope that the Mongols could be turned into allies against Islam, the ultimate foe.

Thus Philip and his party came to the strange capital of the khans, deep in their Asian homeland. This was a 'city' of nomads, a town of tents, each laden with pointless heaps of booty. And yet in this place they found embassies from across the known world and beyond. The Mongols' destruction was terrible, but the unity they had imposed connected empires which had had little knowledge of each other since antiquity.

But Philip found that Ogodai, a clever, impulsive, hard-drinking man, was no Christian, no Prester John. In fact only a few Mongols were Nestorians; the rest adhered to a kind of primitive animism. And besides the Mongols waged war not for religion but for the conquest itself. To

Ogodai even the Pope was no more than the weak leader of a rabble of petty states that would, in due course, be conquered, reduced and assimilated, and that was that. The Pope's embassy failed.

But it was while they remained as guests of the Khan that one of the papal party, a nervous but intelligent young monk called Bohemond, discovered in his pack an 'amulet', as he called it. He had no idea how it had got there.

'Philip eventually examined the amulet for himself,' Thomas whispered. 'He described it to me. It was a sealed box, the size of a man's hand, slim and flat and smooth to the touch. It was pale, cream-coloured, but with coloured markings on its upper surface. It was made of neither wood nor ceramic nor metal – something none could identify. The Christians, huddled in their Mongol tent, exploring this thing, found they could not cut it with a knife, nor would fire burn it.'

But Bohemond himself discovered that if he pressed a certain marking on the upper lid, a green arrow, *the box would speak to him* – in good if stilted Latin, in a tiny insect's voice. The legates were startled, terrified, intrigued. After much praying, and the application of much of their precious stock of holy water, they gathered around the box to hear what the imp in it had to say.

The imp spoke clearly of the future: of the next day, and of the years to come.

Of the next day, it described in detail Ogodai's movements: the hour he would rise, the breakfast he would take, the councillors, ambassadors and generals he would meet, the letters he would dictate and have read to him, the wife he would lie with – and the cup of mare's milk laced with Chinese rice wine that he liked to drink in the middle of the day.

On that cup of mare's milk and wine, said the imp in its tiny voice, the future of the world depended. For it spoke then of what would happen if Ogodai lived – what would become of the world at the feet of the Mongols, in the future.

Mongol armies always advanced in the depths of winter, with their horses fat on the grasses of summer. So it would be, in just a few weeks, that they would fall at last on Vienna. The city would be plundered, torched and razed, and the Viennese scattered to starve on the plains. As the Mongols advanced further west, the Christian princes, hastily uniting, would raise another army, which would meet the Mongols in a pitched battle before Munich. The numbers were well matched. But the Christians would be lured by a false retreat into an ambush, a classic Mongol tactic. Munich would be smashed. The Mongols' advance would be barely interrupted.

Next the Mongol force would split once more into three detachments.

The first would strike at the Low Countries, plundering the rich young trading cities there before shattering them and slaughtering the population in the usual way. Holland's dykes would be broken up; the sea would complete the Mongols' victory.

A second detachment would spend the summer grazing their horses in the plains around the smoking ruins of Paris, while students from what had been the finest university north of the Pyrenees scratched in the rubble for food.

The final Mongol detachment would meanwhile cross the Alps and descend on Italy. The vibrant modern cities of Milan, Genoa, Venice – all put to the sword, all destined never to rise again. And then there was the Eternal City. When the Mongols were done, it would be said that Rome had been reduced to the villages on the seven hills from which the great old city had once coalesced. The Mongols considered the Pope a prince, and therefore no hand would be raised against him. Instead the successor to Saint Peter would be thrust into a sack and trampled to death by horses.

The next season, the squabbling Christian kings of Spain would provide no serious resistance to the Mongol force that marched south through the Pyrenees. And then there was England. The Mongols had learned how to build boats in their campaigns in the far east. By the autumn of that year, London would burn.

So the conquest would be completed. With its great cities shattered, its monasteries and churches broken, Europe would be reduced to a shrunken population living in utter poverty in villages too small to be worth the plunder, ruled brutally by the khans' governors and tax-collectors.

Eventually, the imp said, the Mongols would withdraw, their empire withering away. But the damage would be permanent, Europe cut off from its own antiquity. And, worse, Christ would be lost from the world. With their priests slaughtered, the mass of the population slowly reverted to paganism, finding comfort in the gods they rediscovered in the trees and fields and rivers around them.

Bohemond, Philip and their companions listened to this dreadful account with growing horror.

But it need not be so, the imp whispered. Already grievous damage had been done to the cities of Russia, and even to the great Islamic civilisations of the east, which would never recover their sparkling brilliance of the past. But in the west, Christendom might yet be saved.

A tiny lid opened in the flat top of the box. Inside, revealed to the astonished men, was a pinch of crystals. This, the imp whispered, was a salt of quicksilver. If these crystals were dropped into Ogodai's milk and wine the next day the ruin of Christendom would be averted.

And then the box fell silent, and would not speak again, no matter what markings they pressed. The crystals sat in their little tray, silent, beckoning.

The Christians debated what this all meant. The soldiers like Philip discussed the Mongols' campaigns. The priests and monks explored the theological nature of the imp in the box: was it sent by God, or the devil?

And while they debated, Bohemond slipped away.

'By the end of the next day,' Thomas said, 'the Great Khan was doubled up in pain. His vomit was copious, while bloody diarrhoea hosed from his leathery backside. His doctors could do nothing. By the following morning he was unable even to pass water, and howled in agony. And by the end of the day after that he was dead. It was a horrible death – but not as dreadful as that inflicted on Brother Bohemond, who was discovered skulking in the Khan's tent.'

Like many of the other embassies, the Christian party packed up and fled in haste from the decapitated court. The Mongols' own messengers spread the news of the Khan's death to the generals and governors across their scattered domains.

'And that is why,' Thomas said, 'early in the year 1242, rather than press his conquest west, Sabotai turned back from the walls of Vienna. For all their conquests the Mongols remain tribesmen, bound by oaths of loyalty to their Khan. So when Ogodai died, their leaders were forced by their own laws to return in person to their homeland, to elect a new ruler.'

'And will they not return to Europe?' Saladin asked.

'They haven't yet. They have the rest of the world to occupy them. And as for the amulet – after the envoys had fled from the Mongol city, Philip told me they finally shattered its casing with rocks. Inside they found not the shrivelled corpse of an imp, but bits of wire. Metal discs, like coins, but blank. Other strange little sculptures.'

'Charms, perhaps,' said Saladin.

'Philip thought they were like bits of an engine. But what its function could be, how it worked – even what drove it, for there was no spring, no lever – he had no idea.'

Joan said, 'But whatever it was, why was this amulet put into the luggage of this boy Bohemond?'

'I think that's clear enough. It was put there so Bohemond should kill Ogodai. If he had lived, Christendom was lost. If he died, Christendom was saved. As simple as that. So he had to die.'

'But who could know this? ... Ah,' Joan said. 'A prophet. Or—'

'Or a meddler with time,' Thomas said. 'A Weaver. A man, or an angel or a demon, with the power to speak to the past. A man stranded in this dismal future wrecked by the Khans, who managed to send back this imp-in-a-box – just as somebody, somewhere, some*when*, sent back – perhaps, perhaps! – the designs of your war machines to a young boy's addled head, and somebody else sent al-Hafredi back to the time of Charles Martel, and somebody else whispered in the ear of your ancestress Eadgyth, and, and . . .'

'But this was not the work of al-Hafredi's people.'

'I do not believe so. A different method was used to persuade the minds of men – an imp in a box rather than a human being thrown into history. And, though it is not clear, it seems that the makers of the amulet sought a different future from that described by al-Hafredi.'

Saladin struggled to absorb these dreadful ideas. He feared they were heretical, feared that even to speculate about such matters in the darkness of his own head might be to commit a sin.

But his mother briskly focused on the practicalities. 'I see your point,' she said to Thomas. 'He who sent Ogodai's imp may or may not have been our Weaver. But this does seem to prove that time *can* be spanned by an agent's will, be he human or divine.'

'Exactly.' Thomas's rheumy eyes were bright.

'Well, it's clear what we must do now. The veracity of the Codex is proved to be more than plausible.'

'You never wrote back to your cousin Subh?'

'I was never sure about that. After all Subh is a Muslim. Yet we need the Codex.'

'You're thinking of going to Seville yourself?' Thomas asked cautiously.

'Of course! I will dig up that mosque with my bare hands if needs must.'

'But the armies of the Castilians are moving in on the city. Soon it may be besieged.'

'All the more reason to move quickly, before some other chancer happens on the plans – or worse, Subh herself.' Her eyes were cold. 'I am sure now that this is our opportunity, our chance to revive our family's prospects. We must take it without hesitation.'

Saladin gladly put aside the strange mysteries of the ever-changing tapestry of time, and grasped the essence of this new mission. 'We are going to al-Andalus?' He bunched his fists. 'There are many Muslims there. I shall take the Cross!'

Joan stroked his cheek fondly. 'That's my boy.' She stood. 'We have much to do.' Briskly, still talking, planning, scheming, she led them out of the room.

Thomas hurried after her. 'Of course there is still the question of your enigma: Robert's scrap of cipher, which may or may not have something to do with that phrase in Subh's letter – *Incendium Dei*. As it happens I have heard of a young man who may be able to assist us, another Franciscan, a bright young philosopher at Oxford who is becoming notorious for his radical philosophies. His name is Roger Bacon . . .'

XVI

AD 1247

There was trouble at the pontoon bridge. A suspicious mob, a sus-pected spy, a near-riot – and the potential for real disaster for Seville, if its only bridge across the Guadalquivir were damaged.

This news was brought to Ibrahim's office by a sweating, panicky soldier. Ibrahim summoned Abdul, a captain of the palace guard, and told him to assemble a unit of his troops. Then he ran out of his office, without waiting to see if Abdul and his soldiers followed.

From the emir's palace, the fastest way to get to the bridge was to cut down to the river and follow the bank, and that was the way Ibrahim headed. Even so it was tough going, for every open space, every street was cluttered with refugees and their belongings. Ibrahim was forced to wade through this throng as through a sea. By the river it was almost as bad, but troops stationed here kept a path cleared along the bank, and once he was in sight of the water Ibrahim was able to make faster progress.

It was a bright spring day, he noted absently. The river water glistened prettily, and the orange trees were in bloom. But this year, the hungry would not leave the fruit on the branches long enough to ripen.

It wasn't hard to find the source of the trouble. The mob had caught their man at the abutment of the pontoon bridge. Ragged, already bleeding, his head hidden by a hood, the quarry had backed a few paces onto the bridge.

'Let me scatter them, sir.' Abdul, a veteran of the sieges of Cordoba and Valencia, was a tough, competent man of about thirty-five, who wore a black patch to hide the empty socket from which a Christian arrow had taken his right eye. 'A charge will do it.'

Ibrahim trusted Abdul with his life. But Abdul thought in a soldier's blunt, direct terms. Ibrahim's job was to see the wider picture. 'We can't risk the bridge,' he said. Seville had only two arteries to the wider Muslim world: the river, which was gradually being blockaded by King Fernando's fleet, and this pontoon bridge, which linked the city to the suburb of Triana and the Muslim communities beyond. 'You charge them and they'll be on that bridge for sure. All it will take is one of those idiots with a torch to start chucking fire around, and we're all sunk.'

Abdul pursed his lips. 'Let me guess. You want to go and *talk* to them.'

Ibrahim grinned at the tough soldier. But he wondered, not for the first time, how it was that he, who had always thought his destiny was to be a warrior, had finished up being a cut-price diplomat. 'Our job is to keep order, above all, captain. Let's see if we can do that without breaking any more heads.'

'And when it goes wrong, my boys will sort it all out and save your arse for you. Again. Sir.' But Abdul smiled.

'Fair enough. Wait here.'

Moving rapidly to mask his own fear, Ibrahim walked the last few paces to the bridge, and stood boldly between the mob and its prey. He glanced at the victim, who was a slim man, breathing hard, his face so bloodied it was unrecognisable.

Then Ibrahim turned to face the mob. The crowd was perhaps fifty strong, mostly men, a few women. They were all as ragged and dirty as the man they hunted. Ibrahim knew these people. Without homes, without hope, they were profoundly afraid. But fear was easier to bear if you could find somebody to hate.

He spread his hands to show he was unarmed. Abdul was watching closely, his hand on his scimitar.

Ibrahim called, 'Why are you here? Why do you keep me away from my prayers?'

There was an inchoate growl. One man waved a ragged bit of parchment in the air.

'You.' Ibrahim picked on the man and strode forward. 'Come here!'

The man instinctively stepped forward, and the crowd pressed back. Suddenly the man looked less certain, for he was once again a man, himself, and not a component of the mob.

'Tell me your name,' snapped Ibrahim. 'In me, you face the authority of the vizier. Tell me!'

'I am Gabirol,' he said reluctantly. He was probably no older than Ibrahim.

Ibrahim nodded. He turned to Abdul, who made a show of writing down the man's name. 'All right, Gabirol. My goal here is to secure the peace. That's all I care about. We can't have crowds running around with torches and knives, and we can't have citizens torn apart on our streets—'

'He's no citizen,' Gabirol snapped, and his anger surged. He waved his bit of parchment at the man on the bridge. 'He's a spy! A spy for Fernando, for the Christians.'

A city under threat was rife with rumours, riddled with imagined traitors and spies – and perhaps a few real ones. 'And how do you know that?'

'Because of this! This is what he was carrying when he was found.' He held up the parchment again.

Ibrahim took it gingerly. Streaked with blood, it was covered with sketches of what looked like fish. Perhaps they were anatomical drawings. But when he looked more closely he saw that there were bits of machinery inside each 'fish', gears and levers and pulleys, and sketches of tiny men who pulled on oars or worked at capstans.

He growled, 'Oh, Mother, what have you done?'

Abdul looked at him. 'What was that, sir?'

'Never mind. So, Gabirol, you think he's a spy because of these sketches.'

'Isn't it obvious? Everybody knows Fernando wants to block up the river. Maybe this is the way he's going to do it, with these fancy ships—'

'It's the shape that gives it away.' A woman stepped forward now, her face twisted into a fearful rage.

'What shape?'

'The fish! Everybody knows that's a Christian sign. I've seen it daubed all over the walls of the mosque in Cordoba, a desecration. I've seen it for myself! Doesn't that prove he's a Christian?'

'Oh, for the love of Allah.'

But the mob began to growl again. Ludicrous the root cause might be, but the situation was dangerous.

Ibrahim nodded to Abdul. 'Captain. Take this man.'

Abdul muttered orders. Two of the troops went onto the bridge to seize the 'spy', who did not resist when they took his arms. The rest lined up briskly alongside Ibrahim, forming a barrier between the mob and their prey. They kept their swords in their scabbards, however.

Ibrahim raised his arms again. 'You can see we have taken this man. If he is a spy, we will soon discover the truth and will do something about it. So you don't need to pursue him any further. Go to your homes – go to your prayers. But you with the torches,' he said with a note of command, 'douse them in the river first. The city is too crowded to risk a fire.'

He turned away without waiting to see if they complied. But he murmured to Abdul, 'Make sure they obey.' He turned to the captive. 'And you,' he said, 'are in my charge.' He handed him back his bit of parchment with the fish-ship designs.

The man took it. 'Thank you.'

Although his voice was gruff, Ibrahim thought he recognised his accent. He stepped forward and, carefully, not wishing to exacerbate any injuries, he lifted back the man's hood. His hair was bright blond.

'Peter.'

'Hello, Ibrahim.' The English scholar grinned, then winced as he cracked his bruised lips.

XVII

The palace was as crowded as the rest of the city; anybody who could find shelter with the emir did so. But Ibrahim found an empty room where he arranged for Peter's wounds to be treated by a doctor, and ordered a girl to take him to the baths, and he called for a new set of clothes to replace those ruined by the mob.

By the time Ibrahim came to find him, late that afternoon, Peter was transformed. Sitting on a heap of floor cushions, he gazed out of the arched doorway into the light. His hair had been cut, his stubble shaved, and his skin cleansed of blood. He showed no trace of the beating he had received, save for the sheen of salve applied to his bruises and broken lips, and a little neat stitching in the wound on his forehead. But he had aged since Ibrahim had last seen him; now in his late twenties, he was a little thicker around the neck, his skin of his face less fresh, a little peppering of grey in that golden hair.

The battered bit of parchment, with its images of ships, rested on a low table.

Ibrahim sat down, and Peter offered him orange tea. 'I should thank you,' he began. 'I owe you my life.'

'I'd have done it for anybody. It's my job.'

'Which you do very well, everybody says so—'

'If you'd gone home to England you wouldn't have been in peril in the first place.'

'Why would I want to do that? It's much more interesting here. You know, I believe it's been four years since we last met. It took you a year to fall out with your mother, as I recall,' he said drily.

'And you're still working on this nonsense, after all this time.' Ibrahim reached forward and took the parchment. 'The Engines of God.'

'Four years isn't long,' Peter said. 'Not for a project like this. You have no idea how much ground must be laid before you can take a single step.'

'Why a fish?'

'Pardon?'

'Why build a boat shaped like a fish?'

'Because that's what the sketches say. We are still working from the Sihtric designs.' He meant the sketches he had been able to recover from the records of Sihtric's clerk. It had been a long time since Ibrahim had heard the archaic name of that long-dead priest. Peter went on, 'Oh, I can make deeper guesses about *why*. A fish is comfortable in the water, isn't it? Its smooth shape simply glides through that mysterious substance. Well, then, it stands to reason that if you make a boat with the same profile, it will be similarly advantaged. That's just my guess, though. I don't *know*.

'Progress is slow, Ibrahim. Well, you saw that, before you flounced out of the project. The sketches are partial, incomplete. Many of them are scribbles that would mean far more to the clerk who made them than to us, for whom they were never intended. We have to guess at so much – sizes, weights, materials, gearing. Very often we ask the impossible of our artisans: steel cogs of unimaginable fineness and accuracy, wooden wheels of a seamless perfection. Sometimes we simply don't have the correct materials at all. And, what's still more difficult, we have to make guesses as to the machines' purposes in the first place.'

Ibrahim looked at the designs again. 'It looks as if these stick men are totally enclosed in their fish-boat.'

'So they are. Can you see, they operate their oars and paddles through seals in the skin of the ship, which appears to be a fine metal shell. We are using beaten copper. Some of us speculate that the ship might be sealed so that it can travel not just on the surface of the water, *but beneath it.*'

'How is that possible?'

'Do you really want the details? Look, there are bladders here which, if filled with water, might cause the craft to sink, and if pumped out could make it float. It would certainly make sense of the fish shape, wouldn't it? And think of the advantage, Ibrahim. A boat that could float *under* your enemy's fleet, all unseen, and attack from below.'

Ibrahim tossed aside the bit of parchment. 'This is such a waste of time. It always was.'

'The emir may not think so when we demonstrate our weapons to him.'

'And when will that be?'

Peter shifted, uncomfortable. 'We have a number of designs, partially realised ... We aren't ready yet.'

'Allah preserve us, but the Christian armies are close. Surely even a bookworm like you is aware of that.'

'Of course I am. We're all working as hard as we can, and as fast.'

'What of your conscience, Peter? Are you happy as a Christian to be arming Muslims?'

'I think of myself as a scholar before I'm a Christian. And this is a scholarly project, whatever else it is. I'm *curious*, Ibrahim. Anyway, perhaps our weapons, if they deter Fernando, will prevent war, rather than provoke it. Have you thought of that? In a way we're alike, aren't we, Ibrahim? Both striving to save people from harm, in our different ways.'

Ibrahim thought this was all artifice, and he said nothing. The thoughtful young man he had met five years ago was being eroded away by ambition and a certain flavour of greed – not greed for wealth, but for accomplishment and recognition. He had seen it in scholars before, in his time at the court. Such men would do anything to stand out from their peers.

Peter was watching him. 'You know, we do miss you, Ibrahim. When I first met you I took you for a bone-headed dolt. A slab of righteous muscle.'

'I wasn't twenty years old!'

'Now you're five years older, and your true qualities are emerging. You're no soldier, for all you wear that scimitar at your waist. You're far more than that. You have a set of skills your mother could put to good use – organisation, leadership. You should make your peace with Subh. She misses you.'

'My relationship with my mother is not a matter for you, but for my conscience. And I believe I put my skills to good use here. There is an emergency in the city. Again, even you must be aware of that ...'

Seville's crisis had now lasted nearly a decade, since Cordoba's fall. The city was flooded with refugees from the lost cities to the north. There was a perennial shortage of food, because of the abandonment of the city's hinterland and the disruption to river trade. Every so often the poor sanitation would cause an outbreak of cholera or typhoid or some other hideous disease. Rumours that Fernando's armies had been glimpsed in the heat-haze of the horizon periodically swept the fearful city, causing panic and rioting.

When he had turned up at the vizier's office in the emir's palace, offering to help in any way he could, Ibrahim had found plenty to do. He found he was capable, unexpectedly good at finding solutions to

157

novel problems, and implementing them. Perhaps he had inherited something of his formidable mother's qualities. He rose rapidly in authority, and in the scale of the problems he was given to solve.

Something about the work satisfied a deep spiritual need inside him. He still adhered to the teachings of the Almohads, named for *Al-muwahhidum*, the Oneness of God. In his patient work he felt he was healing damaged lives; it was a work that served God's unity better than any amount of killing, he thought.

'But,' Peter said, 'how long can this continue, Ibrahim? This is a city under stress. King Fernando doesn't even need to attack; the steady pressure he is applying is slowly winning the battle for him. All you are doing here is managing the city's decline.'

'Not necessarily.'

'Of course necessarily; that's the truth. But if your mother's weapons designs were to pay off – if even one of them came to fruition – then the whole situation could be transformed.'

Ibrahim snorted. 'If a miracle happens? If Saladin came back to life and led us to victory?'

'We don't need a miracle. Your mother's engines are taking shape, Ibrahim, manifested in steel and leather and wood, only a short walk from this very room. Don't you think it's your duty to come and see what we have – your duty as an officer of the emirate, and a son?'

Ibrahim stared at him. In the far distance he heard angry shouts, the crash of smashing glass, harsh military orders: the sounds of a disintegrating civilisation. He felt his determination wavering.

XVIII

Thomas Busshe sought out Saladin in northern England, where he had gone to ground three years after he had arrived in Britain. Saladin soon learned that Thomas was coming to tell him that his mother needed him, and he must come back to London.

The monk stayed a single night in the manse itself. It was the home of Saladin's employer, a petty knight called Percival. The next morning, very early, Saladin found Thomas walking in the village. Thomas was showing his age, Saladin thought. His eyes were shadowed, and he looked stiff after his hours on the mead bench with Percival. But here he was, up and about. 'It's the relentless rhythm of a monk's life,' he said. 'You can't get it out of your blood.'

They walked around the village. It was a mean place, a street of long sod-built huts surrounded by a sprawl of plough land. The manse was a small robust house of decently cut stone, which Saladin told Thomas was made of stones robbed from Hadrian's Wall. Thomas seemed to think that was an enchanting idea, the labours of long-dead centurions transformed into the houses of the living.

They came across a group of men setting off for the day's work. They nodded to Saladin, not warmly, but civilly enough. They were skinny men with sallow faces. Hunched against the slight chill of the dewy air, some limping slightly, they were wood-cutters, and they bore adzes and axes and saws. They wore grimy, colourless clothes, breeches, hoses, shirts, kirtles – Saladin knew that these were the only clothes that most of them owned. As they plodded along they sang a song so filthy that Saladin hoped their strong Northumbrian accents, heavily laced with Danish words, would make it incomprehensible to Thomas.

'Many of them are blond,' Thomas said, surprised.

'That's the Viking blood in them. A lot of it about in this area.'

'Do you get on with them?'

Saladin grinned. 'They call me the Saracen, or the Moor, or Muhammad. Ironic, that. But they've never seen anybody like me before.' He grunted. 'In fact most of them have never seen anybody from beyond that hill over there.'

'And all our cathedrals and all our palaces and all our wars rest on the foundation of the toil of the country people, like these.'

'Makes you think,' Saladin said.

'It does indeed. And you found work here.'

'I accompany Percival's bailiff when there's trouble with the tithes,' Saladin said. 'I'm a hired muscle. Every so often we ride to a borough, to Newcastle or Morpeth, so the lord can pay his own tithes, and for the market. I go along to put off the robbers. I enjoy the market. I can buy stuff that reminds me of home, a little. Raisins, cinnamon, figs.'

'The fruit of sunnier lands. And are you happy, Saladin?'

Saladin shrugged. 'Ask those wood-cutters if they're happy. You've got what you've got and you have to put up with it. That or starve. It wasn't easy for me when we first came here to England – how long ago?'

'Three years already.'

'I needed the work. My mother and I had no money left. But I had no close family, nowhere to go.'

'And a face that didn't fit.'

'Yes. I'm grateful to you for finding me that first bit of employment with Umfraville.' A lord with extensive holdings here in the north country, who had made himself rich from a king's commission to protect the main droving routes to the north from the marauding Scots. The Umfravilles' castle at Harbottle on the Coquet was grand. But Saladin didn't have the stomach for the subdued, spiteful, slow-burning sort of war that consumed this border country – subdued but unending, for the nobles who waged it on both sides of the border grew rich from it. He had been glad to move to the pettier house of Percival.

Happy? Happiness was irrelevant in this life, he thought. Content? Yes, perhaps that was the word. Percival was a man of no brain, it seemed to Saladin, and too drunken to formulate any serious ambition. He was happy just to take his villagers' tithe and piss it away into the soak-holes behind his hall. But Saladin had no desire to risk his life supporting the petty ambitions of a more restless lord.

'This will suit me for now,' Saladin said. 'Until something better shows up.' He eyed Thomas. 'But my mother isn't so content, is she?'

'I'm afraid not.'

'I send her my money, you know. Just about all of it, keeping only a little for myself to buy a bit of pepper in Newcastle. I have few needs here; I eat with the lord, sleep in his house, ride his horses. What use is money?'

'She'd be lost without your contribution.'

'You wouldn't let her starve,' Saladin said.

'Well, true. We remember our benefactors. But she's a proud woman, Saladin. She doesn't want charity from a "gaggle of monks", as she calls us.' Thomas sighed. 'But she has ambition enough for a hundred English lords.'

'Jerusalem remains in Saracen hands.'

'So it does. But things have changed, Saladin. You and your mother arrived here without wealth, but with one treasure.'

Saladin said reluctantly, 'Robert's cipher.'

'Yes. Perhaps you remember I found a scholar to study it – another Franciscan, a man called Roger Bacon. Remarkable chap. It's taken him some time—'

'Let me guess. He's worked it out.'

'So he claims. We'll have to judge his results.'

'We?'

'Your mother wants you with her, Saladin. In London, when the truth of the *Incendium Dei* code is revealed.'

Saladin said, 'I always hated that old nonsense about prophecies and codes, Thomas. Maybe it made our family rich in the past. But it never helped us in the Outremer, or since we have come to England. And I never thought it was *real*.' He waved a hand. 'Not compared to this. Land, toil, iron, blood, war – that's the real stuff of life. But my mother wants me with her in case this cracked code reveals secrets that will revive our fortune, and fulfil her life.'

'Yes. And I want you with her,' Thomas said severely, 'in the much more likely case that it does *not*.'

Mulling over Thomas's words, Saladin led him back to the manse.

XIX

Ibrahim and Peter slipped out of Seville.

They came to a hole in the ground just beyond the city walls. It looked like the outlet of a broken sewer or drain. Peter said, 'This is older than the Moorish city – Roman, we think, part of their sewage system. Of course the settlement here was a lot smaller then. The main Roman town, Italica, was some distance away. It's a bit mucky down here—'

'Just get on with it.'

The hole in the ground turned out to be a shaft, deeper than Ibrahim was tall, down which he had to drop. He found himself in a stone-clad tunnel, too low for him to stand up straight. He could see no further than a few paces. There was a smell of damp and rot, but nothing foetid; the sewer was long disused.

Peter used a flint to light a candle. His eyes were pits of shadow. 'Are you all right? Not everybody is fond of the dark.'

Ibrahim took a deep breath. 'I have no love of being buried alive. But it's my mother I'm more frightened of.'

Peter laughed, and clapped him on the back. 'Come. Let's face our nightmares.'

It turned out to be only a short walk, though a clumsy and difficult one, through the low tunnel. Ibrahim stumbled over a broken Roman tile. Then the tunnel opened out, and Ibrahim found himself walking into a big boxy room. Steps cut into the earth led down to a floor some distance beneath him. The walls were stone-clad, the ceiling timbered, and lamps glimmered in alcoves.

And in this chamber, deep underground, machines brooded, dimly glimpsed. There was a great tube mounted on a carriage. An upright wheel turned, a treadmill, with a man inside it to work it. What looked like the skeletal form of a great bird's wing gleamed and creaked. Scholars and artisans moved among these creations, murmuring quietly.

Ibrahim felt deeply uneasy, as if he had descended into a sorcerer's pit.

Peter led him briskly forward. 'This was some kind of water tank,' he said in a murmur to match the subdued voices around them. 'Always built big, those Romans, even when it came to their plumbing!'

'I never knew this place was here.'

'Not many do. It's on no plans; I dare say your emirate doesn't know it exists. When we needed a place to work in secret your mother, ever resourceful, started asking around among the criminal element.'

'Criminal?'

'Smugglers. Hoarders. Even bandits. *They* knew of this hole in the ground. It wasn't hard to take it over, clean it up, extend it a little . . .'

'Ah, the vizier's advisor. How good of you to make time in your busy schedule to visit your mother.'

Ibrahim had not seen his mother for four years. Subh wore a robe, white and pristine despite the dirt, and her hair was piled elaborately on her head, jet black. Unlike Peter she showed not a trace of the passage of time; she was as upright, powerful and magnificent as ever. Peter seemed to cower before her; he was as much in her thrall as ever.

Ibrahim bent forward to embrace his Mother.

But she subtly moved back and offered her hand, cold, the palm oily. 'Let's keep things formal,' she said. She showed not a trace of emotion.

'Mother, you haven't changed.'

'And what of you?' she asked. 'You're clean enough. A smart costume. And well fed, it seems to me.'

'I take only my ration,' he said stiffly, and it was true, though there were many in the palace who did not.

She prodded his belly. 'In that case you're not getting enough exercise.'

'What are you doing here, Mother?'

'You know very well. Building the war engines that might save Seville. Walk with me. See what we have made . . .'

She showed him her marvels. Here was a metal tube that used compressed steam to spit iron balls. Peter called it the 'thunder-mouth', for the great roar it would make when it was fired. Around the perimeter of the treadmill he had noticed was a series of crossbows. An archer sat at the axle, and as the wheel turned one bow after another was brought before him.

'The archer only has to aim and fire,' Peter explained. 'See, the ingenuity is that the mechanisms of the wheel-engine load each bow for him as it turns. So this enables a much faster rate of fire than a conventional bow, without a loss of accuracy.'

There were many such gadgets, most only half-finished, betraying ingenuity but fragility.

Ibrahim refused to be impressed. 'This is all you've achieved, in five years?'

Subh watched him gravely. 'Don't you think anything of our efforts?'

He walked around the workshop. 'Your rapid-firing crossbow machine is vulnerable. A stick poked into the mechanism would jam it.'

Peter said, 'But a row of these machines, fixed to the city walls when the Christians come—'

'They would still break down. Men would do better.' He came to the thunder-mouth. 'This is more promising. More compact than a catapult, perhaps. Faster to reload and reuse. But it does *no more* than a catapult would.' He glanced around. 'I see nothing here which would give one side an overwhelming advantage over the other.'

Peter sighed. 'Well, you're right about that.'

'What we need,' Subh said, 'is *Incendium Dei.*'

'Your mysterious Fire of God.'

'Precisely. The fire that would turn these delicate gadgets into thunderbolts.'

'But you don't have it,' Ibrahim said.

'Joan of the Outremer never replied to my letter. And I regret writing to her now, for I told her something of what *we* have, without learning anything of her. I fear she might become a rival, not an ally.'

'Actually,' Peter said, 'it's not just God's Fire we need, Ibrahim. For these engines to be realised fully we need the original designs.'

'Ah,' Ibrahim said. 'The Codex. The treasure said to be buried under the floor of the great mosque of Seville. Is that why you asked me here? To get me to dig up the mosque?'

'No,' Peter said. 'I invited you here, frankly, because I thought you should be reconciled with your mother.'

'But now that you are here,' Subh said slyly, 'why not? You have the ear of the vizier. If you dropped a word—'

Ibrahim shook his head. 'You have buried yourself in this hole in the ground for too long. Think what the mood is like outside! In this crowded city the faithful wash around the muezzin tower like a sea. If I were to order the mosque floor to be dug up, in the hope of finding plans for super-weapons, I would cause a riot. And besides the imams would never give permission.'

'So you turn your back on us again,' Subh said, her tone poisonous.

'I regret what has happened,' he said. 'Nothing should come between mother and son.'

Subh said, 'But you still think I'm wasting my time down here, don't you? You're just as headstrong and unimaginative as you were as a boy.'

'Yes. I still believe you're wasting your time. And so, it seems, am I.' He turned to leave.

'If you won't help us,' his mother called after him, 'at least don't betray us. Don't let the emir put a stop to our work. Trust me that much.'

He paused. Then, without looking back, he made for the tunnel that led to the air, and the light.

XX

Saladin found London overwhelming, after three years away. When he arrived with Thomas early one morning, the city was blanketed by fog, thick, dense, yellow, stinking. People went around with candles in their hands and bits of moistened cloth held to their faces. Even by the river it was no better, and the ships crept cautiously along, lamps strapped to their prows.

Thomas Busshe led him to the abbey at Westminster, and they waited in a small room where a nervous young novice served them warmed wine. This was a room used by Roger Bacon, this brilliant monk of Thomas's, and Saladin leafed idly through a heap of the scholar's well-read books: a grammar by Donatus, the *Consolation of Philosophy* by somebody called Boethius, Aristotle's logics and metaphysics, with commentaries by later authors – even by an Arab. So many books, Saladin thought. Did the world need them all?

The novice returned and said they had to wait for Bacon.

'For, I'm told,' said Joan, sweeping into the room, 'today's the day for his annual bath, and he's not about to miss that for a couple of ragged refugees from the Outremer.' She was dressed smartly, in a long crimson robe and a white wimple.

Saladin got to his feet and kissed his mother. 'You don't look ragged to me, Mother,' he said.

'Appearance is everything.' She nodded stiffly. 'I thank you for the stipend you send me. I spend it well, I hope.'

'Spend it as you like.'

Her movements as she chose a chair and took her wine were firm and decisive. Her face was still young, he thought, still beautiful; she was only thirty-five years old. She was flushed, though, but not with health.

Flushed with an impatience that had been building all the long years of her exile in England, as she saw it. She eyed her son. 'No wife yet? No grandchildren for me?'

'Not since I last saw you at Christmas,' he said drily. 'And no husband for you, Mother?'

'A husband would only get in the way.'

'He might provide you with an income,' Thomas pointed out.

Joan snorted. 'An income pledged to *his* ambitions, not mine. I've no use for that.'

Thomas looked at them both. 'You are mother and son, but so different. Saladin is finding contentment. He lives simply; he uses the skills God has given him; slowly, patiently, he is building himself a place in this country. He asks nothing, and he resents nothing. But you, madam, are full of anger, aren't you? Rage, even.'

'Rage?' Her cheeks coloured, her eyes glittered, and her lips were thin. 'If you say so. You men of the cloth are so terribly wise.'

'But, Mother,' Saladin said, 'what are you angry about?'

'What do you think?' she flared. 'This is not my country. I despise the weakness of these Christians of the west, who cannot, it seems, summon the will to take back the lands which were lost – our home, Saladin. I have no wealth, no position. I am not respected here. Though my ancestors fought and died to win the Holy Land for Christendom, the people in this country even mock the way I speak. Can they not see who I am – *what* I am?'

Saladin was saddened. 'And is this why you want to build your engines? To change the way people look at you?'

She stared him down.

But if this was true, Saladin saw with dismay, then his mother had no choice but to pursue her dream of engines of war; the logic of her personality dictated it. And, Saladin sensed with dread, he was destined to follow her.

The door crashed open. They all flinched.

A monk burst in, tall, skinny, agitated, and with his tonsured hair comically sticking up around his bald pate. He looked younger than thirty. 'Thomas!' he shouted without preamble. 'Good to see you again. And this must be Joan of Jerusalem, and her son, fascinating, fascinating, you who brought the conundrum of time to my door, you who believe past and future are all muddled up.'

Thomas said, 'Roger—'

The man dumped a leather folder on a low table, and kept talking. 'And why should time *not* be mixed up? All is in flux, the world is an unstable place. Heraclitus pointed out that he was never able to dunk his foot in the same river twice, for it changes with every instant – you see? So why, then, should we imagine that even the river of time is inviolable and unchanging? Perhaps it is more like the fabled Meander in Phrygia, which changes its course with every season, endlessly seeking the perfection of its Platonic ideal. So, then, perhaps history is made and remade, cutting through our lives as a wandering river cuts through sandbanks, for ever seeking some new and more perfect shape. Why not, I say, why not? Shall we get to work?'

Joan turned to Thomas. 'Who *is* this person?'

'One of the liveliest minds of this new age of scholarship, that's who,' said Thomas.

'*One* of . . .'

'Which is why I took your puzzle to him. Joan, Saladin, this is Roger Bacon, born in Ilchester, trained in Oxford, and now lecturing in Westminster.'

'Don't forget Paris,' Bacon put in.

'I have been aware of his career since his student days – oh, a decade back now. You studied the classics at Oxford, did you not, Roger?'

'And geometry, arithmetic, music, astronomy. I worked under Robert Grosseteste.'

'The bishop of Lincoln—'

'Who has led the reintroduction of the works of the Greeks into England.'

'Roger lectured in Paris—'

'I earned my master of arts degree there. I saw Alexander of Hales there, and twice saw William of Auvergne dispute . . .'

This fast-paced duologue was hugely confusing to Saladin, who had heard of none of these scholars.

'I see myself now as a *dominus experimentorum*,' Bacon said.

Joan glanced at Thomas. 'What does that mean?'

'One who studies the physical world,' Thomas said, 'and tinkers with it, in the hope of learning more about the truths of God.'

'I have always "tinkered",' Bacon said. 'I once set up a candle and a mirror in a darkened room, and peered into the eye of a cat. Have you ever tried such a thing, brother Saladin?'

'I can't say I have.'

'You see a carpet of dusky red vessels overlaid by a golden tracery. Quite beautiful, quite mysterious. My study in optics began with those first observations. And if you could look into the head of a man, what would you find? But I have never been able to persuade anybody to sit still long enough to let me see. Ah, well.'

'I thought all truth was to be found in the Bible.'

'Of course, and in the authorities of antiquity. I myself am one of Europe's leading scholars on Aristotle,' Bacon said without a shred of modesty. 'But there are many routes to the same destination, which is God's truth. The role of the natural philosopher is to understand how phenomena reveal that truth. Saint Augustine himself instructed us not to embarrass ourselves by quoting the word of God to contradict some fact of nature, because that would only reveal that we understood neither the word nor the nature. Experimentation: *that* is the way to that deeper truth, that final reconciliation. Or so I am coming to believe. Perhaps you have heard of the work of Master Peter de Maricourt, a Picard who once took the Cross, and subsequently—'

'Yes, yes, Roger,' Thomas cut in. 'But perhaps we should get to the point?'

Bacon smiled, utterly in control. 'Quite right, Father, quite right. You!' He jabbed a finger at the novice, who jumped. 'More wine for our guests. And bring a lamp over here.' He sat before the low table, opened his leather wallet and extracted papers that he proceeded to spread out. 'We have a deep mystery to unravel.'

Saladin murmured to Thomas, 'He's quite a showman, isn't he?'

'And he knows it. But it's not necessarily good for him. Ah, Roger, Roger, how your busy head distracts your pious heart!'

But they sat before Roger Bacon, wide-eyed, as he began to reveal the truth of the *Incendium Dei* cipher.

XXI

'We begin with your fragment of coded text, as Thomas presented it to me,' Bacon said. He spread out a parchment on the table:

BMQVK XESEF EBZKM BMHSM BGNSD DYEED OSMEM HPTVZ
HESZS ZHVH

'I was intrigued by the puzzle ...'

'I knew he would be,' Thomas whispered to Joan. 'Very useful thing about scholars, that curiosity. He didn't even ask for a fee.'

Bacon glanced at Saladin. 'You. Tell me what you see.'

'I'm no scholar—'

'Just answer.'

'I see ten words,' Saladin said. 'Latin letters, not Arabic. I recognise none of the words, though.'

'And nor should you, for they aren't words at all. Even these groupings are a decoy, I quickly realised. This is no sentence. Look at them! What sentence has words of such regular lengths?'

'It is written in a cipher,' said Joan. 'That much is obvious.'

'Yes! But what cipher? What do we known about ciphers? You, Thomas?'

'Just get on with it, Roger.'

'Oh, very well. The first cipher was used by the Spartans, long before the birth of Christ. They had a device called a *scytale*. You would wrap a strip of leather around a baton, and write out your message; once unwrapped the letters are scrambled, you see, illegible to anyone who doesn't have a baton of the same dimensions. Tacitus wrote of codes and ciphers, as did the Greek Polybius. Julius Caesar used a substitution cipher, which depended on a simple cyclic displacement of the alphabet. Caesar used a displacement of three positions, while Augustus later used one.'

'I'll be the one to ask,' Joan said heavily. 'What is a "simple cyclic displacement"?'

Bacon reached for a bit of chalk and scribbled on the tabletop. 'You write out your alphabet. A, B, C, D. And you write it out again with the letters shifted through three spaces, say. D, E, F, G. You have the word you wish to encode, say "CAESAR". And you exchange the true letters for the shifted ones. So C becomes F, A is D, E is H ...'

'I understand,' said Joan.

'Now, history tells us there have been ciphers a good deal more sophisticated than that. Polybius himself described a bilateral substitution system, which means ... never mind! Happily for your weary brains, I soon concluded we aren't dealing with anything much more complex than Caesar's substitutions.'

'Why do you believe that?' Saladin asked.

'This is a message in the Latin alphabet, not Arabic or Persian or Greek. So it is surely a Latin message. The Moors of Spain are developing extremely advanced cryptographic systems, I'm told. But a thousand years after the Caesars, we Latin scholars still lag behind the rest in our ciphers as in everything else. One point on which I kept an open mind was which alphabet we are using here.'

'The Latin one,' said Saladin.

'Ah, but *which* Latin? Caesar used twenty-three letters. We use twenty-five, for we have added U and J. I thought it most likely the classic alphabet was the one employed.

'So I began my analysis. A common technique in breaking ciphers is to study the distribution of letters. The most common symbol is likely to correspond to a common letter in plain language – *E* perhaps, or *S*, or *T*. But this fragment is too short to enable such a count. I experimented with *scytales* of various dimensions, to no avail. And I tried all the possible cyclic permutations, with no luck either. With all the permutations exhausted, I racked my brains for a new way forward.'

Joan murmured, 'And in the end, after much heroic struggle, you found a way, did you?'

Bacon blithely ignored her sarcasm. 'A simple variant on cyclic substitution is to use a key.'

'A key?' Saladin asked.

'Caesar, for instance, could have used his own name.' He wrote it out: CAESAR. 'We must eliminate repetitions.' He crossed out the second A. 'Now we use this five-letter key as the foundation of our cipher.' He wrote out a twenty-three Latin letter alphabet with a code beneath it:

Plain	A B C D E	F G H I K	L M N O P	Q R S T V	X Y Z
Code	C A E S R	B D F G H	I K L M N	O P Q T V	X Y Z

'You see? A substitution with the shift depending on the key word, and with those letters removed. So the word CAESAR now encodes as —' He wrote it out:

ECRQCP

'It's a poor sort of code,' Saladin observed. 'The last few letters are transcribed without change.'

'You're a practical man, I can see that,' Bacon said. 'That's true. But there are easy variants. The simplest is to put the key word at the end of the alphabet, not the beginning, and to proceed backwards.' He scribbled quickly,

Plain	A B C D E	F G H I K	L M N O P	Q R S T V	X Y Z
Code	Z Y X V T	Q P O N M	L K I H G	F D B R S	E A C

'Now all the letters save one have a different symbol.'

'This is all very well,' Joan said, 'but *we* don't have a key, do we?'

'Oh, but we do,' Bacon said. 'You gave it to me – or rather, to Thomas.'

'I did? What key?'

'It was in the letter you received. From your cousin in Spain. The phrase she was particularly interested in, that appeared to be left incomplete on the scrap of parchment you held.'

'*Incendium Dei*,' Saladin said, wide-eyed.

Joan stared at Bacon. 'Can it really be as simple as that?'

Bacon grinned. He now had a full hold on their attention, Saladin thought, and he knew it. 'Shall we try it?' He wiped the table clean of chalk with his sleeve, and began to scribble again. The three of them bent over to see. 'We begin with the key,' Bacon said. He wrote,

INCENDIVM DEI

'The U replaced by V as you see. Next we eliminate duplicates.'

INCEDVM

'There is our key. So we construct our code. I tried out a forward substitution, but succeeded with a backward ...' He scribbled rapidly.

Plain	A B C D E	F G H I K	L M N O P	Q R S T V	X Y Z
Code	Z Y X T S	R Q P O L	K H G F B	A M V D E	C N I

'Now we reconstruct our message. That first B becomes a P, the M becomes R ...'

BMQVK XESEF EBZKM BMHSM BGNSD DYEED OSMEM HPTVZ
HESZS ZHVH
PRGSL CVEVO VPALR PRMER PNYET TBVVT IERVR MHDSA
MVEAE AMSM

Saladin stared at the new string, unreasonably disappointed. 'It's still nonsense.'

Bacon smiled, a magician with another trick to show. 'A simple transposition would be too easy. Our puzzle involves numbers as well as letters. Look at the "sentence" again. Nine "words" of five letters, and one of four. What sentence is as regular as that? What we have here is a simple string of letters, of length – how many, Thomas?'

'I'm not one of your Parisian students,' Thomas growled.

'Just answer,' Joan murmured.

'Forty-nine, then.'

'Good. What's significant about the number forty-nine?'

'Seven sevens,' said Saladin immediately.

'Very good!' said Bacon.

Thomas looked surprised. Saladin said, 'Some of the villagers think it's a lucky number. Seven times seven. That's how I know.'

'Seven squared,' Bacon said. 'That is surely a clue. So now, if we write out the decoded message again, not in these arbitrary blocks of five or four, but in a grid of seven by seven ...'

P R G S L C V
E V O V P A L
R P R M E R P
N Y E T T B V
V T I E R V R
M H D S A M V
E A E A M S M

'It still means nothing to me,' Joan said.

But Thomas was tracing the letters with a chalky fingertip. 'But if you read, not across, but *down* – else why put them in a grid at all? P – E – R ... Give me that chalk, Roger.' He wrote out the letters, column by column, as a single line.

PERNVMERVPYTHAGOREIDESVMTESALPETRAMCARBVM
SVLPVRVM

'Look at this string,' Thomas said, excited. *'Pythagorei* – see it? Surely there is meaning here at last.'

'Good, good,' Bacon said. 'You can imagine the variants I explored before I hit on this correct route through the maze. Now all we have to do is find the breaks between the words ...'

But Thomas was ahead of him, splitting the line with bold slashes.

PER / NVMERV / PYTHAGOREI / DESVMTE / SALPETRAM /
CARBVM / SVLPVRVM

And there, for Saladin, the magic happened, a readable sentence emerging from a clamour of nonsense. He was the first to read it aloud: '"By Pythagoras's number take saltpetre, charcoal, sulphur."'

'Almost there,' said Bacon. 'Almost there.'

'But what does it mean?' Joan said.

'Well, Pythagoras's number is obvious. It is six.'

'It is?'

'Six is the perfect number,' said Saladin.

Thomas raised his eyebrows at him. 'And why is it perfect?'

'Because if you take the numbers that divide into it evenly ...' Saladin took the chalk now, and wrote out, 1,2,3. 'If you add them up you get six again.' 1+2+3=6.

Bacon smiled. 'Once again you surprise us.'

Saladin felt sheepish. 'Another lucky number for the villagers.'

'In fact there are many perfect numbers,' Bacon said. 'Pythagoras did indeed study them. Twenty-eight is the next one. You see, it is divisible by—'

'Never mind,' Joan said hastily. 'So now we have this: "By one, two, three take saltpetre, charcoal, sulphur."'

'Or,' Bacon said, 'three, two, one. In fact those proportions aren't quite correct, but near enough the range that a little trial and error gives you the right product. The value of experimentation,' he said, smiling.

Saladin was mystified again. 'What product?'

'Why, it's obvious – black powder. Haven't you heard of it? The Chinese have studied it for centuries, we're told. They call it the "fire drug". It's said they found it looking for an elixir of life! I had been hoping to obtain samples via the trade routes opened up by the Mongol empire, in order to verify its properties for myself. Now I can begin to experiment with its very manufacture.'

'The manufacture of what?' Joan demanded. 'What does this stuff do, you infuriating monk?'

He didn't seem insulted. 'Well, if you set fire to it—'

'Yes?'

'It explodes.'

XXII

They sat around the low table, heaped with Bacon's papers and covered with chalk scribbles.

'Explodes,' Joan said.

'Somebody,' Bacon said, 'your Weaver of the tapestry of time, Thomas, wants you to make explosions. *Incendium Dei* indeed. I wonder why.'

Joan glanced at Thomas. 'Have you told him of the engines?'

Thomas closed his eyes. 'No. Because I did not have your permission. And because, frankly, I was frightened where it might lead, if *he* knew.'

Bacon's eyes were wide. 'What engines? You must tell me.'

Thomas glanced at Joan. 'You see what I mean?'

Joan said, 'Well, we are committed. And perhaps this strange monk of yours can help us.' She described succinctly the legend of Sihtric and his machines of war, the plans now believed lost beneath the floor of the great mosque of Seville, in faraway al-Andalus.

'But you must retrieve this Codex,' Bacon said. 'You must!'

'Why?'

'Can't you see? Combine these engines of war, engines that roll and swim and even fly, with the black powder, with the Fire of God, and no man could stand before you. Think of it – a miniature Vesuvius loaded on each arrow! . . .'

Saladin's experience of explosions was limited. But once he had seen a forge blow itself apart. He tried to imagine such energies harnessed, launched, and used against the flesh of enemies.

'He's right,' he said reluctantly. 'You told us, Thomas, that Sihtric was dissatisfied with the engines he made. Perhaps this black powder will provide the potency they always lacked.'

Thomas looked pale. 'If it can be made to work – but what a horrible vision of destruction! What man is this Weaver to scatter the seeds of such carnage in our age?'

Roger Bacon seemed to care nothing for that. Saladin saw he was fired only by his curiosity, by the scent of fresh knowledge in his nostrils. 'You must retrieve these designs,' he said rapidly. *'And you must bring them to me.* What you need to make all this work is a *dominus experimentorum.* Such as myself, or an assistant. I can see it now. A scheme of work designed around two elevating principles. First, the verification of the designs, and the physical principles on which they have been based, perhaps principles hitherto unknown to mankind and therefore an everlasting gift to scholarship. Second, the use to which the new understanding may be put, which is the protection of Christendom, and thereby the spiritual welfare of all mankind and the greater glory of God.'

Thomas said, 'You would think, brother, from what you say, that you were being asked to make cathedrals, not weapons.'

'There is no sin in using the power of the mind to build weapons to fight a just war. Why, your Weaver must be a Christian, or he would not have put these engines into the hands of Christians. How can this *not* be God's work?'

'I know very little about the Weaver, and you know less,' Thomas said sternly. 'You must ensure you discuss this work with your confessor, brother. Fully and regularly.'

'Yes, yes.' Bacon leaned towards Joan, eyes bright, like the cat's into which he had spent long hours staring, Saladin thought. 'Bring me your plans, lady. By God's bones, there is no other way – indeed it must be divine providence that brought you to me.

'Give me your plans,' said Roger Bacon, 'and I will build the Engines of God for you.'

XXIII

The guard brought the two of them to Ibrahim's office: the accuser, a middle-aged man, and the accused, a scared-looking girl with a baby in her arms.

Ibn Shaprut sat silently at Ibrahim's side, plucking at his shabby robes. The doctor was a big man who had been a lot bigger before this dreadful summer of siege. Now his grimy, much-patched clothes didn't fit him properly, and Ibrahim sometimes thought his very skin hung loose, drained of fat. However Ibrahim was glad of his steady company and hard-headed advice.

It was an August afternoon in Seville, a city under siege and hot as a furnace. Distantly the muezzins called for prayer. Ibrahim was too busy for prayers. He tried to concentrate on the case.

The accuser was a man called Ali Gurdu. Aged about fifty, his face round as the moon, he looked sleek and prosperous in the middle of a famine that even reached inside the emir's palace, though in August's heat sweat stained his turban a grimy yellow. This man looked suspiciously at Ibn Shaprut. 'Who's he? A lawyer, a magistrate?'

'I'm a doctor,' said Ibn Shaprut.

'What's a doctor got to do with it? This is a case of theft, pure and simple.'

'I rely on his judgement,' said Ibrahim, 'so you will be respectful, Ali Gurdu.'

Ibn Shaprut was watching the girl. 'Your baby is very quiet.'

She smiled thinly. 'He's clever. He's learned not to waste energy crying.' Her voice was scratchy, like an old woman's. Her robe was filthy and torn, her eyes huge in a shrunken face, and the baby in her arms was wrapped in rags. She was called Obona. Ibrahim had had to confirm her age, which was sixteen; he had learned that hunger made you look young, even giving some a kind of ethereal beauty, before it turned you very old indeed.

'You brought him here today,' said Ibn Shaprut. 'You have no family who could have taken him?'

'My parents fled to Granada before the Christian armies came to the walls.'

'Without you?'

'They were ashamed of me. My grandmother stayed, though, and helped me. But she died in the spring.'

'Now you're alone,' said Ibrahim.

'Yes, sir.'

Ali Gurdu clenched a podgy fist. 'You'll be offering her a sugared apricot next. Enough of these questions! She's a thief! That's what this is all about, never mind her baby and her grandmother. She stole from me!'

Ibrahim glanced at his notes. Ali Gurdu described himself as a food merchant. He was steadily selling off a hoard of dried fruit and salted meat and rice. That wasn't quite against the law, even at the exorbitant prices he no doubt charged. But Ibrahim thought there was a stink about the man that was more than just a layer of greasy sweat.

'She came to you as a customer,' he said. 'She bought a bit of salted meat.'

'What meat was that?' Ibn Shaprut asked the girl.

She shrugged. 'Rat, I think. Or cat. What else is there?'

The flesh of a rat, which had no doubt gorged itself on the bodies in the communal graves. 'So you took your bit of rat—'

'She took two sticks,' Ali Gurdu insisted. 'More than she'd paid for.'

'One wasn't enough,' the girl said miserably. 'The baby – I still feed him.'

'That is draining for your body,' Ibn Shaprut said gently. 'I understand.'

'She ran away with the meat she stole.'

'But you didn't chase her,' Ibn Shaprut said. 'She was only caught because she was unlucky enough to run straight into one of Ibrahim's bailiffs. If not for that you'd have said nothing about it.'

Ali Gurdu blustered, 'I was simply slow about it. Shocked. Distressed! I'm not used to such blatant thievery, from a very young girl too. What's the world coming to?'

Ibrahim raised a hand to silence him. 'Obona, how did you pay for this meat? Do you have money?'

She shook her head. 'My parents took what we had. My grandmother had a few coins, but when she was dying I spent the last of those on a bit of water.'

'Yet you must eat,' Ibrahim said. 'Yet you must drink. How did you pay him?'

She glanced at Ali Gurdu, and looked down at her baby, clearly ashamed.

'Well, I think that's clear enough,' Ibrahim said, not bothering to hide his disgust. 'Food for sex, Ali Gurdu? Is that the game?'

Ali Gurdu looked defiant. 'You could call it pity. I mean, look at her. Skin and bone. Who would want her?' He slammed one fat fist into another. 'But it's still theft, that's the top and bottom of it. So what are you going to do about it, "vizier to the vizier"?'

Ibrahim's thirst raged, though there were hours to endure before his next sip of his water ration. He felt fouled by this grubby case, like so many others he had had to deal with.

It was all the fault of the Christians. The Castilians had lain siege around the city in the spring, when King Fernando had assembled a fleet of ships from the coastal waters, forced his way up the Guadalquivir and rammed the pontoon bridge. Thus, after years of pressure, Fernando had at last bottled the city up. As spring gave way to the usual ferocious summer, disease, famine, and worst of all drought had afflicted the city. Fernando seemed content to wait it out, even as his own men dropped of drought and fever. Once there had been rumours of a relieving force coming from Granada. But that *taifa*'s ruler Muhammad Abu Alahmar, concerned above all to secure his own position, submitted to King Fernando and actually *joined in* the siege against his fellow Muslims in Seville.

Sometimes Ibrahim wondered grimly how it would be if the siege never lifted. Would Ibrahim and those like him be forced to administer the death of an entire city, down to the last man, the last child, the last dog and cat?

But meanwhile, today, he had Ali Gurdu and this child-mother Obona to deal with. He glanced at Ibn Shaprut's stern face, seeking guidance.

'Here is my decision. Ali Gurdu, you have a certain usefulness. Men like you, with your grafting and your greed, actually enforce the rationing. You're dribbling out your stock, bit by bit. If you gave it all away there would be a riot, it would be gone in a day, and we'd be a lot worse off.'

'You need me, do you?' Ali Gurdu scoffed.

'But there are limits. We are not like the Christians. We are civilised people, despite the emergency. And if I find you step beyond those limits again, I will impound whatever stock you have left, and I will punish you as I see fit.' He leaned forward. 'Have a care, Ali Gurdu. It will be a different story for men like you when the siege is lifted.'

But Ibrahim thought the worst irony was that if the Christians did take the city, Ali Gurdu might have made himself wealthy enough from the misery of others to be able to buy his way to safety.

'And,' Ali Gurdu said, 'what of her?'

Ibrahim glanced at the wretched girl. 'How would it help anybody if this child was punished?'

'She is a thief!'

Ibrahim said to the girl, 'Well, he's right. You must pay this man back.'

'How can I do that?'

'Catch a rat,' Ibrahim said. 'And don't go to him again, next time you're hungry. Try these people. They are kinder.' He took his wooden pen and scribbled an address on a scrap of old paper and gave it to her. 'Now get out of my sight, both of you.'

He scratched his pen across the case notes and put the parchment aside. Then he stood, stretched, and glanced out of the window at a sky like an oven. He longed for the blessed cool of evening – at least nature lifted its siege, once a day. But Ibrahim's own long day was not done yet.

'Right. That's that. Who's next?'

XXIV

On the parched plain before the walls of Seville, Saladin woke inside his leather tent.

Hanse had died during the night. It had been the fever, of course. Hanse had fallen asleep coughing and puking. Now he was a shapeless, unmoving lump under his sweat-sodden cloak.

And Saladin had slept in a tent with a dead man. With a sudden terror he pushed his way out into the open air, panting.

The sun was still low, but Saladin could already feel its heat on his face. The camp of the Christian army stretched away all around him. Horses wandered apathetically between the rows of tents, and cross-bearing pennants hung limply over a land long stripped of anything edible.

Inside Seville, the muezzins were calling. The pinkish light of day, scattered through the dust rising from the desiccated landscape, reflected from the city walls.

Near the tent, Michael sat cross-legged before the remnants of the night's fire, resting his back on a heap of weapons and chain-mail coats. He was sipping a cup of water and eating dry rice. 'This isn't so bad for soldiering,' Michael said in his coarse shopkeeper's Latin. 'Not so bad.'

Saladin sat heavily beside him. 'What do you mean, not so bad? Hanse's *dead*. Is that his rice?'

Michael grinned and finished off the food. 'Well, he won't be needing it, will he?'

Saladin reached for the flask that contained the last of yesterday's water. There was hardly any left. He felt unreasonably resentful that a third of it had been wasted on a man now dead.

They sat without speaking.

When he had taken the Cross – he wore it proudly on his sleeve even now – and volunteered for Fernando's army, Saladin had joined a company formed from many nations, Christian warriors drawn here from across Europe by the Pope's granting of crusader indulgences – that and the chance to liven up your life by cracking a few Muslim heads. Hanse and Michael were typical, Hanse, blond and a bit frail, from the Low Countries, Michael from England.

It had been curious for Saladin to come up against the Moorish armies, the elite warriors with their quilted light armour, the hard-eyed horsemen from the desert. They were not much like the Saracen troops he had witnessed in the Outremer. Brother Thomas had told him that the Moors of Spain had absorbed the traditions of those who went before them; there were echoes of the post-Roman Visigoths in their cavalry and their colour.

But there had been no serious fighting for months, not since the spring when the siege had been set. There had been deaths among Fernando's forces, a steady stream of fatalities from drought, accident, and especially the plagues that coursed through the polyglot army. It didn't matter much to the generals, Michael said. There were always more volunteers willing to come and join an army on the brink of victory, trickling here from across Spain, indeed across Christendom. And a smart general always factored in the likelihood of losing a proportion of his army to disease. You planned for it, said Michael.

It wasn't really a surprise that Hanse was the first of the three of them to succumb, for he had fried in the Spanish sun. Michael, though, had darkened, his face turning leathery. Saladin wondered if he had a bit of Trojan blood in him, for it was said that it had been Trojans who were the first to colonise England.

'He had been talking of joining King Louis,' Michael said now. 'Hanse, I mean.' King Louis of France was generally believed to be the most pious and accomplished crusader king since Richard the Lionheart. 'Louis is sailing about now, for Cyprus, then on to Egypt.'

'He should have gone,' Saladin said. 'Better than this, sitting around in your own filth for month after month.'

'Maybe. Well, the poor bastard has missed out.'

'On what?'

'The city, when we get into it. They know some tricks, these Saracen women.'

'They are Moors, not Saracens.'

'The emir's whores are the best, if you can get hold of one the other lads haven't been up first. They'll know some tricks.' He laughed lazily.

183

'If the emir hasn't eaten his women by now. Try to find a whore without a bite taken out of her tits, ha ha!'

'I thought you said Moors eat babies.'

'Everybody knows that. But they'll have scoffed *them* all down by now, mate.'

Michael had never, in fact, met a Muslim in his life, save for a few mudejar farmers who had fled at the advance of the Christian army south from Cordoba. He knew nothing of Islam save the name. And yet here he was participating in a world-wide war against it.

Saladin had learned not to express such thoughts. He had had a difficult enough time being accepted by these western Christians without coming across as a Moorish sympathiser.

Their sergeant came by. He was a blunt-spoken Englishman called George, whose father had once fought with Richard the Lionheart, or so he claimed. He carried a big water flask, and an armed soldier watched his back to make sure none was stolen. 'Daily ration for you two arseholes,' he said, pouring the water out into their own flask. He glanced around. 'Where's the other arsehole? Pulling his cock?'

'He's dead,' Saladin said. 'He's a dead arsehole.'

'What, the sickness?'

'I think so.'

'Fair enough. Take him over there.' He pointed to a site near the base of the city walls where units of the army were gathering.

'Why?' Saladin asked.

'New orders. Captain says we're to catapult any dead arseholes over the wall. Let the Moors get the benefit of it.'

Michael laughed. 'They'll probably eat him. Poor old Hanse. He came a long way to be eaten by a starving Saracen whore.'

'Just do it,' the sergeant said, and he moved on.

It took the two of them to shift Hanse out of the tent, Michael at his shoulders, Saladin at his feet. Hanse's guts had emptied before he died. His tunic was crusted with vomit, and pale shit dribbled out of his trousers when they lifted him. What a waste of water, Saladin thought. He tried not to touch Hanse's flesh, or the shit.

'This isn't so bad,' Michael said, grunting as he worked.

XXV

Each day, in the middle of the afternoon, Subh visited Ibrahim at the palace. They were in a city under siege; Ibrahim wanted to be sure his mother was safe, and insisted on seeing her daily. As he was too busy to go to her, she came to him.

Today he found her with Peter, sitting in a well-appointed room that opened onto a broad patio. It was cool in the oven heat of the city. Save only for the loss of the fountain's trickling sound – the fountains had all been dry for months – the room was as it had been for centuries, and the light reflected from the carved stonework washed over Subh's cream-softened skin. She didn't look as if she had been affected by the long months of the siege at all. 'Such a beautiful place,' she said. 'What do you think will happen if the Christians do take the city, Ibrahim? Will they smash up this place? Will all this be lost?'

'I don't think so,' Ibrahim said. 'They're Christians, but not utter barbarians. I hear Fernando is already employing mudejar artisans. Perhaps they will continue to use the palace. They may renovate it, even extend it. Where else in Seville is fit for a king?'

Peter nodded. 'It's more beautiful than anything Christians could build.'

Ibrahim was faintly revolted by the way he disparaged his own culture. In the six years since he had met her Peter had truly become a creature of Subh, subsumed by her more powerful personality.

'But the Christians may disapprove of our decadence,' Subh said. 'They can be stern, these Christians. And we like our luxuries! Speaking of which, you should treat yourself a little more, Ibrahim. You look like a ghost. I told you, you should ignore your own silly rules and eat what you need.'

'I can't break the rationing I myself administer.'

She snorted. 'The common herd can die off and nobody will miss them. *You* are important, and deserve keeping alive.'

'As you are important, I suppose, Mother,' he said. 'And this Christian whelp of yours.'

Peter was indignant. 'I resent that. I don't have to be here. I could just walk out and surrender to Fernando's forces. I only need take my turban off to look like a Christian again.'

'Then why are you here?'

Peter smiled. 'How could I leave when the project is so close to fruition?'

'Ah. Your mysterious engines.'

'We have some news about that, Ibrahim,' Subh said. 'Something to distract you from your grubbing around in this city of the dead and dying.'

Ibrahim glared. 'I'm too busy for riddles. Just tell me what you mean.'

'The thunder-mouth,' the scholar said, 'is ready. My men are hauling it up onto the walls even now. You need to come and see it, Ibrahim.'

Ibrahim was unimpressed, and no doubt it showed in his face.

Subh snapped, 'You disapprove. How typical of you. What if we are saved through *my* vision, Ibrahim, you toiler, you ant? How will that make you feel?' She turned away from him.

'Just come and see it,' Peter urged gently.

XXVI

Saladin was astonished when plump old Thomas Busshe came riding down from Cordoba to see him in the camp.

'You want to be careful, brother,' Michael said to Thomas, laughing. 'Fernando's soldiers will eat that mule for you if you don't keep an eye on it. And if the Saracens get hold of you they'll eat *you*.'

Thomas glanced at him, gasping with exertion. 'My son, in Seville they are Moors, not Saracens.'

'Same thing.' Michael went back to stirring the thick broth of root vegetables, rice and unidentifiable meat that bubbled slowly in the pot on the fire.

Thomas sat on the ground beside Saladin with a thump that sent dust flying up from his mule-blanket. His habit, heavy wool that was completely unsuitable for the climate, was caked with dust and mud and sweat.

'You made a hazardous journey, brother,' Saladin said, offering him his water cup. 'The country is not yet subdued. And this, after all, is a siege.'

'So I was advised. But your mother in Cordoba insisted I come to see you.' He accepted a sip of water gratefully.

'Why? What's so important?'

'Joan has had a letter,' the monk said. 'From Roger Bacon.' And he produced a parchment.

It was more than a year since Bacon had successfully decoded the *Incendium Dei* scrap. Since then he had thrown himself into a vast and secretive project of experimental research, spending his time and energy and all the money he could get hold of on books and instruments and tables, hiring assistants and instructing savants.

'He has been puffed up by his own success in cracking the code.'

'That doesn't surprise me,' Saladin said.

'And now he's looking for engines that can deliver God's fire.'

'But the Codex is buried under the mosque.'

'True. But he's scoured Christendom and beyond for ideas on what *might* be possible. Look at what he speaks of – wagons that move without horses by means of a miraculous force, like the reaping chariots of the ancients, and machines for flight, and so on. He even says there is no doubt that such instruments were built in ancient times and are still being built today. He says he knows of a scholar who tried to build the flying machine ...'

'He speaks of this Aethelmaer of the legend.'

'Perhaps. Or he may mean Ibn Firnas of Cordoba, who also built a flying machine some centuries ago.'

Saladin smiled thinly. 'In Jerusalem I knew a man who sold flying carpets making much the same sort of promises. Well, Bacon is undoubtedly eager to keep our money flowing. Is it possible the ancients really did have such machines, Thomas? In a way it makes the Sihtric designs more plausible, if they are memories of the past, rather than dreams of the future.'

'Well, Aristotle proposes that time is like a great wheel, going around and around endlessly, so that the past *is* the future, and there's no difference. But such speculations don't help us in any practical way. What we need is to get our hands on the Codex, and get it to Bacon, and *then* see what he can do with it—'

There was a spark of light. It came from one of the towers that bristled on the walls of the city, there and gone in a flash, like the sun reflecting from a bit of armour. Saladin stood up to see better. A tiny cloud of white smoke rose from the tower.

All around the camp, men were standing, pointing. In the flat light they looked skinny, skeletal, dead men besieging a city of the dead.

Long heartbeats after the flash of light, a muffled crump reached Saladin's ears, like thunder from a distant storm.

'What,' Thomas asked, 'was *that?*'

'I think we'd better go and find out,' Saladin said.

'I'll get your mule for you, friar,' Michael said. 'If it isn't in somebody's pot by now.'

XXVII

The thunder-mouth had been set up on a look-out platform on top of a tower set in the city walls. Peter and Subh had led Ibrahim up there to see.

The thunder-mouth was a copper tube, shining in the sun. Its muzzle protruded over the battlements, pointing at the Christians' scattered camp. A brazier enclosed the rear of the tube, and when Ibrahim got there a fire was already burning hotly, so intense that it had turned that part of the cylinder red-hot. The brazier was being tended by two of Peter's scholars, who poked at the fire nervously.

Subh looked on with a complacent pride.

Ibrahim walked around the thunder-mouth cautiously. 'Quite a job to haul this thing up here,' he said.

'Oh, yes,' said his mother. 'That alone was a marvel.'

'Well, I hope it's worth the effort.' But, looking at the device now, he doubted it. In the glimmering shadows of the old Roman water tank Peter's machines had looked mysterious, potent, even magical. But here the slim copper tube and the brazier looked absurd, a toy beside the massive stone reality of the walls. 'Does the emir know about this?'

'You're his eyes and ears,' Subh murmured. 'When it all goes to plan, when Christian soldiers are scattered like wheat stalks in a storm, then you can tell him what we have done.'

Ibrahim looked at Peter. This mention of the slaughter of Christians didn't evoke any reaction in him. Obsessed with his machines and his ambitions, in the thrall of Subh, the man was quite without conscience, Ibrahim saw; he was a lost soul.

Peter nodded at the scholars. 'Let's get on with it.'

The two of them approached the thunder-mouth carrying a heavy pail of water between them. Ibrahim saw they were going to tip the water into a kind of funnel mounted over the brazier.

'All that water is coming out of somebody's ration,' Ibrahim said weakly.

'This will put an end to rationing,' Subh said.

Peter pointed. 'The water, poured in here, goes straight down into the hot barrel. It immediately flashes to steam. And steam, as you know, requires more space than water. The steam will roar up the tube and shoot the iron lump out over the walls, as a man spits out a pea, propelling it with his breath, spit it away and into the Christian lines. I am confident of the range. We have tested smaller models; the arithmetic is simple.'

'It will seem a miracle,' Subh said. 'The explosion of the steam, the roar of it as it gushes out of the thunder-mouth – and the iron ball itself, a mass heavier than a man, flying miles through the air. A mouth of thunder indeed.'

'But you haven't tested it,' Ibrahim said.

'Only smaller models. What else could we do, in the conditions of the siege?'

'And what better way to prove it,' Subh said silkily, 'than against live Christians?'

Peter stood straight. 'Do it,' he said to the scholars.

The cowering scholars tipped their great bucket. The water gurgled into the funnel, and through a length of copper pipe that fed it straight through the brazier's coals and into the cylinder. The thunder-mouth shuddered. And in that last heartbeat Ibrahim snatched his mother's arm and pulled her back, putting his body between her and the engine.

Ibrahim was slammed in the back as if by an immense hot fist, and he was thrown forward. An enormous noise crashed painfully into his head. Steam washed over him in a moment, scorching, gone.

He found himself sprawled over his mother. He pushed himself up. His back was tight and sore, burned. His mother seemed unharmed. Lying on the floor, looking up at him, her lips moved. But he could not hear a word she said.

In fact, he realised, he couldn't hear anything at all. He noticed blood trickling from his mother's ears and pooling in her throat. When he touched the sides of his own face, his fingers came away sticky with blood. He felt shocked. He had never heard such a noise, never in his life.

He stood up and turned around.

The thunder-mouth was destroyed, ripped open. The brazier was shattered, its hot coals scattered smoking on the platform. The two scholars lay on their backs, unmoving. He saw with wonder that mis-shapen bits of copper were embedded in the stone wall.

And Peter writhed on the floor. Blood pumped from a dozen wounds punched into body. His face was all but gone, Ibrahim saw, horrified, the skin scorched away, though some awful chance had left his eyeballs intact, staring terrified from lidless sockets.

The thunder-mouth tipped up silently. Ibrahim saw the tube nod down over the battlements, and an iron ball rolled harmlessly out to fall straight down the wall to the ground below.

XXVIII

Saladin and Thomas were not permitted to go with the scouting party to the foot of the walls beneath the strange explosion. But they were able to inspect what was recovered: some twisted bits of metal, and an immense ball of iron.

'An engine,' Thomas said darkly. 'Or the remains of one that failed.'

'Subh,' Saladin said. 'My mother's cousin. She is in there. This proves it.' He glanced at the city walls, and wondered if this remote relative whom he had never met was looking back at him now. 'She must have the engine plans. She must have dug them up from the mosque—'

'Not necessarily. Fernando has the city riddled with his spies. If that were going on we'd have heard about it. Subh's letter to your mother hinted of other designs, sketches developed by Sihtric and his co-workers from the originals – sketches that were not entirely lost when Sihtric died. Perhaps that's what we're seeing here.' He grunted, poking tentatively at a bit of torn copper sheet. 'It would certainly explain why it failed. We may yet not be too late to get to those originals first.'

'I hope so. Or mother will be furious.'

XXIX

Word came from the vizier's office that King Fernando was prepared to accept the surrender of the city on the twenty-third of November. Three days before that cut-off the emir's ministers were to meet with representatives of the King and the Pope, where Fernando's terms would be presented.

Ibrahim was dulled by the months of siege. But Ibn Shaprut counselled him to be hopeful. Perhaps in this moment of surrender the Christians might discover in themselves the mercy of Jesus of which they boasted so loudly.

On the morning of the meeting, Ibrahim woke from a restless night, soon after dawn. He could hear rain hissing down.

Ibrahim left the palace and walked the streets of the city, hoping to clear his head. The rain on his upturned face was light and fresh. The people were coming out of their houses, men and women with scrawny arms protruding from grimy sleeves. They put out pots and bowls and cups to catch the rain. This was the first significant rainfall of the winter, and Ibrahim imagined it cleaning the air, washing away the last of the heat and stench of the filthy summer of siege. The world was being kind to Seville, then, at last.

But it had come too late. The bodies bundled into doorways or heaped in alleyways told him that: the night's dead, dumped by those too weak or apathetic to dispose of them properly. Ibrahim made a mental note of where the corpses lay, so he could brief the day's working parties. But he supposed that in a few more days such problems would be the concern of some Christian soldier, and he, at last, could rest.

He walked down to the river, where no ships sailed this morning, and the waterwheels stood idle. It struck him how very quiet the city was now. There were few animals around; in a starving city the dogs and cats had gone into the pot before the rats. Even the songbirds had been netted, plucked and consumed. Few children too, and fewer old people. Ibn Shaprut the doctor had told him how hunger and disease and drought always took away the very old and the very young, always the most vulnerable.

He tired quickly as he walked, and his burned back still ached sometimes, and the cold of the rain cut into his flesh. After months of rationing there were times he felt so light and flimsy, so detached from reality, that it was as if he had become a ghost, haunting the streets of the city he had tried to help save.

He had wandered far enough. He turned back.

Inside the emir's palace Christian troopers gawped at the tiles and the frescoes, and leered at the Muslim women. The Christians wore chainmail and steel helmets, and had bright red crosses emblazoned on their shoulders. These were *crucesignati*, crusaders, holy warriors, infused by piety and blessed by the Pope. But they were nearly as ragged and half-starved as the surviving population of the city itself.

Ibrahim walked across the patio outside the *turayya*, the hall at the centre of the suite of rooms called the Pleiades, and the grandest in the palace complex. The patio was a lovely rectangular space encompassed by a gallery of delicate trefoil arches. One Christian soldier had taken his boots off and was soothing his filthy, blistered feet in the rainwater trapped in the fish pond. His mate saw Ibrahim pass by and kicked the bather, speaking in rough Latin.

'Get up, Michael, you arse, you're showing us up.'

'Oh, leave me be, Saladin. Arse yourself. This isn't so bad, is it? Not so bad for soldiering ...'

Ibrahim was surprised by that famous Saracen name, Saladin, given to a Christian soldier. But Fernando's army was international, drawn from all across Christendom. 'Saladin' could have come from anywhere.

He walked on into the *turayya* itself, where he found that the discussions had already started. The Christian party had lined up against one wall, and glared at the emir's representatives, led by the vizier, who clustered opposite. Hapless servants, trembling with fear, scurried between the parties with trays of sweetmeats and wine. The Christian leaders were warriors and clerics, knights and princes, envoys of the Pope. Some were both military and pious; Ibrahim saw a man in a tonsure with a chain-mail vest over his monk's habit. And they all wore the shoulder-cross of crusade.

There was only one woman in the Christian party. She was still young, in her thirties perhaps, and quite pretty, with a face like an almond. A fat elderly monk accompanied her. Pretty or not she glared at her Muslim opponents as severely as any of the men.

As for the Moorish party, Ibrahim spotted Ibn Shaprut at its heart – and, he was shocked to see, his own mother stood close by.

He walked up. 'Mother. What are you doing here? It's hardly safe.'

Dressed in a robe as white and clean as mountain snow, her face shining with expensive oils and her hair drawn back under her veil, Subh looked magnificent. Magnificent, but furious. 'Safe? Where is safe? None of us is safe, Ibrahim. Well, none of us save for *him*.' She pointed.

Ibrahim glanced across the room. There was the almond-faced woman, and beside her, talking animatedly to her and her monk companion, was a flabby, sleek, sweating Moor.

'Ali Gurdu,' Ibrahim said with disgust. 'That grafter. I should have cut off his hands and feet while I had the chance.'

'What's done is done,' Ibn Shaprut said. 'You can't blame him for trying to save himself. And he might even help, though he doesn't mean to, if he makes the Christian passage into the city a little easier.'

'"Makes the Christian passage easier",' Subh snapped. 'What are you talking about, you quack? Do you understand nothing of what's happening?'

Ibrahim frowned. 'What do you mean? Fernando has the city. What else can he want?'

'Expulsion,' said Subh.

'What?'

'We must leave. *Every Moor* – all of us who can walk, and even if we can't. That is the condition Fernando is going to impose. Fernando doesn't want a living city. He doesn't want *us*. He only wants the stones, to house a new population of Christians.'

Ibrahim was stunned. The room spun around him, and the rich colours faded to yellow-grey. He felt Ibn Shaprut's strong hands on his shoulders, and he was helped down, to sit on a heap of floor cushions.

Ibn Shaprut offered him a cup of watered wine. 'Drink this.'

Subh stood over him, glaring, a pitiless mother. 'You've worn yourself out, and for nothing. I told you so, but would you listen to me? Now look at you – fainting like an old woman, in this hour of our family's greatest crisis.'

'The family.' His own voice sounded distant to Ibrahim. 'What does the family matter? It hasn't been like this before. Even in Cordoba. There Muslims still live under Christian rule, as once Christians lived under our rule.'

'Things have changed,' Subh said. 'Look at them, Ibrahim. Look at them with those hateful crosses stitched to their shoulders.'

'They won't even know how the city *works*. The city is its people, its history ... This is unthinkable.'

'And yet such things are being thought,' said the doctor. 'You are a sane man, Ibrahim, in a world of the mad. And we men of sanity must cope with the consequences of the decisions of the others. Come, my friend. Stand with me now. In the coming days, the city will ask one last service of you.'

'Yes. One last service.'

'And,' Subh said, glaring at the Christians, 'the family has one great goal to achieve before we abandon this place, as we were forced out of Cordoba.'

Ibrahim knew she meant the Codex, supposedly lost under the floor of the mosque. She was scheming over trifles in this moment of catastrophe for a whole civilisation. He thought she was as insane as the Christians. And yet he must cope with her as well as the city's calamity.

He struggled to rise, leaning on Ibn Shaprut.

XXX

Fernando set a deadline of one month for the evacuation. He told the emir bluntly that he wished to celebrate Christmas Day in Seville's great mosque, reconsecrated as a Christian cathedral.

And in that last month, Ibrahim worked harder even than in the worst days of the siege, as he helped to organise the abandonment of a great city.

When he walked through the streets he found a mood of anger and disbelief about the evacuation. He was shown around houses and gardens, still grand even after the siege, where patios shone and rusted fountains had once bubbled water; he was shown shops and offices and businesses, carefully built up over generations. How could all this be given up for ignorant Christian barbarians to despoil? Some people wouldn't move for sheer stubbornness. And others *hoped*, no matter how sternly Ibrahim spoke of the Christians' ruthless determination. Perhaps you could find some way to accommodate under the Christians. Or perhaps you could simply hide in your home behind a locked door, and somehow everything would turn out all right. Ibrahim knew this was fantasy. He encouraged people to take away the deeds of their houses, to lock the doors, to carry off the keys. This was enough to allow at least some of these desperate new paupers to walk out proudly, bundles on their heads, the deeds tucked carefully inside their djellabas expressing their intention to return. But others were determined to stay, defying the Christians come what may. Often Ibrahim could only walk away.

If there were some who wouldn't leave, there were many more who couldn't, for they were too ill or too young or too old, or damaged by the long siege. So Ibrahim organised parties of refugees who might be able to carry a few of the vulnerable with them. He tried, too, to gather people into parties large enough to resist the predations of the bandits in the country.

And while all this went on, Ibrahim still had a city to run. Even in this last month people still had to eat and drink, sewage had to be taken away, fires controlled, outbreaks of disease contained. Ibn Shaprut told him that it was like tending a dying man, all mundane detail and a steady decline, and an awful knowledge that an utter termination was near.

In the end, as Fernando's deadline neared, the people of the city simply began walking out of the gates to the south and east. These were urban folk, not used even to walking far, and many of them overloaded themselves at the start of their flight. Some even tried to carry out precious bits of furniture, even carpets. You would see these bundles dumped after a few hundred paces, as the harsh landscape quickly took its toll.

Ten thousand people drained out of the city, to vanish into the plains of the south. At the peak of the flight it was an astonishing sight; they turned the roads to the south black.

When they were gone, in the city by night you could see only a scattered flickering of lights across a landscape of gleaming domes and minarets, and the only sounds were the smash of glass, drunken laughter, the occasional scream, and the muezzin's faithful calls. Ibrahim had the oppressive sense of being present at the end of a great phase of history.

Then it was the last week, and then the last day.

And on the morning of the twenty-first of December, the last morning of Moorish Seville, Ibrahim, with Ibn Shaprut at his side, walked the deserted streets one last time. Abandoned bundles littered the cobbles. They saw a scrawny dog nose through one package, looking for food.

'Amazing,' Ibn Shaprut said. 'I thought the dogs had all been eaten.'

'Evidently they're better at hiding than we are. Let's hope they are good at playing the Christian.' Ibrahim reached out to the dog, but it thought he wanted its food and it fled.

Ibn Shaprut held up a hand. 'Listen. Can you hear that?'

There was a soft weeping, so soft they would never have heard it if not for the utter silence of the city. They followed the noise, passing along a street and through an archway, into a small, overgrown patio.

Surrounded by greenery, a girl sat on a stone bench, cradling a baby in a filthy blanket.

Ibn Shaprut approached the girl. When he touched her shoulder she flinched, but the doctor had a soothing manner. 'It's all right. No

Christians here yet. Let me see your baby. I'm a doctor. I might be able to help.'

Gradually she relaxed. Her face was tear-streaked. She wouldn't let go of the child, but held it out so that Ibn Shaprut could examine it. Ibrahim knew nothing of the health of babies, but it was awake, its eyes alert, and it seemed to smile at Ibn Shaprut; there couldn't be much wrong with it.

Ibrahim thought he recognised the girl. 'I know you. That chiseller Ali Gurdu accused you of thieving.'

Her eyes widened. 'Yes. You're the vizier's vizier. That was what they called you.'

He smiled. 'Well, the vizier is long gone. You can call me Ibrahim. And you are Obona.'

'You helped me. You sent me for food from some people, after I got away from Ali Gurdu.'

'Did they help you?'

'Yes. They took me in as a servant. They were decent. But they found a way to flee, and passed me on to another family. They looked after me too.' Tears leaked from her eyes. 'I woke up this morning, the baby woke me crying, and they had gone. I suppose I'm just a burden to people.'

'Don't think that.'

'Is it true, sir, about the Christians?'

'Is what true?'

She whispered it, eyes wide. 'That they eat babies? I'm so afraid – the things people say—'

'No. Don't think such nonsense. Why, the Christians probably say the same sort of things about us.'

'Your baby's fine,' Ibn Shaprut said, standing up. 'Nothing a good feed and a bit of sunshine wouldn't cure.'

She said, 'But everybody's left. Where am I to go?'

Ibrahim glanced at Ibn Shaprut. 'We'll have to leave soon, like everybody else. You can come with us to Granada. But I can make no guarantees about what you'll find there, for we have no arrangements ourselves.'

'Thank you,' she said earnestly. 'That's enough for me. Anything to get away from these Christians—'

'Leave her.' The voice was imperious.

Ibrahim turned. Subh stood in the arched entrance to the patio. Even now, as the city was in its death throes, a haze of perfume hung around her.

'Mother.'

'You weren't hard to find, you know. Plodding around town with this sullen doctor, still doing your duty, even now. You're as pious as a Christian, Ibrahim.'

'I thought you'd gone. I arranged it—'

'I know what you *arranged*. I told you. I'm going nowhere, not until we've been to the mosque.'

'Are you still pursuing that foolishness, even now?'

'You don't understand. Things have changed. *She's* here.'

Ibrahim was baffled and disbelieving. 'Who?'

'Joan. Our cousin of the Outremer. I learned this through Ali Gurdu, who is working with the Christians, and functions as a conduit of information ... Joan, to whom I wrote about the Engines of God, and who never replied, has now come here. It's obvious why. I told you I feared I had made her a rival. She wants the Codex for herself.'

Ibrahim remembered the almond-faced woman in the *turayya*. Could that truly have been his distant cousin from the Outremer, come all this way from lost Jerusalem to dying Seville? How remarkable.

'And,' his mother went on, 'do you know what Ali Gurdu tells me she has done? She has worked her way into the court of King Fernando. She may have warmed the bed of Fernando himself for all I know. And *it was she who hatched the idea of forcing the evacuation of the city*.'

Ibrahim was baffled. 'But why would she want this?'

'Isn't it obvious? She wants the city cleared, so the mosque will be emptied. And there, in the hours before Fernando's first mass, she will have her chance to get her hands on the engine designs. *My* designs.'

'That's absurd.'

'Absurd? The promise of the designs is not absurd. Joan takes it as seriously as I do. Indeed she has travelled from one end of the Mediterranean to the other for the sake of it. I need you to help me thwart her.'

Ibrahim, dismayed, looked into her face, and recognised the same sort of madness that seemed to drive the Christians, a plain, single-minded determination, uncomplicated and unsubtle and uncluttered by reflection. Her purpose had already destroyed Peter. Now the thought of scrabbling around in pursuit of this foolish dream on the floor of an abandoned mosque, in the midst of an epochal tragedy, disgusted him. 'I won't help you with this, mother. I told you. It's over.'

She nodded. 'Then what will you do?'

'As soon as this round is done I'm fetching my pack and leaving with Ibn Shaprut.'

'Then this is where we must say goodbye.'

Something inside Ibrahim broke. 'Give up this madness, Mother, I beg you. Come with us. It's a long walk to Granada. But you will have me.' He gestured at the girl. 'Obona will walk with you. Perhaps you will be able to help her with her baby.' He hoped that would touch his mother's heart.

But Subh looked down at the girl and sneered. 'If you take her you really are a fool. She doesn't need you, don't you see that? She has a pretty face. She can whore herself to the Christians as she once whored for Ali Gurdu. That's what rat-people like her do. But not us, Ibrahim. We're better than the rest. Come with me now, and we will fulfil our family's destiny together. We will change the world.'

Ibrahim looked down at the girl, who was weeping over her baby. 'You shame me, Mother. Go now.' He kept his head bowed.

When he looked up she had gone.

XXXI

So King Fernando walked at last into the city he had besieged for so long. His soldiers lined the way, and cheered. But their voices were small in a city that was an echoing stone shell, and some of the soldiers looked about warily, fearful of Moorish ghosts.

It was three days before Saladin was finally allowed into the city, for the first time since he had accompanied the King's envoys during their negotiations with the emir. He was stunned by the emptiness of the place, compared to the vibrancy he had witnessed only days before. Walking through the innards of this vast stone corpse crushed his soul.

'Not bad work for a Christmas Day,' Michael said to Saladin. 'I mean, the emir's whores have all cleared off to Granada. Nothing left but old ladies and babies. But the lads say that some of those old Saracen chickens have got a bit of juice left in them, if you know what I mean. And there might be a bit of loot to be had, though we're supposed to give it all to the King to pay his mercenaries.' He sniffed, hawked up some snot, spat, and swung his arms as they walked down the empty street. 'There's nothing to buck you up quite so much as a right good sacking on Christmas Day. But still this isn't bad work, not bad at all.'

'Shut up,' said Saladin. 'Oh, shut up.'

'All right. I'm just saying—'

'I know what you're saying—'

'Saladin. Here you are.'

Saladin swung round at the woman's voice. It was his mother.

Michael bowed. 'Lady Joan.' He looked up and leered at her.

'Happy Christmas, Michael,' she said drily. She looked tense, anxious.

'What are you doing here, mother?'

'Looking for you. It took me the devil's own time to find you. That sergeant of yours barely knows where his own backside is, let alone his soldiers. Well, let's get moving. We don't have much time.' She set off down the street, without looking back.

She gave Saladin no choice. He trotted after her. Michael, grinning, followed.

'Mother – where are we going?'

'The mosque, of course. Where else? Thomas Busshe will meet us there. Time is short. The bishops are going to reconsecrate the building this morning. Then the King will hear mass in it this evening. We've only got an hour before the clerics will be swarming all over it.'

Michael asked, 'An hour to do what?'

Joan said, 'To dig up the Codex.'

Saladin had told Michael nothing about his family's strange secret from the past. But Michael picked up those words 'dig up'. 'Buried treasure,' he said, his grin widening. 'Now that's what I'm talking about.'

When they reached the mosque's outer wall, they met Thomas at a gateway that led through to a broad patio where dried-up fountains stood like dead flowers. Thomas was out of breath, and looked anxious. 'This way,' he said, and he hustled them across the patio and through an arched doorway that took them into the mosque itself. 'But,' he panted, 'it isn't good news . . .'

The mosque was immense. Like its great sister in Cordoba, it was a complex of pillars and arches that extended off to infinity in every direction. Just days ago, this place would have been crowded with the Muslim faithful, Saladin supposed, perhaps still praying that Allah would save their city for them. Now there were only soldiers, all of them blazoned with the cross of Christ. In one corner he saw soldiers sleeping, leaning up against the wall. In another, more of them gambled with dice on the polished floor. And in the very heart of the mosque a fire had been built, right in the middle of the floor, and the soldiers were roasting a pig they had robbed from somewhere, no doubt brought here as a deliberate act of disrespect to the vanished Muslims. The smoke licked up and was blackening the fine plasterwork above.

Thomas had brought a few workers with him, off-duty soldiers standing idle with picks and shovels. 'The difficulty is,' he said, 'where are we supposed to dig?'

'I hadn't thought this far ahead,' Joan said. She strode about, looking around at the mosque. 'I think I imagined it would be obvious. That those who buried the designs would leave some clue.'

'None that is apparent,' Thomas said. 'We haven't the time to dig the whole place up, and nor would the King spare us even if we did.'

'Then what are we to do?'

'Ask me.' The woman walked towards them, out of the deeper shadows of the mosque. She wore a veil and a djellaba. She was obviously a Muslim, and had obviously been hiding. The woman removed her veil. She looked about fifty; her face was stern, determined – and familiar.

Michael made a deep growling noise. 'Now that's more like it. Old bones, but well worth jumping on, Saladin my friend, you mark my words—'

'Shut up.'

Joan said, 'I know you. You were in the meeting at the palace with the vizier's staff.'

'In the *turayya*, yes.' She spoke a clear but accented English.

'What do you want here?'

'To meet you. You are here because of me.' The woman smiled, but it was a stern, chilling expression. 'I wrote to you, many years ago. I told you of the existence of the Codex of the Engines of God. I told you where the designs were buried. I hoped for cooperation. We are cousins.'

'You are Subh of Cordoba.'

'And you are Joan of the Outremer.'

The women faced each other. Saladin had rarely sensed such tension between two human beings, even in combat.

'You should have fled with the others,' Saladin said to Subh. 'You must know you have put your life at stake by staying here.'

Joan introduced him. 'This is my son, Saladin.'

'Another relative.' Subh smiled at Saladin, and turned back to Joan. 'I would not leave without what is mine,' she said. 'No – ours.'

Joan said, 'If the Codex exists at all, it is lost under this ocean of flooring.'

'Not lost,' said Subh. 'I know where it is. Precisely.' And she told them of a memoir left by Ibn Hafsun, the *muwallad* who, more than a century ago, had been the man actually to bury the Codex at this site. 'I had a scholar, Peter, who analysed his record and calculated precisely where under the mosque the cache must be. I had hoped we could work together,' she said. 'That is why I wrote to you. In trust. With the two scraps of knowledge that have come down to us, the engine designs and the enigma of the *Incendium Dei*—'

'Tell me where the Codex is.'

'Not until we discuss terms.'

Joan laughed in her face. She turned to Michael. 'Hold her.'

Michael drew his sword. He stepped forward and took Subh's arm. Thomas flinched, upset by the bit of violence.

Subh's face was coldly furious. 'I came here for a civil negotiation.'

Joan said, 'I will not bargain with a defeated Moor.'

204

'You will not find the designs without me.'

'Oh, I will. Perhaps not today. Perhaps not for a year. But with time, there will be a way. Do you doubt that? The only question is, will you cooperate? For, you see, the only chance you have to gain anything from this situation is if you tell me what I wish to know.'

Saladin put a hand on her arm. 'Mother—'

But Joan shook him off.

Subh was beaten, but she was unafraid. 'Very well.' She glared at Michael until he let her go. Then she turned and pointed to the bonfire blazing in the middle of the mosque. 'There. About six paces beyond that bit of arson by your brutish soldiers.'

'Good,' said Joan. 'Let's get on with it.'

Subh stood before her. 'And what of me?'

'What of you? You are Muslim, I am Christian. All over the world, we are at war. And the engine designs are the spoils of war. I told you whatever was necessary to take those spoils.'

Subh stared back at her. 'So you betray me.' She wasn't begging, Saladin saw with grudging admiration. Unarmed, alone, surrounded, she was thinking, trying to find a way into Joan's soul. 'Cousin. We have different faiths. But we are family, you and I – and Saladin. I have a son too, called Ibrahim.'

'I am not like you,' Joan said coldly.

Subh insisted, 'We are the same blood. With roots in this very country, where once a foolish boy called Robert met a girl called Moraima. Is that not a deeper unity than anything else, even than differences in faith? Must it go on and on, Joan, Christian against Muslim, century after century as it has already for half a millennium in Spain, until none of us are left alive?' And she reached out a hand.

Joan pulled back, her face twisted with fury. 'Don't touch me, you witch. You talk to me of blood? Your kind forced me from my home, from Jerusalem. Do you imagine I will forgive that? Do you imagine I will rest until I see the land of Christ restored to Christian hands? Take her out of here,' Joan said to Michael. 'Hand her over to your sergeant, or—'

Without warning Subh let out an extraordinary animal howl. She leapt at Joan and dug fingers arched like claws into her face. Joan screamed and fell backward.

Saladin and Michael rushed forward. They grabbed Subh and hauled her off Joan, but with difficulty, for she was a heavy woman animated by utter rage. At last Michael got his arms clasped around her, pinning her hands to her body.

Joan would have attacked Subh in turn, had not Saladin held her back. Her face was streaming with blood from gouges under her eyes. 'Look at me. Look at me! I'm lucky she didn't take out an eye.'

Michael called, 'What do you want me to do with her, lady?'

Saladin said quickly, 'Mother, she is our cousin.'

'She's a boil that needs to be lanced. Take her,' she said to Michael. 'Do what you want with her, you and your lads. Then throw her out of the city, naked.'

Subh struggled, but Michael grinned and hauled her away to the squad of soldiers playing dice. They laid their hands on her, and pushed her down on the floor of the mosque.

Thomas was ashen. But his eyes were alive with anticipation. 'The Codex. Come. We may not have much time.' He led the way back to the bonfire.

Joan dabbed her torn face with a bit of cloth.

Saladin said, 'You need to find a doctor.'

'Oh, stop your fussing, boy.'

'Did you mean what you said? About the designs – the weapons, and using them to take the Holy Land?'

'Of course I did. It is the most sacred place in the world, Saladin. And our home. We will use the engines for the purpose for which they were intended.'

As a boy in Jerusalem, a 'warrior cub' as Thomas had once called him, Saladin would have applauded such an ambition. But he had grown since those days, grown into a man of twenty-one who had seen much more of the world – and had seen much suffering. 'Mother, are you sure that was the intention? And are you sure that's what we should do?'

'What do you mean?'

'Remember the Dove.' He meant his family's other prophecy, the Testament of Eadgyth, handed down since the days of Robert and his father Orm, a commandment that seemed to warn against the use of Sihtric's Engines of God.

'Gibberish,' she said. 'Meaningless. I care nothing for prophecies. All I care about is acquiring the power to achieve my goals. All I care about is getting hold of those designs, and building the weapons, and turning them on Muslim flesh.'

Saladin heard screams, and the angry shouts of the men. Subh was putting up a fight. 'And what of your cousin?'

'She deserves what's coming to her,' Joan spat. 'I hope they split her open.'

Saladin decided in that moment that he would not follow his mother, not any more, not after this. He would fight for the Holy Land, yes. But he would do it the honourable way, the Pope's way. He would take the Cross again, and join King Louis's crusade in Egypt.

And he would not forget the prophecy of the Dove as long as he lived, and he would pass it on to his own children, and instruct them to pass it on to theirs, so that in the unimaginable future they might make their own judgements about the Engines of God.

They reached the fire. Thomas was rubbing podgy hands. 'Perfect, perfect. All we have to do is retrieve the designs, ship them back to England, and let Roger Bacon get to work.'

Joan, her blood leaking between her fingers, snapped, 'Must we clear this fire first?'

'No need. In fact the fire will help us. Perhaps it was sent by God for that very purpose.' And from his sleeve he drew a packet.

'What's that?'

'A present from Bacon. Black powder.'

Joan grinned, and held out her hand. 'Let me.'

There were howls from the soldiers with Subh. 'Ow!' Saladin heard Michael call. 'The old witch has bitten through my cheek! ... By God's wounds. She's dead! Now, how did she manage that? Poison under her tongue? I think she's defeated us, lads ...'

Joan sprinkled the powder on the floor, on the spot Subh had indicated. Thomas took an ember from the fire and threw it. Fire blossomed, its noise echoing like thunder, beneath the mosque's low ceiling, and the floor broke open.

III

NAVIGATOR

AD 1472–1491

I

In the last days / To the tail of the peacock / He will come: / The spider's spawn, the Christ-bearer / The Dove . . .

Long before he had ever heard of the Testament of Eadgyth, James grew up believing, or at least fearing, that the world's last days were indeed near. Legends of the last days had rattled around the house in Buxton since James had been taken in as a boy, and had listened wide-eyed to the lurid speculations of the older brothers.

As he grew, however, he learned that Franciscans had always been fascinated by legends of the Apocalypse. And as his soul and mind were opened up by the new mood of scholarship that embraced Europe, he thought he became sensible. Pragmatic. He put aside the grim prognostications, the peculiar antique longing for the end of things.

But now the quality of the whispering changed. Dreams that had once clung to the year of Our Lord 1000 accreted like ivy over another milestone year: AD 1500. That was not a remote future. That was a year James expected to live to see; he would not yet be forty.

And when the abbot took him aside one day, and showed him the abbey's secret library, where for two centuries the brothers had been labouring over spidery designs for engines of war – engines that might bring about that final catastrophe – then, in some secret library of his own soul, he began to feel afraid.

For Harry Wooler, it was the Dove himself whose beating wings cast shadows over his own life, on the day his own small world came to a kind of end, as his father lay dying.

Harry, just seventeen years old, was forced to lean over a face already like a skull, smell breath that still stank of ale, and listen while his father whispered in his ear a family tale centuries old, a tale of ancestors called Orm and Eadgyth, and a strange, dark prophecy of a man called the Dove who would shape all history. In the end this morbid tale merged seamlessly into his father's ale-drowned death-rattle. But Harry was the eldest son, and it was his turn to receive the legend, as had his father, an eldest son before him – it was his duty to listen. And after all, his father had driven away everybody else, his mother, his sister, his brothers.

So Harry listened, and after his father died he locked this morbid stuff away in his heart, and tried to imagine it had gone away.

But it had not.

II

AD 1481

The January morning was still grey when Harry Wooler walked into London from the north, passing through the wall at Newgate. It was here that cattle, sheep, pigs and chickens were funnelled into the city to the shouts of the drovers, a steady flow of provision pouring into an ever-hungry gullet. It was like walking into one immense farmyard, Harry thought. Further south he came to the slaughterhouse district where the animals were killed, skinned, and dismembered, and then continued their journey in bits to the butchers' shops and the tanners'. Here he found himself walking on a slick of blood and animal guts, steaming in the cold air, and there was an almighty stink of shit and piss, and the iron tang of blood.

Then he pushed on south to Cheapside, where the farmyard bleats were drowned out by the clank of metal on anvil and the pounding of nails into wood or leather, as the blacksmiths, goldsmiths, silversmiths, tanners, dyers and potters all laboured, and the cowshed stink was replaced by the stench of the fullers' urine jars. Cheapside was a magnificent, unending festival of trade. You could buy anything you wanted here, from a hot veal pie to a flagon of beer, from a Flemish-style hat to Italian-style shoes, from imports like French linen and Spanish silk to eastern spices and Scandinavian walrus ivory – from the words of an apocalyptic preacher that would fire your soul, to the moist quim of a girl to soothe your body. For Harry this was a wonderful place to be, for all the stinks and the filth and the crowding, and the beggars that swarmed like crows pleading for spare farthings.

Harry was Oxford born and bred, but he was a merchant, and England's capital of business felt like a second home to him. And in

Cheapside industry and commerce pulsed as nowhere else in England.

But today Harry was not here for trade.

He pushed further south still, past the walls of Saint Paul's, and through narrowing streets lined with warehouses. Their walls were plastered with posters bearing apocalyptic pronouncements from the Bible. He looked at the posters curiously, for they were printed, a novelty still rare in Oxford.

He came at last to the river bank. He could just make out the brown, filthy water through a forest of cranes and ships' masts and furled sails, and he could hear the cursing of the stevedores in a dozen languages. He was near the old bridge, the only span over the river to the south bank. To his left there was the ugly pile of the Tower, to his right the great palace of Westminster with the abbey beyond, in their suburb around the bend of the river. He turned right and walked perhaps a quarter of a mile along the bank. When he came to the ancient dock road called the Strand he cut north, heading inland past more ware-houses and factories.

And here he found, just where the monk's letter had described, a small, gloomy parish church, its roughly cut stone stained black by city soot. Chantries clustered around the church, chapels devoted to the souls of the long-dead rich. A stone tablet told him that the church was dedicated to Saint Agnes, a virginal martyr of Rome, and his sister's patron saint.

He felt a deep reluctance to enter. But it was to here that he had been summoned.

The letter from the monk had arrived in a pile of business cor-respondence. At his home in Oxford, Harry Wooler had read the letter, from a Carthusian called Geoffrey Cotesford, with a sinking heart, for it concerned a matter of conscience. Harry didn't regard himself as a sinful man, but he preferred to stick to commerce, and leave the affairs of the soul to others. But he could scarcely ignore this summons, for it had concerned his sister, Agnes, lost since Harry was a boy.

The church's heavy wooden door was open. Harry stepped inside. The church was cold, its heavy stone walls sucking out the heat, and the air was thick with incense. A man swept the floor with a cane broom, a portly fellow in a loose black robe, but otherwise the church was empty. Harry knelt at a pew, crossed himself, and uttered brief prayers. Then he walked up the church's central aisle to the altar.

He paused by an elaborate tomb that had been set against one wall, cut from some black stone. It was on two levels. Above rested the figure of a man of about fifty, handsome in life, well-dressed in a robe like a Roman toga, with his hands clasped in prayer. But on the level below lay the same man given up to decay, his clothes rotted to rags, his skin peeled back to reveal a cage of ribs, those praying fingers reduced to bone.

Harry didn't like transi tombs. The hideously realistic corpses always reminded him of his own father's death, and his final morbid mutterings.

But Harry was twenty-five now. He was a merchant, as his father had been before him, and his grandfather too – his family as far back as anybody cared to mention. As their name implied, the Woolers sold prime wool from the heart of England to the continent. Trade was what interested Harry – trade, and stories of exploration, of Prince Henry and his school of navigation in Portugal, of new routes to India and China and perhaps even to countries nobody had even heard of yet. Harry didn't like transi tombs and chantries. He didn't even much like churches, he admitted. Give him Cheapside any day, rather than this!

'You don't seem comfortable.'

The man who had been sweeping was resting on his broom, studying Harry. Harry saw that he had a crucifix on a chain around his neck, and that his black robe looked like a habit.

'I'm sorry, brother. I didn't realise – I would have paid my respects—'

The brother brushed that away. He might have been about forty, a tonsure neatly cut into greying hair. He looked sleek and comfortable, but his brown eyes showed a sharp intelligence. 'And I should not have crept up on you – not before a tomb like this, at any rate! But I don't apologise for reading your soul, for it's written on your face.'

Harry felt resentful. 'I'm not here to pray but to meet a man.'

'Geoffrey Cotesford from York?'

'You know him?'

'Only too well.' The friar stuck out his hand. 'I'm Geoffrey. I am glad to meet you, Harry Wooler.'

Harry shook the hand uncertainly.

'I was early.' The friar held up his broom. 'The door was unlocked – careless, that – and I saw the broom resting against a wall, and I thought I should make myself useful. You have a businesslike look about you – I expected that. I'm here on business myself, in fact.'

'I thought you Carthusians were contemplative.'

'Well, we are, some of us. But we have other vocations. I always had too restless a mind to be bothering God with my fragmentary prayers. So I became involved in my house's business affairs. We Carthusians make a bit of a living from the wool trade too, in fact. And I have always been more interested in the souls of others than in my own, a disadvantage for a contemplative! *Your* soul is as transparently displayed as this poor old fellow's desiccated heart, Harry.'

'It's just so gloomy,' Harry admitted. 'Transi tombs and chantries, monks murmuring your name long after you are dead. The priests say we must all long for the afterlife. Fair enough. But why long for *death*?'

Geoffrey studied him. 'Ah, but death sometimes longs for us. You're a young man, Harry, and like all old fools I envy you your youth. But as you grow older you'll develop a sense of the past. And our past contains a great calamity, a time when the dead invaded the shore of the living.'

'You mean the Mortality.'

'The Great Mortality, yes. The Big Death. My own grandfather told me tales of what *his* grandfather, who lived through it, saw for himself. England used to be crowded, you know! But everybody was stirred around by war, and the cities were brimming with filth ... Well. We were ripe for the plague. In London, *half* the population died off in a few years. Think of how it was for the living, Harry, as all those faces around you melted away. The shock left scars in their souls, I think. No wonder they carved these transi tombs, memorials of a world become a vast boneyard.'

Harry was restless, feeling he was being preached at. 'You wrote to me about Agnes. Where is my sister?'

'Far from here, I'm afraid. She's in York. And you must travel to her; she can't come to you. You'll see why. But she's asking for you. Big brother Harry! And, you know, to understand your sister's situation, you will have to think about history – I mean, your family's. Your ancestors weren't always wool traders. You'll see, you'll see ...'

'My business – I've work to do.'

'I know,' said Geoffrey. 'But you'll come with me even so, won't you? A spark of duty is bright under that woollen merchant's shirt. I see that in you too.'

These words made Harry feel trapped. With a mumbled apology he hurried down the aisle to the door, and drank in the reassuringly foetid air of the Strand.

III

Spain crushed James's soul.

The mule train plodded across a landscape like a vast dusty table, where nothing grew but scrub grass and rough untended olive trees, nothing moved but skinny sheep, and there was no sound but the raucous singing of the muleteers echoing from ruined battlements, and the thin mewl of patient buzzards. And, James knew, the journey could only end with more strangeness. For he was travelling to Seville, where, it was said, the Anti-Christ was soon to be born.

His companion and employer, Grace Bigod, was not sympathetic. She was a formidable woman in her forties, perhaps twenty years older than James. Her face was beautiful in a strong, stern, proud way; her greying blonde hair was swept back from her brow. And, sharp, bored, she picked on James. 'What's the matter, Friar James? All a bit much for you?'

'Everything's so strange.'

'Well, of course it's strange. We're a long way from England now.' Her fine nostrils flared as she sucked in the air. 'Smell it! That spicy dryness, the wind straight off the flats of the Maghrib. My family have roots in the Outremer, you know.'

He nodded. It was well known in James's house in Buxton that Grace and her family were descended from a woman called Joan, who had fled Jerusalem when it fell to the Saracens more than two centuries ago.

'Maybe the country of the Outremer is like this – hot, dry, dusty. Maybe there is something in the very air that pulls at my blood. Or maybe it's the stink of the last Muslims in Spain, holed up in Granada. This is the crucible of the whole world, James! The place where the sword-tip of Christianity meets the scimitar-tip of the Moors, a single point of white heat. What do you think?'

James saw only a landscape wrecked by war and emptied by plague. He turned inward, trying not to see. He longed to be safely enclosed within the reassuring routines of his Franciscan monastery.

But Grace and her forebears were generous supporters of the house, and had been for generations. It was through her family's influence that the house was committed to its strange and dark project, a secretive work centuries old. It was through Grace's influence that James, who longed only for a life of scholarship devoted to the peace of Christ, found himself studying terrible weapons of war.

And it was through her influence, her peculiar desire to bring on the end of the world, that he had been dragged from his book-lined cell and been brought all the way across Europe to this desolate, prickly landscape. Her purpose was to sell her Engines of God to the King and Queen of Spain, and she had a copy of the Codex of Aethelmaer, and a summary of two centuries' worth of its development, tucked in her bags.

James did not want to be here. But there was purpose in all things, he told himself. God would show him the true path through the strange experiences to come. He crossed himself and mumbled a prayer.

Grace watched him, hard-eyed, analytical, and she laughed. She was a vigorous, physical woman. Sometimes she stared at him, as if wondering what shape his body was under his habit. And at night, when they stopped in towns or taverns, she would come close to him, brushing past so he could smell her hair, and see the softness of her skin. James knew she felt not the remotest attraction to him, and that this was all part of her bullying of him. But he was unused to women, and his youthful body's reaction to her teasing left him tormented. She made him feel crushed, pale and pasty and worthless, less than a man. And she knew it.

It was a relief when the caravan at last reached Seville, and James was able to get away from her company, if only for a short while. But Seville had its own mysteries.

The Guadalquivir reminded him a little of the Thames in London. Navigable from the sea, the river was crowded with ships, and the wharves and jetties were a hive of activity, where sailors and dockers, beggars, whores and urchins worked and laughed, fought and argued in a dozen languages – the usual folk of the river, James thought, just as you would find in London. Trade shaped the city's communities too; Seville was home to officers and sailors who had participated in Spain's explorations of the Ocean Sea, and there were Genoese and Florentine bankers and merchants everywhere.

But in other ways Seville was quite unlike London. He walked to the site of a grand cathedral, bristling with scaffolding. It would be the largest in the world, it was said. But it had been built on the site of the city's Moorish mosque, and a surviving muezzin tower still loomed over it; slim and exquisite, the tower would always draw the eye away from the solid pile of the Christian church.

And just over the plaza from the cathedral was an old Moorish fortress-palace which the Moors called the *al-qasr al-Mubarak*, and the Christians called the Alcazar. James peered curiously through its arched doorways. Though the Moors had been expelled from Seville by the city's conquerors, later generations of Christian rulers had brought back craftsmen from Granada to work on these buildings, maintaining and even enhancing them.

Seville was not like London, then, where with their forts and cathedrals the conquering Normans had erased any symbol of the old Saxon state. Here the spirit of the Moors lived on in a Christian country.

Perhaps things were going to change, however. Two hundred and thirty years after its conquest Seville was still the southernmost Christian city in Spain. The great tide of Reconquest had stalled. The Christians were distracted by conflicts between their own rival kingdoms, and their vast project to repopulate the occupied country was diluted by the Mortality; where once the Moors had turned the land green, now only Christian sheep grazed. Seville remained a city on the cusp of a great change, James thought. Perhaps it was no wonder that apocalyptic legends had gathered around the place.

But James, in his first walk around this strange, complicated, muddled city, did not see a need for cleansing, but a kind of mixed-up human vitality he rather relished.

Near the Alcazar he came across two girls who sat on a bench, eating oranges they unpeeled with their thumbs. No older than twelve or thirteen, dark, shy-looking, they giggled with each other as they ate, but kept a wary eye on the folk around them. The girls both had yellow crosses stitched to their blouses. They were Jews, then. They had to wear ugly symbols on their clothing, but at least they were here. In England there were no Jewish girls like this, laughing in the sun and eating oranges.

When the girls saw James watching them, they looked away nervously. Embarrassed, annoyed at himself for frightening them, he hurried on.

He made his way back to the river, and walked to a complicated pontoon bridge of seventeen barges.

And across that bridge he glimpsed the brooding pile of the castle of Triana. It was the headquarters of the Inquisition.

IV

Before travelling to York, Harry returned to Oxford for a few days to put his affairs in order.

Then he joined Geoffrey Cotesford on the great north road, the old Roman route that ran from London to Scotland. Harry would have preferred to make his way by sea, which would have been far more comfortable, but Geoffrey pleaded poverty. So they clattered away in their cart, Harry wincing as they hit every pothole. In places the way was difficult because of fences left untended, bridges unrepaired, work left unfinished for more than a century because there was nobody to do it.

Geoffrey pointed out features of the landscape. 'Still empty – I told you!'

Here was a town half given over to farmland. Here were villages abandoned altogether, the roofless houses slumped like old men, the fields overgrown. Swathes of the country had been given over to herds of sheep, which bleated piously as they nibbled the grass that grew around the ruins. Harry usually rode past such grassy mounds of tumbled walls and abandoned buildings without looking too closely; they were just part of the landscape. But Geoffrey was pitiless.

'The country has a way of cleansing itself. Crows and rats and flies! Even they have a purpose in God's grand scheme. But *we* have never come back, Harry; we have never taken back our villages.'

'Why are we talking about the Big Death again?'

'Because it shaped your family, Harry – or, rather, reshaped it. This is what I have discovered about you. The empty world after the Mortality was quite different from what went before. Suddenly there were too few folk to get the work done; a bad lord could not hold onto a man, for there was always work somewhere else. There were revolts as the nobles tried to stuff everything back into Pandora's box, but it was too late. And opportunities opened up.'

'Such as for my family.'

'Yes! Your grandfathers saw the chance to slip the bonds of allegiance to the lords. You became merchants, wealthy in your own right, and you called yourselves Wooler – you had no surname I can trace before.'

'And before the Mortality? What were we then?'

'You were soldiers – perhaps all the way back to the days of William. It's said you had an ancestor who came over with the Conqueror. But then every family in England says that. Certainly your forefathers fought alongside Edward Longshanks.'

'The Hammer of the Scots.' This story of a lost and different age rather thrilled Harry the merchant.

'And before *that* they rode with him to the Holy Land, for Edward was a great crusader. But to your family the crusades weren't a mere adventure. To them, the Holy Land was home – or had been.'

And he told Harry of his ancestor Saladin, born and raised in the Holy Land, who had come to England, and fought in Spain, and then joined a crusade. Surviving, he returned to England to start a family of his own. 'Saladin was always determined that his family should remember the Testament of Eadgyth; he thought it contained important lessons for the future. Your own father taught it to you, didn't he? But other prophecies accreted around you too . . .'

The news about Saladin was disturbing for Harry. 'Then I might have Saracen blood in my veins.'

'A dash of it, probably,' Geoffrey said. 'Don't worry, I'm keeping this to myself. I wouldn't wish to harm your business reputation. Be grateful there's no sign of Jewry in your blood line. But then, Edward Longshanks expelled all the Jews from England nearly two hundred years ago, by God. We were the first in Europe to do it, and we set a fashion, didn't we?'

Harry, impatient, asked, 'Just tell me simply – why are you so interested in my family's past?'

'Because you will need to understand your own complicated history if you're to understand what has become of your sister. Poor Agnes! I got involved, you know, because my house is not far from the parish church where she lives.'

'She lives *in* a church?'

'You'll see. I was brought to her. But she was calling for you, the brother she hasn't seen for ten years. You always protected her, she said.'

'So I did, I suppose,' Harry said uneasily. 'My father was always short with her. And when he was in his cups – I deflected his blows a few times. He repented before he died; I forgave him.' Harry didn't enjoy talking of his family's past; it hadn't been a happy time. 'But my sister disappeared – she ran away, she was no older than ten. We heard nothing more of her.'

'You didn't try to look for her?'

'At first. But after my father died I took over the business, and found he'd run it down – squandered the legacy of my grandfather. It was hard work restoring it. I had no time.'

'I understand. And in all probability your sister didn't want to be found. But she did not die, Harry; somehow she survived. And she found a place in the world. But eventually her troubles overwhelmed her, and she asked for you. So I came to find you.'

'It's good of you to do this,' Harry said, though he felt resentful rather than grateful. 'To come all this way, to give up your own business for her.'

'You're welcome. But it isn't just charity that motivates me. I rather think your sister's plight has a wider significance.' He eyed Harry. 'I know you're a sceptic, Harry, about matters beyond the material, and that's healthy. But the fact is your family is steeped in prophecy ...'

Harry didn't want to hear this.

They lapsed into silence, as the countryside of England, echoing only to the bleating of the sheep, rolled past them.

V

York, within its rectangle of much-battered, much-repaired walls, was bustling, a city of trade. But it was dominated by its immense cathedral, the newest sections of which, only a few years old, were fresh-cut, bright and sharp. Geoffrey said the minster had been built on the site of a Roman military headquarters, and that the city after the Romans had become a sort of Viking trading capital, a tradition of commerce that still lingered. There were layers of history written in the stones, Geoffrey said, layers that shaped the present.

They stayed the night in the hall of Harry's merchants' guild. It was a grand building, with religious paintings hanging from the stone walls and long tables groaning with food and drink. Harry was made welcome. There was much business to discuss, for Harry only rarely travelled this way, and it was a great relief for him to be able to escape from Geoffrey and history and his family's complicated past, and to immerse himself in the real world of commodities and prices. Geoffrey excused himself and went to sit with the apprentices at the hall's service end. Later Harry found him in the basement, where the guild ran a small hospital for the poor, who were expected to pray for the souls of their benefactors.

In the morning they mounted their cart again and set off to find Harry's sister.

The church she had attached herself to, another Saint Agnes's, was a few miles north of the city walls. It was a small, modest establishment at the centre of a village built of stone recovered from a much larger, abandoned settlement, whose ruins lay all around. The church itself was quite new, in the Perpendicular style. But Harry saw it had been built on older foundations of blackened stone – perhaps a Saxon chapel burned down by the Normans; there had been a lot of that in this area.

They were greeted by the parish priest, a kindly, elderly man called Arthur. It was Arthur who had first called in Geoffrey to help him cope with Agnes's requests. 'But you must understand we very much value your sister's presence with us here,' he told Harry. 'Very much. She brings the love of God into our small lives . . .'

Geoffrey led Harry, not to the door of the church as he had expected, but to a side wall. Here a kind of cell protruded from the church's wall, with no door, and no window save for a slit.

And here, Geoffrey said, was his sister: bricked up in the cell within which she would spend her whole life. Harry stared in horror.

Geoffrey touched his shoulder. 'You must try to understand. This is the life your sister has chosen for herself. And she serves her people, you know. As the father said, most parishes are proud to have an anchoress attached to their church.'

A voice floated up from the slit window. 'Geoffrey Cotesford? Is that you?'

The tone was deeper than it had been, softer, but it was unmistakable. Harry's heart thumped; he had not realised how much he had missed his little sister.

'It is Geoffrey.'

'I knew you'd return.'

'Your faith in your brother was justified too.'

She gasped. 'Harry?'

Harry forced himself to speak. 'I'm here, Agnes.'

'Then come to my window.'

Harry knelt down. The window was a slit, just large enough to pass food and waste. Only a little light leaked into the cell within. He could see another window on the far wall where the anchoress was able to look into the church. The room was simply laid out, with a bed, a bench, a table, a crucifix on the wall. On the table were two books, a leather-bound Bible, and a copy of the *Ancrene Wisse*, the manual of the anchoress. The room's only other feature was a shallow trench in the floor. It puzzled Harry, who knew little of the lifestyle of an anchoress, a walled-in hermit.

And through the squint, this slit window, his sister's familiar blue eyes gazed out at him. 'I prayed you would come. I knew you would. You always did protect me, Harry.'

But, he thought, I did not protect you from this morbid fate. 'I have news of the family,' he said.

'My father is dead,' Agnes said softly. 'I know that much.'

'Mother is well. She misses you.'

'Tell her I pray for her . . .'

Geoffrey interjected gently, 'I will leave you to talk. But we must turn to business. Harry needs to understand why you summoned him, Agnes.'

'I would not have disturbed you,' she said. 'But I had to.'

'Why?'

'Because of what I found. In this cell . . .'

And she spoke of family legends: of Orm, who may or may not have sailed with the Conqueror, and Eadgyth, or Edith, the wife he may or may not have found demented and raving in the ruins of an old Saxon church outside York, while William's Norman thugs rampaged across the north of England.

'Do you know why I was called Agnes? It is part of the old story – my mother told me this – in every generation there is an Agnes, so we remember that Eadgyth's church was dedicated to that saint. And it is said that Eadgyth returned to the church later, when she sickened, and her mind failed. Poor Orm had to seek her here again.

'When I ran away from home, I was only ten years old. I had travelled no further than a day's walk from home. I had no idea what shape England was, Harry! The only place I had ever heard of that had anything to do with the family was Eadgyth's church near York. So I made my way here.'

'This is Eadgyth's church?'

'Rebuilt since then – but yes, it is her church.'

'Quite a journey for a child,' Geoffrey murmured.

'I hardened.'

Harry thought there was a whole desperate saga contained in those two words. He was full of guilt.

She whispered, 'I worked here, on the farms. I knew how to shear a sheep. Then I worked for the parish. And, in time, God and Father Arthur granted me the privilege of this, my enclosed life of prayer. My only stipulation was that my cell had to be here, in this corner of the church, on the old foundations.'

Harry guessed, 'Because this was where Eadgyth had hidden.'

'And where she came back to at the end of her life. I know this, Harry, because *she scraped an account of her visions into the wall*. The lettering is faded and lichen-choked, half-buried by rubble, old-fashioned and hard to decipher – but it is here. And as I dig my trench, I have uncovered it steadily.'

Harry felt a return of that uncomfortable dread, a sense of enclosure. He wanted nothing to do with this antique strangeness. 'I know the story of the man called the Dove,' he said. 'Who will be the spawn of the spider, and so on. And in the last days before the end of the world

225

is due, he must have his head turned west to the Ocean Sea ...'

Geoffrey quoted from memory, '"All this I have witnessed / I and my mothers. / Send the Dove west! O, send him west!"'

'*There is more*,' Agnes whispered. 'Orm remembered twelve lines. That is what we have come to know as Eadgyth's Testament. But there is more.'

'More lines scraped in the wall?'

'Yes,' Geoffrey said. 'Ten more lines, Harry. In which Eadgyth records her vision of what would become of the world if the Testament was *not* fulfilled – of a future in which the Dove turned, not west as he should, but east. I can see you're having trouble believing any of this, Harry. But when I tell you of this hideous future you will see why I summoned you here. Not just for your sister. We have to work out what to do about this. *For we cannot let this dreadful future come about*.' He crossed himself.

Harry felt his whole life hingeing on this moment. He longed to flee from this madness, the woman in the hole, the terrible words scribbled on a wall, the memory of his dying, drunken father. But, as Geoffrey had seen, he had a sense of duty which would not allow him to walk away.

He said impulsively, 'Agnes – never mind prophecies. I still don't understand. What made you do this? Why run away – why throw away your life – why wall yourself up in a cell?'

'For the love of God.'

There must be more. 'And?'

She sighed. 'And because I thought I would be safe,' she said softly. 'If I am in here, far from Oxford, encased in stone, *he* could not reach me again.'

He thought he understood at last. 'Our father.'

'Yes. It was not until Geoffrey came that I learned he was dead.' She closed her eyes.

'What did he do, Agnes?'

'He was maddened. He was drunk. He didn't know what he was doing. I forgive him; I have prayed for him. But I was ten years old. I feared that if I stayed, if I became a woman, and if his seed was planted in me – I left to save myself, and him, from that terrible sin.'

'Oh, Agnes. I didn't know. You say I protected you. But I failed, I failed—'

'It wasn't your fault, but *his*. Agnes is the name he gave me. But Agnes was a holy virgin. I am no Agnes.'

Impulsively he pushed his hand through the slit window. Tentatively his sister clasped his fingers, and then he felt the softness of her cheek on his hand.

Later he asked Geoffrey about the trench in the cell. It was Agnes's own grave, Geoffrey said, a grave she scraped every day, for an anchoress was commanded to keep her death before her eyes at all times. Agnes would live and die in her stone box, and when her life was done she would lower herself into her self-dug tomb.

VI

Grace Bigod and Friar James had come to Seville to meet a man called Diego Ferron, a Dominican friar with contacts in the court of the Spanish monarchs. He was attached to a monastery outside the walls of the city, and had offices, it was said, in the palace complex of the Alcazar itself.

Ferron kept them waiting for days after their arrival. The date he suggested for their meeting, he told them in his note, was 'suitable for our joint purpose'. James didn't know what this meant.

On their tenth day in Seville, Grace and James were at last summoned to Ferron's presence, at a private house in an old part of the city. When they arrived early at his house, they were led by a barefoot servant through a complicated archway into a garden, where water bubbled languidly from a fountain into a pool full of carp. The house was clearly Moorish, presumably abandoned by its owner on the fall of the city more than two hundred years ago. At least the Christian owners of this place had taken care to preserve what they had taken, though the furniture, lumpy wooden chairs, benches and low tables, would not have looked out of place in the home of a well-to-do Englishman, and walls which still bore Arabic inscriptions in praise of Allah were now studded with crucifixes and statues of the Virgin.

Friar Diego Ferron walked in briskly, introduced himself, ensured they had been served with tea and sweetmeats, and sat upright on a severe wooden chair. His habit was adorned with a magnificent black and white cowl made of some very fine wool. He was perhaps forty, his tonsured hair jet black and well groomed. He was a handsome man, his features sharp, his eyes brown, and his skin, shining with oils, was so dark that if not for his vestments James might have thought he was a Moor himself.

James was uneasy in his presence. When the brothers in Buxton had learned he was to meet Dominican friars in Spain, they had laughed. 'They're an odd lot, those Dominicans,' one comfortable old friar had said. Saint Dominic, fired by his experience of the Albigensian heresy in France, had dedicated his order solely to the task of fighting heresy in all its forms. 'And they're worst of all in Spain. Mad as a bat.'

Ferron did not strike James as mad, but businesslike. Certainly he did not waste any time on pleasantries.

He focused his attentions on Grace. 'First let me be sure you understand my role in the court of our glorious monarchs, Fernando of Aragon and Isabel of Castile.' He spoke fluent Latin. 'You wrote to court to request an audience with Tomas de Torquemada. The friar is a Dominican colleague of mine, and was confessor of the Queen.'

'Yes—'

'Friar Torquemada is now working with the Inquisition. The Queen's confessor is now Friar Hernando de Talavera, a Hieronymite. Pious, ascetic – a good man. The second of the Queen's chief prelates is Cardinal de Mendoza, the archbishop of Seville. These persons will be involved in assessing your proposal for the court. I myself am on the staff of Friar Torquemada.'

'You work for the Inquisition, then,' Grace said.

'Yes. But I have good relations with both Friar de Talavera and the archbishop, as well as Friar Torquemada, and so he passed on your request to me as a suitable first point of contact.'

This politicking among holy men baffled James, and dismayed him obscurely.

Grace bowed. 'I'm sure we will be able to do business together, brother.'

'That's what I'm here to find out,' Ferron said slickly, quite coldly. 'For it is business we are talking about, isn't it? You are here to sell arms to the monarchs. These weapons, the Engines of God as you refer to them.'

'There is more to it than that—'

'We have arms. We have cannon, we have arquebuses.'

'But nothing like the weapons I can offer you,' Grace said urgently. 'The engines are founded on the words of a prophecy, retrieved by my ancestor Joan of the Outremer from a cache beneath the mosque of this very city. The designs have been developed in secret for *two hundred years* by Franciscans, followers of the sage Roger Bacon – perhaps you have heard of him. Brother James here has studied the developments closely and can tell you all you wish to know.'

Ferron's glance flickered over James. 'I already know the most salient fact. That these weapons of yours are decidedly expensive.'

'Decidedly better than anything you have. And decidedly what you need for the coming war. I do not mean the conflict with the Moors of Granada. I mean the war to end wars that will follow.' She paused, her face intense, beautiful. 'Brother, I know of this, deep in my bones. My family is of the Outremer, the Holy Land – we lived in Jerusalem itself. We were expelled by the Saracens in the same decade as Seville fell to the Christian armies. This was over two hundred years ago, and we still bear the scars in our souls. They are scars of the long war with the Muslims which has been waged since the death of Muhammad himself. And *it is a war Christendom is losing.*'

Ferron sat back, startled.

She had seized control of the exchange, James saw. They were the same age, roughly, Grace and Ferron. Both strong, both determined, both combative. They would be formidable enemies, still more formidable if they became allies.

James knew, though, that any cold-eyed observer of history would draw the same conclusion as Grace. Ever since the loss of Jerusalem in Joan's day, Christendom had been on the retreat.

The problem was the rise of the Turks. A decade after Seville fell to the Christians, the Mamluk Turks defeated the Mongols – the first significant defeat suffered by the nomads across three continents. It was a turning point for the Islamic empires. The Mamluks, rampant, marched on; within decades they had obliterated the last trace of the old crusader states. Eventually the Mamluks fell to new waves of Mongol invaders. But out of their shattered polities rose a new nation of Turks called the Ottomans, who dismembered what was left of the old East Roman domains. The last Roman emperor died fighting for Constantinople, when the old city fell in 1453. A jubilant Sultan Mehmet crowed that Rome itself was next, that soon he would be feeding his horses on oats from the high altar of Saint Peter's. And in the year 1480, just a year ago, as if making good that promise, Mehmet had assaulted Italy.

'Thus from Jerusalem to Rome Christendom is in retreat,' Grace said relentlessly. 'Only here in Spain are Christian armies taking the fight to the Muslims. Only here, under Isabel and Fernando, are Christians winning. And that,' she said, 'is the key to the future.'

Ferron considered. 'But the monarchs are barely at ease on their own thrones. Their marriage united the Christian kingdoms of Spain, but they must deal with over-mighty nobles, empty coffers, a mixed population of Christians, Jews and Muslims – and, of course, the great canker of Granada, whose emir has refused to pay his proper tribute for fifteen years. The final war against Islam?' He smiled, languid. 'Let's be rid of the Moors in Granada first and then we'll see.'

Grace said urgently, 'Friar Ferron, I accept what you say. But time is short.'

'Tell me what you mean.'

And she told him briefly of another prophecy: her family's legend of the Testament of Eadgyth. Of the mysterious, crucial figure known by his three titles, the Dove, the spawn of the spider, and the Christ-bearer. Of warring destinies, which must be resolved 'in the last days' – which might come as soon as the year 1500.

'We have two decades, then,' Ferron said drily. 'Not long to conclude a war that has lasted for eight hundred years! But why do *you* want this, lady?'

'This is my destiny. My family's destiny, as we have perceived it since the days of Joan of the Outremer.'

Ferron pursed his lips. 'And you are unmarried. No husband – no children.'

'My life has a single purpose, friar. As I said, that has been the case since I was twenty. What need have I of children when I have the Engines of God?'

James shared a glance with Ferron, one of the few times the two of them communicated. Even Ferron looked disturbed by her intensity.

But he steepled his fingers and pressed the tips against his lips. 'What first? We must discuss the provenance of your various prophecies. But it occurs to me that the time is so short that this Dove of yours, if he exists, *must already have been born*. The Holy Brotherhood is rather good at finding people. I'll pass this on; we will find your Dove, if he lives.'

A young monk came into the room and apologetically whispered in Ferron's ear.

Ferron stood. 'We will continue our business later. For now, please, join me. I asked you to delay our meeting until today because I thought that you, as guests in our city, would like to witness the first triumph of the Inquisition.'

Grace stood with polite eagerness. 'And what triumph is that?'

Ferron smiled. 'We call it the Act of Faith.'

Auto-da-fé.

VII

That February day, the procession formed up before Seville's unfinished cathedral. At its head was a company of Dominicans, barefoot, with their heads covered by black and white cowls like Ferron's. They bore the banner of the Inquisition, a knotted cross flanked by the olive branch of peace and the sword of retribution. Behind the monks walked magistrates, then soldiers carrying wood for the fires.

And then came the condemned – seven of them, six men and a woman, flanked by soldiers bearing lances to ensure they could not escape. More hooded monks followed, chanting for repentance, and finally drummers who hammered out a heavy, doleful rhythm.

Ferron led Grace and James to join a gaggle of other notable citizens who trailed the drummers. They passed along narrow streets crowded with people who came to stare at the condemned. Some of them were foreigners, James thought, Portuguese explorers or Italian merchants, ambassadors from an entirely different world, who watched this grue-some parade with sneers of disgust – and yet they watched.

James himself was horribly fascinated by the faces of the condemned. They wore yellow gowns, carried candles, and had nooses around their necks. They were influential conversos – Jews converted to Christianity, or even the descendants of converts – whose treacherous reversion to Judaism had been rooted out, tried and sentenced. One young man looked frightened, and he continually crossed himself and mumbled prayers; if he was secretly Jewish he didn't look it now. The others merely looked stunned, or disbelieving.

The procession snaked out of the city walls to an open field. Here bare wooden stakes had been set up in a row, their purpose blunt and obvious. The condemned were tied to these stakes. One man

232

struggled, another wept, and that younger man crossed himself until his arms were pinned. The rest bore the procedure in stoical silence.

Ferron pointed out one Dominican, a tall, pale figure with a flattened nose, like a boxer's. 'Torquemada,' he murmured. 'Your first contact, madam. Not yet an Inquisitor, actually, but his soul yearns for the good work. Ferociously pious and yet a master of organisation. Perhaps every cleansing needs a cool mind like his!'

The leader of the Dominicans stepped forward, and began to deliver a sermon in windy Spanish, laden with quotations from Revelation.

Ferron whispered to Grace, 'He is Friar Vincent Ojeda, of the Monastery of San Pablo. He led the commission which established the Inquisition in the first place, to root out weakness and treachery in our new state. For connoisseurs of apocalyptic preaching, his sermons are collectors' items,' he said. 'But this is a moment for which he has campaigned all his adult life.'

A portly, intense man, Ojeda was alight with joy in this killing place, James thought. And if James was watching Ojeda, so, he found, Ferron was watching him.

'I wonder what you are thinking, young brother. Your expression is complicated. Are you concerned that the innocent may be wrongly condemned? It is possible; we are human. But remember the words of the Pope's legate at the time of the Albigensian heresy: "Slay all. God will know His own."'

'That would be small comfort were I at the stake today.'

'True, but you aren't at the stake, are you? I've known your type before. You are too intelligent to be truly pious. What do you think of us? What do you think of me?'

James decided to answer honestly. 'I think you are a man of affairs,' he said. 'Of business. Of this world, more than the next. You see this Inquisition as a way for you to achieve your goals, and for your monarchs to build a strong and unified state.'

Ferron's head swivelled, sleek. He said to Grace, 'Your adviser has a mind of his own, I see.'

Grace sneered at James, effortlessly crushing him; he looked away. 'Unfortunately, yes,' she said. 'He's one of the brightest of his generation, so his abbot assured me. And he's an expert on the Engines of God. But he shows an unruly independence of thought.'

'Have you always been "unruly", boy?'

'My father is a farmer,' James admitted. 'We were not rich. As I grew he passed me into the care of the Franciscans. He said I was too intelligent to be of any use behind the plough.'

Ferron barked laughter. 'A sensible man. But I'd have strapped you to the damn plough and beaten the brains out of you. However you're not entirely wrong. One *can* unite one's fellows behind a holy banner. And we need uniting, we squabbling Christians, for we face our mortal enemy in Islam in Granada, and our own cities are full of Moors and Jews. We did not cleanse ourselves in the past, as you English did long ago. But once we have been purified by the Inquisition we will be in a position to conclude a Reconquest that has been stalled for far too long.'

When Ojeda was done thrilling the gathered mob, a notary stepped forward and read out the crimes of each penitent. One had engaged in Jewish rituals; one had mocked the Host which was the body of Christ; one had prepared his lamb meat in accordance with Jewish instruction; and so on. They had all confessed to this when 'put to the question'.

Now the penitents were given one final choice. If they made a full admission of guilt, repented their sins, and converted to the faith of Christ, they would be spared the fire through prior strangulation. All but one man submitted, and knelt before the Inquisitors, who brought out their ropes.

It astonished James how hard it was, even for these practised killers, to crush the life out of a human being; it was long minutes before the last of them succumbed.

When the others slumped lifeless at their posts, the last man was to be burned. A citizen came forward with a brand to light the pyre. He had been promised indulgences for this holy deed. He looked fearful; the brand quivered in his hand.

Ferron, coldly excited, murmured to Grace, 'Look at the faces of the crowd. Look at their pious horror! It all creates an atmosphere. You know, the whole court buzzes with talk of the Anti-Christ, who will be born in Seville.'

Grace said, 'All Europe talks of it. I told you, Christendom resounds to news of the victories in Spain. Perhaps, they say, the King is the Hidden One, he who will defeat the Anti-Christ, and smash Islam, and win Jerusalem.'

'Yes. And perhaps Isabel is the Apocalyptic Woman. Perhaps Isabel and Fernando have been sent to cleanse the world in preparation for the Day of Judgement ... Such things are murmured by the court prelates in the ears of the monarchs. And yet, at moments like these, how plausible they seem.'

James was appalled by such near-blasphemous flattery. But he dared say nothing.

234

Now the flames were licking around the feet of the one surviving penitent. He bore it as long as he could without flinching, but at last the screams were forced out of him, and the mob roared in response.

VIII

AD 1484

The great port of Malaga was the Moors' second city. The city, founded on a huge double fortress that spanned two hills, was built for warfare. And yet ships of many nations clustered in the harbour, including traders from the Christian kingdoms of Spain.

From the deck of his own vessel Harry's pulse quickened as he watched the ships scud to and fro, their sails billowing. This was a place bursting with deals to be done. Perhaps he would be able at least to turn a profit on the trip, once he was done with the murky business that had drawn him here.

It was already three years since Geoffrey Cotesford had reunited him with his sister Agnes, three years spent mainly on patient research by Geoffrey into Harry's family's complicated background – and their scraps of prophecy, principally the Testament of Eadgyth. Harry had been able to get on with his own life, tucking the strange affair away in a corner of his mind. But now that had changed. Geoffrey had unearthed a family of cousins in al-Andalus itself, which was the very eye of the storm the Dove was prophesied to unleash – or so Geoffrey argued from his interpretation of the Testament. Harry had reluctantly agreed to put his own affairs on hold and to come here to resolve this odd business one way or another.

Malaga's harbour was wide but not enclosed, and unprotected from the sea and wind; though the Mediterranean was tideless the landing was choppy. But Harry was a hardened sailor by now, and the turbulent sea did not trouble him.

Once he had disembarked, Harry hired a muleteer and set off for Granada itself.

The country through which he was led was quite unlike any part of England he had seen. Lumpy volcanic hills rippled down to the coast, and black-winged gulls swooped over broken sheets of dark rock that angled out of the ground. It seemed a place of huge rocky violence to Harry. He made notes of his impressions to pass on to Geoffrey Cotesford.

The journey was not long, requiring one overnight stop. Harry found a tavern whose keepers accepted his English coins. The muleteer, a small, swarthy Moor, slept with his animals on a blanket under the stars.

The next day they had to cross the mountain range the Christians called the Sierra Nevada. The muleteer led him through an easy pass without much climbing, and they moved in silence broken only by the complaining snorts of the mules and the soft clank of their bells. Harry looked down over green valleys where farms nestled, replete with figs, oranges and apples, and on the ridges fortresses and watchtowers bristled like the nests of huge birds. On the peaks, even on this bright spring morning, ice gleamed brilliant white. Every element of this landscape reminded Harry he was very far from home. He glimpsed eagles soaring silently.

By evening they were approaching Granada itself. The city's cupolas, towers, gilded domes and tiled roofs rose up out of a sea of green fields that seemed to wash right up to the city walls. The Moors, he was told, took pride in the intensive farming of their land – it was a deliberate contrast to the sheep-strewn wasteland that was all the Christians could make of the country they had conquered. In the city itself he made out the dome of the great mosque, and saw how the suqs clustered around it. And at the very heart of the city was the *al-qala'at al-hamra*, the 'red palace', the complex the Christians called the Alhambra. Long and narrow, sprawling over a hill that dominated the city beneath, it was almost like a great stone ship, Harry thought, its walls a sandstone hull, sailing endlessly through the city it dominated and protected.

Harry had a letter of passage written out in Arabic and Latin. He was here to find his remote cousin, Abdul Ibn Ibrahim, who was on the staff of a vizier, an adviser to the emir. So he was allowed by surly guards to pass through an elaborately arched gateway and into the Alhambra itself, where a slim, young, nervous-looking official in a turban escorted him. He used broken Latin.

The people wore loose robes of white or pale colours, and elaborate turbans glistening with jewellery. The children had quick feet and flashing eyes. He saw groups of men engaged in negotiations in the shade of orange trees, or walking briskly from one building to another.

There was a certain urgency here, he thought. The Christians were on the march; war was not far away.

And he passed a gaggle of young men who walked with a swagger, giggling. Their faces were painted brightly, and their hair was dyed. Harry had heard Christian rumours of the decadence of the court at Granada. A bachelor himself, he made no judgements on what he saw.

This was more than a palace, Harry quickly realised. It was a city within a city, surrounded by an oval of walls perhaps eight hundred paces long by two hundred wide. At its western extremity was the oldest part of the complex, a massive and brooding fortress cut from pale red sandstone – a fort without a moat, for to the Moors water was too precious to waste on mere defence. On the Alhambra's northern wall was a beautiful, oddly delicate palace complex. And to the east was a miniature township, the administrative heart of what was left of al-Andalus, a working community with dwellings, offices, stables, mosques and schools. The gardens were spectacular, lined with the intense green of cypress trees, brilliant with the crimson blossoms of pomegranates, and crowded with roses. Small birds sang everywhere; this island of greenery was a haven for them in a land that was more fit for the buzzards. The air, though, was hot, dense and arid, and Harry found he had to breathe through his nose, or his mouth dried quickly.

Led by his escort, brandishing his safe-conduct from Abdul, he was taken into the palace buildings. He was hurried past rooms full of light and colour, with arabesque mouldings and gold ornamentation, and moulded spires like stalactites suspended from the ceilings. One quite remarkable courtyard had as its centrepiece an alabaster fountain guarded by stone lions; it was surrounded by slim white pillars that supported arcades of open filigree. The architecture here lacked the brutal ordered simplicity of a Norman castle, say. This was a fluid place, airy, light-filled, so delicate Harry could almost imagine its rooms and arches and patios could be picked up by the wind like thistledown.

He was brought to a blocky tower that loomed over the palace complex. And, looking up at the tower's sheer face, he saw what looked like a fishing rod protruding from one window, with a line dangling from it, high in the air.

He found a broad staircase, and climbed up to an open landing. A man was sitting on a ledge, one leg dangling out over infinity. He was indeed holding a fishing rod. At first he didn't notice Harry.

Harry walked to the ledge. He was on the north side of the Alhambra, and below the wall the land fell away. To the north a glen opened up to reveal a river threading through a quilt of terraces, orchards and gardens. The city itself was laid out before him. The sun was setting now, and its light, low and turned red by the dusty air, painted the domes and towers pink. Looking beyond the city to the south he made out the angular peaks of the Sierra Nevada. In the shadows below the icecaps he saw the sparks of fires; he would learn that these were the fires of ice collectors, who travelled up into the mountains with their mules every afternoon, and clambered back down in the night. Thus the ice of the mountains cooled the palace of the emir all summer. A subtle mist rose from that river to the north, and the sounds seemed enhanced, so that Harry could make out a child's laughter, the chime of bells, a guitar's gentle music, and, from the heart of the city, the first wail of a muezzin.

As he stared, wide-eyed as a child, the man on the ledge smiled at him. He was perhaps fifty, with a broad weather-beaten face.

Harry, a little embarrassed, approached him. 'You're fishing,' he said.

'Indeed I am, with a hook baited with flies. I am angling for swallows. Fishing in the sky,' said Abdul Ibn Ibrahim, and his grin widened.

IX

Abdul's office was a pretty room with a fine view, cluttered with scrolls and books and charts and heaps of scribbled-on parchment.

Here Harry and Abdul talked briefly of their lives.

They had little in common, Harry thought. Nearly twice Harry's age, Abdul lived alone. For most of his life he had made a living at sea, a career recorded in his leathery face. But he was a navigator, perhaps strictly an astronomer, not a sailor or a trader. He showed Harry a trophy of those days. It was an astrolabe, a kind of map of the sky compressed down onto a sheet of brass, exquisitely made. It was descended from gadgets devised to show the faithful the correct direction for prayer.

Harry was intrigued to hear that in his youth, some decades ago, Abdul had served on the mysterious Chinese treasure ships that had once plied the Indian Ocean and beyond; Moorish and Arab navigators had always been prized by the Chinese.

Abdul had done well, and by the age of forty-five had been able to retire, 'to tend my garden', he said. But when open hostilities had broken out between the emir and the Christian monarchs he had come to the palace to work for the viziers. 'For this is a struggle for survival,' he told Harry.

Harry, listening patiently while sipping cold pomegranate juice, found it hard to believe that this elegant seafaring Muslim could be any sort of relation. And yet it was true.

Geoffrey Cotesford had discovered this branch of Harry's extended family, which for two centuries had been living in Granada. The first of them had been another Ibrahim. He had fled here from Seville when that city fell to the Christians. He had married a woman called Obona, adopting her child from a previous relationship. In Granada, Ibrahim and Obona lived to old age in peace, raising many children, and the family had prospered ever since. Abdul said the family still remembered Ibrahim. Abdul hoped his own patient service for his emir matched that offered by Ibrahim during the last days of Moorish Seville.

For Ibrahim and Obona, it turned out to be a good time to have come to Granada. The last great wave of Reconquest broke with the fall of Seville. In the natural shelter of the mountains, with support from the Islamic nations of the Maghrib, the wily emirs of Granada had been able to play off one Christian leader against another, and the terrible calamity of the Great Mortality had sapped the Christians' will to expand. Even the fall of the Baghdad caliphate to the Mongols had not harmed al-Andalus, which had gained a further measure of independence. It had been a period of uneasy truce – a peace that had lasted centuries.

But the truth was the emirs of Granada had always been vassals of the Christian kings. In return for security they paid heavy tributes in African gold, a steady bleeding.

And since the time of the Great Mortality, which the Moors called the Annihilation, Granada had slowly declined. It was all because of trade, Abdul told Harry. The strait to Africa had fallen into Christian hands, and Italian merchants monopolised the fruit trade, a vital component of Granada's economy, and drove prices down. But the Christian tribute still had to be paid, the defences maintained. Abdul said, 'I pay my taxes at *three times* the level of a Castilian. No wonder the emirs are unpopular!

'Still, the long truce endured. But it has all changed under our latest emir. The Christians call him Muley Hacen; his name is Abu al-Hasan Ali. He grew up seeing his father bowing before Christians, and he loathed it. About twenty years ago he refused to pay the tribute to Castile, and hasn't since. And three years ago Muley became aggressive, riding out to assault a fortified Christian town. It was a grave miscalculation. These new monarchs, Isabel and Fernando, are united and purposeful.

'And we Moors are suddenly disunited. There have been rebellions. Last year Muley was overthrown in favour of his son, Muhammad Abu Abd Allah, whom the Christians call Boabdil. But Muley's knights still support him. Others back Muley's brother Abu Abd Allah Muhammad az-Zaghall – El Zagal, the "Valiant One". And so it goes. There are rumours Boabdil is concluding secret deals with the Christians. Where once we played off one Christian nation against another, now the wily King Fernando plays us for fools.

'Last winter the long war proper resumed, after a pause for breath that lasted more than two hundred years, when the Christians assaulted a place called Loja. And I came to work in the palace.'

Harry shook his head. 'I can't understand such numbers. Two hundred years? How can a single purpose endure over such a huge time?'

Abdul laughed and topped up his drink. 'Men like you and I, Harry Wooler, traders and sailors, live in the moment, in the business of the world. But popes and caliphs, princes and emirs – those sort of folk like to believe they cast long shadows over history.'

Harry tried to get a sense of this cousin. He seemed intelligent, competent, and with a taste for beautiful things, judging by his clothes, and the wistful glances he cast out of the windows. But he was alone, without a family. Was he a man who preferred men? Whatever his taste he had evidently nothing but failed relationships behind him. And yet he had a place in this city, this ancient civilisation he obviously cherished.

He and Harry could hardly have been less alike, Harry thought. And yet here they were, related, considering working together.

He turned the conversation to the matter of the Testament.

Abdul said, 'I'll tell you the truth. In my family – or my branch of it – we have a sort of memory of prophecies. Of terrible weapons of war, of a man called the Dove, all of that. But if this was ever written down, it was long lost, and reduced to a memory of a memory. I don't think Ibrahim cared much for that sort of stuff. So why have you sought me out? Why come here, to al-Andalus? And why *now*?'

'It was Geoffrey's suggestion ...' Harry had told Abdul of his contact with the monk. Now he produced a parchment on which the first twelve lines of the Testament of Eadgyth were written out.

Abdul lodged small spectacles on his thin nose and scanned it quickly. '"The tail of the peacock",' he read. He looked up. 'There is an old Arab myth, of the Flood—'

'I know,' said Harry. 'Or rather, Geoffrey knows. That's what he found out. He believe that al-Andalus must be the peacock's tail of the Testament.'

'So that tells me why you've come here. But why now?'

And Harry spoke of the 'last days' of the Testament's first line, and how some Christians believed that the year 1500 in the Christian calendar would mark the end of time.

Abdul looked amused at that. 'Muslim scholars rather look down on the Christian calendar. Full of errors! Our calendars and clocks are somewhat superior – the demand for the accurate timing of the calls to prayer five times a day sees to that. But I see the relevance of the date to Christian thinking.'

'When Geoffrey found out about you, he thought you may be able to help understand the prophecy, perhaps even track down the Dove.'

'So I would be an ally in al-Andalus. And,' Abdul said drily, 'I would be committed to help, given that it is my home that will surely be the target of the marvellous weapons of which you speak.'

'What do you think we should do?'

'Think it through,' said Abdul firmly. 'Always the best policy.' He scanned down the Testament. 'Some of this seems quite explicit, doesn't it? A fire consuming "our ocean" – that must be the Mare Nostrum, as the Romans called it, our ocean, the Mediterranean. "God's Engines will ... flame across the lands of spices." A massive war in the east, then, if the Dove turns that way – perhaps a war with the Islamic states which control trade with the spice islands? That much is logical. But why would this Dove, if he exists, wish to travel *west*? To the west is only the Ocean Sea.'

'For trade,' Harry said immediately. 'Perhaps that's a bias in my own thinking. But there is money to be made out there. That's why I would go ...'

For decades European navigators had been probing the Ocean Sea, seeking new trade routes. This drive was a legacy of the Mongols, whose hundred-year peace had briefly united Asia with Europe. Travellers like Marco Polo, following the new continent-spanning trade routes, brought back accounts of great eastern empires. Italian colonies on the Black Sea and the crusader cities in the Levant made a handsome profit as conduits for imports from the east, including sugar, spices and textiles, furs, pelts and hides, wax, honey, amber, metals.

'But it wasn't only wealth that came swarming into Europe along the Mongol trade routes,' Abdul put in darkly. 'The Annihilation dawned in the heart of Asia, and travelled with the traders and their ships out of the east. You can tell from the records ...'

When the Mongol peace ended, the rise of Muslim empires like the Ottomans' cut off the Christian west from the rich markets of the east. Now nobody even knew if the Khans were still on their throne. In the south too Christian traders found themselves boxed in by Muslims, who controlled the spice trade from India and the far east, and whose caravans, snaking across the Sahara, were the only access to the great gold fields of west Africa.

So, in search of new trade routes, the Europeans were taking to the seas.

'It's an exciting time,' Harry said. 'You must have seen the new maps. The ships continue to get better too. The Portuguese, for instance, are inching their way down the west coast of Africa, seeking a sea route to the African gold mines. Some say it might be possible to go all the way down the coast of Africa and find a channel east, through to the Indian Ocean and the spice islands that way. And others are already working their way out west into the Ocean Sea. They are coming to understand how the wind blows, where the great ocean currents flow.

'And we know there are new lands to be found out there. Like Madeira, which the Portuguese control. And the Canaries, which the Spanish have conquered, and they call the Fortunate Isles.'

Abdul said, 'So there are solid reasons for this Dove to turn his energies west.' He fixed Harry with a glare. 'But you haven't told me everything, have you, cousin? If the Dove goes east there will be war between Christians and Muslims – but there is *always* war between Christians and Muslims. What would be so terrible about this one?'

Harry sipped his pomegranate juice. And he showed Abdul the rest of the prophecy, the lines his sister had discovered scratched in the wall of her cell in York.

X

Harry read,

> The Dragon stirs from his eastern throne,
> Walks west.
> The Feathered Serpent, plague-hardened,
> Flies over ocean sea,
> Flies east.
> Serpent and Dragon, the mortal duel
> And Serpent feasts on holy flesh ...

'Geoffrey Cotesford believes he now understands these words, four centuries old. This is how he has interpreted them.

'The Dove is a strong man. Strong, clever, determined. He is a force, elemental, loose in our world. He must be, or else why would the prophecy speak of him? West or east, where he goes others will follow. If he goes west, he will surely lead the conquest of lands teeming with wealth and strange peoples – lands unknown to the ancients, and to our geographers, perhaps. On the other hand, if the Dove turns east, with the same energy and single-minded purpose, he will lead a ferocious war against Islam. And he will use the Engines of God to do it. That's what Geoffrey argues. It all fits together, Geoffrey says.'

'Better weapons are always an advantage,' Abdul said. 'But Muslims aren't fools. Advantages tend not to endure.'

'Yes, that's what Geoffrey says. In time the spies of Islam will acquire the secrets of the engines. And what's more, Islam and Christianity have no means of achieving peace with each other: history shows that, says Geoffrey. So the war will be unending, the destruction on both sides will be multiplied – the use of the engines won't lead to victory but to catastrophe. From London to Baghdad, Geoffrey predicts, not a stone will be left standing. The only victors will be the warlords – whether fighting in the name of Christ or Muhammad it won't matter.

'And like all warlords, like the Mongols, they will need to feed their armies on further expansion. When the destruction of their homelands is complete they will turn their attentions outside Europe, south to Africa – and east into Asia. There will be more carnage. But China, immense, populous and ancient, will survive, as it survived the Mongols.'

'I can believe it,' Abdul said. 'How many warriors could England muster? A few thousand? It's said that the Chinese emperors command an army of a *million* men.' He read, '"The Dragon stirs from his eastern throne, / Walks west." I think I understand.'

Harry nodded. 'Geoffrey says this means that the Chinese will pursue the broken European armies back across the continent, all the way to France, perhaps, and even England. The last remnants of Christianity and Islam alike will become vassals of the Dragon Throne.'

'And when they have taken Europe the Chinese will face the Ocean Sea themselves.' Abdul sat forward, fascinated. 'I sailed with the Chinese, under their great eunuch admirals. Will they take their turn to explore the Ocean Sea?'

'No,' said Harry firmly. 'Not according to the prophecy. Rather, the dangers of the Ocean Sea will come to haunt them ...'

Even if the Dove did not sail west, other Europeans would surely try the journey, fragile ships from Portugal and Spain and England probing ever deeper beyond the curved horizon. Others, then, would fall on the shores of the western countries – not the empires of Asia, but lands unknown to Europe, said Geoffrey.

These more tentative explorations would benefit the strange empires of the west more than the Europeans. The Dove would have conquered – or at least he would have set an example of conquest and colonisation, as opposed to reasonably peaceful contact and trade. These more timid explorers would be overwhelmed. The strange oceanic kings would indulge in trade, but in time they would acquire the newcomers' weapons and ships, take them apart, learn to make their own. They would suffer from plagues brought from Europe, but not in great numbers, and the generations to come would acquire immunity.

And a western empire, ruled by the 'plague-hardened' people of a 'Feathered Serpent', would learn of the rich lands across the Ocean Sea.

'They will come,' said Harry. 'Pushing across the Ocean Sea, a conquering fleet heading east where the Europeans might have gone west.

On the coasts of England, France and Portugal they will fall on an overstretched Chinese empire.'

Abdul read,

> The Feathered Serpent, plague-hardened,
> Flies over ocean sea,
> Flies east.
> Serpent and Dragon, the mortal duel.

'But the western conquerors will unleash a horror not known in our continent since before the Romans.'

'"And Serpent feasts on holy flesh."'

'*They eat the flesh of humans*. They sacrifice human lives in great numbers. Their wars, Geoffrey predicts, will be terrible slave-raids, as captives from across a devastated Europe are hauled to their temples to die under the knives of the priests. Whole populations will be consumed ...

'This, and no more,' Harry said. 'The prophecy lets us see no further.'

Abdul sat as if stunned. Then he got up and paced around the room. He took a bowl of jasmine blossom and breathed deeply of its scent. 'All this,' he said at last, 'if this Dove turns east and not west. But these final lines: "All this I have witnessed / I and my mothers." What does that mean?'

'Geoffrey says that Eadgyth was not a prophet, not a seer who could see the future, but – a puppet. The words were put into her mouth by a Witness, just as the line says, a saint of the far future – a woman, Eadgyth always believed – who will live at a time of the terrible calamity of the western invasion of the east, or at least fears its likelihood. And this person, wishing to avert the horror, will find a way – well, to *speak* to a woman of her own deepest past.'

'How?' Abdul demanded.

Harry smiled. 'If I knew that I'd sell it, and wouldn't be here talking to you. In fact, Geoffrey believes we are dealing with *two* prophecies here – or two witnessings. He says the Dove was *meant* to go west. Somebody *else* found a way to deflect him from his true course – somebody else has already meddled in history, and is trying to send the Dove the wrong way, east, equipped with the Engines of God. And it is a *second* witness who is now trying to reverse things through the Testament.'

Abdul thought that over, and laughed. 'Geoffrey says, Geoffrey says. These scholars are troublesome to men of the world like us. I suppose these Witnesses are scholars too, competing to muck about with history.

And now we're meant to put it all right by packing the Dove off to the west?'

'That's the idea,' Harry said unhappily. 'I suppose the question is, what do we do now?'

Abdul sat again. 'I think we have a responsibility, even if the chance of the witnessing coming true is small, to try to avert this huge destructive disaster of the future of Serpent and Dragon. Anything would be better than that.'

'Agreed. So we must do something about it.'

'Yes. But you feel as uncomfortable about this sort of talk as I do, don't you, Harry?'

Harry shrugged. 'I'm just a merchant. I sell wool. That's all I know.'

'Yes.' Abdul gazed out of the window, and the dusty evening light caught the planes of his face. 'And I, I have always been outside the current of the world. I'm happy with that. Happy to observe, not to be involved. I'm content with my role here in the palace. In Granada, I'm trying to resolve problems, Harry. To save people. To restore equilibrium, if you like.'

'Not to change history.'

'Indeed. And yet here we are.'

Harry nodded. 'Where do we start?'

'We need to find this Dove of yours,' Abdul said firmly. 'For, it seems, all of history turns on his decisions. He must be a navigator, a mariner, a captain, or a ship-owner; he must be seeking sponsorship for his western voyages. These navigators all know each other – and are jealous of each other too. I will see if I can track him down.'

'And then what?'

'Then we will decide what needs to be done to send him on his proper way, off into the Ocean Sea.' He frowned. 'It occurs to me – this strange witnessing has fallen into the hands of our family. But families have a way of proliferating. What if there are others, Harry, others out there like you and me, likewise armed with the Testament of Eadgyth – or worse, the Engines of God? And what if one of those other unknown cousins has decided to work the other way – to send the Dove, not west, but east?'

Harry was appalled; that thought hadn't occurred to him. 'If so they will be looking for the Dove, as we are,' he said.

'True. We must keep our eyes open. And if we encounter them,' Abdul said calmly, 'we must deal with them.' And he pressed his nose to a jasmine petal, as if for comfort.

XI

AD 1485

In the summer of 1485 Grace Bigod, with Friar James in tow, travelled back to Spain. Grace wanted to press her case for the adoption of the Engines of God by the Spanish court.

But the Spanish were at war. This year, Fernando and Isabel were engaged in the siege of a Moorish town the Christians called Ronda.

So James and Grace travelled across the country to Ronda with a raiding party of Castilian soldiers. Moving inland from the coast they crossed a landscape of folded hills and flood plains through which rivers snaked, glistening, and fortified towns sat squat on the hilltops. The scars of the monarchs' war were everywhere, in the burned-out fields, the hulks of abandoned farmhouses, the stinking carcasses littering the roadsides.

The knights called themselves *caballeros*, and they were attended by *hidalgos*, lesser nobles. As they rode they joked, sang and drank. James thought they had a certain lazy arrogance. If they saw a stone wall standing they would run their horses at it to knock it down, if they saw a haystack they would torch it, if they saw a well they would throw stones down it to block it up, if they saw an irrigation channel they would dam it with dead cattle. With their crusaders' crosses stitched to their sleeves they dedicated each new bit of destruction to Saint James the Moorslayer, and they dreamed of what they would do if they found a few plump Moorish women hiding out in the ruins. Thus they wrecked a landscape that had been intensively farmed for seven centuries.

Grace had no sympathy for James's unease at all this. 'You're a hypocrite,' she said bluntly. 'You gladly devote your pious, pointless little life

249

to the development of devastating weapons. And yet you flinch when you see the results.'

James faced his conscience, and he knew she was right. He had had no choice about being assigned by his abbot to the engines project. But he was thirty years old now, and as the years had worn away he had become engaged in the intellectual exercise of the engines for its own challenge. It was thrilling to see these most remarkable toys emerge from heaps of wood and iron, saltpetre, sulphur and carbon – a thrill, his confessor warned him, that might be a compensation for other aspects of his life that he had piously put aside.

But he had, he realised, built a wall in his mind between the development of the engines and their ultimate purpose.

He said unhappily, 'It's just that I didn't expect it to be like *this*.' He waved a hand. 'Is this war? This wanton destruction of property – there will be famine here in the winter – this savagery inflicted on the old and the ill, on women and children.'

She laughed at him. 'What did you expect, chivalry? You ought to read a little more widely, brother. This is the way wars are fought now: French against Flemish, Italian against Italian, Moor against Christian ... Why, we English pioneered the technique, in our long war with the French. You cut off your enemy at the knees by removing his food supply, by shocking his population into terror and submission. There's even a word for it, I'm told: *chevauchée*. Wars are fought like this all over Europe now, like it or not.

'So pray for the souls of the dead children, friar. But remember that the Pope himself says that a war for Christ is a just war, however it's fought. And pray that you're never on the losing side.'

She was a hard, brutal woman. And though she must be near fifty now, the angry lust she had so carelessly stirred in him still flickered. She had made a peculiar enemy of him by the way she had treated him, he thought. He tried to conceal this from her. And he tried to dismiss from his own mind the thoughts he had of her, fantasies of lust and violence, in which he ended her domination of him once and for all.

After days on the road, they arrived at Ronda.

The port of Malaga was the Christians' next strategic objective, as it had been for two years, but its twin fortresses stood strong and stubborn under the command of the formidable El Zagal, and the Christians did not yet have the resources to deal with it. So they had focused their energies on destroying this town, Ronda, thirty miles inland and sixty miles west of Malaga, the key to the western defence of the residual Moorish state.

The site was extraordinary. Ronda sat on top of a butte, a pillar of rock. To the north was a steep-walled gorge. To the south the butte was lower, and here the Moors had built a massive fortification, a curtain wall studded by towers. The only way into the town was by a bridge that spanned the gorge to the north. James, studying this place, thought it was a textbook example of a natural fortress, a definition of impregnability. No wonder the Romans, those great military technicians, had settled here.

But the monarchs of Spain were here to take it, and the siege was laid.

The Christian camp, out of range of the Moorish defenders' cannons, arquebuses and crossbows, was a morass of mud and tents and stinking cesspits, over which a loose cloud of greasy smoke hung day and night. But as they approached, James saw with a helpless thrill that the banners of the monarchs hung over the camp. Fernando and Isabel, the modern champions of Christendom, really were here in person, not half a mile from where James and Grace pitched their own rough leather tent.

But this place of war was not comfortable.

When night fell great cannon began to roar. On the south side of the city, targeting the walls and towers, Fernando had drawn up a battery of immense new Italian guns called bombards. Their unceasing thunder was overwhelming, and the night was a hellish scene of half-naked men, blistered from the heat of the weapons, labouring amid a stink of gunpowder and smoke to load, aim and fire, over and over, the shot gradually battering down the city walls.

And as the day broke the Moors attacked – but they came from the hills, not from the city. James learned that these were the forces of the governor of Ronda. An experienced general called Hamet el Zegri, he had allowed himself to be lured out of his city to raid Christian fields and barns, a revenge for the *chevauchée* of his countryside. But the Christians had sent a cavalry detachment to cut him off from Ronda, and when el Zegri returned he found his town already besieged.

Still, under el Zegri's command the Moors came riding down from their hills, every day. The armies closed amid a roar of cannon and the popping of arquebuses and a clamour of war drums, and to cries of 'For Saint James!' and 'Allah akbar!' When the Christians mounted attacks, the Moorish would kneel in blocks, their pikes at the ready, soaking up the charges, their javelins in quivers to be flung with deadly skill. And the Moorish cavalry, lightly armoured, riding fast under their colourful battle flags, was much more mobile than the Christian knights in their heavier chain-mail and plate.

For all the bustle and excitement of the cavalry charges and the spectacle of the cannon and arquebuses, the real work of killing was done, as it had always been, with pikes and swords and scimitars, wielded by human muscle, one man against another. James was appalled by the utter, fully committed violence of these encounters, even though none of them was conclusive. Isabel had set aside tents to serve as hospitals, but they were overrun, and if you went to that part of the camp the groans of the dying and the stink of rotting flesh were unbearable.

For four nights the bombardment continued, and for four days the Moors attacked. James didn't sleep for a single hour. It was a time of utter misery, for besieged and besiegers. In the Christian camp, the supply lines to Cordoba were fragile, and all there was to eat was a disgusting mixture of flour in pork fat.

Relief came when the last of Ronda's towers was demolished, and the walls crumbled. James stood beside the silent bombards, watching the end game of the siege as the *caballeros* swarmed into the city, and the screams began.

XII

A week after the Moors' capitulation, James and Grace were able to enter Ronda.

Walking in from the Christian army camp they passed a complex of buildings, arched roofs and domes, sheltering in the lee of the smashed city walls. It turned out to be a bathhouse; a marshy, steamy stink lingered in the air around it. The baths were working; on a squat tower the donkey patiently turned its wheel, watched by a Moorish boy with a switch, drawing up river-water to be fed via a slender aqueduct into the baths. Today the men who filed through its rooms were Christian soldiers, but the women who went with them were all Moorish. James wondered how many of them had a choice.

James and Grace made their way over the bridge across the gorge. The bridge was battered, but it had survived the bombardment. The gorge's walls loomed above them, and James peered up curiously. The limestone was cracked vertically and horizontally, heaped up in tremendous blocks as big as houses.

They clambered up steep cobbled paths into the city itself. Squeezed onto its table-top of rock and hemmed in by its walls, Ronda was cramped and crammed. The bombards' shot had created great splashes of shattered stone, as if immense raindrops had fallen from the sky. There was a prevailing stink of rot and raw sewage, even a week after the water supply had been restored. Soldiers worked, picking through the rubble, searching for bodies, pocketing anything worth stealing. No Moors were about. The soldiers said that everybody was either dead, fled or hiding.

With Grace leading the way they cut through the centre of the town, heading for the cliffs on the north-western side. The warren of streets was studded with fine houses, mosques and bazaars.

They came at last to the western boundary of the city, where the town simply came to an abrupt end, for the plateau on which it had been built fell away in columnar limestone cliffs. James looked down over a flood plain, a land of farms and orchards through which a river snaked lazily. It was all so far below him it was like staring down at a vast map. But much of the land was brown or black, the crops and trees burned out, and sluggish threads of smoke rose to pollute the heavy air.

And as he reached the very edge of the cliff James stepped into an updraught of warm air, blowing strongly from the ground below. Down there in the valley a breeze was blowing, but when it reached the vertical cliff face the moving air, with nowhere else to go, washed upwards in an unending invisible stream to ruffle the cloak of a curious English friar. For a heartbeat he was able to lose himself in simple wonder at this unexpected physical phenomenon, a fragment of the rich beauty of God's creation.

Then Grace plucked at his arm. 'Look,' she said. 'Haven't you heard the cheering? *There she is . . .*'

Reluctantly he turned, and immersed himself once more in the affairs of men.

A procession was approaching, advancing along the broad road that lined the cliff: gilded people, merchants and courtiers, senior military men dressed up like peacocks, a splash of Christian colour in this conquered Moorish town. Many of them had crusaders' crosses exquisitely stitched to their shoulders or breasts. There were some Moors in the group, grandly dressed themselves with their jewelled turbans glinting: the rich and powerful under the old regime, he supposed, now hoping to keep their wealth and influence under the town's change of ownership.

At the head of the procession, walking slowly, was a black knot of prelates, somehow sinister in their darkness. And at the heart of this group, shining in a gown of bright colourful silks, was a tall, imposing woman, her features strong, her eyes chips of aquamarine. Her chestnut brown hair was tied back under a small, delicate turban, for when she entered a conquered town she had a custom of dressing respectfully, with a nod to the Moorish style.

It was the Queen, of course, Isabel of Castile. As she passed her soldiers cheered.

'Magnificent, isn't she?'

Diego Ferron had joined them. The Dominican friar, tall and wire-thin, wore a robe so black it seemed to suck the daylight out of the air.

With him was a Moor, a portly man of about fifty with an expressionless, weather-beaten face. He carried a sheaf of documents under one arm, and he waited, eyes empty, at Ferron's side.

Grace took Ferron's hand and kissed it. 'My good friar. You found me, I'm so glad.'

Ferron nodded. He glanced at James and made a curt sign of the cross to him with two upraised fingers. 'And I'm glad you are here at this moment of triumph, madam. Even now King Fernando is composing his letter of jubilation to the Pope, I'm told. Oh, I should introduce my mudejar.'

The Moor smiled. 'I am Abdul Ibn Ibrahim. By profession I am an astronomer. Today I serve the friar.' He said this without apparent bitterness.

Ferron said, 'Actually he is attached to the staff of the emir in Granada. The emir has sent a delegation to Ronda to witness the enactment of the treaty of capitulation. We do try to be civilised about these things. And so I am shadowed by this mudejar. Well, he is useful; his Latin is quite good.'

James introduced himself. 'And this is the lady Grace Bigod, of Buxton – we are from England.'

The Moor's eyes glinted. 'I know who you are.'

It was a remark that puzzled James. But Abdul said no more.

Ferron said, 'Ah, the Queen is nearing us . . .'

They applauded as Isabel with her retinue continued her progress down the road.

Ferron watched admiringly. 'I've met her several times. A remarkable mix of courage, piety, and sheer glamour! In her way, you know, she is as valuable to the cause of Christendom as ten thousand knights, for the men love her in a way they will never love Fernando, though they admire his cunning and leadership. And she is competent too. Since the fall of Ronda she has already rededicated the main mosque, and ordered cart-loads of sacred books and crosses to be shipped in from Cordoba and Seville, along with good Christian settlers to occupy the abandoned properties. Thus she has completed the city's conquest by her cleansing.'

James asked pointedly, 'And the Jews and conversos? Are they to be cleansed too?'

Ferron smiled thinly at him. 'Torquemada is here himself.' Torquemada was now the Grand Inquisitor for all of Spain. 'Even with Brother Torquemada's famed efficiency, the courts have yet to process more than a handful of cases. But we are making progress.'

James's soul turned at this brusque summary. Since he had last visited Spain he had found out more about Ferron, who, as it turned out, was from a converso family himself – and Grace, of course, likely had her veins polluted by Saracen blood. Was this why they were so enthusiastic about the Inquisition's dreadful cleansing? For no matter how hard they scrubbed, they could not remove the impurities from their own bodies.

Ferron went on, 'In the meantime, lady, we have business to discuss. I told you the Inquisition has ears and eyes everywhere. We are almost as ubiquitous as God Himself, our admirers say – and our enemies. *I believe we may have found your Dove.* Come, we must talk.' He offered his arm, and they walked off, without looking back to see if James and Abdul followed.

XIII

Friar Ferron escorted them to the palace of the Moorish governor of Ronda, called the Mondragon, which had been given over to officers of the Inquisition. The palace was only a short walk along the road that followed the cliff top. They walked through light-filled rooms to a colonnaded courtyard, and then passed on through a horseshoe arch into a small garden that overlooked the cliff itself, with a remarkable view of the flood plain below.

The mudejar Abdul brought out a tray of tea.

Grace glanced at Abdul. 'Are you sure it's safe to talk of these matters in front of him?'

'The mudejar? Of course. He is an ambassador to one defeated Moorish city from another which soon will be defeated. What harm can he do? We will speak freely, and forget he even exists.'

Grace leaned forward eagerly. 'Tell me of this Dove, then.'

Ferron said, 'I cast a net for men of his sort, and have caught what looks like a promising fish. He came to our attention – I mean the Inquisition's – because he intends to travel to Cordoba, to the monarchs' court, where he hopes to present his case.'

'A case to do what?'

Ferron smiled. 'To sail the Ocean Sea. To go west, if he can.'

'Then such a man exists,' Grace breathed.

'Oh, yes. He was born in Genoa, this man, the son of a clothier. He is now thirty-four years old. It seems he was educated in a school run by the clothiers' guild. But his learning is poor,' he said dismissively. 'He was restless, as many of that Italian breed are. He ran off to sea; he served on ships from his youth. He has sailed to Chios in the Aegean, and as far as Iceland in the Ocean Sea; he has visited Ireland, England, Flanders, and sailed down the African coast. He became a competent navigator, mapmaker and ship's master, it seems. He made his money from his petty bits of commerce, as men of his kind do.

'But his fortunes changed, this poor Dove's, when he made a good marriage. He wed into a noble Portuguese family called Perestrelo. And this is where the dream was born. For his father-in-law, who died before the Dove married his daughter, served as a captain during the colonisation of Madeira, led by Henry the Navigator. The Perestrelos were given some land on the island of Porto Santo, off Madeira. Here it was that our Dove settled with his wife, and he began to go through his dead father-in-law's maps and accounts of his explorations. He learned first hand how a new land may be made to turn a profit for its discoverer, and the nation that sponsors him.

'And his eyes were drawn west. Porto Santo, I am told, is a haven for those who sail out into the fringe of the Ocean Sea in their little ships, explorers hunting down the African coast, slavers seeking a supply base. And many of them bring back tales of marvellous lands which lie to the west, always just out of sight . . .'

Out of all these fragments, in the head of the clothier's son, a most remarkable dream was born.

Ferron said, 'Perhaps if you sail west and keep on sailing, it would be more than new lands, new Madeiras, that you would find. For if the world is round, then perhaps you could sail *around* it. Perhaps you would end up coming around the curve of the earth and arrive in the *east* . . .'

James was astounded. He was educated; he knew his geography, and the shape of the world. But this was a category of journey that had never occurred to him before. 'Can it be possible?'

'Oh, yes,' Ferron said. 'Why, it was a dream of Pedro, elder brother of Henry the Navigator, half a century ago. And there are strong commercial reasons to try it. Some say that if the Muslims block the way to the east – well, then, on a round world, perhaps a route can be found to the far east, by sailing *west.*'

'And that is the Dove's dream,' Grace said.

Ferron sneered. 'You can just see this little man, the jumped-up Genoan, his poorly educated mind struggling to make sense of the tavern legends he so credulously devours. But he is devout, I'll give him that. It's not just trade he's after. He's said to have concocted a scheme to contact the Mongol Khan, if he still reigns, and to persuade him to join an attack on the Islamic states from the east. Our clothier's son dreams of liberating Jerusalem!'

'All right,' Grace said. 'But so what? You say men have had this sort of dream before. What makes this "Dove" different?'

Ferron said, 'For one thing, the plausibility of his case. The seed of his dream may have been travellers' tales, but he has been trying, in his dogged, uneducated way, to assemble a rational case, based on the testimony of the ancients and other arcana. Second, he has added a gloss of a divine mission, which will appeal to our monarchs. You could even see it as fitting in with the greater project of the Hidden One to rule the whole world; after all you must discover a land before you can conquer it. Third, there is his sheer determination. Anybody who has met him says this of him. He is obsessed where those who went before him were not, and he may succeed in his dream of going west merely because of that.'

'Or perhaps,' James said, 'he just wants to get out from under the shadow of his father-in-law. That would be human.'

'Well, if he wants to impress his wife he's sadly too late,' Ferron said. 'She died last year, leaving our Dove with a chick, a son. Perhaps that death released our dreamer from the damp prison of Porto Santo. Within months he had travelled to Lisbon and petitioned the Portuguese court to fund his westward expedition. In return he wanted a share of the profits, a hereditary nobility and to be named governor of any lands he found.'

Grace smiled. 'This little man thinks big.'

'You can't blame him for that. Joao turned him down. He left Portugal – although that may not be unconnected to the fact that his wife's family were implicated in a murky little plot to assassinate the King. And so, early this year, our Dove came to Spain. He's here now, in a little port called Palos. And as I say we've learned that he intends to come to Cordoba to present his case to the monarchs.'

Grace nodded. 'And you do believe he is the figure predicted in Eadgyth's Testament?'

'Oh, yes.'

James said, 'His father was a clothier, you said, friar. What kind of clothier?'

'A *weaver*. This man is the son of a weaver. Just as your prophecy says.'

And James remembered the line: *the spider's spawn*. The weaver of a web.

Abdul asked, 'And if I may, what is his name?'

'His Italian mother called him Cristoforo, his Portuguese wife Cristovao. In his workaday commercial Latin he is Christophorus. We in Spain must, I suppose, call him Cristobal.'

'Christophorus. *Christo ferens*,' said Grace slowly. 'The Christ-bearer. And the surname?'

259

Ferron smiled, anticipating her reaction. 'He will be called Colon here – Colombo in Genoa and Portugal – Columbus in Latin.'

Grace clapped her hands, delighted as a child. 'Columbus – the Dove! Can it really be as simple as that? The spider-spawn, the Christ-bearer, the Dove – Christopher Columbus!'

But James, shocked, thought there was nothing simple about a four-hundred-year-old prophecy coming true.

Ferron said, 'Well, it seems that all hinges on this man. Spain is drained by war; the monarchs won't buy *everything* that is presented to them. If this man is funded to go west, they will not spend on your engines – as I am coming to believe they must, if the world's final war is to be won. What we must do, then, is recruit this Dove, this Colon, to our cause. We must make him forget the western Ocean. We must make *him* long for the engines, and the glorious war to come.'

'"And the Dove will fly east",' James breathed.

The mudejar Abdul was staring intently at Ferron, absorbing every word.

XIV

Abdul Ibn Ibrahim, a big, heavy-set man, his sailor's face leathery and creased, would have looked out of place in London, Harry thought, even if it hadn't been for the turban on his head. He had come to England to tell Harry and Geoffrey what he had learned of this man, this putative Dove, Cristobal Colon.

Colon had joined the court of the Spanish monarchs at Cordoba. 'The monarchs have turned the capital of the caliphate, a city of scholarship, into an armed camp, the headquarters of their war on the Moors,' Abdul said bleakly. 'It is full of weapons shops, everywhere soldiers drink and whore, and in the shadow of the mosque drums beat, horses parade and the armies of the nobles stage mock battles ...'

When he had first landed at the small port called Palos, seeking somewhere safe for his child to stay, Colon had settled on a Franciscan priory called La Rabida, outside the town. It was a lucky stop, for he quickly found allies in the priory's father superior, Juan Perez, and in a visiting brother called Antonio de Marchena. These two had become stout supporters. And it was a letter from de Marchena of Palos that had served as an introduction to the Queen's confessor.

So Colon got his chance to present his petition to the monarchs' council. But this was quickly rejected.

'He was turned down for his sheer implausibility,' said Abdul. 'This Colon is not a scholar, and when he gets into debates about the shape of the world with sea captains and geographers, it shows.'

But Colon showed the qualities of iron determination of which the Testament hinted, 'heart stout, mind clear'. He found a way to make a direct appeal to the monarchs.

'And he immediately snagged the attention of Queen Isabel,' Abdul said. 'After all she has Portuguese ancestry. Colon's father-in-law went exploring in the Ocean Sea with Prince Henry, the Queen's own great-uncle. I think her blood was stirred at the thought of doing some exploring of her own.' He raised an eyebrow. 'He is a handsome man too, striking. And a lusty one. I'll say no more than that!

'The monarchs were interested, despite the implausibility of his case. I think it was Colon's wild promises of gold from Cathay that most attracted them. The monarchs need funds to fight their war against Islam.'

Geoffrey asked, 'Then they might support his case?'

'They have appointed a *junta*, a commission of geographers and navigators and sea captains, under the leadership of the Queen's confessor, to investigate his proposition.'

To Harry, all this was the stuff of a personal nightmare. He felt this figure, Colon, was emerging from a mist of chaos, from the Testament's obscure old language, from the ramblings of his dying ale-soaked father, into the cold light of actuality.

Geoffrey sensed his unease. 'Have courage, Harry.'

Harry tried to focus on the practical. 'Is there any sense in this talk of crossing the Ocean Sea in the first place, and of vast unknown empires? If not, we can dismiss it all as fancy.'

Geoffrey asked, 'What do *you* think?'

Harry shrugged. 'I'm no navigator. The journey I made from London to Malaga was my longest sea voyage. I only know what I've heard.'

'Which is?'

'That the world is a dangerous place. The Romans called the Ocean Sea the Mare Ignotum, the unknown, and not for nothing. They say that to the west is a Sea of Doom, a place of vast whirlpools that can crush a ship like a fly in a child's fist. If you go south towards the equator you sail into the Torrid Zone, where the sun's heat turns you black before the flesh boils off your bones. And the world is not a sphere, as the ancients believed, but a sort of pear-shape, with a great extension to the extreme east where the earthly paradise resides.' He felt uncomfortable, as Abdul listened to this in cold silence. 'This is what has been said by mariners to me.'

'All right,' Abdul said. 'But what mariners? Europeans, that's who, who have barely ventured out of the puddle that is the Mediterranean. But the Chinese have gone much further, and learned much more ...'

And he spoke of his time on the treasure ships.

'You should have seen them, cousin. They were not like our little ships at all. Like floating cities, they were, with a great square bow at the front, topped by serpents' eyes. Nine masts bore huge red silk sails.

The ships were built in compartments, so they could not be sunk. They had holds full of preserved food, and immense tanks of fresh water, and they grew soya beans on board, and they kept otters in their holds to catch fish – they could stay at sea for months! And the officers enjoyed banquets and dances, and the company of courtesans.

'It's all gone now. There was upheaval at court, a fire in the Forbidden City, a lot of bad omens – the eunuch admirals were retired, the ships broken up. The mandarins at court adhere to the principles of *tao* – order, stability, harmony of all things. That sort of thinking doesn't sit well with the exploration of the unknown. I suppose in the end the Chinese decided China is world enough for them.

'But in the heyday of these tremendous ships, only a few decades ago, the Chinese ventured far over the oceans – around India, as far as the coast of Africa, and to the south-east, where they discovered huge masses of land and strange peoples unknown to Europeans.

'Listen to me. I once met a man who had worked in the Forbidden City. In a zoo there, he said, the eunuch explorers had brought back specimens from a dry southern land. There were strange skinny people with black skin and flat noses and curly hair. There were trees that kept their leaves and shed their bark. There were huge creatures with faces like a deer's and back legs like huge levers, that carried their young around in a flap of skin on their belly . . .'

Harry smiled. 'I too have heard such tavern tales.'

'All right, all right. I'll tell you this. The Chinese learned far more about the shape of the world than any European, thanks to us Moors, and thanks to their own expertise.

'Do you know any navigation, cousin? To fix your position on the round earth you need to know two numbers, your latitude and longitude. Latitude tells you how far north you are of the equator. That's easy. You just look for how high the Pole Star is; the higher in the sky, the further north you must have sailed, until it would be over your head if you sailed all the way to the north pole itself.

'Longitude, the angular distance travelled east or west, is trickier, for the sky itself spins about the earth. The Chinese developed a method using eclipses of the moon. Such events are visible all across the world. A legion of astronomers scattered across the world, all studying the elevation of the stars at that precise moment, would be able to map the earth's curve—'

Harry held up his hands. 'Enough. I'm better at figuring accounts than the geometry of the stars.'

'My point is that the Chinese *know* how big the world is. And they would tell you that it would be a *long* journey if you were to try to sail west from Lisbon, say, to China. But on the other hand,' Abdul said thoughtfully, 'that big Ocean Sea has plenty of room for an unknown continent or two. The Chinese never sailed far enough to find out.'

Geoffrey thought this through. 'Then you're saying,' he said carefully, 'that the prophecy of the Dove, the invasion of Europe by people from the west, could have a basis in truth.'

'I'm saying it's not impossible.' Abdul looked at the two of them. 'All this will take years to come to fruition, one way or another. The monarchs have other matters to deal with before they fund Ocean crossings. And the Engines of God need development before they kill anyone save by accident. We have time yet to deflect history's course.'

Harry's heart sank at that thought. 'So we can't be rid of this any time soon.'

'Not yet,' said Geoffrey grimly. 'Be patient.'

XV

AD 1488

The Derbyshire country under its lid of low cloud was a dark green mouth, damp and enclosing, and the abandoned village was a field of worn-down hummocks. Though it was not long after noon, the light already seemed to be fading. As he followed James and Grace into the village, Friar Diego Ferron, tall, thin, almost spectral, held up the hem of his expensive robe, as if trying to avoid any contact with the English mud.

James couldn't help but see the murky, unsatisfactory English December day through Ferron's eyes. A greater contrast to the dry brilliance of southern Spain was hard to imagine. After all they were here to impress another man from the Mediterranean, Bartolomeo Colon, the brother of navigator Cristobal. Bartolomeo had come to England to seek support for Cristobal's adventure from King Henry, for after three years of fruitlessly pestering the Spanish monarchs Cristobal was casting his net wider. Grace and Ferron had seized the chance to impress one of the Colons with a demonstration of their Engines of God. If Ferron was instantly put off by the English weather, would Bartolomeo be too?

But then Diego Ferron was a uniquely unpleasant man, James told himself. Though they had worked together for seven years now on the continuing development of the Engines of God and on following the progress of Cristobal Colon, Ferron's stern, cruel piety appealed to James no more now than it ever had.

So James was spitefully glad when a hatch in the ground opened up under Ferron's feet, and the friar jumped back.

Grace said quickly, 'There's no need for alarm. Prepare to be impressed, brother. James?'

James led Grace and Ferron down muddy steps into a dark hall in the earth, leading off into the dark. Lamps burned in alcoves on the walls, and a greyer light diffused into the corridor from air vents.

A wagon was waiting at the bottom of the stair. A squat platform, it had a large crossbow-like mechanism mounted on its upper surface, and a fifth wheel attached to a rudder on a pivot at the back. With no horse or bullock in sight, there seemed no way it could be moved. James guided Grace and a bewildered Ferron to sit on two leather seats at the front of the vehicle. He himself took the rear seat, took hold of the rudder, and unclipped a latch on the crossbow.

The wagon moved off down the corridor, smoothly and silently. Ferron sat bolt upright, his large delicate hands white as they gripped the edge of his seat.

James, enjoying the moment, said nothing of the wagon, but described the background to work that had progressed in utter secrecy for more than two centuries since the time of Roger Bacon. 'We are working in a continuing tradition. In ancient times, thinkers like Archimedes applied their intellect to the design of weapons and defences. In more recent decades engineers like Taccola, Buonaccorso Ghiberti and Francesco di Giorgio Martini have developed military treatises. And we have had some fruitful correspondence with an artist and philosopher called Leonardo da Vinci, who is developing war engines for the Duke of Milan. But our engines are rather more advanced than his – of course we have had some centuries' start ...'

Ferron had said nothing since the wagon began to move. Now he spoke at last, his voice tight. 'This cart of yours.'

'Yes?'

'It has no horses. No bullock. No slaves to pull it.'

'Of course not.'

'*Yet it moves*. What witchcraft is this?'

James grinned behind Ferron's back. 'No witchcraft. It propels itself. This mechanism – you see, it is rather like a crossbow – when wound back stores energy which, if released, is transmitted to gears that drive the wheels.

'Most of our designs are based on five simple machines studied since antiquity: I mean the winch, the lever, the pulley, the wedge and the screw. As to energy sources we use weights, heat – I mean trapped steam – human and animal muscle, wind or water power, and spring energy, as on this wagon. That, and Bacon's black powder. The principle of the wagon is simple. The engineering challenge was in designing differential gears so the wheels can move independently ...'

266

Grace leaned back. 'Enough,' she whispered to James. 'We're here to impress the man, not to terrify him.'

James nodded. But he couldn't be bothered to suppress his grin. Thirty-three years old, he felt confident and in command – and he felt like taking a little petty revenge on these rather monstrous figures who had dominated his life.

The wagon slowed. James latched the spring drive, applied the brakes to the rear wheel, and the wagon came to a slightly juddering halt. Without much dignity Ferron scrambled off his seat to the dirt floor.

They passed through an arched doorway and walked down further steps to emerge into a large chamber, walled with rough stone blocks and lit up by more torches and oil lamps. It was a cave, but a vast one; from its cathedral-like roof stalactites dangled like icicles.

And in the shadows obscure engines loomed, their metal flanks gleaming with oil. Monks scurried around the machines. There was a low hum of conversation, the clank of hammers on metal – and a shriek of released steam, which made them all jump.

A shadow like a bat's rattled across the roof, and settled into a corner.

'Welcome,' James said, 'to our manufactory.'

'This is a cave,' Ferron said, wondering.

'Oh, yes,' Grace said. 'This shire is riddled with them. Limestone country, you see. And up above there's nobody around for miles; the country has yet to recover from the Great Mortality. In fact we moved here after the plague, decades ago; already nearly a century had passed since Bacon's first instructions, and we needed the room. In time the brothers have spread out through a whole complex of these caverns, quarrying out tunnels and passageways as they went. Like moles with tonsures!' She seemed to find the notion comical. 'An ideal place for work like this – heavy, noisy – if you want to keep it secret.'

They walked towards the machines. Ferron asked, 'Secret? From whom?'

Grace shrugged. 'The seventh King Henry isn't long on his throne. These brothers haven't toiled for centuries to put bombards in the hands of one pretender to the English crown or another.'

Ferron nodded. 'We have a higher purpose than the ambitions of kings, we are waging a war which transcends all others. You have chosen the right course – you and your forebears, for centuries.' He had recovered his composure, James noticed, amused.

Now they were walking among the engines. They passed wheeled platforms, and huge hulls like steel houses, and blunt cannons whose mouths gaped, and more exotic forms yet, complicated masses of machinery with no clear purpose. On one bench lay a huge skeletal wing, twice the length of a man's body. There was a stink of oil and hot metal, the air was dense with steam, and the labouring monks, wide-eyed in the gloom, scurried out of their way.

James said, 'It might seem simple to translate given designs into actuality. In fact much of our work is at a more basic level, as we learn to make the components required by our engines. Steel hard enough to make screws and gears that will not shear was a particular challenge. Advanced cannons need just the right casting, loading, lighting and cooling if we are to increase their capacities and speed of fire.'

Ferron confessed, 'I understand little of what I am seeing.'

'The engineering detail doesn't matter,' Grace said. 'Our purpose is only to show you the scope of the work here. The practical demonstration aboveground later will show you all you need to know.'

Ferron smiled thinly. 'A demonstration? I'll look forward to it. And all of this comes from the fevered brow of this Roger Bacon?'

'He worked from the designs and recipes in the Codex of Aethelmaer, returned from its hiding place in Seville ...'

Bacon had quickly abandoned his Aristotelian studies and had thrown himself into experimental, secretive research. He had recruited students and assistants, and had discreetly sounded out like-minded savants across Europe. He appointed a Picard called Peter de Maricourt as his *domum experimentorum*, and it was de Maricourt who had set out the design for the first laboratory-manufactory.

The work progressed quickly. But as he aged, Bacon himself became more difficult. He had always been a man who craved attention and recognition. He campaigned for the acquisition of more experimental knowledge about the natural world, and began to compile a vast encyclopaedia of all the known sciences. But he made plenty of enemies by expressing his strong contempt for those who did not share his passions, and he was severely disciplined by superiors who thought he was out of control. Bacon, ever grandiose, appealed over their heads, even direct to Pope Clement. The death of Clement ended his ambitions, and his career.

His superiors excluded him from the manufactory, and in the end actually imprisoned him for his indiscipline and suspected heresies; his whirling mind was confined to a cell for thirteen years. When released, he was exhausted; his final works remained incomplete.

Ferron listened to this soberly. 'But after Bacon, for two hundred years, underground, all invisible, the monks of his great manufactory have toiled at weapons of war. Yes? Quite remarkable. You know, I am told Colon has used Bacon's writings in trying to construct his own case for the monarchs. In his *Opus Majus* Bacon surveys geographical understanding, and argues, for example, *against* the existence of a Torrid Zone below the equator.'

Grace said, 'Perhaps we can use that to persuade Colon and his brother to accept these, the fruits of Bacon's genius.'

'It's possible.'

They moved through a low passage into another, smaller chamber. Here only enclosed oil lamps burned, and the murky air stank of dung and piss. Ferron recoiled, and with an impatient snap Grace summoned forward a novice, who presented each of them with a scented napkin to hold over their noses.

Here gunpowder was manufactured, according to Bacon's carefully researched recipes. It was kept separate for safety, and for the foul air; the brothers assigned to this work didn't last long.

James said, 'We mix the ingredients with mortars and pestles, or with these wooden stamps.' He showed Ferron a clunky device, all levers of iron and mallets of wood. 'We need to combine the powder into granules of varying sizes, depending on the application. Granule size determines burning rate; you don't want your powder to burn so rapidly it shatters your bombard's casing. So we mix up the powder with a binding agent. Sometimes it's water and wine, but in fact urine is best.'

'As I can smell,' Ferron said drily. 'And the ingredients?'

'The best charcoal is free of knots, and made of coppiced wood – hazel or ash, gathered in the spring and so full of sap. We import our sulphur from the volcanoes of Iceland, the purest in the world. The saltpetre is more difficult, and needs manufacture.' He showed Ferron a series of vats, from which a murky water was poured one to the next. 'Saltpetre is made from dung.'

The monks filled a pit with layers of quicklime, cow manure, wood ash and vegetable waste. They turned this regularly, moistening its surface. It was important that the matter was not allowed to get too wet, or too dry. After some months of this a whitish efflorescence would appear on the surface of the heap, which the monks scraped off and collected. The powder was dissolved in water, which was then passed through the series of vats.

'This is saltpetre,' James said. 'The Arabs call it "Chinese snow". The saltpetre stays dissolved where other salts precipitate out. It's an intricate technique, worked out over centuries by the Chinese among others—'

'The Arabs have such processes now. They've been firing cannon at Christians for a hundred years – more, I think.'

'Yes,' James said patiently, 'but thanks to the Codex, Bacon had saltpetre, and the recipe for black powder, decades earlier than otherwise. The scholars believe that as a result we have a lead of a *century* or more over the Arabs in the exploitation of these secrets. And *that* is how these engines will win the holy war.'

'It's quite an industry then,' Ferron said. 'All this material flowing into this dungeon, sulphur from the mountains of Iceland and manure from the farms of Derbyshire, and then the ingenuity of the burrowing monks here. I suppose it would be inappropriate if it did not take intelligence and effort to make this devilish dust, this gunpowder, that can slay so many men. But I wonder how its victims would feel if they knew the shot that killed them was propelled by an alchemy of dung? ...'

They walked back to the main manufactory. A winged form flapped noisily beneath the vaulting roof.

Ferron looked up nervously. 'If that was a bat it was a big one.'

James grinned. 'Not a bat. A man.'

XVI

Abdul leaned over his tankard of English beer, and spoke softly to Harry and Geoffrey.

'As you know I have tracked this man, this Cristobal Colon, since he first came to the attention of the Inquisition. His career since then has done nothing to dissuade me that he is indeed the man of whom your Testament speaks.'

Posing as a mudejar Muslim, Abdul continued to work with Diego Ferron. He had come to England once more, this time as part of Ferron's retinue. Now he had met Harry Wooler and Geoffrey Cotesford in this small tavern in the town of Buxton – which he said he had heard of; it was a spa town the Romans had called Aquae Arnemetiae. They all spoke quietly, as if one of the gawping locals might be a spy for the Spanish Inquisition.

They were all growing older, Harry thought, the three of them, filling out, their necks thickening and hair greying. He was in his thirties himself. And yet here they were furtively huddled once again, still pursuing the obscure project that had obsessed them for years.

Abdul went on, 'You know that Colon has been refused several times already. I was there when Colon gave a grand presentation of his case in the ancient Moorish university of Salamanca. But in January of last year they turned him down again.'

Geoffrey said, 'And still he doesn't give up?'

'Not at all. He hangs around the court, begging for audiences, assembling more evidence from legend, sea-farers' tales, Arab geographies and the works of the ancients. To the rest of the court he has become a comical figure, I think. A bore and a charlatan. Yet he still seems to appeal to Isabel. She has even been paying him living expenses.

'But you must understand that all this time the monarchs have been prosecuting their war against the Moors. It's been a bloody summer,' Abdul said, remembering. 'I saw too much of it. Malaga's resistance was strong. When the fortress fell at last, the population was divided up among the Spanish nobles for slavery, like so many cattle. The emirate at Granada, divided against itself, could do nothing . . . I think it's clear to everyone that if Fernando and Isabel ever do support Colon's venture overseas, it will only be after the conclusion of the war with the Moors.

'But Colon's time may be running out. Just this month he has been in Portugal to hear the testament of Bartolomeo Dias, who has sailed down the coast of Africa past the equator, proving by the way there is no Torrid Zone, and discovering a cape where he was able to turn east.'

Geoffrey frowned. 'I'm no geographer. I'm not sure I see the significance.'

Harry said, 'Dias believes he has discovered a sea route to the spice islands by sailing *east* around the southern tip of Africa, rather than west across the Ocean Sea.'

'Ah,' said Geoffrey. 'So Colon's voyage west would have no purpose.'

'Worse,' Abdul said with a smile. 'Dias is a hero. He is getting the attention and fame Colon craves! I told you Colon is a shallow man.'

'And that's why he has sent his brother to sound out the King of England,' Geoffrey said.

'Yes. Even the dogged Colon is despairing of the Spanish monarchs.'

'But he mustn't be allowed to give up,' Geoffrey said. 'Let's hope our "man from Cathay" works his magic.'

Harry frowned. 'A man from Cathay?'

Abdul grinned. 'Actually it was my idea.'

Geoffrey said, 'We have been trying to support Colon's case by feeding his camp selected bits of scholarship on the size of the earth, what might lie beyond the sea, and so on. Colon's ally Friar Antonio de Marchena of Palos is a fellow Franciscan, and I was able to use him as a conduit to reach Colon. But we thought we needed something more dramatic to impress the monarchs.'

Abdul said, 'One of Colon's sea stories is that when he voyaged to Iceland, he was told of corpses, washed up on a western shore of Ireland, strange men with yellow skin and dark hair, in a boat that was a hollowed-out log. Colon never saw these corpses. Yet he believed they must have come from China, washed across the ocean by a current.'

'So,' Geoffrey said, 'Abdul suggested repeating the trick.'

'I arranged for a corpse to be dumped on the shore near Palos. As it happens,' Abdul said grimly, 'the south of Spain has not been short of corpses these last few years. I ensured the man, a Christian, had

272

drowned. I dyed his skin yellow-brown with tea, and added some tattoos for good measure. And I cut him around his eyes, for everybody knows that the Chinese have odd narrow eyes with folds of skin across the corners. Such a corpse at Palos was bound to come to Colon's attention, and so it did. Now he parades around the court with diagrams of the wretched man, and even dried bits of flayed skin to show off my fake tattoos.'

Geoffrey laughed. 'Gruesome but ingenious.'

'But will it be enough?' Harry said gloomily. 'All we have to turn Colon's head is a bit of scholarship and a dubious corpse, against Grace Bigod's engines . . .'

'It will have to be enough,' Geoffrey said.

Abdul said with a trace of bitterness, 'Of course Grace and Ferron do not admit to their clients how much Bacon's work was helped by the studies performed for my ancestress Subh by *Moorish* scholars and artisans. After all, Sihtric took his designs to al-Andalus because he knew the best scholarship in Europe was available there. When Joan of the Outremer took possession of the Codex, she plundered what had been achieved there as well, though all Subh's Moorish workers had fled from the approach of the Christians. It is part of a wider story, as Christendom plunders al-Andalus of learning as well as gold—'

'And thereby rediscovers its own lost past,' Geoffrey said gently. 'Can that be such a bad thing, Abdul?'

'Yes, if Moorish scholarship is now to be turned against the Moors!'

Geoffrey pulled his lip. 'Well, we must have patience. We will watch Grace Bigod's display of fire, and see what we can learn. Now. Who can spare a penny for more of this filthy beer?'

XVII

The December day dawned bright and clear. Even in mid-morning the sun was still low over the abandoned village, so that the hummocks and green-clad shells of the ruined houses cast long shadows over the dewy ground.

And James, looking down on this scene from his ridge, could already hear the crump of explosions, the cries of men, and the clanking, hissing noises of monstrous engines. He grinned with anticipation. Let Bartolomeo Colon be unmoved by *this*!

As for himself, since before dawn James had been atop this rough limestone ridge, making ready. He was wearing leather trousers and a close-fitting quilted coat that he belted tight around his body. He knew from earlier trials that the wind and grit would get in his eyes, and so he wore a special cap with a long peak and panels protruding before his cheeks. He tied its strap under his chin before donning his gloves.

Now four novices approached, each bearing an iron egg. These were slim ovals, each the size of a sleeping pigeon, with sprawling tails. The novices trod warily, nervous, trying not to tremble. They hung the eggs from James's belt, and he tested the leather tabs he had to pull to release them.

Next his engine had to be assembled around his body.

First came the 'muscle', as he thought of it. This was a box of canes several feet tall. It had complicated 'shoulder' mechanisms, and at its heart was a powerful crossbow as thick as his arm, already wound back. It had quickly been learned that a man's muscles were too feeble to beat the great wings; but the crossbow would suffice. This frame was lowered onto his shoulders and strapped to his torso by a cradle of leather bands.

James's shoulder units had to be tested. These were elaborate arrangements of rods, shafts, gears, pulleys and ropes at either side of the muscle frame that would translate the crossbow's unwinding into complex movements, up and down, twisting. The shoulders, carefully oiled, worked flawlessly. The novices added a vertical 'tail' of wood and feathers fixed on a strut to the back of the central frame.

And now came the wings, each borne on the backs of more sweating novices. They climbed stepladders to either side of James, and pushed the wings' joints into their attachments in the shoulder units and strapped them into place with more leather belts. The wings, spread, were like tents made of young fir, fustian, starched taffeta and feathers, and the morning light shadowed their internal skeletons.

The supervising friar ordered one last test of the mechanism. With utmost caution the wings, still supported by the novices, were lifted and lowered, twisting as they did so, and the feathers spread and closed, each pasted by hand to its own tiny cog wheel. The flight of birds had been carefully studied by Bacon and his followers for two hundred years. It was clear that the air was a fluid through which birds swam, as fish and seals swam through water. This elaborate machinery had been designed, after generations of paper designs, model-making and trial and error, to copy exactly that flapping, swimming motion.

But at this moment the theory, the mechanics, didn't matter at all to James, compared to the sheer beauty of the engine above him. He was thrilled that he had used his master's seniority to become the soul of this fantastic creation.

The supervising friar, a blunt practical man with wild grey hair around his tonsure, now faced James. 'Ready?'

James grinned and nodded.

The friar yanked at a rope. The crossbow was unlatched, and flexed, and immediately its elastic energy was poured through gears and pulleys into the shoulders. The wings flapped and twisted, James's harness tugged at his chest, and he was dragged up into the air.

The ground fell away, and the novices' upturned faces were like coins on a table. They were clapping and cheering. The landscape opened up beneath him, and he saw the shape of the limestone ridge from which he had launched, and the plain before it, and the ruined village where engines crawled and gunpowder flashed.

His heart raced with excitement, and a bit of fear, and he felt his loins tense up. He had admitted to nobody, not even his confessor, the extraordinary erotic thrill this hurling into the air gave him. If he could never have a woman, at least he had *this*. And as the air washed around him the face of Grace Bigod swam into his mind, elegant, cold, sneering.

Already the crossbow was running down, but it had lifted James high enough for his purpose. He had to work quickly. He pulled strings to latch the crossbow, and others to lock the wings, outstretched with the feathers closed and banked. Then, with a grunting effort, he leaned forward, and the leather cradle into which he was strapped pivoted, so that he was suspended beneath the wings, belly down.

He glided forward, wings rigid as a coasting seagull's. He was falling, of course, falling like a dead leaf. But he should reach the battlefield, and that was enough for him to do his job.

He looked down at the ruined village. More hapless novices were defending a 'fortress', crudely constructed of heaped-up stone from the village. They were equipped with weapons of a conventional sort, crossbows, longbows, arquebuses and cannon, and had even had some rudimentary training in using them.

But huge machines crawled relentlessly towards the village, spitting fire. James made out the gun carriage nicknamed the 'organ-pipes'. Between two massive wheels was suspended an axle with a triangular cross-section. On each of the axle's three faces had been fixed a dozen cannon, in a row like the pipes of a church organ. These fired together, lit simultaneously by spring-loaded flints. Then, dragged by unhappy mules, the engine trundled forward until the axle turned and another bank of cannon was brought into play.

Other engines displayed different solutions to the challenge of multiplying fire. Here was a great wheel set horizontally, mounted with cannon spread radially like the petals of a daisy, which turned and spat fire when each gun was brought to the right position.

And now, shaking itself to life with a series of crashing explosions, here came the most spectacular machine of all. It was the *testudo*, named by the brothers after the famous formation of the Roman legions. It was a great shell of steel, immensely heavy, tough enough to withstand a direct hit from any of the defenders' petty weapons. Cannon fired from ports in all the forward angles, and as it advanced it shook and shuddered, smoke billowing from its ports from the internal detonations that drove it forward. It was unstoppable, inhuman. The *testudo* simply crushed a crumbling stone wall beneath its great hidden wheels, and the defenders, their shot and bolts and arrows simply bouncing off the mighty shell, fled, probably terrified out of their wits by the noise alone.

From James's elevated vantage he could smell nothing of the battle; he could hear little save the distant crump of explosions and the shouting of men like birds' cries, sounds drowned by the hiss of the wind in his wings, and his own rapid breathing. It was like watching a battle played out with toys, he thought – distant and abstract enough to quash his

276

own conscience, and to allow him to savour the exhilaration of his extraordinary flight over these engines of carnage.

Now it was time for James himself to deliver the finishing blow. He tugged on guide ropes so that his wooden bird swooped to a line that led straight to the mock fortress. He glanced to his left to the observers' canvas pavilion, to see if Bartolomeo Colon and the rest were watching him. He saw Grace in a bright purple gown. He grinned, and the wind was cold on his teeth, and his heart beat even faster.

He banked over the fortress. As his huge shadow crossed the village some of the defenders ran, their superstitious fear overwhelming them, though they knew it was James. Now he pulled at the leather tags at his belt, one, two, three, four. The metal eggs were released and fell straight down, their bird-like shapes cutting through the air, the fins at their backs stabilising their fall.

All four landed in the heart of the fortress, splashing fire as they hit. The noise of the explosions hit him, and a sudden updraught of hot air pushed him higher. He whooped with an unreasonable joy. James was a man of peace, but he was young enough to relish the sheer exhilaration of such a complicated and dangerous game.

And as the fires bloomed he thought of Grace, Grace pushed down before him, Grace begging for his forgiveness – begging him to *stop*.

He looked over at the pavilion. Grace and the others were standing and pointing – not towards James and the fortress, but east. James craned his neck to see that way.

Something was wrong.

XVIII

'The *testudo*,' Ferron said weakly, 'is astounding. Devilish!'

'Not the devil,' Grace said smoothly. 'It is all the work of man, his imagination divinely inspired.'

'But how is it possible for such a weight even to drag itself over the earth? There must be a herd of horses in there.' He cupped his ears in gloved hands. 'And the *noise*—'

'Not horses. Bacon's black powder.' And, sitting beside Ferron in the wooden viewing stand, she tried to explain how the gunpowder had been harnessed into an engine. 'There are a series of pistons. When the gunpowder charge explodes above each piston, air is forced out of a chamber of iron, and the piston is dragged up, as a man inhaling may draw a feather into his mouth. That motion is translated into a turning of the great wheels, by a complicated mechanism James could no doubt describe for you. And so the steel beast travels forward, powered by a beating heart, each pulse a detonation that could kill ten men ...'

While Bartolomeo Colon stared, fascinated, it seemed to be too much for Ferron. He held his hands over his ears, flinching from each new explosion. 'Devilish,' he repeated. 'Devilish.'

She tried to distract him with the manufactory's new sort of arquebus; one of them was set up on display before them. 'Then consider this, brother. The old sort of hand gun, as Isabel is deploying against the Moors even now, is slow to reload, and unreliable to fire, for you must apply a flame to the powder that propels the shot. Now we have a new sort of gun – based, again, on the designs in the Codex – which is fired not by flame but by a spark.' She showed him how, when a trigger was pulled, a hammer slammed a bit of flint against a steel plate; the resulting sparks were funnelled into a chamber to ignite the gunpowder.

Ferron was distracted by the glistening mechanism as she operated it. 'I see,' he said. 'I see.'

'It is still difficult to reload – we will work on that – but the reliability is so much improved, the weapon is so much safer, that it will be as if we have double the number of soldiers in the field. And furthermore—'

'What,' Ferron said, pointing, 'is *that*?'

It was a woman – young, scrawny, dirty. Grace had no idea who she was. She was running. She fled *towards* the battlefield. Grace could not have imagined a more unexpected sight.

And now monks followed her, grimy, blinking in the light. They too ran towards the noise and smoke of the field, not pursuing the girl, just running. But one of them called over his shoulder to the spectators in the viewing stand. 'The manufactory! Get away, my lady – the manufactory!'

'Dear God,' Ferron said.

Grace was bewildered, unable to understand what was happening. 'I think—'

The explosion was a roar, all around her. She was thrown forward onto the ground, helpless as a doll.

From the air, James saw fire erupt from the ground, a line of searing fountains. Monks and novices squirmed out of hatches like moles emerging from their holes, and ran off. James understood immediately. The fire was breaking out of the ground through the air vents of the underground manufactory. The explosions must have come from within the compound. It was the store of gunpowder, it could only be that. Some accidental spark had ignited it – or perhaps, he thought suddenly, it had been deliberate.

James had to concentrate on his own flight. His mechanical bird was dipping towards the ground. He had only a few heartbeats left in which he could control his descent. He scanned the ground anxiously, looking for a clear space to land.

But a fresh set of explosions broke out over the location of the main manufactory, distracting him, and James saw bones hurled into the sky. The gunpowder must have broken open a plague pit. It was an extraordinary, unnatural sight to see those bones go flying up into the air and then fall back, a grotesque parody of the Day of Judgement.

XIX

Harry, with Abdul and Geoffrey, had been watching the display from a distance, with appalled fascination. The wooden bird in the sky especially was an awful, unnatural sight.

But when the fires began to erupt from the ground they all knew something had gone badly wrong. Abandoning all attempts to conceal themselves, they ran towards the party coming from the viewing pavilion.

They met the others not far from the entrance to the manufactory. The explosions had stopped now, but smoke still poured from the ground. No more monks clambered out of the hatches, and Harry wondered how many had died that day.

Diego Ferron was unmistakable, a tall, pale cleric. He was holding a woman by her hair, a wretched, skinny girl in a grubby white gown. Beside Ferron and his captive was Grace Bigod. She was a hard woman of nearly fifty, her face smeared with soot and twisted in fury. It was the first time Harry had met this remote cousin.

Ferron seemed surprised to see Abdul with two strangers, but his rage overwhelmed him. In accented Latin he cried, 'Ruined! Destroyed! Centuries of work lost!'

'Not lost,' said Grace, her voice trembling, 'Just delayed. We have lost our engines, but those in the field survive, and we have the designs—'

'Lost because of this Christian witch!' He twisted the girl's hair and threw her to the ground.

She lifted her head. She looked straight at Harry. Her hair fell away from a bruised face.

'Agnes!' He could not have been more shocked if his sister had been raised from the dead. 'But you are in your cell in York.'

'Evidently not,' she said. Her voice was a scratch, and she coughed, her lungs full of smoke.

Grace looked at Harry and Geoffrey. 'Who *are* you?'

Harry ignored her and spoke to his sister. 'And you – you caused this destruction?'

She whispered, 'You are a good man, Harry, a good brother. But you are not strong enough to do what is necessary. I prayed. God spoke to me. My mission was clear. It was worth breaking out of my cell for this, wasn't it?' She forced a smile, and suddenly she looked as she had when she was a little girl.

His heart broke. He stepped forward. 'Oh, Agnes—'

But Ferron blocked his way. 'Keep away. This witch is for the Inquisition. Keep away, I say!' And he brought his gloved hand slamming down on the top of Harry's head.

The world peeled away into darkness.

XX

AD 1489

Seville was cold that February morning, and the wind that funnelled along the Guadalquivir was biting. It was a disappointment for Geoffrey, who had at least expected to be able to warm his English blood as a reward for undertaking this hellish trip.

It was a relief to get out of the open air and duck into the great cathedral, where he was supposed to meet Abdul.

In the still, incense-laden calm, he genuflected and crossed himself. The cathedral was a cavern of sandstone and marble. His gaze was drawn upwards to a vaulting roof that was filled with a golden light cast from huge stained-glass windows, a hint of heaven. There was nothing on this scale in England. The cathedral was a sink of wealth; it was expensive, tacky, uplifting, crushing; and it was certainly a monument to the untrammelled power of the Church in Spain.

Abdul Ibn Ibrahim met him just inside the doorway. His turban and long Moorish cloak looked thoroughly out of place in this Christian space.

Geoffrey greeted him. 'I'm surprised they let you in.'

The Moor shrugged. 'We Muslims are not barred. Perhaps the priests hope that I will be converted by the sheer stony mass of this place.' He grinned, comfortable in himself. 'So you arrived safely. What do you think of Spain, of Seville?'

'Overwhelming. Like this cathedral.'

Abdul glanced around. 'I think it's all a bit tasteless myself. However the cathedral's not meant for me, is it? Come,' he said cheerfully. 'Let me show you what is said to be the finest Moorish monument in Christian Spain.'

It turned out he meant the old mosque's muezzin tower, called by Christians the Giralda, which still stood. There was a doorway to it from the cathedral interior, and Abdul led Geoffrey up a series of broad ramps. Geoffrey had been expecting a staircase, but Abdul said the ramps had been designed this way so that guards on horseback could climb the tower. The ascent was easy but long, and Geoffrey, not a young man, was wheezing when he reached the top.

Here, huddling in his cloak against the wind, Geoffrey looked out over the roof of the cathedral, crowded with buttresses and pinnacles. It was as if he stood on the back of some huge stone beast. The city beyond was a patchwork of patios and domes that looked very Moorish to his untrained eye. But when he looked to the west, across the busy river with its pontoon bridge, he made out the hateful pile of Triana.

Abdul followed his gaze. 'You may not be able to help her,' he murmured. 'Agnes Wooler. The Inquisition is nothing if not relentless.'

'I can try. I was present at the destruction of the engines, but Ferron has no reason to suspect I had any involvement in that catastrophe – indeed, I didn't, not directly. And I am a Franciscan, quite senior in the order; I have letters from the church authorities in England. Ferron cannot deny me access to her hearing. At least I may learn what Agnes is forced to say to her interrogators. Then we may be forewarned for the battle to come over Colon.'

The Moor studied him. 'I don't believe you have come all this way just for the lofty purposes of prophecies. I know you by now, Geoffrey Cotesford. You care for people more than for ideas. You are here to save Agnes, an English girl who has fallen into the hands of the Spanish Inquisition.'

Geoffrey felt his anger mount, as it had so often whenever he reflected on that dreadful day in Derbyshire when Diego Ferron had effectively kidnapped Agnes Wooler. 'England is not Spain. In England we have a common-law writ known as *habeas corpus*. It dates back centuries, to the day the barons tempered King John's powers with the Magna Carta. Ever since it has served to preserve individual liberty by testing the legality of detentions. If she had not been removed from England, Agnes Wooler would be protected by such traditions, such laws. But not here, not here! Not in this country poisoned by war, and by the fear of the other.'

Abdul laid a calming hand on his arm. 'I'm afraid you can be sure that the Inquisition will extract everything she knows from poor Agnes before they are done. As for us, your name will surely be protected, but mine may not. And if I am implicated, I won't be able to help you further with the matter of Colon.'

'You must think of yourself, then,' Geoffrey said.

Abdul shook his head. 'No. We serve a greater cause, you and I.'

'Yes, we do, by God – by Allah! Thank you, my friend. But it comes to something when my most robust ally, here in this most ardently Christian of cities, is a Moor!'

The morning was advancing, and Abdul suggested they descend and return to the city for lunch. Geoffrey glanced once more over the cathedral's sprawling bulk. Far below he glimpsed a patio with orange trees, a relic of the Moorish origins of this huge church, where a boy sat on a low wall plucking at a guitar, and a girl danced before him, her arms raised, her feet clattering on the ground, her movements sensuous despite the February cold. The music drifted up to him through the rustle of the wind, a liquid sound. But the boy's song sounded almost like a muezzin's wail. In this city the Moorish face was only ever poorly disguised by the Christian mask, Geoffrey thought.

He followed Abdul down the ramps, where once the hooves of horses had clattered.

XXI

The courtroom was a cold stone room in the bowels of the Triana, windowless, its walls smeared with lamp black. Guards stood by the door and at the back of the room. They were beefy soldiers of the Holy Brotherhood, the religious police of Fernando and Isabel.

The panel of inquisitors was led by Diego Ferron himself. Two more clerics sat at either side of him. A pile of papers and books of procedure cluttered the desk before them, and a clerk made continual notes. The Inquisition was nothing if not orderly.

The only observer here was Geoffrey Cotesford, who sat as bravely as he could on a hard wooden chair. The chair had been brought into the room especially for him; Diego Ferron had made it clear that he was not welcome here.

An immense and detailed crucifix hung from one wall. Geoffrey reluctantly studied the image of Christ, whose wounds gaped. He supposed that he was the only one in the room who was aware of the irony of that gruesome sculpture of a victim of torture, suspended in such a place as this.

At last Agnes was produced. She was half dragged into the room by two more heavy-set brothers. She was wearing a grimy, colourless shift, stained brown with old blood, and her hair was matted and filthy. The size of the two soldiers with her was absurd, Geoffrey thought; either of them could have broken her with a single blow. She looked dimly around, at Ferron and his colleagues, and at the crucified Christ. There was a smell of decay about her, of shit and piss and blood. But her shrunken face had an odd, unearthly beauty about it.

And then she turned and looked directly at Geoffrey, and her eyes widened.

Geoffrey forced himself to smile at her, and made a blessing with two fingers. How she must blame him for prising her out of her anchoress's seclusion!

She dropped her head.

Ferron watched this coldly. Then he nodded to the brothers. 'Release her.'

The brothers let go of the girl's arms. She slumped to her hands and knees, and Geoffrey saw her back for the first time. Bloody stripes were clearly visible through the thin cloth of her shift.

Geoffrey found himself on his feet. 'This is an outrage. She has been whipped!'

Ferron turned that stern glare on him. 'All due and lawful process has been followed. The girl was given thirty days' grace in which to make her full and voluntary confession. When the thirty days expired, she was encouraged further to speak.'

'You call this *encouragement*?'

'And when she still failed to speak, she has been brought before the court. Perhaps she will speak here. But you, friar, will keep your silence, or you will be ejected.'

Geoffrey sat, fuming.

Ferron fixed the girl with his cold judgemental stare. 'Agnes Wooler. You are guilty of wanton destruction. You have damaged an ancient project with holy and pious purposes: you have blunted the swords of our new crusade. And, further, you took many lives in the process.'

Geoffrey put in, 'No. No lives were lost. She gave the friars in that manufactory sufficient warning. Whatever you think of her actions against the engines, she's not guilty of murder.'

Ferron ignored him again. 'Further I put it to you, Agnes Wooler, that you have been complicit in the corruption of a supplicant at the court of Fernando and Isabel, whom God has chosen as His emissaries on earth in this dark time. I mean Cristobal Colon, the navigator.' And Ferron spoke evenly about the 'Chinese' body discovered on the shore at Palos. Colon had believed this to be a relic washed east from Asia. But the body had been examined by a physician, who argued from blood-pooling that its tattoos had been applied *after death*. Its strange eye-folds were artificial too, the result of a bit of surgery, again performed after death. 'The body was a fake, designed to baffle Cristobal Colon and to thwart the holy purpose of the monarchs.'

Ferron produced other bits of evidence, selected bits of scholarship fed to Colon. 'There's really quite a conspiracy, it seems, to pour this nonsense of westward voyages into Colon's head. And it can't be a coincidence that your destruction of God's engines happened to occur

286

on the very day that Colon's brother Bartolomeo was there to see it.'

Geoffrey was depressed at how much Ferron knew. Piously cruel he might be, but Ferron was evidently no fool. He tried to protest. 'What on earth can this wretched English girl have to do with the goings-on at the royal court of Spain? She's spent most of her adult life in York, locked up in the cell of an anchoress!'

Ferron said smoothly, 'That's what we're here to find out. Now you are put to the question, Agnes Wooler. Unburden your soul. I want you to tell me first the names of your co-conspirators. And when you are cleansed of that, we can move on to the detail of your further sins.'

Agnes, shaking, raised her upper body so she was kneeling before Ferron. She would not reply.

One of Ferron's aides whispered in his ear. Ferron nodded. 'That's enough time.' But before he proceeded, he hesitated. He said to Geoffrey, 'We are not monsters, Geoffrey Cotesford, whatever you English think of us. Hardened by the war against the Muslims we may be, but we are civilised, and pious in all things. And there is a process I must now follow, laid down by the Grand Inquisitor and sanctioned by the monarchs: a process tested in the law and the eyes of God. A process of five steps, at any of which a penitent may turn back to God and spare herself further suffering.'

Geoffrey said nothing.

Ferron turned to Agnes. 'You refuse to speak, Agnes Wooler. You understand that if you do not cooperate, further proceedings will follow.' After waiting for Agnes to respond Ferron nodded to a clerk, who made a cross in a book. Evidently that warning was the first step of the process.

Ferron stood. 'Bring her,' he snapped to the brothers, and he led the way out of the room. The brothers took Agnes's arms, hauled her to her feet, and dragged her after the others.

The room was suddenly empty, save for Geoffrey. He stood, his heart hammering, and he hurried out of the room after the rest.

They walked along a short corridor, lined with little offices inside which more churchmen laboured at mounds of paperwork. Geoffrey was reminded again that the Inquisition was a marvel of bureaucracy as well as cruelty. None of the clerks looked up from their work as the English girl was dragged past.

They came to a spiral staircase, its steps worn stone slabs, and down it they went, down into the deeper dark. At the foot of the stair they came to another room, bigger but no more brightly lit than the court office above. There was no furniture here, but the room was dominated by two pieces of equipment: a table fitted with leather straps and a kind of winch, and an odd arrangement like a ladder tilted up on trestles, around which stood buckets of water.

Geoffrey noticed mundane details. Channels cut in the floor, leading to drains. A thick oaken door that looked impervious to noise. He felt very cold.

Agnes was made to stand before the table device. A soldier's gloved hand under her chin ensured she saw it.

'Step two,' Ferron said. 'Agnes Wooler, you are being shown these instruments of God's mercy. Do you understand what they are? Repent now and spare yourself this righteous pain.'

Agnes stared dully, but said nothing.

The clerk made another cross in his book, and Ferron said, 'Step three.'

One of the brothers closed his huge fist at the neck of Agnes's shift, and pulled. The filthy cloth ripped easily, and she was left naked, surrounded by men, in the middle of the cold room. She hunched her shoulders against the cold, but did not try to cover herself. Geoffrey knew she was nearly thirty years old, but she was so emaciated she looked like a child, her ribs showing, her legs like saplings. The flesh between her legs was stained with piss, shit and blood, and her back was marked with bloody weals. The brothers leered at her shrivelled dugs, the patch of auburn hair between her legs.

Again Ferron asked her to confess. When she did not speak, Ferron said, 'The fourth step.'

The brothers grabbed her and pushed her onto the table. They took hold of her wrists and ankles, pulled them back so her arms and legs were stretched, and fixed her in place with tight bonds of metal and leather. Agnes did not resist. One brother went to the winch at the top of the table. He tugged it experimentally; the table creaked, and the mechanism under it, a mesh of gears and levers, shuddered as if eager.

Agnes lay passively, her body a white strip of fragile flesh laid over wood and iron.

Ferron stood over her. 'Have pity on yourself, child,' he said. 'You were an anchoress. You don't deserve this. Just tell me the truth.'

She whispered, 'I know only one truth. That my father's love doomed me to this.'

Ferron frowned, clearly wondering what new heresy this was. But Geoffrey knew that the father she spoke of wasn't God.

Ferron ran out of patience. He glanced at the brother at the winch, who spat on his hands.

'Step five.'

The brother hauled. As gears bit and ropes tightened, the wooden tabletop lengthened, creaking. Agnes screamed, the noise huge in the confined room.

But still she would not speak. Ferron ordered the winch turned again, and then again.

Geoffrey forced himself to watch. He heard a ripping, cracking sound. Agnes's knees and elbows turned red and lumpy, and her shoulders were oddly twisted. Of course it would be the joints that would fail first, he thought helplessly, not the bones.

Still she did not talk.

Ferron made a curt gesture. 'Enough. Keep her conscious. We'll try the water.'

The brother at the head of the table released a latch, and let the winch spin loose. The brothers removed the buckles and clasps. Agnes didn't move. One brother slid his arms underneath her and lifted her. When her knees bent and her arms fell forward she was convulsed, and her screams became bestial.

But she was lowered onto the tilted ladder, with her head above her feet. Again she was strapped in place. Her head was pinned down by a metal band around her forehead. Twigs were forced into her nostrils, coated with fat so they plugged her nose.

Guards stood by, one holding a cloth and a bit of metal, the other a bucket of water.

Ferron leaned over Agnes. 'Can you hear me, Agnes? God doesn't want to see you suffer. If you choose to confess, after it begins, then all you have to do is look at me, as you are now. Do you understand? Is there anything you wish to say to me now?'

'He called me his Agnes,' she whispered. 'His precious Agnes. I was no Agnes when he was done with me ...'

Geoffrey's heart broke a little more.

Ferron, baffled, irritated, turned away. 'Do it,' he snapped to the brothers.

The one with the cloth stepped up. With casual, brutal strength he grabbed Agnes's cheeks, forced her jaws open and pushed his metal frame through her lips. It was like a funnel, Geoffrey saw, that kept the mouth wide open. Now the brother laid the centre of his cloth over the funnel and stepped back.

Agnes was still, save for her eyes, which flickered back and forth over distorted cheeks.

The other brother stepped up with his bucket of water. With care, he poured a bit of water onto the cloth. The water's weight forced the cloth into Agnes's mouth. The brother kept pouring, and Geoffrey saw that the cloth was drawn deeper into Agnes's throat. At last she swallowed, convulsively, and she coughed and choked, but she could not get the cloth out of her throat. Still the brother poured, and again she gagged, each swallow drawing the cloth deeper down her throat. Soon Geoffrey saw that she was close to panic, her battered body fighting back, immersed in a fear of drowning, of suffocating.

Ferron leaned over her. 'All you have to do is look at me,' he murmured. 'Just look at me and I'll tell them to stop.'

But, though she jerked and thrashed her head against its metal bond, she kept her eyes closed. Ferron nodded for the brothers to continue.

As the brothers poured more water into her, bucket after bucket, and more of the cloth was drawn into her throat and belly, and her stomach began to bloat, a grotesque swelling under her gaunt ribs.

Geoffrey, in torment himself, understood the logic. Ferron, as a man of God, wasn't supposed to draw blood. And nor was he supposed to allow his victims to die. This punishment with water, which would leave no mark, was a method devised with stunning ingenuity to fit this contradictory logic perfectly. It was even cheap, for the cloth and metal frame could be used again.

A full hour after it had begun, still Agnes would not speak. So Ferron nodded to the brothers, who lifted up the ladder, with the girl's broken body still fixed to it, and turned it so her feet were higher than her head. As her bloated belly pressed on her heart and lungs, through her crammed throat Agnes let out an animal roar of pain and terror.

Geoffrey could stand it no more. He lunged at Ferron. 'You monster, Ferron! How can you imagine that *this* serves the purposes of Christ? ...' But a brother grabbed him, pinning his arms.

XXII

On the morning of the execution of Agnes Wooler, Geoffrey Cotesford came early to the place of burning. It was another grim February day.

Eight years after the first *auto-da-fé*, the burning place outside the walls of Seville had come to be known as the *quemadero*. A platform had been set down here, with blunt stone pillars, strong and reusable. On the four sides of the platform statues of prophets stood, glaring sternly at those brought here. This morning, wood was piled up around each of the pillars.

From this place hundreds of souls had already been despatched, wisping to heaven or hell like the greasy smoke from their owners' crisping bodies.

As the morning brightened, others gathered for the show, men, women, even some children. Geoffrey had expected that. But the mood among these onlookers was not as he had anticipated. They seemed dull, almost numbed. Perhaps the Inquisition had dug too deep into the vitals of the nation. You came to watch, but not with relish, for you could not be sure you were safe yourself.

At last the procession reached the *quemadero*. The crowd murmured and shuffled, and some crossed themselves. Led by Ferron and other inquisitors and flanked by soldiers of the Holy Brotherhood, there were perhaps twenty of the condemned. All carried lit candles. The men walked barefoot, and their feet were white from the cold. But the women were stripped naked, and though their bodies were shrivelled from their captivity they had to suffer taunts from the crowd.

It was this type of detail, this repulsive lasciviousness at a place of death, that convinced Geoffrey that whatever motivated the Inquisition it was nothing to do with God. If Christ were here, He would surely have stepped forward to protect these suffering ones, even if it meant He had to die in their place. But Christ was not here. Only Geoffrey Cotesford, weak, cold, ashamed.

There among the huddle of women was Agnes. Geoffrey was surprised she could walk at all. She carried her candle in one hand, for her other arm hung limp. The shoulder looked dislocated; the pain of it, weeks after her first punishment, must have been agonising.

He couldn't help but call, 'Agnes!'

She looked around dimly. Her eyes seemed unfocused.

He didn't know what to say. 'I'm sorry,' he said. 'I'll pray for you. I can't help you—'

'I can, though.'

The voice in his ear was startling. It was Abdul Ibn Ibrahim, and he was grinning. He held a bundle of documents.

'Abdul? What are you doing here?'

'Being my deceitful, conniving, conspiratorial self.'

'I don't understand.'

'The Inquisition,' he said, 'is the logic of our times – of *your* times, of this age of Christendom. The Reconquest and all your crusading has militarised Christianity, which was once a faith of love. Frightened and ignorant, terrified by the march of infidels, stirred up by holy fools and greedy monarchs, you fall willingly into the thrall of these perverted prelates. Well, there's nothing I can do about the flaws in Christian souls. But perhaps I can save one helpless woman. Come.' And he strode forward, boldly approaching Ferron.

Geoffrey, confused, could only follow.

Abdul stood right in front of Ferron, forcing the whole procession to stop. The situation couldn't have been more public, with the inquisitors, the brothers, the crowd, even the condemned looking on.

Ferron glared at Abdul and asked him why he was here.

'It's a matter of grave concern,' Abdul said. He tapped his sheaf of documents. 'I must discuss it with you.'

'What, here? *Now?*'

'There is no time to delay. Please, brother. It is a matter of death, or life.'

'Whose life? Whose death?'

'Yours,' said Abdul.

Ferron stared. Then he allowed Abdul to draw him aside, but he waved the procession forward. As the brothers made the condemned kneel before the posts, he snapped, 'Make it quick, mudejar.'

Abdul indicated the sheaf of papers. 'A witness has come forward. To testify against *you*, brother. He has the testimonies of others to back him up.'

Ferron stiffened. 'And what is his allegation?'

For answer, Abdul held out his hand. It contained a round sliver of bread, a communion wafer. 'This was found in your office.'

And Geoffrey immediately understood.

At the heart of the crimes routinely alleged of conversos, supposedly lapsing from Christianity to Judaism, was the theft of consecrated wafers. It was easy; when fed it by a priest you could just slip a wafer under your tongue and keep it there, unconsumed. But, once consecrated in the Holy Mass, its substance had been transformed into the flesh of Christ, and so the wafer held potent magic. For example, some years back there had been a rumour of a conspiracy to spike the water supply of Seville with communion wafers and the mashed-up heart of a Christian boy, a blasphemous toxin that would drive Christians insane.

There was fear in Ferron's eyes; it was well known he was of converso blood himself, and this was a silent accusation of a very grave crime. 'Who gave you this?'

'Well, you aren't entitled to know that,' Abdul said. 'Strictly speaking, by the rules of your Inquisition, I shouldn't be showing you this evidence at all, for you don't have the right to see it. And of course you are presumed guilty once an allegation is made. Have I got that right?'

'It's a lie. An evil, devil-spawned, malicious lie.'

'I'm glad to hear it,' said Abdul heartily. 'Then the processes of the Inquisition will have no difficulty establishing exactly that fact. But perhaps it would be better to save everybody the trouble of putting you to the question.'

'What is it you want, mudejar?'

'Agnes Wooler.'

Ferron stared at him, and then looked at Geoffrey. 'I nearly broke this girl seeking answers about her conspiracy. But those answers were staring me in the face, all the time. If I ever see you again—'

Abdul grinned, and he held up his fist, enclosing the host. 'Threats are so ugly.'

Ferron turned away. He walked onto the *quemadero*, grabbed Agnes by her good arm, and marched her away from her stake. Another inquisitor flapped after him, muttering about irregularities, but Ferron waved him away.

He brought Agnes to Abdul and Geoffrey. She looked grotesque, her feet and hands blue with the cold, her nipples hard as pink pebbles. Her bruised face was empty.

Abdul dropped the communion wafer into Ferron's hand. In return

Ferron released the girl. She stumbled, and Geoffrey took her thin, shivering form in his arms.

Ferron glared at Abdul and Geoffrey. 'This isn't over.' He turned away.

Geoffrey nodded. 'So the battle for the future is joined.'

'But for now,' Abdul said, 'we must concentrate on the needs of the present.' He took off his thick Moorish cloak and wrapped it around Agnes's bare shoulders.

XXIII

AD 1491

James loved to climb into the hot, silent air over Granada, to escape the squabbles of mankind and the conundrums of morality, to ascend into the realm of birds, and clouds, and stars, and God. The clean, harsh breeze of Spain was even more conducive to supporting his flight than the soggy air over England's green hills. And in long hours of practice he had learned to coax his machine ever higher into the sky, even after the elastic energy of its launching crossbow was exhausted. The trick was to seek out rising masses of warm air, invisible fountains in an atmosphere like an ocean, that would lift him up like a leaf on a breeze.

And, that bright October day, he had never seen anything quite as extraordinary as Granada, the last Moorish kingdom, and the Christian military city drawn up before it.

The Alhambra was like a vast ship stranded in the middle of the land, like the Ark fallen on Ararat. Somewhere in that fortress poor Boabdil was holed up, perhaps the last emir al-Andalus would ever know. The city of Granada was a splash of grey around the Alhambra itself, studded with the glittering gold of mosque roofs. The air over the city was brown with smoke this morning, for Granada was swollen with refugees. And he could make out a thin black line of caravans and mule trains heading south, Muslims fleeing further towards the Strait and the welcoming lands of Africa.

As he wheeled away from the fortress James flew over Santa Fé – 'Holy Faith', the Christian city-camp set out on the plain before Granada. Within a circle of walls and ditches it was a crucifix of buildings, with a glittering pile of weapons where the crucifix's upright and crosspiece intersected. Santa Fé looked solid, centuries old, and yet it had been

295

thrown up virtually overnight when the monarchs had brought their armies to within sight of the Alhambra. The speed of the construction had bewildered the Muslim defenders, but it was another of Fernando's ruses; the 'city' was more wood frame and cloth than stone.

So at last the war had come to Granada itself. It was now two years since the final defeat for El Zagal, the Valiant, brother of the dead emir Muley Hacen. Now there was only Boabdil, an emir so hapless that the Christians called him El Chico, the little one, and even he called himself the Unfortunate. Defeated and imprisoned more than once, he had already agreed terms of a final surrender. But his own people were revolted by the way he had rejoiced at his uncle's fall, and Boabdil had been forced to make a show of resistance. So Granada was besieged, with sixty thousand *caballeros* assembling at Santa Fé.

And in that long summer of siege and negotiation and simmering tension, of almost gladiatorial combat between Christian and Muslim champions, Cristobal Colon had once more been summoned to court. There would be yet another hearing of his case, here in Santa Fé, and one more chance for Grace Bigod and Diego Ferron to make their counter-case. Three years after the disaster of the burning-out of the manufactory of the Engines of God, Grace and Ferron still hoped that Colon, who clearly believed himself a man of destiny, could be seduced into leading a new army east in a final war against Islam.

And here was James, flying high in the air, ready to play his part. James's flying machine had been unharmed by the sabotage of the manufactory. So the plan was that as the latest debate over Colon's destiny reached its turning-point, the minds and souls of the court would be uplifted by the vision of a man-machine in the sky, with the cross of Christ painted bright red on its gossamer wings, suspended in the air like an image of the returned Virgin Mary, who in the last days would be seen in the sky with the moon at her feet.

James had become increasingly uneasy about the ardour of Grace and Ferron. He continued to find it difficult to reconcile a war against the Muslims with his own personal relationship with Christ, the prince of peace. They, however, both longed for the final cleansing war against Islam, to be waged with Grace's machines – and Ferron, burning with an Inquisitor's cruel moral certainty, really seemed to have come to believe in the approach of the end days.

But James banished his doubts and fears by pouring his energy and imagination into mastering his man-bird. He couldn't believe that the sheer beauty of the flying machine could be *sinful*, no matter for what purpose men intended to use it.

So he flew high over Santa Fé, making a circle over that shining heap of weapons. He saw a few faces turned up towards him, pale dots lifted to the sky. He was so high they would surely believe him an eagle or a buzzard, for you didn't expect to see men suspended in the air. The shock would be tremendous when James came dipping down out of the sky and all could see it was a man, not a bird, suspended by the ingenuity of the human mind, and that the cross of Christ burned on his wings. He grinned at the thought of it, and made a mental note to admit his sin of pride to his confessor.

Then he tugged at the cables that controlled his wings and ducked away, soaring over the Alhambra and heading for his landing site.

XXIV

On the ground, at the heart of Santa Fé, Harry Wooler peered up at the hovering bird – if it was a bird. He hadn't forgotten what he had seen over Derbyshire, on that dramatic day of destruction three years ago. He said to Geoffrey, 'If he drops any of those eggs of fire this city of wood and cloth will burn like a hundred-year-old timber pile.'

Geoffrey Cotesford peered up, uninterested. 'One toy machine in the air won't make much difference. The boy flying that thing is a Franciscan, you know. James of Buxton, a bright lad according to his abbot. Now his head has been turned by these gadgets, by all this talk of war. As I've researched these prophecies I've discovered they have a peculiarly corrupting effect on scholars and holy men who should know better. A priest called Sihtric, who lived through the Conquest. A scholar from Oxford called Peter, who was burned to death during the siege of Seville. And now this James. A waste of good brains, a steady seducing of souls away from God's true purpose . . .'

They were walking down a broad street of trampled earth. This was a military camp, and in the low buildings around them the soldiers did what soldiers always did: ate, slept, wrestled, picked their feet, and complained about the food. There was a surprising number of Muslims here, talking to Christian officers in tight, tense groups. Even while the siege of Granada continued, Boabdil's court was in negotiation with the Christian monarchs about the terms of his almost inevitable capitulation.

And Geoffrey spoke of Cristobal Colon.

'Since the destruction of the manufactory, that day when Bartolomeo Colon was driven away from England with the stink of smoke in his nostrils, we have been winning the argument. Now we are approaching the culmination of years of work, Harry. Cristobal Colon has a thorough and well-worked-out case for his journey to the west.'

Harry said gloomily, 'But Colon has plenty of enemies at court, who think he's an obsessive buffoon, and sometimes it's hard not to agree with them. And after all these years he's growing sick of Spain. He thinks he's being strung along. It's said he's planning to approach the King of France next.'

'Have faith, Harry,' Geoffrey said with good humour. 'Have patience! It has been a long haul, but just a little further. This chap de Santangel, who Colon is meeting today, is more businesslike than most courtiers.' A wealthy Aragonese, Luis de Santangel's family had served Fernando's ancestors for centuries as merchants and lawyers. Now de Santangel was treasurer of the Holy Brotherhood, the monarchs' religious police. Geoffrey said, 'De Santangel is a man of money, not of God. He will see Colon's plan as a good business proposition, and I am confident he will back our case. You'd get on with him, Harry.' He grinned. 'Two men of business together, carving up the future! I can see it now.'

Harry wasn't in the mood to be teased. 'But Grace Bigod is here at the court. Hovering around that monster Ferron, damn his cold heart. Ferron longs for war, you know, and so does she. I think they've both gone mad.'

Geoffrey shrugged. 'Grace *must* continue. She has invested her whole life in this project, even passing up her chance of children and grand-children. But whatever Grace and Ferron do or say, it is a critical time.

'The monarchs' heads are full of fantasies. Isabel dreams of explor-ation. And on the other hand Fernando really believes, I think, that he is the Hidden One, the new King David who will return the Ark of the Covenant to the City of David, thus heralding the Second Coming of Christ, and the kingdom of God upon the earth. And so on! Thus the monarchs are predisposed to be swayed either way – west with Colon to find a new world, or east with the Engines of God to continue the logic of their Reconquest.

'This is the time. The war against the Muslims is almost won. Soon, for a brief moment, the souls of the monarchs will be fluid, their purposes fulfilled, their dreams unlocked. And in this moment the future must be fixed. It is now or never for Colon, and the rest of us – perhaps the whole world.'

Harry felt he had already burned up too many years of his working life on this extraordinary project. 'Let's hope that we really are reaching the end of this long game, Geoffrey, one way or another.'

The friar nodded. 'Yes. But, remember, Harry, the true game of the future is only about to begin.'

And at that moment Harry saw Abdul Ibn Ibrahim walking towards them. He was carrying a small wooden box.

Geoffrey rushed to him and clasped his arms. 'Abdul! I didn't know you were here. I haven't seen you since that terrible day in Seville. What became of you?'

Abdul's face was stony. 'I was forced to leave Seville, of course. I returned to Granada, where I went back to the emir's court. Now I find myself working on the finer points of our capitulation treaty.'

Harry was as glad to see Abdul as Geoffrey was. But he could see how grim his mood was. 'What's wrong, Abdul? You know I'll always be grateful to you for having saved Agnes from Ferron.'

Abdul sighed. 'But it is Ferron who has sent me here today.'

'*Ferron* did?'

'He sought me out. And he gave me this, to present to you.' He handed Harry the box.

Harry took it. It was finely made of cedarwood, an expensive gift.

Abdul said, 'Ferron's message is this. You must not support your champion any more, Harry. When Colon presents his case you must speak out *against* the arguments you have helped him develop. Otherwise you must stay as silent as your sister.'

Harry was confused, but frightened. 'My sister's safe in England. And she's never been silent.'

Abdul said nothing.

Geoffrey touched Harry's shoulder. 'Open the box, Harry.'

The lid lifted easily, on oiled hinges. Inside was a glass vial, which contained a slab of meat, pickled in some preserving liquid. It took Harry long heartbeats to recognise what it was, from the bloody stump, the shape of the tip. It was a human tongue, severed at the root. In the lid of the box a note was tucked. Harry took this and unfolded it, and read: 'AGNES WOOLER.'

'He took her back,' Geoffrey raged. 'He took her back!'

XXV

In the monarchs' audience chamber expensive tapestries hung from the walls, showing such scenes as the Virgin Mary hovering, ethereal, over crusaders who stormed the walls of Jerusalem. And the wooden floor was covered with rich Persian carpets, a gift from Boabdil in Granada to his effective masters. This chamber, at the heart of Santa Fé, was grander than any room Harry had ever been in, even if it was just a mock-up of wood and waxed cloth. And it was full of courtiers. They reminded Harry of exotic birds, preening and gossiping, curious about the latest trial of a favourite of the Queen.

They were curious because here, on benches before a throne-like chair, opposing factions prepared to debate once again the matter of Cristobal Colon.

The throne was occupied today by Luis de Santangel. A portly, sensible-looking man of perhaps forty, dressed expensively, he looked what he was: heavy with money, and an influence at the court. Even if he approved Colon's proposal it would not be the final verdict, which as always lay with the monarchs. But his word carried a good deal of weight.

Harry, Geoffrey Cotesford and Abdul Ibrahim were here under the sponsorship of Antonio de Marchena, the friar from the monastery of La Rabida at Palos who had supported Colon's dream of sailing the Ocean Sea since he had first come to Spain.

Opposing them was Hernando de Talavera, once Isabel's confessor and still the court's principal theologian, and his party of sea captains, geographers and astronomers, and a few clerics. While de Marchena had always supported Colon, Talavera had opposed his case just as steadfastly since he had first presented it six long years ago. Over the years, as Colon refused to give up and disappear, Talavera had grown steadily more exasperated, and was now quite determined Colon would never get his ships.

And, sitting in the front row of courtiers, there was Diego Ferron, who campaigned for Colon to become, not an admiral of the Ocean Sea, but a general of the final war with Islam, leading forces equipped with Grace's Engines of God. Ferron had Moorish attendants with him: a slim, dark woman wearing a jewelled veil, and a servant girl who sat silently at his feet, face covered by her veil, even her eyes invisible. It seemed strange to Harry that this man who was arguing for the violent destruction of Islam should have Muslim servants, but these were the last days of Granada, and Boabdil, cornered and compromised, was lavish in his gifts of people as well as objects to the court of the monarchs.

Harry stared at Ferron, but he would not look back. After Agnes's destruction of the engines there was only hatred between the two camps, he thought, a hatred that could surely only end with the destruction of one or other of them – and, perhaps, of Agnes.

Now a shiver of excitement ran around the crowded room. Harry looked around.

A man strode boldly into the room. He was dressed in a long black robe like a monk's habit, and he carried a bundle of maps and books under his arm. He was tall, and his swept-back hair was almost pure white, with at the temples traces of a vanishing russet red. His brow was broad, and his imposing face was dominated by a strong nose; his skin was somewhat freckled, a sea-farer's face, and his eyes were grey-green – the colour of the ocean, Harry thought. He looked like a Roman senator, a revenant from a grander age than this. Yet there was anxiety in his sea-green eyes as he fumbled to lay out his charts and books on a table before de Santangel. Some of the courtiers even laughed. And, Harry thought, looking at that shock of white hair, though he was only just forty years old he was already growing old in the pursuit of his single dream.

In all the long years Harry had been tracking his career, this was the first time he had seen the man in the flesh. This was Cristobal Colon, Christophorus Columbus, a man who seemed to Harry to have been made flesh from the flimsy fragments of prophecies and augurs written down centuries before he had been born. A man about whom history pivoted.

Harry found himself hoping that Colon would lose his argument yet again. For if Colon by some chance swayed de Santangel, Harry knew that he was going to have to stand on his feet and shout Colon down, betraying years of effort by himself and his friends. Harry prayed that this convoluted dilemma could be resolved in some way that spared him making such a dreadful decision.

Without preamble Colon began to speak. It was a case he had set out many times before, and he told it clearly, with a deep, strong voice. But his tone was laced with impatience that he was forced to go through all this again, and his Spanish was poor, his Italian accent thick, and he stumbled over his words.

He began by quoting the authorities of antiquity. He leaned heavily on the great Ptolemy, who in the second century had presented a clear and consistent model of the world, around which the sun and stars rotated on crystal spheres. Colon knew Ptolemy through a three-centuries-old Latin translation of a book called the *Almagest* that had been preserved by the Arabs.

He referred too to the work of Pope Pius II, who before his elevation had written a book developing Ptolemy's ideas, and a cardinal called Pierre d'Ailly whose *Image of the World* had presented strong views on the relative sizes of Asia and the Ocean Sea. He read extracts from Roger Bacon's *Opus Majus*, which was a synthesis of Ptolemy's vision with more recent work by Christian and Muslim geographers. Bacon argued that there was no significant land mass to be found save those already known: Asia, Africa and Europe.

Ferron scowled as Grace's own engineer was quoted against her case.

Summing up these ideas, Colon presented a map drawn for him by one Martin Behaim, with a relatively narrow Ocean Sea and only a scattering of islands between Europe and Asia. If Colon's arguments were correct then a voyage west across the Ocean Sea to the riches of the east, thus closing a circle around the curve of the earth, ought to be a trivial matter.

Colon was interrupted by a weary-looking geographer from Talavera's party, who presented rebuttals he had been forced to make many times before. All this was supposition, he said, addressing de Santangel. 'Nobody would argue with the bulk of Ptolemy's ideas, so lucidly set down in a greater age than this, and preserved through the ignorant copying-down of the Arabs. Of course the earth sits at the centre of the universe; that much is obvious to a child.

'But as to the size of the earth, even the great Ptolemy is only one authority among a range with differing views. Centuries before Ptolemy was born the Greek Eratosthenes computed the earth's circumference from the angle of shadows cast by the sun, and derived a figure somewhat greater than Ptolemy's. These "authorities" like d'Ailly have clearly been *selected* by the gentleman because their estimates of the earth's figure all lie at the *lower* end of the range of accepted possibilities, the mean of which lies, I should judge, somewhere around *four times* bigger than that shown in the gentleman's charts. And if that is so, if we were so foolish as to set off a boat into the western sea, the crew would never return – and nor would our money!' That won a laugh.

But Harry knew he had a point, as he and Geoffrey had indeed selected many of the more helpful authorities and fed them to Colon.

Colon, however, was undeterred. He said simply that nobody could prove his figures right until the earth was sailed all the way around, but nobody could prove them wrong either.

He went on to the next leg of his case, that a voyage across the Ocean Sea would be no more than an extrapolation of journeys of exploration that had already been made – mostly by the Portuguese, he pointed out to the Spanish court. He spoke of developments in shipbuilding, and of the discovery of hitherto unknown islands in the Ocean Sea, from Madeira and the Canaries to the Azores.

And he spoke of earlier attempts to sail west across the Ocean Sea. He had collected many such tales in his years on Porto Santo and in Portugal. One Diogo de Tieve had sailed steadily south-west from the Azores, coming to a place where the condition of the sea and the circling of land birds indicated that land lay to the west, but he had had to return before it was reached. A Genoese merchant called Luca de Cazana had mounted several voyages that sailed west from the Azores for a hundred leagues or more, but in vain. Colon said that even unsuccessful explorations returned useful information about the state of the winds and the ocean currents. Colon himself had sailed far down the coast of Africa, and, he claimed, knew the Ocean Sea as well as any man alive.

Now he moved on to older legends. He referred to stories of the voyages of Saint Brendan and other Irish monks who had supposedly sailed far to the west across the north of the Ocean Sea, encountering mountains of ice and other strange phenomena. He quoted from the sagas of the Vikings, who, as was well known, had built churches in a western land so rich and warm that vines grew readily, so extensive it had never been explored properly.

Colon turned at last to what he believed to be the strongest plank of his argument: his own personal experience. He spoke of evidence he had seen with his own eyes, relics from the lands across the sea fortuitously washed east: bits of carved wood, branches of unfamiliar species of trees, even war canoes carved from single logs. It had been such bits of evidence, Colon said, which had been the seed of his own quest to go west.

Concluding, Colon spoke of the riches of the east, and quoted at length the biography of Marco Polo, who had crossed China in the days of the Mongol Peace. And Colon spoke of his dream of a grand alliance of western Christendom with the armies of the Khan and the wealth of the domain of Prester John, all linked by Colon's mighty new trans-oceanic trade routes: a grand alliance that would fall upon the great Islamic states from the east and wipe them from the earth, at last liberating Jerusalem from the hands of the infidel.

One by one the court's experts rose to counter aspects of Colon's case.

Harry half listened. Of course, he thought, there was a hope, just a grain of it, that Colon might actually be *right*. Much of Colon's evidence was faked by Harry, Geoffrey and Abdul. But not all of it.

And if anybody could succeed at this venture it would be Colon. He was a vision of doggedness, of determination. Where others had tentatively probed a little way west before running for home, if Colon ever got his ships he would keep right on going come what may.

Yet, Harry thought sadly, Colon was at the same time an unimpressive figure. His poor education showed in the stumbles in his Spanish, and in his sometimes weak grasp of scholarship. Snobs about the new printing presses mocked men like Colon, who now found learned material much too easy to get hold of, and regurgitated it, half-digested, in pursuit of their own pet theories. Such nostalgics pined for the good old days when books were so rare and expensive that scholarship was properly kept in the hands of the privileged few.

But, Harry thought, his soul stirring, if the prophecies were right, these flawed arguments by a flawed man might yet result in a bold stroke that would transform the fortunes of mankind for ever.

The last speaker was Diego Ferron. 'This is all fanciful. Legend. Tittle-tattle from drunk sailors. It is the mission of this court to prosecute holy war. But the way to do that is to drive *east*, straight for the exposed belly of Islam, not to follow some fool's errand to the west. The monarchs' money should be spent on weapons, not ships, not thrown into the endless Ocean Sea in pursuit of a dream . . .'

De Santangel heard him out. Then he got to his feet.

And just as he did so there was a murmur at the back of the court. Harry turned.

Amid a flurry of bowing and murmured obsequies Queen Isabel walked in. Flanked by soldiers of the Holy Brotherhood and trailed by bishops, nobles and other courtiers, she was dressed for the field in a practical-looking gown of crushed velvet, and her famous chestnut hair was pulled back from a still-beautiful face. She had a quality of light about her that changed the very room, Harry thought.

She smiled almost fondly at Colon, who bowed with a flourish.

XXVI

Isabel took the seat de Santangel had vacated. She murmured to the financier that she was sorry to have missed Colon's presentation but looked forward to his judgement.

De Santangel, glorying, showed off. He walked back and forth, stroking his bearded chin. 'I'll tell you what I think of all this, good Colon. I can see you're a man of substance: of good bearing, of integrity, of faith, of belief – and of determination, which is what a man needs to get along in business.

'But I can also see that the case you've spouted is a lot of bilge. No, no,' and he held up a hand as Colon made to protest, 'I don't want to hear it all trotted out again. Once is enough, thanks! But what I will say is that it's *bound* to be a lot of bilge, because the truth is nobody can say what lies on the other side of the Ocean Sea until somebody goes out there to see for himself. Am I right? So that's the bare bones of the case.

'Now, I'm a man of business, and I'm used to estimating risk. And as I see it the risk to the monarchs is low. All we have to fund is the first voyage, for if you succeed subsequent voyages will be paid for out of the profits, and if you fail, for instance if you don't come back, we just won't go out again. All you want is three ships. You're asking for, what, five million maravedis? Why, I'd be prepared to put up my own house as collateral on that much if necessary.

'And why? Because the returns are potentially huge. The Portuguese are already sucking in profits from Madeira; we are already making money from the Canaries. Now, I'm no geographer and I don't know if you'll find a way to Asia or not. But it stands to reason that there's *something* out there, because God surely wouldn't make a world half-covered with an ocean good for nothing but fish!

'Our new kingdom of Spain has grown from nothing to cover the whole peninsula, in a few centuries. Now, it seems to me, we have the chance to build a new Spanish empire that could grow much further, beyond all imagination. Why, the monarchs could be compared in future to – to—'

Abdul said drily, 'Alexander the Great?'

'Exactly! And on the other hand if we *don't* take this chance some other petty king or grasping prince, from Portugal or England or France, will take it instead, and we'll be for ever in their shade.

'And I'll tell you something else. *We need the money*. For centuries we lived off a tithe of Moorish gold. Now we're funding the war with money confiscated from the Jews by the Inquisition. But the Moors are all but defeated. And if some have their way,' and he eyed the Inquisitors, 'we'll soon be driving the last Jew out of Spain, and half our merchant class and a good chunk of our wealth will go with them, and *then* we're going to need a new source of funds.

'Cristobal Colon, you may be a genius or as mad as a grasshopper in a hat, I'm not qualified to judge. But you offer a vision of virtually unlimited wealth, for a price that represents an affordable risk. And for that reason I'll be recommending strongly to their noble majesties,' and he bowed to Isabel, 'that they fund your mission. Let it not be said that such great and noble monarchs denied themselves a grand chance to probe the secrets of the very universe over a pittance.

'And as for the proposal that Colon should become a general in God's army,' he concluded, glancing at Ferron, 'God has many generals, but *we* have only one Cristobal Colon. He is meant for discovery, not war, friar!'

So, Harry realised, his and Geoffrey's years of work and scheming – and perhaps a manipulation of history centuries deep – were coming to fruition in this very room.

And Harry himself had to ruin it. He gazed at Ferron, who met his eyes calmly. Anger flared in Harry. Perhaps he would defy this monster even now.

But then Ferron turned to his serving girl, who had knelt, silent and still as a statue, throughout Colon's presentation. Ferron slid back the veil from the girl's face.

It was, of course, Agnes. Her chin was bruised, her nose a little bloody. Her eyes were empty, unfocused, and a little drool laced her lips. It was clear she was drugged.

Harry knew he had no choice. Reluctantly, he stood. The Queen, de Santangel, even Colon, turned to him curiously.

307

Geoffrey plucked at his sleeve. 'In God's name sit down. We have won! There's no more to be said.'

But Harry shook him off. 'I must speak.' He turned to de Santangel, his head full of devastating arguments against Colon – not least the fact that some of his evidence was simple fakery, planted by Geoffrey and himself. He prepared to speak.

And Ferron's other Moorish companion, the tall woman, leapt to her feet. From beneath her loose white robes she produced a blade, long and sharp and polished.

With a strangled cry she hurled herself at the Queen. Isabel stared, with no time to react.

But as the woman's arm descended, as the blade fell towards the Queen's breast, Abdul Ibn Ibrahim threw himself between the killer and her target. He took the first strike in his arm, but he stayed on his feet and spun around, trying to get hold of the killer. His reward was another stabbing, this time in the chest. Blood spurted from the wound, frothy with air, and Abdul gurgled, as if drowning.

But the blade was caught, perhaps on Abdul's ribs, and the killer could not draw it out. The Holy Brothers, had time to fall on the assassin and club her to the ground.

The audience erupted in screams and panic, as bishops and nobles scrambled to get out of the room. Colon stood beside the monarch fiercely, protecting her with his bulk.

Harry ran to Agnes, and scooped her up in his arms. She was as limp as a puppet, her eyes rolling in her head. But she was alive.

He turned to see the Holy Brothers holding down the would-be killer. He got a clear view of her face for the first time.

Her skin darkened, her hair blackened, it was Grace Bigod.

XXVII

James saw the courtiers spilling out of the audience chamber. From his elevated viewpoint they boiled like ants over the ground. He grinned, and swept lower. If Grace and Ferron had arranged for the inquiry into Colon to come out into the open air to see his display in the sky, this was his cue.

But the crowd seemed disorderly. People were running away from the chamber – and likewise soldiers were running towards the mocked-up building. Even from up here he could hear screams. And now he saw a knot of the heavy-set brothers hustling out of the chamber, escorting a finely dressed woman who could only be the Queen. Something had gone wrong. Nobody was looking up. He would have to descend to see what was going on – and to make people look at him.

Tugging on his control lines he dipped his left wing, and banked that way. But then a gust of wind washed over the wing, and it pulled out of his grasp. He felt the machine slide further to the left, and the strengthening breeze made it impossible to pull the wing back. He fought with his control lines and kicked at his machine's tail. Struts snapped with sharp cracks.

And he slid into a tight spiral, spinning ever leftward, that drove him towards the ground. As the wind pushed back the skin of his face, as his speed rose and he spun like a leaf, he screamed in longing and fear: 'Grace, Grace!'

XXVIII

It was a huge relief for Harry to get out of the chaotic confines of the audience chamber and into the clear Spanish air. He still had his sister in his arms. Geoffrey stood by him, panting with shock and fear.

The army camp was in chaos. The attempt on Isabel's life had been like a stick thrust into a beehive. Soldiers ran everywhere. There were screams, and the crack of arquebuses. Muslims, who an hour ago had been able to go about their business unmolested, now ran for their lives. It was a grim irony, Harry thought, that it had been a Muslim who in fact had saved the Christian Queen, and a Christian who had tried to kill her.

'But I don't understand,' he said. 'I don't understand.'

'Evidently Grace didn't know of Ferron's scheme with Agnes,' Geoffrey said grimly. 'Our opponents didn't even trust each other! Grace saw she was losing the argument, Harry. She saw we were winning. And that couldn't be allowed. She was a woman who had come to *need* her murderous war, the glory of her weapons. She would even impersonate a Muslim, she would murder the greatest Christian queen, in order to win the argument – and to provoke needless slaughter.'

'And Abdul—'

'Abdul, in that flash as the blade descended towards Isabel, saw the opposite. The Moors are already defeated, here in Spain; Boabdil, for all he is despised, is doing a decent job of negotiating a surrender with honour. But if Isabel had been killed Fernando and his soldiers would have vented their fury on Granada. And in the east, the sultans would have responded to such a massacre as they have always threatened to do, beginning with reprisals against the Christians in Jerusalem, and against our holy sites.'

'And then the holy war would have been inevitable.'

'Yes. Abdul saw it all in a flash. He gave his life to save a Christian monarch, and to avert global disaster.'

'We have all spoken of such possibilities,' Harry said. 'But it was Abdul who acted.'

'He was a better man than either of us,' Geoffrey murmured, calming. 'He has saved countless lives, beginning with Isabel's. Perhaps he has saved the future.'

Something in the sky caught Harry's eye. It was like a bird, yet massive, more ungainly, high in the air. And it was spinning, spinning towards the ground, as if it had broken a wing.

'Is that a man? Is that James of Buxton? Are men meant to fly, Geoffrey?'

'If so, not here, not now.'

The fragile contraption, all struts and feathers, tumbled down, out of sight. It didn't seem to matter. Harry held Agnes close, murmuring to her, longing for her to wake from her drugged stupor.

EPILOGUE
AD 1492

I

There was much excitement around the harbour of Palos this August morning. The place was crowded with curious Christians, many still wearing their crusader shoulder flashes, and with Jews desperate to flee a country that had rejected them.

Harry and Geoffrey walked a good distance, pushing through the crowds, trying to get a glimpse of the explorers. In the end they climbed a steep slope, just outside the town, from which they could see the harbour and the three ships it cradled.

It was a modest fleet. There were the two caravels, called the *Pinta* and the *Santa Clara*, the latter more commonly known as the *Nina* after its owner, a man called Juan Nino. And there was the one larger carrack called the *Santa Maria*, but often called *La Gallega* as it had been built in Galicia. The *Santa Maria* carried square sails on a foremast and mainmast, and a triangular lateen sail on a mizzenmast at the rear. The *Pinta* was rigged like the *Santa Maria*, but the *Nina* relied on lateen sails. The two caravels especially were graceful, slim little ships.

In these last minutes before they cast off Harry could see the figures of the crew loading their ships, bustling around the decks and the stout castles at prow and stern. The men looked somehow too large for their ships, which were only some fifty or sixty feet long; they were terribly tiny ships to challenge a world ocean. Harry remembered Abdul telling him that the *rudders* on some Chinese vessels were almost the size of a ship like the *Nina*.

And yet it was not the Chinese who sailed today, but Cristobal Colon.

'Modest they may be, yes,' Geoffrey said, when Harry voiced these thoughts. 'But look at them, Harry, bristling in the water, full of purpose.

315

Henry the Navigator would be proud to see the day – even if they are Spanish ships sailing from a Spanish port.'

'It's turning out to be quite a year for Cristobal,' Harry said.

'Quite a year for Spain!'

The door to Colon's ocean adventure had finally opened in November of last year, when Boabdil, the last emir of al-Andalus, signed a treaty of surrender. On 6 January 1492, the monarchs themselves entered Granada. They were dressed respectfully in the Moorish style, Isabel radiant in a turban and an embroidered caftan, but the sweet voices of the royal choir sang hymns to Christ, which echoed through the empty stone streets. It was a tremendous victory for Christendom, the conclusion of eight centuries of dedicated reconquest, and the news of it rang out across Europe.

And in April Colon was summoned to the monarchs' court once more. The monarchs received him in the Alhambra itself, in a chamber the Moors had called the Hall of the Mexuar, a room in the oldest part of the palace where the daylight was filtered through the stained glass of a lantern roof. In this architectural triumph of a vanquished people, amid rooms inscribed with Moorish slogans – *Wa la ghalib illa Allah,* there is no conqueror but Allah – Colon's contract documents were sealed. He was given a letter from Fernando and Isabel to the Great Khan of the Mongols. And as a final flourish Colon begged the monarchs to devote all the treasure raised by his expedition to the reconquest of Jerusalem.

But Colon would not be able to sail from Seville or Malaga, for those great ports were choked with fleeing Jews.

He headed for little Palos on the Tinto estuary instead; Colon was glad to honour the town where he had found such support from the brothers of La Rabida. But on the road Colon was caught up in great chains of refugees, more Jews, struggling to get to the coast. Some of them carried shards of the shattered tombstones of their ancestors. They were dusty, exhausted, ill; some helpless mothers even gave birth on the road. But their rabbis made the women sing and play tambourines to raise the people's spirits. And even when Colon reached Palos he had trouble securing ships, for all the masters were busy with the urgent task of transporting Jews.

Just at this moment when it was preparing to reach out across the world, Spain was cleansing itself.

Geoffrey said, 'What a terrible mistake the expulsion could prove to be! Torquemada's bitter heart may be brimming. But Spain is stripping herself of her most industrious citizens – of a whole class of bankers and moneylenders, artists and administrators; no *hidalgo* or *caballero* would lower himself to such work. Just as she is on the verge of empire, Spain is ridding herself of the talents she needs to run it. Ha!

'And the Moors will surely follow the Jews out of Spain sooner or later, whatever promises the monarchs have made. What will become of the Moors I don't know, for though their ancestors came from the deserts of Africa and Araby, they don't belong there now any more than you or I would have a place in the German forests of our own forebears. Perhaps they will simply dissipate, a vanished people, leaving behind their palaces and books, and the future will wonder that a Muslim nation once flourished in western Europe ...'

Harry had had enough of the grand sweep of history. 'Well, all I want is to get back to my own life,' he said firmly. 'I'm thirty-six years old now, brother, and feeling it. I have spent too long on the past; I want to think of the future. If I can find a wife, have some children—'

'Good for you.'

'And I want to get back to trade. If there's profit to be made from this adventure, I want a share in generating it – and spending it. The Spanish aren't the only explorers. I have been corresponding with an Italian adventurer called Jacobo Caboto who is going to approach King Henry with a proposal to try to find a route to Asia through the northern seas, following in the wake of the long-dead Vikings.'

Geoffrey grunted. 'Perhaps you will find Vinland, if not China.'

'And what next for you, Geoffrey?'

Geoffrey thought, tugging at his lip. 'I have been contemplating this muddy business we have been involved in. I want to do something about it. We have been at the focus of a battle between two time-meddling agents, the Weaver who fed the designs of the Engines of God back to Aethelred and Aethelmaer, and the Witness who spoke to Eadgyth.

'*And there is evidence of other tampering*, Harry. Your remote ancestor Sihtric, dead four centuries, made marginal notes on his copy of the Engine Codex. He believed he had found evidence that the Weaver, or another agent, tried to avert the course of the Norman Conquest of England. And even earlier, in the deep and ancient days when the Romans ruled Britain, another meddler, or the same one, tried to arrange the assassination of the Emperor Constantine. I have tried to map all this.'

He produced a parchment on which he had scribbled a kind of tapestry. He explained that the long warp threads were the true course of history, the wefts the deflections of history, or attempted deflections – he had found no less than six of them, from the failed assassination of Constantine to the amulet of Bohemond which resulted in the murder of the Mongol Khan.

317

Harry gaped. 'That's astonishing.'

'Yet it seems to be true. But after all this meddling, what is left? What is true, what is right? What *should* our destiny be? The tapestry of time, rent apart and rewoven over and over, has become a shabby, worthless rag.'

'And you're thinking of doing something about it?'

Geoffrey's gaze was distant. 'What if I could speak to a Weaver of my own, off in some future time? I don't know how – perhaps I will write and speak and have my words printed up in a thousand copies, so that they never die. Or perhaps I will simply take my testament to my grave, and one day, when my body is exhumed, my words will rise with me.'

'What will you say?'

'I will ask for help. I will ask that these meddlers, the Weavers and the Witnesses and the whole pack of them, be halted from their tampering with time's tapestry. That an end be put to it, and history be allowed to resume its proper course.'

Harry looked around the world, at the huge blue sky of Spain, the shoulders of the land around the harbour, the endless shimmering sea. He felt the heat of the sun on his neck, smelled the ocean salt, heard the cry of seabirds who wheeled far above. It was all so vivid, so specific, so real, that it seemed impossible to him that it could all be *changed* on a whim.

But of all the elements in the pretty panorama before him, the most vivid and exciting were the brave forms of Colon's three ships.

At last the ships cast off, to distant cheers from the crowds who thronged the harbour. They put out to sea towed by launches, but soon their sails billowed with the offshore wind, and they surged into the waters of the Ocean Sea, the cross of Christ bright red on their sails.

'He has gone,' Harry said.

'Yes. In this moment it changes,' Geoffrey murmured. 'If Colon is right, perhaps this is the moment when Christendom will win a world, and will never again be threatened, its destiny never again subject to the whim of history, a battle turned, a ruler dying. Certainly the dark future warned of by Eadgyth's Witness has vanished, like so many others: whole histories that never existed, and never *will* exist. Millions of lives, generations of men and women living and loving, fighting and dying, marching off into the future like legions – all of them wiped out!'

Harry said, 'But after all this, Geoffrey, as Colon sails, has the world changed for the better, or worse?'

'I doubt if even the Lord God would answer that with confidence, my friend.'

They watched until the three fragile ships, pressing ever west, disappeared over the curve of the round world. Harry felt as if a nightmare that had plagued him since his father's death was at last sailing out of his head.

Then, thirsty for wine, they made their way back down the slope and into the town.

II

The elderly parish priest, the same Arthur who had cherished her before, walked with Agnes to the church.

It was a hot, humid day, and England was a feverish green, lacking colour now the flowers of early summer had gone, and the air was full of busy insects. It was quite a contrast to the brilliant, arid severity of Spain. Yet Agnes was glad to be back, for this was her home. Even the ache in her damaged mouth didn't seem so bad here.

They came to her old cell, still fixed on the wall of the church. It was strange to Agnes to peer on it from outside. It looked so tiny, yet once it had been her whole world.

But it had changed. The squint, the one tiny window, had been stopped up with loose brick.

Arthur said regretfully, 'I'm afraid we have to contain her. The noises she makes are sometimes rather disturbing. The screams, you know. The yelling in half a dozen languages. Some of my flock believe she is possessed, not by the Holy Spirit but by His malevolent counterpart. Oh, we miss you, Agnes! There's no other word for it. My flock were drawn to your piety and your patience. They loved you in a way they will never love *her.*'

Somewhere in Agnes's bruised heart, she was touched. She had a bit of parchment with her and some charcoal. She scribbled, *But she more interesting. True word of God in her rambling. Truth that underlies the universe. Chaos of it all.*

He looked at her strangely. 'You have changed. You have been hurt.'

Hurt long before I went into cell. Won't go back. Other plans.

He nodded, accepting, regretful, wary.

On impulse Agnes bent and pulled one brick out of the stopped-up squint.

There was a rat-like scrabbling, and a single pale eye was pressed to the hole, its pupil huge from the darkness within. '*You*. You hell-spawned witch! I should have destroyed you while I had the chance—'

Agnes rammed the brick back in the hole.

'You see what I mean about stopping her up,' said the priest, troubled.

Better this than Inquisition. By the time she's got her grave dug out she'll find peace.

'I pray you are right,' said the priest.

Agnes and Arthur walked away from the church, while the verdant life of the English summer rustled and swarmed around them. But if she listened hard, Agnes could still make out the cries of the woman trapped in the brick cell.

'I am Grace Bigod. My ancestors fought with the Conqueror, took the Cross, and built a holy kingdom in the Outremer. I do not deserve this – not this! Let me out, oh, let me out . . .'

Afterword

I'm very grateful to Adam Roberts for his expert assistance with the Latin of the *Incendium Dei* cryptogram.

A general history of Islamic Spain is Richard Fletcher's *Moorish Spain* (Weidenfield & Nicolson, 1992). I have used Fletcher, and the Encyclopaedia Britannica (2001 edition), as references for variant spellings of personal names, both Moorish and Christianised.

I also used Fletcher as a reference for spellings of Spanish place names, which varied through the period covered here, and many sites had both Christian and Moorish names. I have used the term 'al-Andalus' to mean that part of the Iberian peninsula under the control of the Moors at any given time, and 'Spain' to mean the Iberian peninsula itself; the peninsula of course includes modern Spain and Portugal, both of which coalesced as political entities during the period up to 1492. Regarding names in England I have generally defaulted to modern versions. In all my choices I have aimed primarily for clarity.

The words 'crusade' and 'crusader', which I have used here for clarity, are relatively modern terms, derived from the twelfth-century term *crucesignati* (signed by the cross).

The historical 'turning point' at Poitiers, AD 732, was regarded by Edward Gibbon as 'an encounter which would change the history of the world'. In his *Decline and Fall of the Roman Empire* (1776–1788), Gibbon opined that following an Arab victory, 'Perhaps the interpretation of the Koran would now be taught in the schools of Oxford, and her pulpits might demonstrate to a circumcised people the sanctity and truth of the revelation of Mahomet.' A more recent essay covering Poitiers is by Barry S. Strauss in *What If?* (Putnam's, 1999); in the same volume Cecelia Holland speculates on the turning-back of the Mongols in 1242.

An account of the English opposition after the Norman Conquest is Peter Rex's *The English Resistance* (Tempus, 2004).

The eleventh-century 'flying monk' Aethelmaer of Malmesbury (or Eilmer, Elmer or Oliver) was an historical character, mentioned in William of Malmesbury's twelfth-century history *Gesta Regum Anglorum*

322

('The History of the English Kings'). I have based some of Aethelmaer's (fictitious) engine designs on the sketches of Leonardo da Vinci (1452–1519), including the gunpowder engine; see for example *Leonardo da Vinci's Machines* by Marco Cianchi (Becocci Editore, 1984). The career of the ninth-century Moorish aviator Ibn Firnas is described in, for example, the *Dictionary of Scientific Biography* (Scribner). An airport to the north of Baghdad is named after him, as is a crater on the Moon.

Roger Bacon, born c. 1220, was another historical character, a philosopher, educational reformer and an early proponent of experimental science. Bacon was indeed the first European to describe the properties of gunpowder, and he speculated on its use in weaponry. This was largely based on a study of Chinese firecrackers brought to him from the Mongol court by a missionary called William Ruysbroek, a few years after the date of Bacon's fictitious encounter with the Engines of God shown here (Part II Chapter XXII). However (in our timeline) the manufacture of gunpowder remained unknown in the west for decades after Bacon, and the flintlock musket was not developed until c. 1550. See Brian Clegg's *The First Scientist: A Life of Roger Bacon* (Constable, 2003), *Gunpowder* by Clive Ponting (Chatto & Windus, 2005), and Joseph Needham's *Science and Civilisation in China* (Cambridge University Press, 1962).

A recent reference on the Black Death is *The Great Mortality* by John Kelly (Fourth Estate, 2005). The notion that the Chinese in their great age of exploration in the fifteenth century might have reached Australia and perhaps gone much further is set out in Gavin Menzies's *1421: The Year China Discovered America* (Transworld, 2002).

A solid reference on the life of Columbus, based on the primary sources, is *The Worlds of Christopher Columbus* by William D. Phillips and Carla Rahn Phillips (Cambridge, 1992). A recent study of the events of the years leading up to 1492 is James Reston's *Dogs of God: Columbus, the Inquisition and the Defeat of the Moors* (Doubleday, 2005).

My research for this book took me to Ronda, Granada, Cordoba, Seville and elsewhere in Andalucia, as well as locations closer to home such as Harbottle in Northumberland. As I noted in the first book of this series, there is no substitute for visiting such wonderful places.

Any errors or inaccuracies are my sole responsibility.

Stephen Baxter
Northumberland
February 2007